D0810620

Praise for *Summer Secrets*

"Barbara Freethy writes with bright assurance, exploring the bonds of sisterhood and the excitement of blue-water sailing."
—Luanne Rice

"Told with wisdom and clarity, [Barbara Feethy's] story of love, forgiveness, letting go, and starting over will linger in your heart long after the book is closed."—Susan Wiggs

Praise for Barbara Freethy

"Barbara Freethy is a fresh and exciting voice in women's romantic fiction."
—Susan Elizabeth Phillips

"Barbara Freethy is a highly talented author, who puts her own unforgettable twist on an emotional and complex drama."
—*Romantic Times*

"Superlative."—Debbie Macomber

"Barbara Freethy delivers strong and compelling prose."—*Publishers Weekly*

"Freethy has once again penned an exceptional piece of fiction."—*Library Journal*

Turn the page for an excerpt from Summer Secrets . . .

"Don't go after my sisters, Tyler. That would be a big mistake."

Tyler sent her a long, measuring look. "I believe it would be," he said.

"Good. Then we understand each other." Kate turned to escort him out of the room, but he caught her by the arm.

"Not so fast."

It wasn't fear that drove the shiver down her spine, but an undeniable attraction, and Kate couldn't afford an attraction to this man. She couldn't let herself like him or trust him. She had family to protect, not to mention her heart.

"We're not done," he added.

"Yes, we are. I don't trust you. I don't believe you're here for a simple story."

"And I don't believe nothing happened during your race. I think you're hiding something."

"Believe what you want. I don't have anything to gain by talking to you."

"You may have nothing to gain, but I suspect you have something to lose."

He had no idea how much. And she desperately hoped he would never find out.

SUMMER
SECRETS

Barbara Freethy

AN ONYX BOOK

ONYX
Published by New American Library, a division of
Penguin Group (USA) Inc., 375 Hudson Street,
New York, New York 10014, U.S.A.
Penguin Books Ltd, 80 Strand,
London WC2R 0RL, England
Penguin Books Australia Ltd, 250 Camberwell Road,
Camberwell, Victoria 3124, Australia
Penguin Books Canada Ltd, 10 Alcorn Avenue,
Toronto, Ontario, Canada M4V 3B2
Penguin Books (N.Z.) Ltd, Cnr Rosedale and Airborne Roads,
Albany, Auckland 1310, New Zealand

Penguin Books Ltd, Registered Offices:
80 Strand, London WC2R 0RL, England

First published by Onyx, an imprint of New American Library,
a division of Penguin Group (USA) Inc.

ISBN 0-7394-3392-X

 REGISTERED TRADEMARK—MARCA REGISTRADA

Printed in the United States of America

PUBLISHER'S NOTE
This is a work of fiction. Names, characters, places, and incidents either are
the product of the author's imagination or are used fictitiously, and any resem-
blance to actual persons, living or dead, business establishments, events, or
locales is entirely coincidental.

*To my daughter, Kristen, who inspires me
every day and wanted a dedication
that did not include her brother*

Acknowledgments

Many thanks to everyone at the Jane Rotrosen Agency, especially Andrea Cirillo and Kara Cesare, for their wonderful ideas and unending support. Thanks also go to my fabulous editor, Ellen Edwards, who has a keen eye and always asks the tough questions. I couldn't have finished this book without the support of my writer friends, Carol Grace, Lynn Hanna, Barbara McMahon, Candice Hern, Casey Claybourne, and Kate Moore, who also asked many questions and even helped me find a few answers along the way, especially when it came to sailboat racing. Finally, thanks to my family for encouragement and inspiration.

Prologue

Ship's log, *Moon Dancer,* July 10
Wind: 40 knots, gusting to 65 knots
Sea Conditions: rough, choppy, wild
Weather Forecast: rain, thunder, lightning

Kate McKenna's fingers tightened around the pen in her hand as the *Moon Dancer* surfed up one wave and down the next. The ship's log told nothing of their real journey, revealed none of the hardships, the secrets, the heartbreak, the danger they now faced. She wanted to write it down, but she couldn't. Her father's instructions were explicit: Nothing but the facts.

She couldn't write that she was worried, but she was. The weather was turning, the barometer dropping. A big storm was coming. If they changed course, they would lose valuable time, and her father would not consider that option. They were currently in second place—second place and heading straight into the fury of the sea. She could hear the winds beginning to howl. She feared there would be hell to pay this night. Everyone's nerves were already on edge. Arguments could be heard in every corner of the boat. She wanted to make it all go away. She wanted to take her sisters and go home, but home was at the other end of the ocean.

"Kate, get up here!" someone yelled.

She ran up on deck, shocked to the core by the intensity of the storm. The spray blew so hard it almost took the skin off her face. She knew she had to move, had to help her father reef down the sails to the storm jib. But all she could do was stare at the oncoming wave. It must be forty feet high and growing. Any second it would crash over their boat. How on earth would they survive?

And, if they didn't, would anyone ever know the true story of their race around the world?

Chapter One

Eight years later . . .

"The wind blew and the waves crashed as the mighty dragon sank into the sea to hide in the dark depths of the ocean until the next sailor came too close to the baby dragons. The end."

Kate McKenna smiled at the enraptured looks on the faces before her. Ranging in age from three to ten, the children sat on thick, plump cushions on the floor in a corner of her store, Fantasia. They came three times a week to hear her read stories or tell tales. At first they were chatty and restless, but once the story took hold, they were hers completely. Although it wasn't the most profitable part of her bookstore business, it was by far the most enjoyable.

"Tell us another one," the little girl sitting next to her pleaded.

"One more," the other children chorused.

Kate was tempted to give in, but the clock on the wall read five minutes to six, and she was eager to close on time this Friday night. It had been a long, busy week, and she had inventory to unpack before the weekend tourist crowds descended. "That's all for today," she said, getting to her feet. Although the children protested, the group gradually drifted from the store, a few mothers making purchases on their way out the door.

"Great story," Theresa Delantoni said. "Did you make that up as you went along, or did you read it somewhere?"

"A little of both," Kate told her assistant. "My dad used to tell us stories about dragons that lived under the sea. One time we were sailing just outside the Caribbean, and the sea suddenly seemed to catch fire. Dragons, I thought, just like my father said. It turned out to be phosphorus algae. But my sisters and I preferred the fire-breathing dragon story."

"A romantic at heart."

"It's a weakness, I admit."

"Speaking of romance"—Theresa's cheeks dimpled into an excited smile—"it's my anniversary, and I have to go. I promised I wouldn't be late, because our baby-sitter can only give us two hours." Theresa took her purse out of the drawer behind the counter. "I hate to leave you with all those boxes to unpack."

"But you will." Kate followed her to the door. "Don't think twice. You deserve a night off with that darling husband of yours."

Theresa blushed. "Thanks. After eight years of marriage and two babies who need a lot of attention, sometimes I forget how lucky I am."

"You are lucky."

"And you are great with kids. You should think about having some of your own."

"It's easy to be great for an hour."

"Brrr," Theresa said as they walked out of the store together. She stopped to zip up her sweater. "The wind is picking up."

"Out of the southwest," Kate said automatically, her experienced nautical eye already gauging the knots to be between twelve and fifteen. "There's a storm coming. It should be here by six o'clock. Take an umbrella with you."

"You're better than a weather man," Theresa said with a laugh. "Don't stay too late, now. People will start to suspect you don't have a life."

Kate made a face at her friend. "I have a fine life." Theresa was halfway to her car and didn't bother to reply. "I have a great life," Kate repeated. After all, she lived in Castleton, one of the most beautiful spots in the world, a large island off the coast of Washington State, one of the several hundred islands that made up the archipelago known as the San Juans.

Her bookstore at the northern end of Pacific Avenue had an incredible view of the deep blue waters of Puget Sound. It was only one of the interesting, quaint shops that ran down a two-mile cobblestone strip to Rose Harbor, a busy marina that filled every July with boats in town for the annual Castleton Invitational Sailboat Races.

Castleton was known for its rugged beauty: fir- and evergreen-covered hillsides and more than one hundred miles of driftwood-strewn beaches. Most of the island traffic came via the Washington State Ferry, although boaters were plentiful, and small private planes could land at the Castleton Airport. The unpredictable southwesterly winds created swirling, dangerous currents along many of the beaches and had driven a few boats to ground on their way to shelter in the harbor. But the winds didn't stop the boats from coming or the sailors from congregating. Tales of sails and storms could be overheard in every restaurant, café, and business in town. There were more boat slips in the marina than there were parking spaces downtown. The lives of Castleton's residents weren't just by the sea, they were about the sea.

Kate loved her view of the waterfront—loved the one from her house in the hills even better—but more than anything she appreciated the fact that the view didn't change every day. Maybe some would call that boring, but she found it comforting.

The wind lifted the hair off the back of her neck,

changing that feeling of comfort to one of uneasiness. Wind in her life had meant change. Her father, Duncan McKenna, a sailing man from the top of his head to the tips of his toes, always relished the wind's arrival. Kate could remember many a time when he had jumped to his feet at the first hint of a breeze. A smile would spread across his weatherbeaten cheeks as he'd stand on the deck of their boat, pumping his fist triumphantly in the air, his eyes focused on the distant horizon. *The wind's up, Katie girl,* he'd say. *It's time to go.*

And they'd go—wherever the wind took them. They'd sail with it, into it, against it. They'd lash out in anger when it blew too hard, then cry in frustration when it vanished completely. Her life had been formed, shaped, and controlled by the wind. She'd thought of it as a friend; she'd thought of it as a monster. Well, no more.

She had a home now, an address, a mailbox, a garden. She might live by the water, but she didn't live on it. The wind meant nothing more to her than an extra sweater and a bowl of soup for dinner. It didn't mean that her life was about to change. Why couldn't she believe that?

Because of the boats.

They'd been sailing into the harbor for the past week, every day a few more, each one bigger, brighter, and better than the last. There was an energy in the air, a sense of excitement, purpose, adventure. In just a few days the race would begin, and next Saturday the biggest and brightest would race around the island in the Castleton Invitational. Two days later, the boats would be off again, racing to San Francisco and then on to Hawaii for the Pacific Cup. The sailors would battle the elements and one another. In the end, only one would be victorious.

Kate didn't appreciate the direction of her thoughts. She didn't want to think about the boats or the damn race. Ten days. It would all be over in ten days, she reminded herself as she walked back into the store and shut the door firmly behind her. She could handle the pleasure cruisers, the fishermen, the tourists interested in whale watching; what she couldn't handle were the racers, the fanatical sailors who lived to battle the ocean, to conquer new seas. She knew those men and women too well. Once, she'd been one of them.

The door to her store opened, accompanied by a melodious jangle from the wind chimes that hung outside. A man entered, dressed in khaki pants and a navy blue polo shirt. He had the look of a man on business. There was an energy in his movements, a gleam in his deep blue eyes, and an impression of power and purpose in his stance. As he ran an impatient hand through his dark brown hair, Kate felt her pulse quicken. Strangers came into her store all the time—asking for books, directions, information about the island—but none of those strangers had given her heart such a jump start. Maybe Theresa was right. She definitely needed to get out more.

"Hello." His voice had a bit of a drawl to it. The South? Texas? She wasn't sure where he'd come from, but she had a feeling it had been a long journey.

"Hello," she said. "Can I help you?"

"I certainly hope so."

"I'm betting you need directions, not a book."

He gave her a curious smile. "Now, why would you bet that?"

"You don't look like an armchair adventurer."

"You can tell that just by looking?"

She shrugged. "What can I say? I'm good."

"Not that good. I don't need directions."

"Oh. A book about sailing, then?"

"Wrong again."

Kate studied him thoughtfully. He hadn't stood still since he walked into the store, shifting his feet, tapping his fingers on the counter. He looked like a man who couldn't stop running even when he was tired. Hardly one to settle into a recliner with a good book.

However, she couldn't refute the fact that he had come into the bookstore of his own free will, so he must have had a reason.

"I know." She snapped her fingers. "Gift book. You need a book for Aunt Sally or Cousin Mary, or maybe the girlfriend whose birthday you forgot."

He laughed. "No Aunt Sally. No Cousin Mary. And, regretfully, no girlfriend."

Kate had to bite back the incredulous *really* that threatened to push past her lips. She settled for "Interesting. So what do you want?"

"I'm looking for someone."

"Aren't we all?"

"You're very quick."

He was quick, too, and it had been awhile since she'd flirted with a man. Not that she was flirting—she was just being friendly. "So, who are you looking for?"

He hesitated, and it was the small pause that made Kate tense. That and the way his gaze settled on her face. It had been eight years since someone had come looking for her. It wasn't likely this man was here for that reason, though. What were the odds? A million to one.

"A woman," he said slowly.

Kate licked her lips, trying not to turn away from the long, deep look he was giving her.

"I think I've found her," he added.

So much for odds.

"It's you, isn't it? Kate McKenna?" He smiled with satisfaction. "The oldest sister in the fearsome foursome that raced around the world in a sailboat. I recognize you from the photographs."

"Who wants to know?"

"Tyler Jamison." He stuck out his hand.

Kate gave his hand a brief shake. "What do you want?"

"A story."

"You're a reporter?" She had to admit she was surprised. She'd once been able to spot a reporter from a block away. She'd gotten complacent. That would have to change right now. "I can't imagine why you'd be looking for me. That race was a long time ago."

"Eight years. That would make you twenty-eight, right?"

Kate walked over to the door and turned the sign to *closed*. If only she'd done it five minutes earlier, she would have missed this man. Not that he wouldn't have come back in the morning. He had a look of stubborn persistence about him. She suspected that he was a man who usually got what he wanted.

"I'd like to do a follow-up story on what's become of one of the most interesting sailing crews in ocean-racing history," Tyler continued. "It would tie in nicely with the upcoming sailboat races."

"I don't race anymore, but I'm sure I can find you some interesting racers to talk to. Take Morgan Hunt, for instance. He raced in the Sydney to Hobart last year and could tell you tales that would curl your toes."

"I'll keep that in mind. But I'd like to start with you and your sisters. Your father, too."

Duncan McKenna would love the publicity, adore being in the spotlight, but Lord only knew what he'd say once his tongue got going, especially if his tongue had been loosened by a few pints of beer, which would no doubt be the case.

"My father loves to talk about the past," Kate said, "but just like those fishermen whose stories of catches grow bigger by the year, so do my father's stories about that race. You can't believe a thing he says."

"What about you? You'd tell me the real story, wouldn't you?"

"Sure." She gave him what she hoped was a casual shrug. "Let's see. We sailed forever it seemed. Some days were windy; some were hot. The wind ran fast, then slow. One week turned into the next with more of the same. The food was terrible. The seas were treacherous. The stars were always fantastic. That's about it."

"Short and succinct. Surely you can do better than that, Miss McKenna. A woman who appreciates books should be able to tell a better story."

"I sell books—I don't write them. Besides, there were a dozen news stories about the race in the weeks that followed our return. Everything that needed to be said was said. If you're interested, I'm sure you could find them on the Internet or in the library." She paused. "Do you write for a sailing magazine?"

"I'm a freelancer. I go where the story takes me."

Kate frowned. This was great. Just great. Another man who went with the wind. Why did they always stir up trouble in her life? "Well, there's no story here. We're all very boring. I run this bookstore, not exactly a hotbed of commerce, as you can see." She swept her hand around the room, forcing him to look at the cozy chairs by the window, the neatly stacked shelves of mysteries, fiction, fantasy, romance, children's books, and, of course, the ever-popular books on seafaring.

Although she was trying to downplay the bookstore, she couldn't stop the sense of pride that ran through her as she looked around the room that she had decorated, remembering the care she'd taken with the children's corner now brightened by posters and stuffed animals. She'd turned the bookstore into a home away from home, a place of delicious escape. It hadn't been easy to build a business from nothing. But somehow she'd done it.

"It's nice," Tyler said. "From sailboat racer to bookstore owner. Sounds like an interesting journey. Tell me more."

She'd walked right into that one. "It's not interesting at all. Trust me."

"You're avoiding my questions. Why?"

"I'm not avoiding anything," she said with a laugh

that even to her own ears sounded nervous. "It's like this—I was barely out of my awkward teenage years during that trip. I'm grown-up now. I don't particularly want to rehash that time in my life. It was no big deal."

"It was a huge deal. Most people who win ocean races are seasoned sailors, sponsored by big corporations, sailing million-dollar boats. But the McKenna family beat them all. I can't understand why you don't want to talk about it. It must have been the biggest and best thing that ever happened to you."

"We had fifteen minutes of fame a long time ago. And our race was different. It wasn't filled with racing syndicates but with amateur sailors who had a passion for sailing and a longing for adventure. The racing world has changed. No one cares what happened to us."

"I do."

"Why?" Something about him didn't ring true. He seemed too confident, too purposeful to be after a fluff story. "Why do you care?"

"I like to write about adventurers, ordinary people who accomplish extraordinary things. And I'm fascinated by the thought of three girls and their father alone on the ocean, battling not only the other racers but the wind, the icebergs, fifty-foot waves. I've read some accounts of the trip, especially the harrowing details of the terrible storm during the second-to-last leg of the race. I can't imagine what you must have gone through."

There was a passion in his voice that bespoke a genuine interest, but why now? Why after all these years? Why this man—who had appeared out of nowhere and didn't seem to work for anyone? Why him?

"You look familiar," she said, studying the sharply drawn lines of his face. "Where have I seen you before?"

"I just have one of those faces. An average, everyday Joe." He paused. "So, what do you say? Will you talk to me? Or do I need to track down your sisters, Ashley and Caroline?"

Kate couldn't let him talk to Ashley or Caroline. She couldn't let this go any further. She had to get rid of him. But how?

"You're stalling," Tyler said. "I can see the wheels turning in your head."

"Don't be silly. I'm just busy. I have boxes to unpack before tomorrow, so I'm afraid we'll have to do this some other time."

The phone behind the counter rang, and she reached for it immediately, grateful for the interruption. "Fantasia," she said cheerfully. Her heart sank as she heard a familiar voice on the other end of the line. Will Jenkins ran the Oyster Bar on the waterfront, her father's favorite hangout. "How bad is he?" The answer put her heart into another nosedive. "I'll be right there. Yes, I know. Thanks, Will."

"Trouble?" Tyler inquired as she hung up the phone.

"No." She opened the drawer and pulled out her purse and keys. "I have to go. And so do you."

"You look upset."

"I'm fine." She opened the door, the breeze once again sending goose bumps down her arms. There was change in the air. She could feel it all around her.

"You don't look fine. Is someone hurt?" Tyler waited while she locked the door behind him. "Can I help?"

Kate told herself not to be taken in by the concern in his eyes. He was a reporter. He just wanted a story. "No one can help. You should go home. Back to wherever you came from."

"Thanks, but I think I'll stay a while. With all these sailors in town, I'm sure someone around here will talk to me."

"Suit yourself."

Kate hurried to her car, which she kept parked in

back of her store. Tyler Jamison was a problem she hadn't anticipated, but right now she had a more pressing matter to deal with. She turned on the ignition and let out the brake. Her small Volkswagen Bug shook with another gust of wind. Her father always said if you can't own the wind, you have to ride it out. She had a feeling this was going to be one wild ride.

"Get me another beer," Duncan McKenna demanded as he put his fist down on top of the bar. He'd meant to slam it down hard, make the glasses jump, but he was too tired. "There was a time when a man could get a beer around here, Will."

The bartender finished drying off a glass at the other end of the bar. "You've had your limit, Duncan. You'll get no more from me tonight. You need to go home and sleep it off."

Sleep it off? He couldn't sleep. Hadn't for years. Oh, he dropped off now and then once the liquor took hold of his mind and gave him a blessed few hours of peace. But that didn't happen often, especially lately.

"Dammit, Will, I need a drink. I need one bad." He could hear the desperation in his voice, but he couldn't stop it. The need had been building in him all day, growing fiercer with each boat that sailed into the harbor, each dream of a journey, of a race to be sailed and to be won. That had been his world. God, how he missed it, missed the pitch of the waves, the power of the wind, the thrill of the race. Missed the pounding of his heart, the spine-tingling, palm-sweating moments when all would be won or all would be lost. What a rush his life had been.

"I need a drink," he repeated.

Will walked down the length of the bar and gave him a hard look. "It won't do you no good, Duncan. I called Kate, and she's on her way."

"Why the hell did you call her?"

"Because you need a ride. You've been in here all day."

"I can get myself home." Duncan tried to stand up, but the room spun around, so he sat back down and held on to the edge of the bar for dear life.

"Sure you can," Will said dryly. "Just sit there. Don't try to leave."

"I'll do what I want," Duncan snapped. "I've been around the world upside down and backward. I won the goddamn Winston Around-the-World-Challenge. No one thought we could do it. But we did, me and my girls." He paused and let out a weary sigh. "We were the best, Will. The very best. My girls got heart, just like their old man. They don't quit. I don't quit. McKennas don't quit."

"Yeah, yeah, I know."

And he did know because he'd heard it all before. Will was only a few years younger than Duncan, and he'd been tending bar for more than twenty years. Duncan couldn't understand how a man could be happy staying in one place for so long. Twenty years ago, Will had had hair on his head, a flat stomach, and girls lining up three-deep to flirt with him. Now he was bald, soft in the middle, and married to a librarian. Hell of a life he'd made for himself.

Will walked away to serve another customer at the end of the bar. Duncan turned his head and saw a woman sitting at a nearby table. As she moved, her hair caught the light, and he lost his breath at the glorious, fiery shade of red. Eleanor, he thought impossibly. His beloved Nora had hair the same color, and deep blue eyes that a man could drown in. He'd gone overboard the first time he'd seen her standing on the docks in a summer dress that showed off her long legs. His gut twisted in pain at the memory. Eleven years she'd been gone, but he still missed her. His heart felt as heavy as a stone. He wanted a drink. He wanted oblivion. He wanted . . . so many things.

"Dad?"

He tried to focus, but he couldn't see clearly. It's

the alcohol, he told himself, but when he wiped the back of his hand across his eyes, it came away wet.

"Are you all right?" Kate asked with concern on her face.

Kate had the look of Nora in her eyes, but her hair was blond, her skin a golden brown and free of the beautiful freckles that had kissed Nora's nose. Kate's face was stronger, too, her jaw as stubborn as his own. There were other differences as well. Nora's love had never wavered. But Kate's . . .

"The boats are coming, Katie girl. There's a wind brewing. You know what that means? You know where we should be?"

"Not today," Kate replied.

"You never want to sail anymore. I don't know why." He shook his head, trying to concentrate, but his head felt thick, his brain slow. "What happened to us, Katie?"

"Let's go home."

Home? Where was home? He'd had to sell the *Moon Dancer*. It had almost broken his heart, selling his beloved boat. Now he lived in a small old sailboat. He'd wanted to call the boat *Nora*, but he couldn't quite bring himself to paint his wife's name on the side. Nora wouldn't have been proud of this boat or of him. Kate wasn't proud of him, either.

"I'm sorry, Katie. You know how sorry I am?"

"You're always sorry when you drink." Kate put out her hand to him. "Let's go home."

"I can't go now. I'm telling Will here about our big race."

"He's heard it before. I'm sorry, Will," Kate said.

"It's no problem," Will replied.

"What are you apologizing for?" Duncan demanded. "I ain't done nothing. And I'm your father. You don't apologize for me." He got to his feet, wanting to remind her that he was bigger and stronger and older than her, but the sudden motion caused him to sway unsteadily. Before he knew it, Kate had a hand on his arm. He wanted to shrug her away. In fact, he would do just that as soon as he caught his breath, got his bearings.

"Need some help?" a man asked.

Before Duncan could answer, Kate said, "What are you doing here?"

"I was thirsty."

"Can't blame a man for being thirsty, Katie girl," Duncan said, feeling more weary by the second. "I gotta sit down."

The man grabbed Duncan's other arm as he started to slip out of Kate's grasp. "Your car?" he asked.

"I don't want to go home," Duncan complained. "I want another drink."

"The alcohol is going to kill you, Dad," Kate told him as she and the man managed to walk Duncan out of the bar and into the parking lot.

"Better the alcohol than the loneliness," Duncan murmured. Kate pushed him into the front seat of her car. His eyes closed and he drifted away. He was finally able to sleep.

Kate saw her father slump sideways in his seat. For a moment she felt a surge of panic that he wasn't just sleeping, that something was happening to him, that he was sick or— No, she couldn't think the word, much less say it. Her father was strong as an ox. He wasn't even that old, barely sixty. He was just drunk. A terrible, lousy drunk. A terrible, lousy father for that matter. Why was she worried about losing him when it was so apparent that she'd lost him a long time ago?

"You'll need help getting him out of the car," Tyler said, interrupting her thoughts.

She'd almost forgotten he was standing there. "You've gotten yourself quite a headline, haven't you? 'Victorious sailor turns into worthless drunk.' "

"Is that how you think of your father?"

"No, but it's probably what you'll say."

"How do you know what I'll say?"

"I've been interviewed before, had my words twisted."

"Is that where your resistance comes from?" he asked with a thoughtful expression on his face. "I'm not interested in embarrassing you, Miss McKenna. I just want an interesting story. Fame, success, adventure—those are things that change people's lives forever. Most people never experience even one of those, much less all three, the way you did."

Kate didn't know what to say. She needed time to think, to figure out the best way to handle this man. Maybe if she told him just enough, he would go away. But what would be enough? Would he start digging? And if he did, what would he find?

"I need to take care of my father," she said. "Maybe tomorrow, if you want to stop by the bookstore, we can talk."

He sent her a skeptical look. "Why the change of heart?"

"You don't look like someone who gives up."

"That's true." Tyler tipped his head toward the car. "Will your father be all right? I could follow you home, help you get him into the house."

"No, thank you."

"Where is home, anyway? I don't think you said."

"I don't think I did." Kate got into her car and shut the door. "I don't know what to do about him," she muttered, glancing over at her father. Duncan's response was a very unhelpful snort. She'd have to take care of Tyler Jamison herself.

Tyler stared down the road long after Kate's taillights had disappeared. What had seemed so simple had suddenly taken on new and disturbing dimensions. The first was Kate herself. She wasn't what he'd expected. For some reason, he'd thought tomboy, tough girl, overachiever, but she hadn't looked all that tough in a pair of black capri pants and a clingy T-shirt that matched her light blue eyes. Her blond hair had fallen loosely around her shoulders, and she'd moved with a feminine grace, spoken with a soft voice. She had a great smile, too, he thought, the kind that invited you to come in and stay awhile, the same way her friendly little bookstore invited customers to stop in and browse. Not that she'd been all that friendly when she'd discovered he was a reporter. Despite her casual manner, he'd sensed a wall going up between them with every question that he asked.

Tyler reached into his pocket and pulled out a folded piece of paper. It was a magazine cover from eight years ago. Three blond, sunburned girls stood on the deck of a sailboat, holding an enormous silver trophy in their hands, their proud, beaming father in the background. The McKennas had conquered the world's toughest oceans. But were there secrets behind those smiles? Was there another story of their trip, one that hadn't been printed? Tyler suspected the answer to both questions was yes.

In fact, if one looked closely at the picture, only Duncan looked really happy. The girls appeared shell-shocked. It was the only word he could think of to describe their expressions. Maybe he was reading more than was there. He'd spent most of his life living by the facts and only the facts, but this story was different. This story was personal.

Kate McKenna hadn't wanted to talk to him. As she said, it was an old story, so why the resistance? She was hiding something. A drunken father? Not the biggest secret in the world. There had to be something more. Tyler had a hunch he knew what that something was.

He folded the magazine cover, slipped it into his pocket, and took out his cell phone. He punched in a familiar number, then waited.

"Jamison residence." Shelly Thompson, Mark's private nurse, answered the phone in her no-nosense voice.

"Shelly. It's Tyler. How's Mark doing today?"

"Not good. He tried to stand, but his legs couldn't support his weight. He's very depressed."

Tyler let out a sigh filled with frustration, helplessness, and anger, emotions that swamped him every time he thought about his younger brother who had once been such an accomplished athlete. "Can I talk to him?"

"I think he's asleep. Do you want me to wake him?"

"No. But when he gets up, tell him I found the McKenna sisters." Tyler ended the call, slipping the phone back into his pocket. The McKenna sisters might be good at keeping secrets, but he was even better at uncovering them.

Chapter Two

Ashley McKenna tapped her foot nervously on the dock that bobbed beneath her feet. The swells grew larger with each passing minute as storm clouds came in from the west. "We need to do this soon," she told the man on the deck of the boat she was about to photograph. "We're losing the light."

"We've got one more guy to get in the picture. He should be here any second. Hang on."

Hang on. Sure she could do that. As a photographer, she was used to waiting patiently for the right shot. But not when she was standing so close to the water, not when she could see the waves beginning to churn. She sent a longing look behind her. She'd much rather be on solid ground than standing out here in her impractical high heels with her skirt blowing up around her legs like a Marilyn Monroe photo. For the hundredth time she wished she'd had time to change, but she'd rushed from shooting the ribbon cutting of the new maritime museum to this assignment, photographing the crews and boats entered in the Castleton Invitational.

Water splashed over the side of the dock, and she took a hasty step backward. She felt small and vulnerable on this bobbing piece of wood with a storm blow-

ing in. The sea had often made her feel that way. Her
father had always told her to look the ocean right in
the eye, never back down, never give up, never give
in. There was a time when those brave, fighting words
had given her courage. Then she'd learned through
hard experience that the ocean didn't back down or
give in, either. That if it was man or woman against
nature, nature would win.

Ashley shivered as she glanced at the boat, watching
the men scurry back and forth, checking the sails and
completing the chores necessary to settle in for the
night. A strong gust of wind blew strands of her long
blond hair across her face. Setting her camera bag on
the dock, she knelt down and dug into her purse for
an elastic band.

She should have cut her hair years ago. In fact, she
considered chopping it off every six weeks, but she
never quite got up the nerve. As a result, her hair
dipped down to her waist. It made her look too young,
and it was often tangled, but in a small way it made
her feel closer to her mother. Ashley had inherited her
mother's red streaks, making her more of a strawberry
blonde than her sisters. But it wasn't just the color
that reminded her of Nora McKenna, it was the memories of her mother brushing her hair every night, one
hundred strokes exactly. Those nights had been a long
time ago, but she still missed them. Sentimental tears
blurred her vision.

She told herself to stop being so emotional. She was
an adult now, twenty-six years old, an independent
woman with a career. It was time to grow up, to stop
being sensitive. Her sisters certainly didn't cry at every
Hallmark commercial. They didn't wax sentimental
about family moments from a lifetime ago. And she
shouldn't, either.

As Ashley pulled the elastic band out of her purse,
the dock rolled, and she had to put down one hand
on the wood to steady herself. She made the mistake
of looking at the gap between the dock and the boat,

at the greenish-blue water rising up and down, up and down. The sight was mesmerizing. She wanted to look away, but she couldn't. How many times had she stared at the water? How many times had it been her friend as she played with the dolphins and swam in the waves? Those were the times to remember, she told herself desperately. Not the other times, when the waves grew as high as skyscrapers, when the water threatened to swallow everything within its reach. Her body began to sway. She was afraid to move, afraid to get sucked into that terrible vortex where nothing ever came back.

"Ashley? Ashley? Is that you?"

She heard her name called from a great distance, but when she looked up she found a man standing right next to her. Faded blue jeans covered a pair of long, lean legs and a navy muscle T-shirt hung loosely around his waist. As her gaze traveled up his body, she told herself to look away before she got to the dimple in the chin, the slightly crooked nose broken by a football when he was twelve years old, and the sandy-colored hair streaked with blond highlights that he'd never had to pay a dime for. Unfortunately, she couldn't stop herself from meeting his gold-flecked brown eyes.

"Sean," she murmured.

"Ashley," he said, watching as she slowly got to her feet.

Even in her heels, Sean Amberson towered over her, six foot four inches of solid male. He was broader across the chest now, and his upper arms rippled with muscles honed by years of building and sailing boats. She cleared her throat, trying to calm the sudden racing of her pulse. It was bad enough the wind was blowing; now she had Sean to deal with as well. She'd known he'd come back again. His parents still lived on the island, still ran the boat-building business that would one day go to Sean. But knowing he would come home and seeing him in the flesh were two very different things.

"When did you get back?" she forced herself to ask.

"Yesterday. Did you miss me?"

"I—" Ashley shrugged helplessly. "It's been a long time."

"Almost two years since my last visit, and I think you managed to dodge me the entire week I was here."

"I don't remember."

"Sure you do. You developed a sudden and very contagious case of the flu, as I recall. Wouldn't even open your door. I had to yell at you from the hallway of your apartment building. The time before that, you claimed you had poison ivy, and the time before that—"

"Stop it. I can't help it if I'm sick when you happen to come to town." She refused to admit she'd been hiding out in her apartment on any of those occasions. The wind blew her hair in front of her face, and she remembered the elastic band in her hand. She quickly pulled her hair back into a ponytail, acutely aware of his very long and intent stare.

"I'm glad you didn't cut your hair," he said. "It's still incredible."

Ashley swallowed hard, the husky note in his voice stirring up unwanted emotions. She'd loved this man once, loved him more than anyone or anything. But it was over. It had been over for more years than he'd been gone. She just wished he'd go away again, because it was easier when he wasn't around. She could almost forget. She could almost move on. "So is this just a family weekend visit?" she asked, hoping it wouldn't be longer than that.

"Not exactly. I'm racing in the Castleton."

"You can't be serious. You said you'd never race."

"Never is a long time. I just finished refurbishing Stan Baker's boat, the *Freedom Rider*. He asked me

to race it with him in the Castleton and on to Hawaii.
I thought it was about time I raced in one of the boats
I helped build."

"You're not a racer."

"Who says I can't be?"

"You can't race, Sean. Your parents would die."

"My parents won't die, but I suppose it's possible I
might." His gaze bored into hers, searching for an
answer she couldn't give him.

"Why risk it?" she asked instead.

"Because I'm . . ." He shook his head. "I'm restless.
I can't settle in anywhere. College didn't work out.
The jobs I've had never seem to last."

"You always have your family business. I've heard
your father say he wants you to come home and run
the business." Not that she wanted that to happen. If
Sean ever came home for good, she'd have to leave.
This island wasn't big enough for the both of them.
Sean took up too much space. He'd always made her
feel small—it wasn't just his height but his personality.
He was a man in constant motion, impatient, energized, restless. He made her tense; he made her a little
bit crazy. Make that a lot crazy.

"I'm sure you'd prefer that I stay far away," he said.

"I don't care what you do."

"Dammit, Ashley." He slapped his hand against his
jeans in a gesture of frustration. "Don't say that.
Don't pretend. Don't act like we never meant anything to each other."

"What we had was over a long time ago."

"Yeah, so you said."

"You can't possibly still care," she murmured.

He stared at her for a long minute, then shook his
head. "Of course I don't still care."

It was the answer she wanted, but it still hurt. Not
that she'd let him see that. "I didn't think so," she
said. "You probably have a girlfriend, don't you?"

"More than one. What about you? Dating anyone
these days?"

"Sure," she lied, knowing that the last date she'd gone on had been at least six months ago.

"You'll have to introduce us. Is it a local guy?"

"Uh . . ." She shifted her camera bag on her shoulder, relieved when a man ran by her and jumped on the boat she was supposed to photograph. "Are you the last one?" she called.

"Yes. We just need one minute," he replied.

"You're photographing the crews for the Castleton?" Sean asked.

She nodded. "I wish they'd hurry up."

"My mom said a bunch of your photographs are displayed in the Main Street Gallery."

"Janine is a friend. They're not that good."

"I bet they are. I remember when your mom gave you your first camera. You were hooked. You wouldn't go anywhere without that thing, and you were always snapping shots of me doing something stupid."

"Which was fairly often," she said, thinking back to those carefree days before everything had gotten so complicated. "But you rarely stood still long enough for me to get a good shot."

He grinned, and for a brief moment he was her best friend in the world again, the boy who'd started kindergarten with her, who'd joined her in food fights, backyard picnics, and neighborhood ball games. He'd been her first dance, her first kiss, her first promise of love. And now—now he was nothing. They couldn't be together, and she couldn't tell him why.

His grin faded, and their eyes met in a long, poignant moment of desire and regret.

"God, Ash," he murmured. "I told myself I wouldn't do this, wouldn't try to talk to you about what happened. I told myself I was only beating a dead horse. But, dammit, it's still here, whatever this thing is between us. I can feel it right now."

"It's just the . . . the wind," she said desperately. "It makes me edgy."

As she finished speaking, the dock took a big roll, sending her stumbling. She grabbed Sean's arm like a lifeline, terrified of ending up in the water.

"Easy," he said.

"I have to get out of here." But she couldn't let go of Sean's arm. What if she fell? The water would be cold. It would make her heart stop. It would rush over her head. She'd have to fight to get back to the surface. Her clothes would drag her down.

"Ashley," Sean said sharply. "What the hell is wrong with you?"

She sent him a blank look. "What?"

"You're white as a sheet."

His words slowly sank in. She realized she was letting him see a side of herself she didn't want anyone to see. "I'm okay." She took a deep breath and forced herself to let go of his arm. "I just felt dizzy for a minute. I guess I didn't eat enough today."

"You don't look like you eat much any day. You're thin as a rail."

Ashley didn't comment, her attention drawn to the crew member on the boat waving her over. "Are you ready?" she asked.

"Yes, but we've changed our minds on the angle. We'd like to have you shoot from onboard, not from the dock. Get the pier in the background and the banner for the race."

Ashley stiffened. She had already shot three boats and their crews from the safety of the docks. It was a good shot. She didn't need to get on the boat. "I think it's better from here."

"No, we want you onboard. Come on." He extended his hand to help her cross.

Ashley looked from his hand to the water that separated the boat from the dock. It was only a foot or two, barely anything. She wouldn't slip or fall. She couldn't. It was perfectly safe. But the swells were lifting the boat and pushing it farther away. What if the line got loose? What if she couldn't get back?

Feelings of panic swamped her. Her breath came faster. Her hands tingled. But she couldn't let on. No one could know. No one could ever know.

"It's getting dark. The clouds are rolling in," Sean said as he watched her measure the distance between the boat and the dock. "Maybe you should wait until tomorrow."

"It's too dark," she told the man on the boat. "We'll have to reschedule. I'm sorry, but I know you wouldn't be happy with the photos in this kind of light. I'll come by tomorrow. We'll do it then."

"Hey, wait a second," the man called after her, but Ashley had already begun walking down the dock, and she didn't stop until she reached solid ground.

She didn't realize Sean had followed her until she stopped abruptly and he barreled into the back of her.

"Sorry," he said.

"It's fine. I'm fine."

"No, you're not. It's still with you, isn't it?"

"I don't know what you're talking about." She looked away from his probing gaze.

"I'm talking about the fear on your face when you considered getting on that boat. I saw it before, when you first got back from the race. I wish you'd tell me what happened to make you so afraid."

"Nothing happened. I just got tired of living on a boat. So tired I can't stand the thought of getting on another one."

"Even after all this time?" he asked, a skeptical note in his voice. "It's been eight years."

"I know how long it's been," she snapped as she looked back at him. "I have to go. I have to talk to Caroline. I'm worried about her."

"Why? What's going on with your baby sister?"

Ashley hesitated, not one to share family business, but talking about Caroline was preferable to talking about herself or her irrational fears. "It seems that Caroline is dating Mike Stanaway."

Sean raised an eyebrow. "He's at least ten years

older than her. Maybe fifteen. Not to mention . . .
Well, let's just say he has some problems."

"I know, that's why I need to talk to her. Not that
she'll listen, but I have to try."

"I could go with you," Sean offered.

"No," she said abruptly. "You know how defensive
Caroline can be when she feels she's being ambushed.
I'll see you around."

Ashley walked away, wondering if he'd call her
back, but he didn't. As she headed toward Caroline's
salon, her thoughts weren't on her sister but on the
man she'd left behind. She wondered why it never got
any easier to walk away from him. Lord knew she'd
had enough practice. For a brief second, she was
tempted to look back, to see if he was still standing
there, still watching her, still wanting her—the way
she still wanted him.

"Phone for you, Caroline," the receptionist at
Noel's Hair Salon said. "Line one."

"Just a second." Caroline squeezed the last bit of
blond hair color out of the plastic bottle and looked
at her client in the mirror. "We'll let this sit for a
while. Can I get you a magazine?"

"I brought a book," Peggy Marsh replied. "And
take your time. This is the first bit of peace and quiet
I've had all week. The kids have been driving me
crazy. Take my advice, Caroline, do not rush into the
marriage and children thing. Enjoy this time of your
life."

"I'll keep that in mind." Caroline certainly wasn't
pushing for marriage or kids. She was twenty-four
years old and had plenty of time to do both. Someday,
when she was ready. Right now she had her job as a
stylist at Noel's Salon and a small apartment in a
building just a few blocks away. She was happy. Most
of the time. Sort of.

It was probably the wind that was making her restless. She was like her father in that regard. A good

stiff breeze always got her itchy to go somewhere. But she couldn't go anywhere. She had another haircut in ten minutes.

She walked over to the reception desk and picked up the phone. "Hello."

"It's me, Kate."

"What's up?" Caroline couldn't help tensing at the sound of her older sister's voice. She had things she needed to talk to Kate about, but now wasn't the time or the place. Not that she knew when that time or place would be.

"It's Dad," Kate said with a weary note in her voice.

"Where is he?"

"Sleeping on my couch. I was lucky to get him this far. He really tied one on today. Will called me to come and pick him up."

"It's hard for him with all the boats coming to town. It makes him want to be out there with the other racers. He misses the life he used to have."

"And that's an excuse for drinking himself into oblivion? How can you defend him?"

"Someone has to," Caroline snapped. Kate had always been hard on their father. She didn't understand him. She never had.

There was a pause on the other end of the phone. "Look, Caroline, that's not really why I'm calling. Although it's a lot easier to defend Dad when you aren't the one constantly called to come and pick him up from some bar. I'm sorry if I'm a little out of patience, but I'm just sick of it."

"Hey, they can call me anytime. But everyone knows you're in charge."

"I never said that."

"Oh, please, Kate. You've always been in charge."

"Fine. Whatever. We have another problem."

"What? I have a haircut to do." Caroline looked up as the front door to the salon opened and a man walked in. He must be her seven-o'clock appointment.

"A reporter came into the store today," Kate continued. "His name is Tyler Jamison. He wants to do a story on us—a where-are-they-now piece."

Caroline didn't know what to say. The reporters had stopped coming around years ago, and they'd all begun to breathe easier. Lulled into a false sense of security, she realized now. "What did you tell him?"

"That we had nothing to say. That there was no story."

"Did he believe you?"

"I don't know. He seems very persistent. I just wanted to warn you not to talk to him if he comes around. Don't let yourself get taken in."

The way you usually do. Caroline could hear the unspoken words as clearly as if Kate had said them out loud. "As if I would," she said, once again feeling defensive. "Ashley is the one you should warn. She's so nervous all the time. There's no telling what she'd say."

"I left her a message to call me, but if you see her first, let her know."

"I will." Caroline paused, wishing there was something else to say. When had it become so difficult to talk to Kate? They'd once been close. Kate had been her idol, her big sister, the one who told incredible stories, made her laugh, made her feel safe when the world outside got too scary. But things had changed. There was too much they couldn't talk about. It was easier to speak of nothing than worry about crossing a line that wasn't supposed to be crossed.

Caroline hung up the phone and walked back to her station. "Sisters," she murmured, meeting Peggy's gaze in the mirror.

Peggy nodded. "You love 'em and you hate 'em."

"Exactly. I have another client, so why don't you move into this seat, and I'll put the hot lights on you. We'll see if we can't speed this process up a bit." Caroline moved Peggy to the station next to hers. She adjusted the octopus-style lights and said, "Let me know if it gets too hot."

"I love your color," Peggy said.

"You do? I did some experimenting." Caroline glanced at her reflection. Her hair was dark blond with brown streaks that were emphasized by a short, spiky cut and a lot of mousse.

"You look hip," Peggy said wistfully. "I haven't been hip in a while."

"Kate thinks I should go back to my natural color."

"Which is what?"

"I don't remember," Caroline said with a laugh.

"Caroline, your client is here," the receptionist, Erica Connors, interrupted, tipping her head toward the man leafing through a magazine in the waiting area. "A hunk," Erica mouthed silently.

Caroline had to admit the guy was exceptionally good-looking, not in a pretty-boy sense, but in a mountain-climbing, ocean-racing kind of way. When he stood up, she saw that he was well over six feet tall, and as he walked toward her she got the full benefit of his sexy smile.

"Caroline?" he asked.

"Yes."

"I need a haircut."

"You've come to the right place." She motioned him toward the chair Peggy had just vacated. "Can I get you a cold drink or some coffee?"

"No, thanks." He sat down in her chair, and she looked at him in the mirror. His face was well-defined, with a square forehead, a strong jaw, intelligent eyes, and thick, black lashes that were wasted on a man.

"What do you think?" he asked.

"Uh, what?"

"About my hair? How short should I go?"

His hair, right. She was supposed to be concentrating on his hair, which actually was fairly spectacular— dark brown, thick, naturally curly she suspected as she ran her fingers through the strands. It was already well styled. In fact, it didn't look like it needed much more than a trim, if that.

"A quarter inch," she said, meeting his gaze in the mirror. "Unless you had something else in mind? A buzz cut perhaps." She laughed at his wary expression. "Just kidding. I had you worried there for a second, didn't I?"

"For a second."

"Shampoo first?"

"If you want to just wet it down, that's fine."

"Whatever you like." She pulled out a plastic cover-up to protect his clothes and used the spray bottle to wet down his hair. "So, where are you from? You've got a touch of the South in your voice."

"Good ear. Texas."

"You're a long way from home. Are you here for the races?"

"As a matter of fact, I am. What about you? Are you a native?"

"I was born here, if that's what you mean." She ran a comb through his hair and picked up her scissors.

"Have you lived anywhere else?"

Caroline didn't know how to answer that question. Did sailing across several oceans count as actually living somewhere else? "I've been around. Are you crewing for someone?"

"I haven't firmed up my plans yet."

"Waiting for the best offer?"

"You could say that. Have you done any racing yourself?"

"Some."

"But you're not involved this year?"

"No, I have other things I'm more interested in right now." She paused, pulling up strands of hair so she could measure the cut. "How does that look?"

"Perfect."

"Mousse, gel, blow-dry?"

"No to all three."

"A natural kind of guy. Or you're just cheap."

"It's raining outside," he said with a grin.

"Then you're a smart guy." Caroline pulled off the cover-up and shook out the loose hair. "You can pay Erica at the desk," she said as he stood up.

"Maybe I could buy you a drink, hear more about your racing experience."

A date with a fascinating stranger? She'd be crazy to say no. In fact, every instinct in her body told her to say yes. Especially since Mike had already canceled their plans for the evening, and she didn't particularly want to be alone.

"I'd like to show off my haircut," he said persuasively.

God, his smile was hot! Reason warred with impulse. "I have to finish a highlight. It will be at least another thirty minutes."

"I can meet you. I saw a bar down by the wharf."

"How about some food instead? There's a terrific seafood restaurant a few blocks from here, called the Castaway. It's on Gilmore Street. When you leave here, turn left at the next corner and go down about four blocks."

"Sounds good. An hour?"

"Sure."

"Good. I'll see you there."

"See you there," she repeated softly, as he handed Erica a twenty and told her to keep the change. Caroline was still staring when he went through the door, caught up in genuine appreciation of his nicely rounded butt. It wasn't until Peggy began to cough that she turned away. She forced herself not to say a word until she heard the door close behind him.

Erica let out a whoop and jumped up from her desk. "You got yourself a real hottie there, Caroline," she said with twenty-year-old candor.

"He's all right."

"Honey, he's better than all right," Peggy said. "If I wasn't married, with enough stretch marks to make a map of Washington on my hips, I'd have gone for him myself."

"Did you see his ass?" Erica asked.

"I wouldn't mind getting my hands on those abs," Peggy said.

Caroline groaned. "You are both terrible. Why do I suddenly feel like we're twelve and at a slumber party?"

"Hey, it's not like a gorgeous stranger walks in here every day of the week," Erica said. "Usually it's cranky old ladies or middle-aged marrieds, present company excluded, of course."

Peggy laughed. "Believe me, at this moment, with my head covered in tinfoil, I'm happy that the only name you called me was 'middle-aged married.' But you look great, Caroline. It's no wonder he went for you."

"Do you think so? The skirt isn't too short?" Caroline looked at her reflection in the mirror. Her black skirt was as mini as they came, her stomach bared by a short, cropped, purple V-necked top that would have showed off some generous cleavage if she had any. Unfortunately, Kate was the only one of the sisters with more than a boyish bosom.

"You look terrific," Peggy assured her.

"I look like I've been at work all day."

"A little lipstick, some blush, you'll be good as new."

They both turned as the door to the salon opened once again. "Oh, it's just you," Caroline said with disappointment as her sister Ashley walked into the room. Normally, Caroline got along much better with Ashley than with Kate, but at the moment she wasn't particularly interested in talking to either of her sisters.

"Gee, thanks. Who did you think I was?" Ashley asked.

"A hottie," Erica said irrepressibly. "This incredible man came in to get his hair cut, and he made a move on Caroline. She's going to meet him for dinner as soon as Peggy's hair is done baking."

"Thanks for sharing," Caroline said with an annoyed look in Erica's direction.

"Who is this guy?" Ashley asked. "Does he have a name?"

It was only then that Caroline realized she didn't know his name. Had he said it? She tended to think of her clients by their appointment time or what they were having done. But he must have said his name. What was it?

"You don't know his name?" Ashley asked when she didn't reply. "And you're having dinner with him? How can you go out with him, if you don't know his name?" Ashley's brows knit together in a familiar worried line. "I don't like the sound of this at all."

"I know his name. I just don't remember it. For heaven's sake, Ashley, I'm not sixteen. It's just dinner in a public place."

"But he's a stranger."

"You worry too much."

"And you don't worry enough. It's raining out there, too."

Caroline realized her sister's agitation had more to do with the storm than with her. "Are you okay?"

"I'm fine," Ashley said evasively. "I came to check on you."

"Fine here, too."

"Well, good. Why don't you cancel your date and have dinner with Kate and me instead?"

"Kate has Dad on her couch."

"Oh."

"Don't say anything," Caroline warned her.

"I wasn't going to. What could I say, anyway?"

Silence fell between them as they both avoided a subject neither wanted to cover. "Did you want anything else?" Caroline prodded.

"Yes. Rumor has it you're dating Mike Stanaway."

"So what if I am?"

"He's too old for you. And isn't he still married?"

"He's separated."

"Caroline—"

"Ashley, I have work to finish. You don't have anything to worry about. Mike and I are just friends. Trust me."

"Are you sure?"

"Positive. Now, I really need to finish Peggy's hair."

"I guess I'll see you later," Ashley said after a moment. "But I think you should be careful about meeting this strange guy."

"He's not strange. He's just a stranger."

Ashley didn't look convinced as she said good-bye to her sister and dashed out of the salon into the rain.

"He's not a stranger, exactly. I have his name written right here," Erica said triumphantly, holding up the appointment book. "Tyler Jamison. Now you know who he is."

Caroline's stomach flipped over. Tyler Jamison? Wasn't that the name of the reporter Kate had warned her about? *Don't let yourself get taken in.* Kate's voice rang through her head. Caroline frowned. She hated it when her sister was right.

"Yeah, now I know who he is," she said heavily. And she also knew exactly what she had to do.

Chapter Three

"So what was it about me that made you think I was the most gullible? Because I'm the youngest? Because I have a reputation of being an airhead? What was it exactly?" Caroline set her purple purse on the table in front of Tyler, then sat down across from him in the lounge of the Castaway.

"You've spoken to your sister." Tyler took a drink from his frosted beer glass. He'd had a feeling Caroline would catch on to him sooner rather than later. But he'd taken a shot, and in the end he'd gotten what he wanted. She was sitting across from him. Mad as hell, maybe, but definitely within conversational distance. "Can I get you a drink?"

"No."

"Are you sure?" he asked as a waiter came up to take her drink order. "Our table won't be ready for a few minutes."

"Fine. I'll have a mineral water," Caroline said, forcing a tight smile as she said hello to the waiter. "Hi, Bobby. How are you?"

"Great," Bobby said. "No cosmopolitan for you, tonight?"

"Just the mineral water." She turned back to Tyler. "And I won't be staying for dinner."

Tyler hoped he could change her mind. "Why don't we start over? I'm Tyler Jamison."

"What do you want?" Caroline asked. "And why didn't you just tell me who you were when you came into the salon? I knew your hair didn't really need cutting, but I thought you were one of those types who has to have his hair perfect at all times."

Tyler put a self-conscious hand to his head, aware that he hadn't even looked at his hair since walking four blocks to the restaurant in the wind and rain.

"I can see I was wrong about that," Caroline said.

Tyler smiled. "Listen, I probably should have introduced myself, but you were busy, and your sister gave me the cold shoulder earlier, so I thought it might be better if we had a chance to speak in private. I did give my name to the receptionist at the salon. I didn't realize you weren't aware who I was." Actually, he had realized early on in their conversation but had decided to see how far he could take it.

Caroline appeared somewhat mollified, but she still had her arms crossed defiantly in front of her. "Fine. What is it you want to know?"

"I'd like to write a follow-up story about your family and the race, what happened then, what's happening now. I'd put the photograph of the three of you holding the Winston trophy right next to a photograph of the three of you today. Say where you are in your lives now, how the race may have changed you, that kind of thing. Where-are-they-now pieces are quite popular these days."

"I'm sure Kate told you we weren't interested."

"I thought you might have a different opinion. And I didn't think you'd want your older sister to speak for you."

Caroline sat up straighter in her seat. Tyler could see he'd hit a nerve with that one. Caroline was not about to let Kate speak for her, that was quite clear. He had a feeling this sister was his way into the family.

"I speak for myself," she replied. "But, that said, I

can't imagine what you'd write about us that would be at all interesting. We're not exactly living a wild and crazy life here on Castleton Island."

"True, but I'd like to know how hard or how easy it was to go from sailboat racer to hair stylist."

Caroline gave him a wide, toothy grin that made her look young, fresh, full of life. "That sounds like a headline that will sell about ten copies. Tell me something. Are you even a good reporter?"

"I've done all right," he said, biting back a smile. "And the value of the article would, of course, depend on how forthcoming you and your sisters are with the interesting details that people want to know."

"I barely remember the details now. Our journey was well documented in the logs we showed to the press at the end of the race."

"I've seen them—a page-turning discussion of the fish world, a little about your struggles with a geometry correspondence class, Ashley's reluctance to put a worm on a fishhook, and Kate's fascination with the brightness of the stars and planets as seen from each of the different hemispheres. Incredibly juicy stuff."

"Hey, I told you we were boring. Even when we were racing, there were a lot of days at sea where nothing happened. You've heard the expression 'in the doldrums'? We got stuck in them for days. Just lying there waiting and praying for a wisp of wind to get us on our way. Sometimes I wanted to scream or pull out a paddle and start rowing. Once Kate and I did that just to be funny. Dad wasn't amused. Thought we were breaking the rule about not using anything other than our sails."

"You and Kate, huh? Are you two the closest?"

"We're sisters."

"That's not what I asked." He paused. "I haven't met Ashley yet. What's she like?"

"Quiet, pretty, sensitive. But I didn't come down here to tell you that."

"Why did you come?"

"Because I said I would. And because I didn't want you to think I was an idiot. I'm not. I was just distracted earlier. Otherwise, I would have seen right through you." Caroline lifted her chin in the air, the gesture filled with bravado.

Tyler nodded approvingly. "I understand, and I like your style." But he thought her words had an edge of desperation to them, as if she wanted to make sure he understood that she was smart and capable. He had a feeling Caroline had been trying to prove herself for some time.

"I don't care if you like me or you don't. That's the end of our discussion. I'm not interested in a story, and my sisters aren't, either."

Tyler considered her words, then leaned forward in his chair. "You know, Miss McKenna, you and your sister are awfully secretive for no apparent reason. Most people who win races love to talk about them."

"So go talk to them."

"Can't. My curiosity is piqued."

"Curiosity killed the cat."

"Hmm, what should I make of that?"

"It's just an expression." She paused as the waiter set down her mineral water. "I really can't stay," she said when they were alone again.

"Why don't you have your drink and give me the opportunity to change your mind?"

"That won't happen. I'm not as gullible as some people seem to think."

"Like Kate," he said, taking a wild guess.

"I didn't say that."

"You didn't have to. You're the baby sister. Did Kate try to boss you around when you were at sea?"

Caroline rolled her eyes. "She bosses me wherever we are."

"But on a boat, in close quarters, I would imagine not everyone gets to be chief."

"Daddy was the chief."

"Daddy," he murmured, taking another sip of his

beer. "I met him earlier, you know—your father. He was three sheets to the wind."

"His favorite place to be." Caroline picked up her glass, running her finger around the edge. "But he's a good man. He did his best by us. And he did accomplish an amazing feat. People forget that nowadays."

Tyler put his elbows on the table and leaned in, sensing he'd just gotten the opening he needed. "They won't forget if you let me tell the story again, and not just that story, but the one you're living now. Your father could have it all back, the glory days of his life. What's the harm in that?" Caroline didn't reply right away, and he could see the indecision in her eyes. "This could be a good thing for you and your family."

Before she could answer, a loud group of men entered the lounge, their voices high and filled with energy.

"Damn," Caroline muttered, looking past him. "Just what I need."

Tyler followed her gaze to the four men sitting down at a table near the door. "Friends of yours?"

"Kiwis," she said.

Tyler raised an eyebrow. "Are we talking fruit here?"

"New Zealanders."

"Ah. And we don't like Kiwis?"

"My father is an Aussie. There's a long-standing rivalry between Aussies and Kiwis in ocean racing," she explained, tensing even further as one of the men approached their table.

"Caroline," he said in a loud, boisterous voice. "Just the person I was looking for. Did you hear who's coming to town?"

"Do I care?"

"You should. Or at least your father should."

"What are you talking about?"

"The *Moon Dancer* is a last-minute entry in the race. She should be here by Monday."

Tyler watched Caroline's face pale as the news registered. The *Moon Dancer* was the name of the Mc-Kennas' boat. Now it was back, apparently with a different owner. He didn't know the significance of this news, but it seemed to disturb Caroline.

"That's not possible," she said.

"Oh, but it is, and guess who bought it?" The man paused dramatically. "Good old K.C. Wales. I can't wait to see Duncan's face when he finds out his nemesis is coming to town on his boat."

"He won't care a bit."

The sailor laughed. "Yeah, sure. See you around."

"That's your boat he was talking about, right?" Tyler asked.

"What?" Caroline sent him a blank look.

"Your boat. The *Moon Dancer*. The one you sailed around the world."

"Yes, it was our boat," Caroline said slowly. "I can't believe that K.C. bought it, or that he's bringing it here. My dad will go crazy when he sees her. Kate, too. And Ashley . . ." Caroline shook her head. "This is bad, very bad."

"Why?"

"A lot of memories. I should tell my father and my sisters." She started to get up, then sat back down in her seat. "I don't want to tell them."

"Why not?"

"Because it will hurt. I don't have the stomach for it."

He raised an eyebrow. "Three ear piercings, a tattoo on your shoulder, a naval ring, and you don't have the stomach for a little pain?"

"Not that kind of pain." She frowned at the mineral water in front of her. "I need a real drink."

"I'll get you one." He put up his hand to motion for the waiter.

"No. Wait, never mind," she said hurriedly.

Tyler put down his hand.

"I'd rather eat instead. I wonder when our table will be ready?"

"I can check."

"I'll do that. Is it under your name or an alias?"

"My name." He watched her walk away. She was careful not to go near the bar, but he did see her fling a somewhat desperate look in that direction. Was Caroline a drinker? She'd said she'd wanted a drink, but then changed her mind. And the waiter had seemed surprised she'd ordered a mineral water. Not that it meant anything, but her behavior was a bit off, he thought. As a reporter, he'd become very good at paying attention to the details. It wasn't what a subject said or did that was important but what they didn't say or didn't do.

With an alcoholic father, it was certainly possible that Caroline had her own problems with alcohol. He made a mental note to check it out. Mark would definitely want that information. Tyler raised his beer glass to his lips. He had a feeling things were about to get interesting.

Kate opened her door just before nine o'clock that night to find Caroline on the porch. It was a little surprising, since none of her family was prone to dropping in, to suddenly have Ashley in the kitchen making tea, Duncan in the living room sleeping it off, and Caroline on her doorstep looking guilty about something. "You talked to him, didn't you?"

"He didn't tell me his name right away," Caroline said defensively as she entered the hallway. "Where's Dad?"

"Can't you hear the snoring?"

Caroline peeked into the living room where their father lay sprawled on his back amid Kate's fluffy sofa cushions. "He looks tired. And his face is all red."

Kate followed her younger sister's gaze and saw exactly what Caroline saw and more, not just the weary lines, or the red face, but the thin translucent skin on his arms and hands, the lack of meat on his bones. Their father had always been big and stronger than most, but he was fading away like an old photograph, and she didn't know how to make it stop.

"We should do something for him," Caroline said, echoing Kate's thoughts.

"Like what?"

"I don't know, something. He looks pathetic. I don't like seeing him like this."

Duncan had always been Caroline's hero, even when he was at his most unheroic. Most of the time, Kate tried to protect Caroline from seeing moments such as these. Perhaps that had been a mistake. But she was so used to being the big sister she couldn't stop the nurturing instincts from kicking into gear. "Come into the kitchen. Ashley brought over her chocolate cookies, and she's making tea."

"That sounds good. I'm still hungry."

"You mean he didn't buy you dinner?" Kate asked wryly as she followed Caroline down the hall and into the kitchen.

"Who didn't buy you dinner?" Ashley asked from the kitchen counter where she was pouring tea into a cup. "Hi, Caroline. Do you want some tea?"

"Just cookies." Caroline grabbed one off the plate on the counter and took a seat at the kitchen table. One bite brought a squeal of delight. "These are heaven. I swear, if you weren't a photographer, you could be a chef."

"All I can make are cookies and tea," Ashley said. "Not exactly chef material."

"Don't forget your famous blueberry pancakes or your turkey stuffing," Kate reminded Ashley. "You're always too humble."

"Makes a change from you," Caroline said.

Kate made a face at Caroline, who stuck her tongue out in response. They both burst out laughing. Kate was amazed how good the sound made her feel. It had been awhile since she'd had both her sisters together in one place.

Ashley handed Kate a cup of tea, then sat down at

the table. "So who didn't buy you dinner, Caroline? It wasn't that strange man you were going to meet, was it?"

"You knew?" Kate asked in surprise. "You knew she was meeting Tyler Jamison, and you didn't stop her?"

"Tyler Jamison? The reporter you just told me about?" Ashley asked in confusion. "That's who Caroline met for dinner?"

"Exactly."

"But why?"

"I have no idea. I told her to stay away from him."

"Okay, both of you, breathe," Caroline said. "Yes, I met the reporter for dinner, and yes, I did eat, but as you know I can always eat more. Before you ask, I didn't tell him anything. So chill out. We have bigger fish to fry. The *Moon Dancer* was sold to K.C. Wales. He's planning to race her in the Castleton, then on to Hawaii. They should be here by Monday."

Ashley put a hand to her heart. "K.C. Wales? Oh, dear."

"Dad will freak." Caroline picked up another cookie. "You'll have to tell him, Kate."

"Why me?"

"You're the oldest, the most responsible, the most understanding."

"Since when?" Kate asked. "According to you, I'm bossy, opinionated, and critical."

"That, too," Caroline said. "But I'm Dad's baby, and you know he never takes anything I say seriously. And Ashley can't do it because . . . well, she just can't do it."

"I could do it," Ashley said. "But it would come better from you, Kate. You always know the right thing to say."

Once again, both sisters looked to Kate for the answer to their problem. They'd played out this scene many times before—Caroline eating chocolate, Ashley biting her fingernails while Kate paced. As before,

Kate wanted to say something reassuring. She wanted to give them the answers they were looking for, but words were difficult to find.

Her mother would have known what to say. She'd understood each of them and had passed on special pieces of herself: sensitivity to Ashley, passion to Caroline, and loyalty to Kate. It was that loyalty they needed now. Kate had promised her mother that she would protect her sisters and look out for her father, and she'd do it now, just as she had done before.

"It's funny how life goes merrily along and then, boom, the past comes back and bites you in the butt," Caroline said with her usual descriptiveness.

"I wonder if the *Moon Dancer* still looks the same," Ashley said quietly. "I wonder if Mom's curtains are hanging in the master cabin."

"What I wonder is why K.C. bought the boat," Kate said. "He must know that Dad will hate him for it."

"I doubt he cares," Caroline replied. "He was always more interested in winning than in friendship."

"Not always." Kate shook her head, confused by the turn of events. K.C. had once been a friend, then an enemy. What was he now?

"Did I tell you that Sean is back, too?" Ashley asked. "I saw him down at the docks. He says he's going to race in the Castleton. Now that I know the *Moon Dancer* is in the race, I have an even worse feeling about it. Look, I've got goose bumps," she said, holding out her arm.

"You're too thin—that's why you have goose bumps," Caroline retorted. "And you knew Sean would come back again. His family is here."

"I know, but I'm not ready to deal with him."

"You'll never be ready."

"Okay, let's put Sean aside for the moment," Kate cut in, knowing that Ashley and Caroline had never seen eye-to-eye on that subject. "What did you tell Tyler Jamison about us, Caroline?"

"I told him to leave us alone. But . . ."

Kate groaned. "Please don't let there be a but."

"He might be able to do us some good. Dad would love to be in the spotlight again. It would give him a reason to get up in the morning. It could turn his life around."

"It could turn his life upside down. Are you actually telling me you think that an article about us is a good idea?" Kate didn't give Caroline a chance to respond. "What do you think Dad will tell Tyler? What do you think he remembers about the race? About the storm? What do you think will come out when he's wasted out of his mind? It's crazy."

"She's right," Ashley said, siding with Kate. "We can't let a reporter into our lives. There are too many people who could be affected, like Sean. I knew the wind would bring trouble. I just knew it."

"So did I," Kate agreed.

"Well, I didn't. I thought it was a grand wind, and a great storm while it lasted," Caroline said. "You two have forgotten how to live. We used to be brave. We used to be adventurous. Kate, you used to climb to the top of the sail without any fear. Ashley, you used to dive to the bottom of the sea. What happened to us?"

"You know what happened," Kate said pointedly.

"I'm not sure I do, not really. We've never talked—"

"And we're not going to talk now," Kate interrupted. "We can't. There's too much at stake. We have lives to live, maybe not wild and adventurous, but good solid lives, the kind Mom wanted us to have."

"I want more than good and solid. And you should want more, too," Caroline muttered.

Maybe she did once in a while, Kate thought, not that she'd admit that to her baby sister. But Tyler Jamison's appearance in her bookstore had sent an unexpected burst of adrenaline through her bloodstream. And she'd enjoyed the heady rush far more than she should have.

"I wonder why this reporter came to town now?" Ashley mused. "It's not the tenth anniversary of the race. Why is he interested in us? It seems like he came out of nowhere for no reason. And who does he write for, anyway?"

"He's a freelancer, or so he said," Kate replied. "He told me that there is a lot of interest in sailboat racing, and because we don't fit the traditional mold of a racing syndicate, we're of even more interest to the general public. It makes some sense. I know short biographies are popular right now, but I still don't have a good feeling about this. My instincts tell me that he came looking for something in particular."

"I agree," Caroline said. "The fact that he didn't tell me who he was, that he asked me out to dinner without revealing his identity, goes along with the idea that he's playing some sort of game. He's good at the game, too. He's very charming."

And attractive, Kate thought. But it didn't matter. Charm and good looks would not destroy her family. He'd have to come up with something more than that.

"If none of us talk, there won't be a story," she said decisively. "We have to stick together, protect one another, the way we used to do. Remember?" Kate walked over to the table and took each of her sister's hands in hers. "Circle," she said.

"We're not kids anymore," Caroline complained, but she did as Kate wanted by placing her other hand in Ashley's, forming a circle.

"All for one," Kate said.

"And one for all," her sisters repeated. A reassuring squeeze went from hand to hand.

Their unity had gotten them past a lot of hardships. With any luck it would get them past one very persistent reporter.

*   *   *

It was past ten that night when Tyler finally picked up the phone to call his brother. He knew it wasn't too late to call. Mark had always been a night owl. Catch him in the morning, and he was a grumpy bear. But, after nine o'clock at night, he was ready to party—at least in the old days. Mark's life had changed drastically since the car accident a month earlier.

Tyler could still remember getting the call. He'd been in a hotel room in London, covering a summit meeting. The phone had rung in the middle of the night and he'd known, even before he answered it, that bad news was coming. Those first words had stopped his heart: *Your brother has been in an accident. You should come as soon as possible.*

His immediate reaction had been a silent, desperate prayer: *Please let him be all right.* Then he'd asked about Mark's eight-year-old daughter, Amelia, and Mark's wife, Susan. Amelia had made it. Susan had died on the way to the hospital. And Mark was in surgery to save his life.

The time it took to get from London to San Antonio, Texas, had been the longest hours of Tyler's life. He'd made a million promises to God along the way, using every bargaining chip he could think of to plead for his brother's life. Amelia would need her father to help her get over the tragedy of her mother's death. Mark had to survive to take care of his child. And Tyler couldn't lose his brother. Not when they'd just begun to get close again. So he'd begged God for a miracle and promised he would do anything and everything he could to protect Mark and Amelia from any further pain. He would make himself responsible for them. He hadn't known then just how far that promise would take him.

"Hello?" Mark said, his voice coming over the phone.

"How's it going, little brother?" Tyler deliberately put a cheerful note in his voice, trying to sound casual, as if this was any other conversation they'd had over the years.

"Not so good," Mark replied, making no effort to aid in the pretense of normalcy.

"What's wrong?"

"What isn't wrong? Do you have any news? Shelly said you found the McKenna sisters. Did you talk to any of them?"

"Yes, I spoke to two of them—Kate, the oldest, and Caroline, the youngest. Kate runs a bookstore and appears to run the family, too. She's smart, responsible, wary, doesn't let her thoughts show. Caroline is a firecracker, impulsive, headstrong, wants to be taken seriously and doesn't like big sister calling the shots. I still have to track down Ashley."

"Did they tell you anything?"

Tyler wanted to ease his brother's mind. But he didn't have the information Mark wanted. "Not yet. They're not particularly interested in a follow-up story. In fact, they're more secretive than I expected. I also met their father, Duncan. He was bombed out of his mind. Kate was called to take care of him, and I got the feeling this was definitely not the first time. I think it's likely he has a drinking problem."

"He's not important. I don't care about him. It's his daughters. One of them—" Mark's voice caught on a sob of emotion. "Amelia is all I have left. I promised Susan. She was dying, Tyler, and she knew it. I can still see the fear in her eyes. She was afraid, not for herself but for me and for Amelia."

"I know," Tyler said tightly. "You won't lose Amelia. Trust me."

"I do trust you. But it's a hell of a big problem even for you, big brother."

And he'd been a hell of a big brother, Tyler thought, as a shaft of pain ran through him. He'd missed a lot of years of his brother's life. "Get some sleep," he said gruffly. "I'll call you as soon as I know anything. And I won't give up. No matter what the McKenna sisters throw in my path."

Chapter Four

Kate stared at the blanket tossed haphazardly on the living room floor. Her father was gone. She'd planned on offering him a cup of coffee, some breakfast, and a stern warning not to speak to Tyler Jamison. But Duncan had already left. He'd always been one to get up with the sun, hangover or not. He was probably on his way back to his boat or maybe to the Oyster Bar for a Bloody Mary.

As she picked up the blanket, she caught a whiff of her father's aftershave. The musky scent reminded her of childhood, the scent forever linked to her father, to childish hugs and Daddy's strong arms. He'd once been her hero, her protector, the man who stood taller than all the rest. She remembered sitting on the floor by his feet listening to him tell stories about his adventures at sea. His words would sweep her away. She could smell the sea and feel the splash of the waves, and she would shiver with the imagined wind. She couldn't have stopped listening if she tried, and she never tried, because having her father at home was always special. He was gone a lot in her early childhood, running fishing boats, charters, whatever he could do to make a living. His frequent absences had made his rare presence that much more special, a time to be treasured, as her mother often said.

But those times of treasuring had created a man who took for granted the devotion of his family, Kate thought now. And once her mother had passed on, the responsibility of taking care of Duncan had fallen to her, the eldest child. She'd cooked and cleaned and mothered her sisters and tried to make sure her father's life always ran smoothly. She'd supported his every decision, including the one that had taken them to sea for three long years, always believing in her heart that Daddy knew best.

As a grown woman, she realized that Daddy hadn't known best for a very long time, and somewhere along the way their roles had reversed. Duncan had become the child, and she had become the parent. It was not the role she craved. And she couldn't help but wish for the impossible, that he would wake up one day and be the father she craved, the kind of man who would listen and advise, who would laugh with her and come to her bookstore and tell her he was proud of her. But he had never been that kind of father. Proud of her, yes, but only when it came to sailing. The rest of her life—her interests, her emotions, her ambitions—had never been of concern to him. If it didn't touch his life, he just didn't care that much.

Sometimes she hated him for not caring. But most of the time she loved him. He was her father, and she was supposed to love him. In the still of her heart, she could hear her mother's voice: *Your father is the most special man in the world. You are a very lucky little girl.*

Maybe she just hadn't figured out the special part yet. Kate sighed, as she took the blanket into the laundry room and tossed it in the pile to be washed. As for lucky, well, she could use a little luck right now, because she had a feeling her father was the least of her problems. No doubt that reporter would be waiting for her when she got to the bookstore. He certainly didn't act like a man who gave up easily.

As she returned to the kitchen her eye caught on the laptop computer on the counter. She hadn't had a chance to look last night, but maybe she should make the time now.

Taking the computer over to the kitchen table, she got it started, then poured herself a cup of coffee. When she was logged on to the Internet, she quickly did a search on the name Tyler Jamison. If he was a reporter, he'd no doubt published some stories somewhere, and she was more than a little curious as to where.

The answer wasn't long in coming, but it was long in detail.

Tyler Jamison reporting from Somalia for *Time* magazine

An in-depth look at India's Kashmir region by Tyler Jamison

Japan's new royalty, Tyler Jamison, *U.S. News and World Report*

Kate's jaw dropped farther with each entry. It couldn't be the same man. A foreign correspondent, a man who covered war, whose words had been printed in every national magazine—that kind of reporter didn't write about sailboat races in Puget Sound. Something was definitely wrong. Either Tyler Jamison wasn't really Tyler Jamison, or he'd come to Castleton for another reason.

Maybe there was a photograph of him somewhere, she thought, hastily clicking on each of the entries and scanning the articles for a picture. She had barely started when the doorbell rang. For a split second, she thought it might be one of her sisters, or her father, but the second decisive ring told her that the man she was researching was probably closer than she thought.

She walked down the hall to the front door and opened it. She was right.

Tyler Jamison wore jeans and a short-sleeved polo shirt this morning. His eyes didn't look nearly as tired as they had the day before, and he'd obviously showered only a short time earlier, as his dark hair was still damp and there was a glow to his cleanly shaven face. Or maybe it was just the glow that came from his eyes. He really had incredible eyes, a much darker blue than her own. They reminded her of the deep waters of the ocean. She just hoped he wouldn't prove as dangerous or as deadly as the sea.

"Good morning. Can I interest you in some bagels?" He held out the white paper bag in his hand. "I don't know about you, but I always think better on a full stomach."

"Come on in," she said wryly as he brushed past her without an invitation.

"Thanks, I think I will."

"How did you find me?"

"The island isn't that big, Kate, and everyone knows you. You don't mind if I call you Kate, do you?"

"Would it matter?"

He smiled in reply. "Are you ready for your interview? You did tell me we could talk today."

"I said you should come by the store, not my house."

"We'll have more privacy here." Tyler walked into the living room, his sharp gaze taking in every detail.

She knew what he saw, a comfortable, feminine room, with pastel colors, puffy white couches, throw rugs that warmed up the hardwood floor, and small lamps on every table. This was her haven, her home, and she'd make no apologies for the decor. Her years on a sailboat had left her with a distinct longing for a place of her own that didn't rock with the waves or blow in the wind, a house she could make a home, with a garden and trees, with roots that went deep into the ground.

"Landscapes," Tyler mused, surprising her with his words.

Kate followed his glance to the pictures of hillsides and meadows, flowers and trees on the walls. "You don't like landscapes?"

"They're okay. But where's the sea? The lighthouses? The piers? The boats?"

"Just a few miles down the road."

"No reason to put them on the wall?"

"None whatsoever." She met his gaze head-on. "Do you find that surprising?"

Tyler nodded. "Among other things. Are you going to talk to me, Kate?"

"I might." She still didn't know how to handle him. She'd dreamed about him last night, the first time in a long time a man's face that wasn't Jeremy's had appeared in her dreams. But she didn't want this man in her dreams, or in her house for that matter.

Tyler walked over to the mantle and studied the portrait hanging over the fireplace. It was Kate's favorite picture—the McKenna women, Nora, Kate, Caroline, and Ashley. They'd had the portrait painted for her father's birthday when Kate was fourteen years old, Ashley twelve and Caroline ten. She could still see her father unwrapping the portrait, the love, joy, and pride lighting up his eyes when he saw it. He'd jumped to his feet, grabbed her mother in a huge bear hug, and swung her around until she was dizzy. Next he'd picked up Kate and spun her, then done the same with each of her sisters. There had been so much laughter that day, so much love.

"Your mother?" Tyler asked, drawing her attention back to him.

"Yes."

"You look like her."

"I've always thought Ashley looked the most like her."

"I haven't met Ashley yet."

And it was going to stay that way, if Kate had her wish.

"What happened to your mother?" Tyler asked.

"She died of cancer when I was seventeen years old."

"I'm sorry."

"So am I."

"Was she a sailor?"

"Yes, but she didn't like sailing far from home. A spin around the islands was enough for her. She was an artist, a dreamer. She used to design sails, not for money, just for friends. I think she was more of an armchair adventurer than anything else." Kate let out a small sigh, feeling a wave of longing and nostalgia that never seemed to go away completely. It had been years since her mother's death, but she still missed her. "I wish she could have seen my bookstore. I think she would have liked it." She stopped abruptly, remembering whom she was talking to.

"Don't stop now. You're on a roll." Tyler sent her a curious look. "We don't have to be adversaries. I'm not sure why, but I get the feeling that you don't want me here. In fact, I believe you'd like to send me away as quickly as possible. I just don't know why."

"What are you really after?" she asked, deciding it was time to turn the tables. "You don't write stories about ocean racers, not even world-class ones. You write about wars and emperors and international economies. You've had bylines in every national magazine. And I think somewhere along the way you've won a journalistic award or two."

His eyes narrowed with a glint of admiration. "You did some checking."

"Is that a problem? Do you have something to hide?"

"Not at all. I'm just not used to being on the other side of the research."

"So, tell me, Mr. Jamison, why would a man comfortable in the hottest spots of the world want to re-create an old story that wasn't that exciting to begin with?"

"Again, I think you underestimate the level of interest in your experience. But, to answer your question, I wanted a change of pace. It's been an intense few years for me. After a while there's only so much blood and carnage you can absorb without going a little crazy."

"I can imagine," she murmured.

"No, you can't."

She started to reply, then hesitated, seeing a grimness on his face that bespoke things she probably couldn't imagine. "I'm sorry. I didn't mean to make it sound—"

"Why don't we talk about you?" He moved closer, invading her personal space, making her feel very aware of herself as a woman. She hadn't spent much time on men or relationships in the past few years, keeping herself busy with family, friends, her home, and her business. It seemed to be enough most days. But not today, not with this man standing so close, his warm breath brushing her cheek, his lips within kissing distance.

Kate cleared her throat, feeling distinctly warm and foolish as she took a step back. Tyler Jamison wasn't interested in her. He was after a story, and he wasn't above using his appeal to get it. She'd have to be careful. She sat down on the edge of the couch and waved her hand toward a nearby chair. "What do you want to know about me?" she asked as he took a seat.

"When did your family decide to race around the world?"

"It wasn't a family decision. My father decided for us. After my mom died, we were at loose ends. My dad wasn't good at homework and carpools, so he decided to take us to sea. He'd always been a sailor. He was in the navy in his early years, raced as a younger man, then settled down to running charters around Puget Sound once he married my mother. He always felt more comfortable on water than on land. He had itchy feet. My mother was the only person who could keep him in one place. Once she was gone, he couldn't settle down."

"Sounds like he loved her."

"He did. Very much, I think. He was different with her. I think she understood him in a way that I've certainly never been able to."

"A different relationship—husband/wife, father/daughter."

"Yes."

"So you took to the sea. What happened next?"

"At first we just sailed. That lasted about six months. Then a short race came up, and we joined in. After our first win, my dad wanted another and another. It became a fever. He filled up our future with big dreams of big races. We were somewhat limited, because our boat was built for cruising as well as racing. We weren't as big, sleek, or powerful as the boats used by the racing syndicates. But my dad was determined to win an around-the-world race. The Winston came up in one of the off years between the Whitbread and America's Cup. It was a different kind of race, one for both amateurs and professionals; the class level of the boats made sure of that. The crews were limited to no more than six. There was more time built into the race and into the layovers."

"But there were only four of you. Why not fill out the crew with a couple of hefty guys?"

She smiled at the familiar criticism. So many people had suggested that they take on additional crew members. The initial reports of the race had all predicted that the McKennas would finish last, if they finished at all.

"We were good at what we did," she said. "I think we proved we were quite capable of winning without two hefty guys."

"Good point. What happened to the boat after you came home? It's my understanding that it's now owned by someone else."

"Yes. We sold it when we returned home."

"Why?"

Kate thought for a moment, wondering how she could answer that without drawing additional questions. "That part of our life was over," she said finally. "We needed the money for other things."

"What other things?"

"Just things."

Tyler tapped his foot against the floor. "Okay. Tell me this, how will you feel when you see your boat come sailing back into the harbor on Monday?"

"How do you know about that?" she asked sharply, then remembered he'd had dinner with her sister. "That's right. You were out with Caroline last night."

"Yes."

"Why did you ask her out?"

"I thought she'd be more forthcoming than you."

"And was she?"

"You know she wasn't. She was as evasive as you are, although a bit more colorful in her language."

Kate could believe that. Caroline had always loved a good swear word. "What else do you want to know?" she asked, checking her watch. "I have to get to the bookstore."

"Did you ever want to quit the race?"

"Yes. But my father was determined, obsessed with getting to the finish line. Once we began, nothing and no one could stop him."

"I guess that's how you win races."

"I guess." She hadn't let herself think about the race in a very long time. There were too many emotions wrapped up in that part of her life, incredible joy, horrific pain. Standing up abruptly, she said, "We're done."

"We're just beginning," Tyler said as he also stood up.

"If you want more information, go to the library."

"I thought we were getting along, breaking the ice." His soft smile was meant to take the edge off her mood, but it wasn't enough. She'd started to feel the pain again. She couldn't go back there. She wouldn't go back there.

Tyler reached out and touched the side of her face with his hand. The heat burned through her skin, the intimate gesture startling her.

"What put that look of enormous hurt into your eyes?" he asked softly, his gaze intent on hers.

"Nothing. You're imagining things." She wanted to look away from him, but she couldn't seem to break the connection between them. "You're staring at me."

"You're staring at me," he murmured.

And she was, dammit. Why now? Why did her sleeping libido have to suddenly wake up now?

"Was it a man?" Tyler asked.

"What?" Caught up in her physical reaction to him, she'd completely lost the thread of their conversation.

"Was it a man who hurt you?"

"No," she said quickly.

"Did something happen to one of your sisters while you were racing?"

"Why would you ask that?"

"Because you're their protector. And anything that hurts them hurts you. Am I right?"

She was relieved that the conversation had turned to her sisters. "I'm the oldest," she replied. "I do what I have to do."

"I can understand that."

"Because you're the oldest, too," she guessed. "Which explains why you're so bossy."

Tyler frowned. "I think that word refers to ten-year-old girls named Lucy."

"Don't go after my sisters, Tyler. That would be a big mistake."

Tyler sent her a long, measuring look. "I believe it would be."

"Good. Then we understand each other." She turned to escort him out of the room, but he caught her by the arm.

"Not so fast."

It wasn't fear that drove the shiver down her spine but an undeniable attraction, and Kate couldn't afford an attraction to this man. She couldn't let herself like him or trust him. She had family to protect, not to mention her heart.

"We're not done," he added.

"Yes, we are. I don't trust you. I don't believe you're here for a simple story."

"And I don't believe nothing happened during your race. I think you're hiding something."

"Believe what you want. I don't have anything to gain by talking to you."

"You may have nothing to gain, but I suspect that you have something to lose."

He had no idea how much. And she desperately hoped he would never find out. Before she could reply, the doorbell rang once again. Her house had never been this busy, but she was grateful for the distraction. She pulled her arm away from his hand. "I need to get that." Opening the door, she found Ashley on the doorstep.

Ashley's eyes were wild, her long hair tangled and falling around her face and shoulders. "I can't do it, Kate. I can't get on the damn boat. The wind has died down, but I still feel a breeze, and it's too much." Ashley's words tumbled out in a rush as she stepped into the hallway. "If I don't photograph all the crews, Mr. Conway will give the assignment to someone else, and I really need the money. But I can't get on the damn boat. What's wrong with me? Why do I have to be so afraid all the time?" She waved her hand in frustration, the action sending her purse flying to the ground, the contents spilling on the floor. "Dammit. I can't do anything right."

"Oh, Ash," Kate said, putting a calming hand on her sister's arm. "It's going to be fine."

"No, it's not." Ashley stopped abruptly as Tyler squatted down to collect the things that had spilled from her purse. "Who are you?"

Tyler. Kate had forgotten he was there. Damn. What had Ashley said?

"Tyler Jamison," he said as he stood up and handed Ashley her purse. "You must be Ashley."

"The reporter?" Ashley looked from Tyler to Kate in confusion. "You're talking to the reporter, but you said—"

Kate cut Ashley off with a warning glance. "I said that he was very persistent, and he is."

"Right. I'm sorry I interrupted you."

"Oh, this must have come out of your purse, too," Tyler said, handing Ashley a small bottle of pills.

"Thank you," Ashley said hastily, sticking the pills in her purse. "I should go."

"You don't have to go. Mr. Jamison was just leaving." Kate sent Tyler a pointed look, willing him to just go. She needed to deal with Ashley in private.

"All right. I'll go," Tyler said. "It was nice to meet you, Ashley. I'll talk to you later, Kate."

"Sure, whatever." Kate shut the door behind him and turned to her sister. "Now then, tell me again why you're so upset."

"One of the boat crews is insisting that I photograph them from the deck of the boat. I've made up two excuses already, and I'm going to lose the assignment if I don't take their picture the way they want it." She shook her head in frustration. "It gets harder every day, Kate. I lived on a boat for three years, and now I can't get on one for twenty seconds. It's stupid. I thought the fear would have gone away by now, but it's worse than it was eight years ago. It's as if every day the fear pushes me back another step. I used to be able to go out on the Sound, remember? When we first got back, I went on some day trips. I was nervous, but I made it. But each time I went out got shorter and shorter. Now I can't even get on a damn boat."

Kate saw the frustration and pain in Ashley's eyes and wanted so badly to make it all right again, but

Ashley's fears ran deep, probably deeper than Kate even realized. She'd told herself in recent months that Ashley was doing better, that she was fine. It was easier to believe they were all okay now, to pretend that the past no longer had the power to hurt. But it was clear that Ashley wasn't better, and pretending otherwise would only make it worse. "Do you want me to go with you?" Kate asked. "Maybe it would help."

"I can't ask you to do that," Ashley said, but there was a plea in her eyes that told Kate not to give up too easily.

"I want to do it. I want to help you. It will be fine, you'll see. We'll go together and you'll snap their pictures, and it will be over before you know it. Not nearly as bad as a root canal, I promise."

"I'm such an idiot."

"No, you're not."

Ashley drew in a deep breath and let it out. "You know, just telling you about it actually makes me feel like I can do it."

"You *can* do it. Remember, the boat isn't going anywhere."

"I know. My fear is ridiculous. Even if the boat got loose, I could swim back."

"You could sail back."

Ashley gave her a reluctant smile. "Yeah, I could do that, too." She paused. "What did you say to the reporter? What was his name again?"

"Tyler Jamison, and I said as little as possible. I don't trust him, Ash. He's got a hidden agenda, but I don't know what it is."

"It's been so long. I didn't think anyone . . ."

"I know."

"What are we going to do?"

"I'm thinking we should check him out at the same time he's checking us out. I already did a brief search on the Internet. He's been all over the world, covering major stories."

"That doesn't sound good."

"No, it doesn't. I'd like to find out why he has developed a sudden interest in ocean racing."

"If he's been all over the world, maybe we ran into him before and just don't remember?"

Kate thought about the rugged, dark-haired man who had just left her house and knew deep in her soul that if she'd ever met him before, she would have remembered. "If our paths crossed, I don't think we knew it. But it might be interesting to find out what Mr. Jamison was doing eight years ago."

"Do you think you can?"

"I'm sure going to try."

"I'd like to look at news articles that appeared eight years ago in reference to the McKenna family's racing victory," Tyler told the librarian. Castleton's library was little more than a two-story Victorian house, but since the McKennas were local, he figured he might get lucky.

"Oh, well, that's easy," the librarian replied. "We photocopied and laminated every article we could find, seeing as how the McKennas are hometown heroes. We were so proud of them, you know. They were amazing."

Tyler nodded. "That's what I understand." He followed the librarian into the next room.

"This is where we keep everything on sailing. Racing, boats, maps—you name it, it's here. And this is the McKenna shelf," she added, pointing to several notebooks. "Do you mind if I ask why you're so interested? It was a long time ago."

"I'm writing an article on ocean racing featuring famous crews. A where-are-they-now piece."

"Well, they're all right here," she said with a gleam in her eye. "And all quite single. Are you single, Mr. . . . ?"

"Jamison. Tyler Jamison. And, yes, I'm single." If

the woman asking him had been less than seventy years old, he might have felt awkward, but she was clearly not asking for herself.

"Really? A handsome man like you—what are the girls thinking? Why, if I were twenty years younger, I'd go after you myself."

"I would count myself lucky."

"Oh, you're a charmer, you are. Well, I'll leave you to your reading. Let me know if you need anything. My name is Sheryl Martin, and I'll be here until we close at five."

"Thank you." Tyler pulled out the first notebook and sat down at a nearby table. He'd already read through several articles on the race that he'd found on the Internet, but most of those articles had been about the race itself: winners of each leg, time handicaps, and weather conditions. Nothing that helped his cause.

He turned to the first page. The headline stated FIVE RACERS LOST AT SEA.

Tyler had read a little about the storm but hadn't thought much about it, since the McKennas had come through unscathed. Now he wondered if that storm had caused some trauma. Ashley seemed to have a surprising fear of the water. His mind darted back to the bottle of pills that had fallen from her purse. The label had read Xanax. He wasn't positive, but he thought Xanax was an antianxiety medication. It would make sense. Ashley had appeared more than a little anxious. Something else to file away, he thought with a pleased nod. He was making headway, slowly but surely.

Tyler skimmed the article, but there was no mention made of the McKennas or the *Moon Dancer*. Instead, the article focused on a boat that had capsized, losing all but one of her entire crew to the raging sea. Turning the page, he found more reports on the storm, quotes from some of the sailors.

"The winds were screaming. It was a scene from hell."

"The waves were three stories high. I couldn't tell if I was on the boat or in the water."

"There were Maydays and distress calls every-where. Flares popping up all over the place like the Fourth of July. We were no longer racing. We were simply trying to survive."

Tyler wanted a quote from one of the McKennas. He wanted to know what they had been thinking, what they had been feeling. It sounded terrifying. Certainly something that could bring on a water phobia—maybe even a need to drink, he thought, his mind turning to Caroline and to Duncan. But what about Kate? She didn't have any noticeable vices or inconsistencies. Had the storm affected her in some way? He'd have to find out. Mark was counting on him.

He wondered if Kate had somehow connected him to Mark. It seemed unlikely; they didn't share the same last name since Mark's stepfather had adopted him. But she'd obviously been on the Internet. What else had she come up with?

Tyler shook his head. Too many questions, not enough answers. The second notebook focused on the end of the race. There were photos taken of the *Moon Dancer*'s arrival in Castleton, most of which he'd seen before. Although the official finish line had been in San Francisco, there had been a victory celebration at Rose Harbor when the *Moon Dancer* had sailed home a week later.

It occurred to him that it must have been a strange few days, the time between the end of the race and the sail home. Anticlimactic for sure, but what else? Had the McKennas simply sailed home, gotten off their boat, and said good-bye to sailing forever? According to Kate, that was the scenario. He studied the girls' faces as they waved from the deck of the boat. They looked weathered, exhausted, and completely overwhelmed. He supposed those were natural responses to a race that had gone on for eleven long months. But he knew something else had happened during those eleven months, something no one wanted to talk about.

Turning the page, he found a photo of Ashley and a young man. The caption: *Sean Amberson welcomes home high school sweetheart, Ashley McKenna.*

Amberson? Wasn't that the name of one of the men lost at sea?

Tyler flipped back to the article on the storm, tracing the names of the five sailors lost with his finger. The final name was Jeremy Amberson. The brother of Ashley's boyfriend? That was an interesting connection. Sean Amberson sounded like someone who might have insight into the McKenna family, especially Ashley. If he couldn't get answers from the McKenna sisters, maybe he could get them from their friends.

Chapter Five

"Ready?" Kate asked, watching Ashley take a deep breath before boarding the sailboat. "They're waiting for you."

"Thanks for coming with me. I know you should be at work."

"It's fine. Theresa handles the store as well as I do. Although I hate to admit that. You know me, control freak to the end."

Ashley nodded, but Kate could tell her sister wasn't listening. Her mind was wrestling with the task ahead of her. It saddened Kate to see her once-courageous sister battling simple and often imagined fears. At one time, she had been so decisive, so eager to explore the unknown. Now there always seemed to be a battle going on between mind and body, between right and wrong, truth and lies.

"Here I go." Ashley squared her shoulders and lifted her chin. She called to one of the crew that she was coming aboard. An eager male came to assist her, stretching out a strong, secure hand for Ashley to take. And she did, stepping onto the boat with just a bit of a stumble.

Kate watched while Ashley went into photographer mode. With the camera in her hand and the vast expanse of water at her back, she seemed able to keep the fear at bay as she instructed them on where to stand and where to look.

While Ashley took care of business, Kate looked around. It was a beautiful day. The stormy night had blown away all the dust, leaving the sky a bright, brilliant blue, and the water glistened like diamonds in the sunlight. There were colors everywhere, from the sails on the boats to the multicolored roses in planters along the waterfront that gave Rose Harbor its name. There was excitement in the air, too. The slips were filling up with boats, the local bars teeming with racers looking for crews.

For a moment, Kate felt a strange sense of yearning that she didn't begin to understand. She'd turned her back on this world a long time ago. And she didn't regret it. She didn't miss the life she'd led. Not for a second. She knew how quickly the magic could go, the wind could change, the race could turn from one of friendly competition to cutthroat obsession. Out in the middle of the ocean anything could happen. The sea could swallow up a boat without anyone knowing. People could disappear.

Kate turned her back on the water and tried to quell the sudden nausea in her stomach. She shouldn't have come down here. She should have stayed safe at home or in the bookstore. God, she was getting as bad as Ashley.

"Kate?"

"Sean," Kate murmured in surprise as he approached. "Ashley said you were back." She slipped her hands in the pockets of her slacks. She always felt awkward around Sean, especially since he'd grown into a man, a man who reminded her of Jeremy.

"What are you doing down here?" he asked.

"I came along with Ashley." Kate tipped her head in Ashley's direction.

"Ah, she got on the boat. I guess the sun brought out her courage."

Kate looked away. His brown eyes were too familiar.

"It's all right. I know I remind you of my brother," he said quietly. "I figure that's why you avoid me."

"I don't mean to," she said, forcing herself to meet his gaze.

"It's just easier if I'm not around."

"Ashley said you came back to race in the Castleton."

He nodded. "I thought it was about time. So many of these racers remind me of Jeremy—young, reckless, willing to sign on with anyone to go anywhere. Do you remember the first Castleton that Jeremy sailed in?"

"I—I don't know."

"He was fourteen, but he lied and said he was eighteen. By the time my parents found out, he was halfway across Puget Sound. He was fearless. I admired him so much."

"Why are you racing now, Sean?" she asked, searching his eyes for the answer, but she couldn't find one. "Why would you want to do the one thing that will hurt your family even more?"

"Because I need to know. I need to feel what Jeremy felt. I don't think I can let him go until I know what he went through, what he experienced, what he saw. I've never been more than a couple of miles offshore. I can't imagine what it would feel like to be two or three days from land."

"It feels lonely and scary. Everything is bigger than you are—the waves, the wind, the sky. I've never felt so helpless, so vulnerable."

"That's not the way Jeremy described it. He talked about how fast the boat rode the waves, how the wind sounded like a song, and how the spray in his face made him feel alive."

Sean's words, actually Jeremy's words, stole the breath from her chest. She remembered Jeremy saying the same things to her. She could still feel the breeze on her neck as his arms crept around her waist and could hear the words he whispered into her ear: *The wind is playing our song, listen.*

"I have to go," Kate said quickly. "Could you tell Ashley that I needed to get back to the bookstore?"

"You don't have to run away. I'll leave."

"It's not you."

"Sure it is. You don't like to talk about Jeremy. No one does. My father hasn't mentioned his name in years. Sometimes I catch my mother looking at a photo, but as soon as I come in, she hides it away. Maybe that's why I can't let him go."

"It's been a long time, Sean."

"I know. Every year I think I'll move on. But changing locations hasn't helped. I've been in more cities than I can count in the last few years. The only place I haven't gone is the middle of the ocean, the place where Jeremy died."

"There aren't any answers out there. There aren't any answers anywhere."

"I know it was an accident, a risk Jeremy was willing to take to do the one thing he loved most. I've heard it all, Kate. But, dammit, it still doesn't make it easier." He ran a hand through his hair in frustration. "I can't let go. Believe me, I've tried."

Kate wished she had an answer for him, and as she watched Sean's gaze turn to Ashley, she realized that he hadn't let go of Ashley either. There was a naked need on his face that made her ache for him.

"I'm sorry," she murmured.

"You don't have anything to apologize for. It's my problem. I'll deal with it." He walked away with a brisk, impatient stride, as if he were sorry he'd stopped at all and wanted to get away as quickly as possible.

"I'm done," Ashley said, getting off the boat with a relieved sigh. "I did it."

"I knew you could."

"Was that Sean I saw?"

"Yeah."

"He looked mad."

"He is mad, and by that I mean crazy. Wanting to race in the Castleton, wanting to follow in Jeremy's footsteps. His parents must be beside themselves. I hope he changes his mind. It's not going to solve or change anything." She paused. "He's still in love with you."

"No, he's not," Ashley said immediately. "He told me he has lots of girlfriends."

"Yeah, that's why he's here alone and wanting to sail to the edge of the world."

"We don't even know each other anymore. Aside from last night's short conversation, it's been years since we talked, spent time together. It's over. And I don't want to talk about him."

"Okay. I have to get to work, anyway."

"Why now?" Ashley asked abruptly.

"Because I've been gone half the day."

"Not work. I mean, why now, why is the reporter here? Why is Sean wanting to crew? Wanting to follow in Jeremy's footsteps? What happened, Kate? Why is it all coming back now?"

"I wish I knew. Just when you think it's safe to go back into the water . . ." she wisecracked.

"Hush. You know that movie gave me nightmares for weeks."

"Not me. Out there the sharks were the least of our worries."

Kate was reminded of sharks a few hours later when Tyler walked into her bookstore just before closing time. He'd pulled a dark blue sweater over his polo shirt, which should have made him look casual and friendly. But the way he moved, the way he looked at her, reminded her of the sharks that had circled their boat from time to time. They'd come close, then disappear, then pop up again. You could never be truly sure they were gone. You could never be truly sure that they wouldn't attack even if they weren't provoked. She'd learned to respect the sharks as much as she'd respected the sea. She didn't want to respect Tyler, but she had a feeling it would be even worse to underestimate him.

"I'm back," Tyler said, a challenging glint in his eyes as he approached the counter.

"I figured you would be." Kate fiddled with a stack of flyers. "So what do you want now?"

"The pleasure of your company."

"Yeah, right. You have more questions."

"A few."

"Maybe I could find you something more interesting to write about than my family," she suggested, searching her brain for an idea.

"Okay, shoot. What have you got?"

"Micky Davis said he saw a mermaid off the coast of Florida last year."

"After how many drinks? Nice try, but I don't do alien stories."

Kate thought for another moment. "The owner of the *Sally McGee,* that's the racing yacht that came in third in our race, just got married for the sixth time, and, get this, the first wife, the third wife, and the sixth wife are all named Sally."

Tyler grinned. "You just made that up."

"I didn't. I swear. He said Sally was a lucky name for him."

"Not if he was married six times."

"Good point."

"Tell me about the storm," he said.

She stiffened. "Last night's storm? Well, I think we got about a half inch of rain."

"You know what storm I mean, the one that almost sent your entire race fleet to the bottom of the sea."

"Well, it was terrifying. Huge waves, monster winds. I can't describe it. It was like a freight train bearing down on us. But we battled, and we came through it. There's really nothing else to say." Or, at least anything else she wanted to say.

"Did anyone get hurt?"

"Just bumps and bruises, that sort of thing."

"What would you have done out there in the middle of the ocean if someone had been injured?"

"We had a good first aid kit. Dad knew the basics, or at least enough to keep us stable until we got to port."

"Quite a man, your father. And you, too. I'm still baffled as to how three young girls could handle a boat of that size. You're not exactly built like an Amazon."

"Thank you, I think."

"It was a compliment."

"I'm glad to hear it. My sisters and I were good sailors. We learned to sail the same time we learned to walk. It was second nature to us. Some jobs required more strength than others, but we were extremely fit. My father insisted on fitness even when we were small children. Some kids get bedtime stories, but we got personal training—sit-ups, push-ups, leg lifts, weights."

"Sounds like a slave driver."

"Well, he did tell us a few stories while we were working out."

"Stories about what?"

"Sailing, of course. They were always tales that involved great courage, determination, physical, and mental strength. They were meant to inspire us. My father taught us how to use our minds and our bodies to make things happen that seemed impossible. And that's exactly what we did when we raced, we accomplished the impossible."

"Is that a note of admiration in your voice?"

She sighed. "I think it might be."

He rested his elbows on the counter as he studied her thoughtfully. "You and your father have a complicated relationship, don't you?"

"That's an understatement."

"And neither one of you race anymore. I can't help but wonder why."

"We lived a lifetime in those eleven months, Tyler, not to mention the two years of sailing that came before the race. It was enough."

"That's the first time you've called me Tyler." He tilted his head. "I think I like it. Makes it seem like we're getting along."

"Well, I wouldn't get carried away unless I start calling you Ty."

"I'll keep that in mind. Now, how about some dinner?"

Kate immediately shook her head. It was hard enough to get through five minutes of conversation with him. She certainly couldn't do dinner. "No."

"Why not?"

"I don't want to have dinner with you because, frankly, I don't want to talk to you and find my innocent statements written up in some magazine in a few months."

"We can go off the record."

"I'm not stupid. There is no off the record with reporters, especially not a reporter who has interviewed Fidel Castro."

Tyler grinned. "More research?"

"You're not hard to find on the Internet. In fact, you've led a very busy life. You don't seem to stay home much. Where is home, by the way?"

"Now, that's the kind of question I'd be happy to answer over dinner."

"I'm still not interested."

"What if I tell you about my tattoo?"

"I don't care about a tattoo."

"It has a woman's name on it."

Kate's eyes widened. She had to admit she was curious. "You actually did that? Tattooed a woman's name on your body? I hope she's still in your life."

He shook his head. "A youthful mistake. I've made

a few others, too. If you buy me a drink, I might tell you about them."

"Buy you a drink? I don't think so. You're definitely paying."

"Then we're going to dinner?"

He sounded far too satisfied with the turn of the conversation. "A drink, that's all," she replied firmly.

"All right, I guess I can find someone else to have dinner with." He paused. "Maybe I'll ask Sean."

Sean? How did he know Sean? Not that Sean was a secret or anything. But dammit all. She didn't want Tyler talking about her family all over town. Nor did she want him talking to Sean's parents about either of their sons.

"You don't know Sean," she said.

"I hear he and Ashley were childhood sweethearts. In fact, he was one of the first to greet her when she got off the boat. I saw a photograph of them."

"If that's the best you've got, I think your reputation as an investigative reporter is overrated."

He laughed. "Point taken. Have pity on me and join me for dinner. I obviously need a face-to-face interview."

"Fine, you win. We'll have dinner, and for every question I have to answer about my personal life, you have to do the same."

"Deal. I'll show you my tattoo, you can show me—" His gaze traveled down her face to her chest.

"Nothing," she interrupted, crossing her arms somewhat self-consciously. "I will be showing you nothing."

His smile grew broader. "Too bad. So, what time can you go?"

"An hour. The Fisherman is very good. It's at the end of Main Street. I can meet you there at six o'clock." She waved her hand toward the door. "The sooner you go, the sooner I'll be able to leave."

He moved away from the counter, then paused. "Always punctual? Early? Or never punctual, always late?"

"Which would irritate you the most? Never mind. I know."

"You don't know."

"I do," she said with a laugh. "You're type A—intense, driven, ambitious, stubborn, and absolutely always on time. Never early, because you wouldn't want to waste a second waiting, which means a woman who takes an hour in the bathroom would drive you nuts."

"But you're not that kind of woman," he returned. "You're the oldest child, the responsible one. You're smart, determined, protective, and you hate to fail. Being late would seem like a failure to get somewhere on time. I'll see you at six."

Tyler smiled to himself as he walked away from the store. He felt good, invigorated, and it wasn't the late-afternoon breeze or the beautiful view of the harbor that made him feel alive; it was the woman he'd left behind. He couldn't remember the last time a simple conversation had given him such a charge. He just hoped Kate showed up for dinner. While he might be making a mistake in liking her, he wouldn't make the mistake of trusting her.

His cell phone rang, and he pulled it out of his pocket, not particularly happy to see his brother's number on the small screen. "Hey, what's up?"

"That's what I want to know. What's going on?" Mark asked, impatience in his voice. "You said you'd call me today."

"The day isn't over yet."

"I can't stand the waiting. Just give me something, please."

"Well, I met Ashley today," Tyler replied. "She's a very tense, uptight woman. And she carries around antianxiety medication in her purse. She also seems to have a fear of the water, which is odd, considering the sailing background."

"That's something, I guess," Mark said, hope evident in his voice. "What about Kate?"

"I'm having dinner with her tonight. I wish I could

move faster, but if I tip my hand, who knows what will happen?"

"I agree, but you can't move too slowly, Tyler. I got an e-mail from George today. He received a letter from an attorney out of Seattle by the name of Steve Watson. Mr. Watson states quite clearly that he believes George handled a private adoption in Hawaii eight years ago and he has some questions about the way the matter was managed and the welfare of the child involved."

"Damn. That was fast."

"My thoughts exactly. He's already found George. How long will it take him to find me and Amelia?"

"George won't talk."

"But someone else might. And I'm a single, disabled father without a job. Hell, a job is the least of my worries. I can't even walk. But that doesn't matter, because I'd cut off both legs before I'd give up my daughter. You've got to help us, Tyler. You've got to find out the truth. I need to know which of the McKenna sisters is Amelia's mother."

"I understand," Tyler said in frustration. He just wished Mark hadn't cut corners in the first place.

Mark and Susan hadn't asked many questions when their lawyer, George Murphy, showed up with a baby girl eight years earlier. They'd been trying for a few years to adopt, and Amelia had looked like a gift from God; a gift they'd paid George Murphy very well for, Tyler thought cynically. If he'd known what his brother was up to, he would have told him to ask more questions, like why there was no signature from the birth mother giving up her rights to the child. The only reason they knew the baby belonged to one of the McKenna girls was because the baby had come with a locket, the name Nora McKenna engraved on the back, the picture inside matching the one he'd seen of Kate's mother. Nora McKenna was definitely Amelia's grandmother. Unfortunately, they still didn't know which of the sisters was Amelia's mother. Duncan had apparently given the baby to a doctor in Hawaii, who had been paid handsomely for his silence. The timing had coincided with the last stop in the race. One of the McKenna sisters had given birth to a baby during that race—but, surprisingly, there was absolutely no record of that birth, no photographs of a pregnant girl onboard the boat, nothing.

"You have to find Amelia's biological mother before she finds me," Mark added. "And once you find her, you have to find a way to discredit her. If this Ashley has prescription medication that makes her look like an unfit mother, then we can use that."

"Ashley may not be the mother."

"But she might be. Until we know for sure, we need to dig up information on each of the women. I have to have something to fight with. The more dirt you can get the better. I'll do whatever I have to do to protect Amelia."

"So will I," Tyler promised. His niece had already lost her mother; he wouldn't let Amelia lose her father, too. They deserved to be together. No matter how they'd started out, they were a family now, and if Tyler had anything to say about it, they would stay that way.

Chapter Six

The family picture evolved slowly, first the father, then the mother, the son, the daughter, and finally the dog. Ashley stared at the photograph she was developing in her makeshift darkroom, which also served as the bathroom in her one-bedroom apartment. It had been a good day of work. After she'd left the marina, she'd joined the Haroldsons for their family reunion picnic at Stern Grove. She'd snapped a dozen photographs of the large clan and the individual families who had come from far and wide to spend the weekend together playing volleyball, barbecuing burgers, and laughing a lot. The Haroldsons had treated her like part of the family, and she'd enjoyed herself, too.

Stern Grove was a forested area set deep in the center of the island—no sign of water, just tall trees, thick bushes, and plenty of flowers. It was one of Ashley's favorite spots, and one she'd photographed many times. She'd had a picnic at Stern Grove with Sean once. They must have been eleven or twelve, and their picnic fare had consisted of peanut butter and jelly sandwiches, apples, and Twinkies. She smiled at the memory, wishing all her memories could be so happy and carefree.

Although, it wasn't her memories that were the problem these days; it was Sean's presence on the island. She no longer had the luxury of roaming freely without worrying about running into him. She'd already bumped into him twice in as many days. And, with race week coming up, they'd be crossing each other's paths constantly. How on earth was she going to handle him?

The doorbell rang, and she started. What if it was Sean? Her pulse sped up at the thought. She wanted to see him almost as much as she didn't want to see him. But, if it was him, she had to answer the door; she simply could not allow him to go on thinking that she was avoiding him. It made it all seem that much more important. She just had to act casual, as if she didn't care, as if it really was over between them.

Squaring her shoulders, she walked out of the darkroom, closing the door behind her. A quick glance at her small apartment reminded her that it was in its usual state of disarray. Her kitchen table was covered with photographs, her coffee table piled high with more of the same. She liked to think of her space as controlled chaos, but in truth it was more chaos than control. Her attention span had never been particularly long; she was known for starting one thing, getting distracted, and never coming back to it. She picked up the half-eaten sandwich she'd made for lunch and tossed it in the wastebasket as she headed for the door.

"I'm coming," she called. She threw open the door, and her jaw dropped open in surprise, for standing in front of her was the last person she'd ever expected to see there: Sean's mother, Naomi Amberson.

Ashley stared at her in dismay. They'd shared a few hellos and how are yous over the years, even conversed about the weather or some island happening, but they hadn't had a private conversation in years, and Ashley didn't particularly want to start now.

"I should have called," Naomi said, holding her purse tightly in both hands. "But I need to speak to you. It's important. May I come in?"

"Of course." Ashley stepped back as Naomi entered the room. A petite brunette, Naomi barely reached five feet. But what she lacked in height, she made up for in the sheer force of her personality. She'd always ruled the Amberson household, despite the fact that her husband and sons topped her by a good twelve inches. She knew what she wanted, and she knew how to get it. And what she wanted always had to do with her family's happiness—which made Ashley uneasy. Why did Naomi need to speak to her now?

"Do you want to sit down? Can I get you a drink?" Ashley asked.

Naomi shook her head. Standing stiffly in the middle of the living room, she looked as uncomfortable as Ashley felt. "I'll get right to the point. Sean has signed on to race in the Castleton. I want you to talk him out of it."

"Me? I can't talk him out of it."

"You're the *only* one who can."

"Sean and I aren't even friends anymore. He's been gone for years. We barely know each other."

Naomi dismissed that with a shake of her head. "Sean has been in love with you since he was twelve years old."

"But that was a long time ago," Ashley protested, not liking the look in Naomi's eyes. "We had a teenage crush, that's it."

"I know my son. That was never it. But we can argue about that later. Right now, I need you to focus on getting Sean out of that race." Naomi's lips drew together in a tight line. "I can't lose him, Ashley."

"I'm sure he'll be all right," she said tentatively.

"The only way I can be sure is if he doesn't go. If you were a mother, you'd understand how hard it is to watch your child head straight for danger. I can't let him do it. Not without trying to stop him. Will you help me?"

Naomi's pain was so palpable Ashley could feel it coursing straight through her. But she didn't know what to say.

"You're my only hope," Naomi continued. "His father and I have tried. Sean seems determined to do this, as some sort of quest to retrace Jeremy's path. But I don't want him to go down that path. The sea already took one of my sons; I won't let it take another. You were out there once, Ashley. You saw how horrible it could be. You saw what the sea could do to a boat and a few men who thought they were invincible."

Yes, she had seen all that. In fact she still saw it now in her dreams—in her nightmares.

"I don't want to lose Sean. I don't want to spend the next year worrying about whether or not there's a storm blowing his way. I want him on solid ground. I want him to be safe. Please, Ashley, you have to try."

"All right. I'll try," she replied and saw the relief on Naomi's face. It was the least she could do.

She should have been late, Kate thought as she pulled into the parking lot next to the Fisherman restaurant exactly on time. She'd wanted to make Tyler wait for her. He thought he had her pegged, and he was right, dammit. Both her watch and the clock in her car read exactly six o'clock. She was embarrassingly punctual.

Stalling, she tilted the rearview mirror and checked her face one last time. With the blush on her cheeks, the light blue shadow on her lids, and the soft pink on her lips, she almost didn't recognize herself. Why on earth had she put on makeup for this guy? This wasn't a date. It wasn't even a friendly dinner. It was a battle. She couldn't let herself forget that, couldn't let herself get lost in a pair of incredible dark blue

eyes that reminded her of the waters of the Mediter-
ranean.

Moving the mirror back into place, she wondered if
she was doing the right thing. Just because she'd
agreed to have dinner with Tyler to head him off from
other sources didn't mean he wouldn't go after Sean
or Ashley or Caroline tomorrow. In fact, he probably
would. Which meant this dinner was a complete waste
of time. Of course, if she were honest, she'd have to
admit that having dinner with him appealed to her on
a personal level. And, obviously, if having dinner with
a reporter was appealing, she needed to get out more.
She needed to work on a social life. That was it. She
was a little lonely. It wasn't a crime. People got lonely,
especially people who'd been working nonstop the
past few years.

Maybe she'd call someone tomorrow. Maybe Neal
Davis. He'd asked her out before. And he was nice
looking, not to mention responsible, decent, kind . . .
boring. Or maybe it was just his job. There wasn't a
lot of excitement in the accounting field. But he did
a heck of a job on her books. No, not Neal. He knew
her finances. Dating someone who knew your finances
wasn't a good idea. Maybe Connor O'Brien, one of
the bartenders at the Oyster Bar. No, she couldn't
date a bartender. Besides, Connor knew her father
and had heard many stories about her. How embarrassing would that be?

Maybe dating an out-of-town stranger was a good
idea. Someone who wouldn't be around forever. Not
that she was dating Tyler Jamison. Good heavens,
where was her mind going?

Kate banged her head gently against the steering
wheel, hoping to knock some sense into herself. She
was attracted to Tyler, no doubt about it. But she
didn't want to be attracted, didn't want little shivers
running down her spine. They reminded her of the
past, of feelings she didn't want to feel again. Love
hurt. It was an irrefutable, inescapable fact of life. She

knew that without a doubt. But she also knew that
someday she would have to try again, that she wanted
the things that came with love, like marriage and children. She just had to find the right man, one who
didn't sail into the wind, didn't lead with his heart,
didn't do anything remotely dangerous or risky. Someone who wasn't anything like Jeremy.

She knew she hadn't completely let her first love
go. Eight years had passed, and Jeremy still had a grip
on her heart. It was funny, in an odd way, because
Jeremy had never been possessive. He'd been too busy
leading his own life to worry about what she was
doing, who she was seeing. He'd trusted in their love,
figured it would always be there. Even when her father
had taken her to sea, Jeremy had assured her that
they'd still be together when she got back. He hadn't
worried about anything. He had taken life as it came,
and he'd lived every minute of it. He wouldn't want
her wasting her time like this. He'd want her to move
on. In fact, he was probably looking down on her right
now, tilting his head to the right the way he'd always
done when her behavior confused him, muttering,
*Katie, what are you thinking? Life is going to pass you
by while you're making all your plans.*

So, she'd stop making so many plans, stop trying to
second-guess Tyler Jamison and his intentions. It was
just dinner. She'd survive. And she'd handle whatever
came her way. Checking her watch, she was relieved
to see a good ten minutes had passed. She was now
sociably late. Getting out of her car, she walked into
the restaurant, prepared to look like she'd almost forgotten their date.

Kate was disappointed not to find Tyler cooling
his heels on one of the nearby benches. She walked
into the dining room, a large airy room with windows
overlooking the water. Fishnets hung from the ceil-
ing, poles decorated the walls, and photographs of
fishermen displaying their prize catches covered
every other available space. The room was crowded,

but there was no ambitious, handsome reporter at any of the tables.

Tyler could not be late. He wouldn't take the chance that she'd wait for him. And she wouldn't wait for him. She tapped her foot impatiently as she considered her options. It would serve him right if she left. Then again, she'd just be delaying the inevitable. The sooner she steered Tyler Jamison in another direction, the sooner she could get back to her life. Maybe she'd wait a minute—or two.

"It was a beautiful spinnaker run down the coast," one sailor said.

"Magic conditions," another man added.

"Twenty-four hours later, we had gale force winds of ninety miles per hour and waves eighty feet high."

"I thought we were going to die."

A murmur of admiration broke around the table, and more and more people gathered around the group of sailors talking about their experience in the southern seas. Tyler looked to his right where Sean Amberson was perched on a bar stool, nursing his way through yet another beer. He was listening to the stories with an odd look in his eyes, as if a part of him wanted to listen and a part of him didn't.

After leaving Kate's bookstore, Tyler had gone to the Oyster Bar to look for Duncan McKenna. Instead, he'd found Ashley's friend, Sean, and managed to strike up a conversation. They hadn't exchanged more than a sentence before the boisterous crowd at a nearby table captured their attention with swaggering stories of a ferocious storm. While he'd found their comments entertaining, Tyler was more interested in talking to Sean, if he could get his attention again.

"Sounds like a hell of a trip," Tyler said.

Sean nodded, his face somewhat grim. "My brother, Jeremy, used to talk about the Furious Fifties."

"The what?"

"Furious Fifties—the high-latitude zones known for winds gusting to seventy knots. Jeremy said that when you sail through them, you feel like you're flying."

"Sounds terrifying but also exciting. Are you a racer, too?"

"I'm thinking about it," Sean replied, draining his glass. He set it down on the bar and motioned for the bartender to give him a refill.

Tyler checked his watch. He was running late, and he doubted Kate would wait for him. Of course, she was probably late herself; no way would she want to prove him right about her punctuality. But he hated to leave Sean without getting whatever information he could. Maybe it was time to go for the jugular.

"I understand your brother, Jeremy, was one of the sailors lost in the Winston race," Tyler said. It was probably a painful subject, but, then again, Jeremy had been gone for eight years.

"That's right," Sean said curtly, now eyeing Tyler somewhat suspiciously. "Who are you, anyway?"

"I'm a reporter. I'm writing a story on sailboat racers. I'm particularly interested in ocean racing and the McKenna family. In fact, I'd like to do a follow-up piece on the sisters and their father."

"Good luck," Sean said, a cynical note in his voice.

"Do I need it?"

"With Duncan, no. With the sisters, yes. They don't talk about the race."

"Why is that?"

Sean shrugged. "Who knows why they do anything?"

"You're a friend of theirs, aren't you? I saw a photograph of you and Ashley taken after the race."

"I used to be." Sean's eyes darkened with something—regret, anger, Tyler couldn't quite tell. "Ashley and I hung out together when we were kids. But when she came back from sailing around the world, it was over. She was a different girl."

"How so?"

"She wouldn't go near the water or boats, for one thing."

"Why not?"

"I don't know. Not much of what she did made sense to me. It doesn't matter anymore. It's all in the past."

Sean didn't sound like a man who was done with the past, Tyler thought. Nor did he sound like he was done with Ashley. Which was all well and good, but it didn't help Tyler's search. Although, he mused, Ashley had been in love with Sean when she left, but changed when she came back. Maybe she was the one who'd gotten pregnant. Maybe by another guy. Feeling alone, afraid, she'd given up the baby. And when she returned home, she couldn't look Sean in the eye, couldn't go back to him without admitting everything that had happened to her. Ashley would have been eighteen when the race ended. As a young girl who'd given up a baby, she could have been traumatized.

It made sense, but he was only speculating. He still had no hard facts and too many questions. For instance, why hide the pregnancy? Not only why, but how? Hadn't anyone seen a pregnant girl on the *Moon Dancer*? Hadn't anyone taken a photograph? Sure, they were at sea, but there were ports of call throughout the race. That part baffled him.

"Do you think there was someone else?" Tyler asked Sean, returning to the subject at hand.

"What do you mean?" Sean seemed confused by the question.

"Another guy. Someone Ashley met while she was sailing around the world."

"No," Sean said forcefully. "Absolutely not. They were on a boat, the three of them and their dad. There wasn't anyone else around."

"But they stopped along the way, and she was gone a long time."

"Something else happened. Something to do with Kate and Jeremy, I think."

"Your brother had a relationship with Kate?" Tyler asked, his pulse jumping with this new information.

Sean nodded. "They were going to get married."

Married? The thought stuck in Tyler's throat. Kate was going to get married? Why hadn't that been in any of the news reports?

"After they got back?"

"Yeah, they'd even set a date for a month after the race. My mother had the church booked and the band picked out. I was going to be the best man." Sean let out a long, heartfelt sigh. "And then that damn storm blew everything to bits."

"Why were they racing on separate boats?" Tyler asked. "It seems like Jeremy would have been a nice addition to the *Moon Dancer*."

"Duncan wouldn't take Jeremy on as crew. He wanted to win the race with just his family. At least, that's what he said. Duncan and Jeremy rubbed each other the wrong way sometimes, even though they were a lot alike. I wish he had taken Jeremy onboard. Then he'd still be alive." Sean set down his glass. "I've got to go. I hope you find what you're looking for."

Tyler hoped so, too. He knew one thing for sure: He now had a lot more questions for Kate.

Kate tapped her fingernails on the bar and stared moodily into her diet Coke. Times like this she wished she drank. But her father's nasty habit had cured her of that desire years ago. After her mother died, Duncan's drinking had spun out of control, and it had been left to Kate to make sure her sisters got what they needed while Duncan was partying it up or sleeping it off. She'd thought things would get better when they went to sea. It was one of the reasons why she hadn't fought him on going. Leaving her life and her friends had seemed like a small trade-off if they could find their way back to becoming a family again. For the most part, life at sea was better. Duncan didn't drink as much when they were racing. He'd let loose when they got to port, but on the ocean he'd managed to keep it together, at least most of the time.

Looking back, she realized now how naive she had been. There had been so many dangers that she hadn't seen, hadn't even imagined. The ocean had toyed with them like a cat plays with a mouse, sucking them into a game they couldn't win, but one they couldn't stop playing, either. Not even now.

There was solid ground under her feet, but sometimes she still felt as if she was moving, as if her world was rocking. She'd turned her backyard into a garden worthy of the cover of a landscaping magazine just because it made her feel better to dig her hands into the dirt and hold on. She'd planted roses, foxgloves, hollyhocks, and violets, a cornucopia of colors that wouldn't remind her of the endless blue of the sea and the sky. She'd built a trellis for the roses to climb, and she'd planted several fruit trees with roots deep in the ground. She wished she could be there now, feeling those roots between her fingers. She wanted something to hold on to, something strong and unmoving. Her hand curled around the glass in front of her. It was cool and wet, slippery. A shiver ran down her spine, the memory of hands slipping. She'd tried to hold on. She'd tried desperately to hold on.

"Kate? Are you all right?"

"What?" She looked up in confusion to find the bartender, Keith Brenner, staring at her with concern.

"You look like you're about to break that glass." He tipped his head toward her diet Coke. "And I'd hate to have to charge you for it."

Her knuckles were white, her fingers leaving prints on the moist glass as she forced herself to let go. "Sorry. I was thinking about something else."

"Like the guy you're waiting for?"

"Who said it was a guy?"

"It's Saturday night. You're wearing makeup, looking annoyed, checking your watch. Gotta be a guy. Want to tell your friendly bartender about it?"

"No."

Keith grinned. "Just think of me as Dear Abby."

Kate rolled her eyes. Keith Brenner was one of the local boys she'd grown up with. "You're a worse gossip than Caroline. I wouldn't tell you what kind of perfume I wear."

Keith laughed. "White Dove."

Her jaw dropped open in shock. "How do you know that?"

"Jeremy gave you White Dove for Valentine's Day one year. Remember? I was with him when he bought it. In fact, I had to lend him money to pay for it. Frankly, I couldn't believe the kind of cash Jeremy wanted to spend on a chick. He was crazy."

Jeremy had been crazy, Kate thought as Keith moved down the bar to help another customer. Crazy in love. And she'd felt the same way. He was bold, daring, and impulsive—and he'd brought out those traits in her, encouraging her to dream big, think large, live life. Jeremy had put the sun back in her life after her mother died. He'd always been a good friend, but after her mother passed on, he had become everything. Leaving him behind had been the hardest thing she'd ever done. But Jeremy had promised he'd see her again. Somewhere out there in the middle of the ocean when she least expected it, there he'd be. And there he'd been.

She smiled, thinking of the first time she'd seen him after two years apart. He'd been standing on the deck of a beautiful sailboat, his brown hair so long he could have pulled it back in a ponytail, an earring in one ear, a tattoo on one arm, both new since the last time she'd seen him. He'd looked like a pirate, a sexy pirate. And she'd fallen in love all over again.

Everyone had told her they were too young to be in love. It was just a crush, a youthful infatuation that would fade with the years. The years that they wouldn't have.

Kate took a sip of her diet Coke and tried to focus on the present, the future. She'd learned to play keep-away with her thoughts a long time ago, but sometimes the effort it took was exhausting.

"Drinking in a bar? I'm shocked." She heard a familiar male voice behind her.

"Dad?" Kate looked over to find her father standing next to her bar stool. Duncan didn't usually frequent the touristy restaurant bars, preferring the more casual atmosphere of the pubs along the waterfront where the sailors and the fishermen hung out.

"What? You don't recognize me all dressed up?" He pulled together the edges of a well worn navy blue sports coat. "Your mother used to love this on me."

Which went to show just how old the jacket was. As she took in Duncan's freshly showered and shaved appearance, Kate's stomach muscles tightened. She didn't like the look of this, didn't like it at all. "What are you doing here?"

"I have a meeting."

There was a rare sparkle in his eyes. He was up to something, probably something she did not want to know about. Still, she had to ask. "A meeting with whom?"

"Rick Beardsley," he said smugly.

"The owner of *Summer Seas*?" she asked, naming one of the entries in the Castleton Invitational. The *Summer Seas* had undergone several owners in the last five years, Rick Beardsley being the most recent. Rick had been on the sailing circuit for years and had garnered himself quite a reputation for being a daring, no-holds-barred racer, a man cut from the same cloth as her father.

"The one and only," Duncan replied. "He wants to hire an experienced skipper." Her father stood taller with each word, pride throwing back his shoulders and lifting his chin.

"You?"

"Why not me? I am the best in the world." He grinned as Keith came over to take his order. "Isn't that right, Keith?"

"Whatever you say, Mr. McKenna," Keith replied. "What can I get you?"

"Your best whiskey and a round for everyone here at the bar," Duncan said, waving hello to three lucky tourists. "Whatever you're having," he told them. "I'm celebrating tonight."

Kate sighed as her father moved down the bar to shake the hands of three complete strangers. Duncan had always been one for grand gestures. As for strangers, they were just friends he hadn't met yet.

"Dad," she said when he returned to her side, "you promised me you wouldn't race again."

"Now, Katie girl—"

"Don't you 'Katie girl' me. You promised. We made a deal."

"It was a long time ago. I need to do something. I need this."

"You can't have *this*," she hissed, dropping her voice down a notch as she realized they were still the center of attention. "Pick something else. Find yourself another hobby. Take up flying. Join the circus. I don't care what you do, as long as you don't race."

He paled, but his eyes had a steel glint in them, a glint she remembered all too well.

"I'm still your father. You don't talk to me like that."

"You haven't been my father for a long time." The words struck him hard. She could tell by the sudden catch of his breath. But she didn't regret them. He'd promised. She'd begged, and he'd promised. And now he was breaking that promise, like he'd broken so many others. "Why can't you just do this for me?" she pleaded. "We went through so much . . ."

"I need to race again. It's important to me. I'm dying inside." He put his hand to his heart in yet another dramatic gesture. "I need to be on the water. I need to feel the wind in my hair, the ocean in my face."

"You don't need to race to feel those things. You can just go for a sail."

"I need the excitement, the rush, the speed, the power." For the first time in a long while his eyes were clear and purposeful, instead of dull and vague. He'd come alive. "Ah, Katie girl, aren't you tired of dragging me out of bars?"

It was the first time he'd ever acknowledged that she did.

"I can't go on like I've been going on," he continued. "If I could get out there on the ocean, see the distant horizon, the endless possibilities in front of me, I could breathe again. Haven't I paid enough penance, Katie, or will you be leaving me in purgatory forever?"

"I'm not your jailer. That's your conscience. Or maybe you don't have a conscience. Because if you did, you wouldn't break your promise. You wouldn't race again." She scrambled off her bar stool, her eyes blurring with angry tears. "Do what you want. You always have, and you always will."

Kate hurried out of the bar, wanting to put as much distance between her father and herself as she could. She threw open the door to the restaurant and ran smack into Tyler.

He caught her by the arm. "Kate? What's wrong?"

"You're late."

"And you're angry," he said slowly. "Are you crying?"

"No, I'm not crying." She pulled away from him. "I'm tired, and I'm going home." She headed down the stairs to the parking lot, a part of her hoping he would follow. She fumbled with her keys as she reached her car, dropping them on the ground in her haste. Tyler picked them up before she could move.

"You're not going anywhere until you can see straight," he said.

"I'm fine."

"You're furious. At me?"

"Yes, you're late," she repeated.

"I'm sorry."

"Well, you blew it." She tried to grab her keys out of his hand, but he was too quick for her.

"Not so fast. Tell me what's wrong."

"I've had it," she replied. "I've had it with lies. I've had it with people making promises that they have no intention of keeping. They just say the words they think you want to hear, then they do whatever they want. And no one changes. People say they'll change, but they don't. No matter how hard you try, what you say, you can't make them do what they don't want to do. I give up. I quit. I'm throwing in the towel, putting up the white flag. I just wish I had a handkerchief or something. But you don't have one, because you're not a gentleman, and men don't carry handkerchiefs anymore, and it's all such a mess!"

"Are you finished?" he asked gently.

"I don't know yet."

"Well, while you're thinking, I do believe I have a napkin." He reached into his pocket. "Will this help?"

Kate took it and wiped her eyes. "Sorry," she muttered, feeling more embarrassed with each passing moment. "I got a little carried away."

"A little?"

"A lot," she admitted.

"Who got you so mad?"

"My father. He drives me crazy."

Tyler nodded in understanding. "That I can relate to. What did he do?"

"He's in there having a meeting." She tipped her head toward the restaurant. "He is trying to get back into racing. Someone actually wants him on his boat."

"Why is that so surprising, given your father's track record? From what I've read about him, he was an amazing sailor. I think one of the sailing magazines called him 'a genius at working the sails,' at taking the best advantage of the wind.''

She suddenly realized who she was talking to. "He's too old to race," she said, which was only part of the truth. "And that genius quote probably came from my father.''

"But he was good, wasn't he?"

"Yes, he was good," she admitted reluctantly. "Sometimes brilliantly good. But that was before, and this is now. And, more important, he promised he wouldn't race again.''

"Why?"

"It doesn't matter why. And it's none of your business, anyway.''

"All right, I'll drop it—for now. Are you hungry?"

"I'm not going back in there.''

"Then we'll go somewhere else. Your pick.''

She wavered between wanting to go home and not wanting to be alone with her thoughts and memories.

"Come on, say yes," Tyler prodded. "You can order the most expensive item on the menu and eat until you drop, my treat.''

His wheedling smile suddenly reminded her of just who she was dealing with, a man who could probably charm the socks off her, not to mention a few other important items of clothing. "I feel like I'm choosing between the devil I know and the devil I don't know," she muttered.

"Is that a yes?"

"I'm going to regret this.''

"Don't worry, I'll still respect you in the morning.''

She smiled as she was meant to, but deep down she had a feeling that his respect wouldn't survive the wrong answer to the wrong question. She would have to be careful, because she had a lot more to lose than respect.

Chapter Seven

Ashley tried to tell herself that it would be impossible to find Sean on a Saturday night. He could be anywhere—a restaurant, a bar, the movies, making out on some girl's couch. The possibilities were limitless. She could only try so hard to find him. She couldn't work miracles. Maybe she'd just wait until tomorrow.

Or she could walk down to the marina and check the family boat that Sean had always been fond of sleeping on.

Indecisive and more than a little reluctant to actually locate Sean, she paused in front of the travel agency on Main Street. The windows were decorated with flyers inviting her to summer in Savannah, wine and dine in the Napa Valley, take a ferry ride to Vancouver, or sail on a fancy yacht to San Francisco. None of those places appealed to her. If she went anywhere, it would be somewhere in the middle of the country, maybe Kansas, some place where water came out of wells in the ground, where the hills rose up like protective guardians and the endless plains made her feel safe and secure.

Who was she kidding? She wasn't going to Kansas. She wasn't going anywhere. She loved this island, loved the forested hills, the quiet coves, the pretty neighborhoods. This was home. It always had been, and it always would be. She could still remember the first time she'd seen the island after years at sea. A huge weight had slipped from her shoulders when she stepped off the boat and onto solid ground. She'd let out her breath after months of holding it. The island felt safe. The thought had come into her mind and never left. Just as she could never leave.

Unless . . . What if Sean came back to live? If she did convince him not to race in the Castleton, that might mean he would stay on the island, take over the family business. What would she do then? She wouldn't be able to avoid him. And avoiding him wasn't even her biggest worry—giving in was more the concern. If he still wanted her, if he tried to kiss her, tried to persuade her they should get back together, how would she keep saying no?

Maybe he wouldn't stay. Maybe he wouldn't race, either. The best scenario was if he just went back to wherever he'd been and stayed there for another eight years.

Turning away from the window, she trudged down the street, avoiding the bars overflowing with Saturday night sailors. She could almost hear their conversations, arguments about which boat was faster, who had the best crew, where the winds would be the strongest. Every one of those sailors would have the most information they could have, the best boat, the most experienced crew, the strongest and bravest men, but none of it would matter in the end. The ocean was the ultimate equalizer. It was Mount Everest in constant motion. Everyone wanted to conquer the sea, but no one could.

As she neared the marina, the noise began to fade and the shadows lengthened. She passed by a couple kissing in a doorway. The man's hands were under the woman's shirt, and they were moving their bodies together in such an intimate way it looked as if they were having sex with their clothes on. Ashley caught herself staring, feeling a rush of warmth course through her body. How long had it been since she'd kissed a man like that, felt passionate, out of control, full of desire?

"Maybe we should tell them to get a room," Sean said, coming up behind her.

She whirled around in surprise, embarrassed to be caught watching. "You startled me."

"Sorry. What are you doing down here?"

"Looking for you. I thought you might be on your boat."

"Now you're scaring me. Why on earth would you come looking for me?"

"I want to talk to you. Can you sit for a minute?" Ashley walked over to a nearby bench and sat down. Sean took a seat beside her, resting his elbows on his knees as he stared straight ahead.

Ashley crossed her legs, then uncrossed them. She smoothed out the sides of her jeans, then played with the necklace that hung around her neck. Sean didn't say a word. She didn't, either. The silence wasn't comfortable. The tension grew with each passing second.

"Your mother came to see me," Ashley said finally, knowing she had to say something.

"So that's why you came looking for me."

"She's worried about you. She doesn't want you to race in the Castleton, although I think it's the on-to-Hawaii part of it that really bothers her."

"So she said."

Ashley could tell that Sean wasn't in a particularly flexible frame of mind. Casting him a sideways glance, she was struck by the shadow of beard along his jaw, the lean lines of his face, the strength of his chin. It occurred to her how much he had changed. This wasn't the boy she'd fallen in love with. This was a man. A stranger almost. Their private conversations had ended years ago. The time when she had known his every thought, his every dream, was far in the past. She had no idea what he was thinking now, no idea whatsoever.

"I don't know you anymore," she said softly, not realizing she'd spoken aloud until he turned his head, his eyes dark and somber.

"Did you just figure that out?"

"Maybe I did." The realization fueled the sadness that ran deep within her. The only person who had ever really known her was Sean. Not even in her sisters had she confided some of the things she'd told Sean all those years ago. She'd trusted him. He'd trusted her. And that was the crux of the problem. His trust had been misplaced.

"What do you want, Ash?" Sean muttered, his voice edged with annoyance. "Why did you really come looking for me? I have a hard time believing you're at all concerned about anything I do."

"Your mother was very persuasive. I couldn't say no."

"You can say no to me, but you can't say no to my mother?" he asked with a skeptical look in his eyes. He started to stand up, but Ashley put her hand on his arm, the touch between them shocking in its heat and intensity. Their eyes met for a long, long moment.

"It's still there," he muttered. "You can tell me whatever you want, but I can feel it right now, and so can you."

She dropped her hand, her voice unsteady as she said, "This isn't about us, it's about you. Your safety. Your life. Your future. I don't want you to go chasing after Jeremy. You're never going to be able to catch him. You have to let go."

"He was my brother. I can't let him go."

"Whether you let go or not, he'll still be dead. And whether you sail in his wake won't matter a bit to Jeremy, but it will matter to your parents. They don't want to lose you, too."

"I don't want to hurt my parents, but this is something I feel like I have to do. I was fifteen when you left and sixteen when Jeremy took off. I felt like the two people I cared about the most were somewhere in the world having this incredible life while I was plodding away here in town, going to school, doing my homework. I wasn't living the way you were, the way Jeremy was. Whenever he'd call, my parents and I would crowd around the phone, eager to hear every word that came out of his mouth. And when my dad would hang up the phone, he'd look at my mother with incredible pride in his eyes and say, 'That's our son, Naomi. Isn't he something else?' " Sean paused. "They've never said that about me. Why should they? I haven't done anything exceptional."

"I'm sure they're proud of you."

"How could they be? I dropped out of college halfway through. I've changed jobs as often as I've changed my shirt. I've been drifting. And when they asked me to come back and work in the family business, I said no. Believe me, they're nowhere near proud."

"You're just figuring out what you want to do. There's no crime in that."

"Then why are you trying to stop me from racing?"

"Because I don't think you'll find what you want to do out on the ocean. It's a hard life, and it's lonely. And you've never liked being stuck in small spaces."

"How would you know what I like anymore?"

She looked into his eyes and saw anger, but also truth. Some of the things they knew about each other would never change. "You don't have to prove anything, Sean."

"Don't I?" He paused. "I know why you broke up with me when you got back. You'd had all these incredible adventures, and I was just the small-town guy you'd left behind, who'd never understand what you'd seen, what you'd done. That's why you blew me off."

Ashley tucked her hair behind her ear as she looked away from him. It was all so much more complicated than he realized. "I didn't come back to town thinking any less of you. It was me. I was different. I was the one who had changed, who had done things I wasn't proud of."

"I don't understand."

"I kissed someone else," she said impulsively, not really meaning to say the words, but there they were.

He stared at her. "What?"

"I kissed someone else while I was gone."

He cleared his throat. "Okay, well . . . You were young. We were apart for a long time. Why didn't you tell me? We could have started over. I can't believe you broke up with me because you kissed another guy, someone you were probably never going to see again. Why didn't you trust me?"

"It was Jeremy." Ashley looked him straight in the eye so there could be no mistake. "I kissed Jeremy."

Tyler sat back in his chair as the waiter filled their coffee cups. Choosing a noncombative approach, he'd talked to Kate about the menu, the weather, local sports teams, the latest bestsellers, and finally the quality of the Italian pasta they'd just consumed, at a tiny restaurant named Piccolo's hidden on one of Castleton's backstreets. He'd enjoyed getting to know her better, which only made his job that much more difficult. He had to start asking questions, but he selfishly didn't want to raise the wall back between them, which in turn made him feel guilty.

He had no business liking Kate. His brother's family was at stake. Kate could be Amelia's mother. She could be the one hunting down his brother, threatening the life Mark had built with his daughter. And even if she wasn't the mother, she was the sister. She'd support Ashley or Caroline to the bitter end. And he'd support Mark. They'd never be on the same side. Never.

Kate set her spoon on the table. "It's time, isn't it?"

"Excuse me?"

"To discuss what you really want to discuss. I have to tell you that despite the fact you've stuffed me full of tortellini, I'm still not interested in an interview. I don't trust you. I don't think you're being completely up-front about your intentions."

"I don't trust you, either," Tyler said with a smile. While he didn't trust her, he did admire her spirit. He liked being with a woman who gave as good as she got, who could keep up with the conversation, anticipate the twists and turns before he did. He'd always liked a challenging puzzle, and Kate was certainly that. He still didn't know who she really was, but he damn sure wanted to find out. Before he could say so, a woman stopped by their table. She had her hands full with two small children who had probably put some of the weary lines on her face.

"Kate, I'm sorry to interrupt, but I just wanted to say thank you for the casserole. It was incredible and very much appreciated."

"You're welcome," Kate said, smiling at the children. "Hello, Sammy, Joe. Did you like my noodles?"

"They loved them," the woman answered. "In fact, they want to know why I can't cook like that." The woman sent Tyler a curious look. Kate intercepted the look and, after a moment's hesitation, said, "This is Tyler Jamison. My friend, Ruth Lewis."

"Nice to meet you," Ruth said, her brown eyes very curious. "Are you here for the race?"

"Yes, I am."

"My husband, Larry, was going to race but he had an accident a few days ago."

"I'm sorry," Tyler murmured.

"Oh, he'll be okay. He just won't be able to race until next year. Kate saved me by making me enough dinners to fill my freezer."

"It was nothing. I like to cook," Kate said with a dismissive wave of her hand. "And let me know if you need anything else. Oh, I also picked out a few books for Larry in case he goes crazy waiting for that leg to heal. I'll bring them by tomorrow."

"I can stop by the bookstore and get them."

"It's not a problem."

"Thanks again," Ruth said. "I hope you enjoy Castleton, Mr. Jamison."

"I'm sure I will." Tyler paused, waiting until Ruth and her children had walked out of the dining room. "So you're a good neighbor and a good cook. I'm impressed. Was that a skill you learned after your mother died?"

"Actually before. My grandmother taught me. She used to live with us when I was really small. She'd cook all the meals. I think she and my mother carved out their territories early, and they rarely crossed the lines."

"Your mother's mother or your father's mother?"

"My father's mother. She could make a feast out of nothing. She'd take celery and carrots and onions and turn it into a thick, rich stew. It was like magic."

He leaned forward, captivated by the softness in her voice when she spoke of her grandmother. He had a feeling Kate was a woman who still believed in magic. He wondered if she could possibly rub off on him, but he doubted it. The thick skin he'd grown repelled magic and all other silly sentimental notions.

"My grandmother died when I was eleven," Kate added. "After that, my mom and I split the cooking and, when my mom got sick, it became my job."

"And are you as good a cook or magician as your grandmother?"

"Oh, no, I'm not nearly as good. I've never quite mastered the concept of completely letting the recipe go and making it up as I go along. My grandmother knew instinctively what would work and what wouldn't. I still need a cookbook and a measuring cup. What about you?"

"Me? I need a microwave and a frozen dinner. Or a good take-out menu."

Kate laughed, and the warm sound ran through him like a pretty song that he wanted to hear over and over again. She picked up her coffee cup and took a sip. "This is one thing I've never been able to master, a perfect cup of coffee."

"Now, that's something I am good at, as long as you like your coffee strong and black."

"Actually a little hazelnut and vanilla are my preference."

"That's sissy coffee."

"I don't have anything to prove." Kate sat back in her seat. "Thanks for the dinner. It was a nice break."

"You're welcome. But I'm sure there must be lots of men on this island interested in giving you a break."

"Is that a roundabout way of asking me if I'm seeing someone?"

"Are you?"

She hesitated. "Not that it's any of your business, but, no, not at the moment. I do get asked out. Friday night dates and sometimes Saturday nights. Just because I was free tonight does not mean that I'm not usually busy on the weekends."

"I believe you," he said with amusement.

She made a face at him. "Actually, I'm not all that busy. I've even been accused of not having a life."

"Something else we have in common."

Disbelief flashed through her eyes. "That's a stretch. I can't believe you don't have a social life." She paused. "So, what's wrong with you?"

"I don't think there's anything wrong with me."

"There must be, if the girls are turning you down."

"I may have heard a few comments about working too much." Along with not being able to open up, not trusting anyone with personal information, not sharing his thoughts, not putting his heart into the relationship, and numerous other complaints. Tyler didn't really understand why the women he'd dated felt they had a reason to complain. He'd never promised to give his heart. He'd never led anyone on. But it didn't matter. Women who started off okay with casual inevitably ended up wanting more, a lot more.

"Travels all the time, doesn't want to commit, here today, gone tomorrow," Kate said with a knowing nod. "Ambitious, competitive, willing to sacrifice anyone and anything for what you want. I know the type. I grew up with one."

"Your father?"

"Yes. He's a charming man, gregarious, fun loving, a storyteller. Most people think he's a terrific guy. Kind of like you, I bet. But my father has a dark side, an obsessive nature, an ambition that knows no bounds." Her blue eyes filled with shadows. "He has a desire to win at all costs."

"And you think I'm like that?" Tyler asked, annoyed by her assessment. She didn't know the first thing about him, didn't know where he'd come from, what he'd been through, what winning even meant to a man who'd lost everything very early in life.

She stared at him for a long moment. "Aren't you?"

"No, but I know someone who is like that. My own father."

"What do you mean?"

He didn't answer right away. Talking about himself had never come easy. And his natural reticence had been increased by his father's constant reminders: *No one needs to know who we are, where we come from, what we're doing here. Just keep quiet. Mind your own business, and make sure they mind theirs.*

"Tyler?" Kate prodded. "You were saying?"

"Never mind."

"You can't do that. You can't start and not finish."

"You do it all the time."

"Tell me something about yourself. Give me one good reason why I shouldn't walk out the door right now and watch my back where you're concerned."

He couldn't afford to have her walk out the door or start watching her back. He'd have to tell her something, but what?

"Forget it," she said abruptly, reaching for her purse. "I think it's time I went home."

"All right. You win. Put your purse down."

She hesitated, her handbag firmly planted on her lap. "I will after you start talking."

"You know, if you're this demanding on sharing personal information, there may be a reason why you aren't busy on Saturday nights."

"And if you're this secretive, it's no wonder you aren't married or involved in a serious relationship."

"Are we even again?" he asked, feeling ridiculously charged up by their exchange.

"Stalling, stalling, stalling," she said, putting the strap of her purse over one shoulder.

"Fine. What do you want to know?"

"Start with something easy. Tell me about your childhood, your family."

"My family isn't easy."

"Tell me about them anyway. Think of it as a way of gaining my trust. That should give you some motivation."

He debated just how much to tell. Hell, with the way things were going, she probably wouldn't believe him anyway. "Okay. I was born in San Antonio."

"Texas. I knew I heard an accent."

"I lived there until I was twelve. That's when my parents divorced."

"That must have been difficult."

"It was, but it got worse. A few weeks after the separation, my father picked me up from school one day and told me my mother didn't want me anymore. She couldn't handle two boys, and my brother was younger, so I had to go with him. I didn't have a change of clothes or a toothbrush. Or a chance to say good-bye."

Tyler's chest tightened at the thought of Mark waiting on the porch for him, hoping to play catch or throw a football or follow his big brother around. With their dad gone and their mother interested in dating, Mark had only had him. And, that day, Tyler hadn't come home to take care of his younger brother. Damn.

"Oh, my God," Kate breathed. "That's awful."

He hated her look of pity. Hated himself even more for sharing something with her that he hadn't shared with anyone else. He didn't know why he had told her. He could have told her anything. She wouldn't have known if it was the truth or not.

"Your mother must have tried to find you," Kate said. "Where did you and your dad go?"

"All over the country." Endless motel rooms, dive apartments, cities that looked the same. "It took me awhile to figure out that we were hiding. My father had these letters, you see, from my mom and my brother. They told me how much they loved me and how someday we'd be together, but for now it was better if we were apart. I stupidly believed the letters were genuine. And more letters and postcards followed those, including a note that told me they had moved to a new house. There was even a goddamn description of the new house. I was completely taken in."

"Oh, Tyler. How could you have known? Your father sounds like he was very clever. And you were just a kid. How could you not believe him?"

"By being smarter. I should have found a way to call home. In the beginning I was angry. I didn't want to call. If they didn't want me, then I didn't want them. But I started to waver with time, started to talk about a visit. That's when my dad pulled out his ace."

"What was that?"

"He told me there was a fire. The house was gone. My mother and brother were killed. We only had each other. And you know what else he did? He made up an obituary. That's how sick and twisted he was. And

I bought it," he said in self-disgust. "I was an idiot. I look back now and see that I had countless opportunities to figure things out." He doubted he'd ever be able to forgive himself for being so trusting. "At any rate, by the time my mom caught up with us, six years had passed. I was eighteen years old. I didn't need a mother anymore, and even though she was happy to see me, she didn't really need another kid. She'd gotten remarried. My brother had been officially adopted by his stepfather. My mother had another child, a girl. Life had moved on for all of us."

"That's a terrible story." She gave him a searching look. "You're not lying, are you?"

"I'm telling you the truth."

"About this."

"About this," he agreed.

Kate sat back in her chair. "Well . . . I don't know what to say."

"Don't say anything. I only told you because I know what it's like to live with a father who's willing to do whatever it takes to get what he wants."

"My dad looks like a saint in comparison."

"It's all in the perspective, isn't it?"

"Where is your mother today?"

"Dallas."

"And your father?"

"He died a couple years ago." Tyler picked up his coffee cup, feeling somewhat embarrassed by his confidence. She was going to think he was a real head case. "I wonder what they put in this coffee. I don't usually spill my guts like that."

"It's truth serum. That's why I brought you here."

He appreciated the light tease in her voice. She was letting him off the hook instead of going after him when he was down. She wouldn't make a very good reporter, but she might just make a good friend. Not that they were going to be friends, he reminded himself. That wasn't possible.

"It's interesting to me that you picked a career that

would take you on the road," she said. "Seems like you would have wanted to settle in one place, put down roots, reconnect with your family, your mother and your brother."

"Is that what you wanted?" he asked, countering her question with one of his own. "Did those years at sea make you yearn for the hard ground under your feet?"

"Absolutely. When I first got back, I'd lie in my bed at night and feel the boat rocking beneath me. It took weeks to get my land legs back, to get comfortable with steadiness."

"And you don't miss the rush of the sea?"

"I should tell you that I don't miss it at all."

"But . . ."

"Maybe a little. I don't miss the racing. But sometimes I miss the wonder of it all, the incredible sunsets, the awesome quiet, the sense of being a part of something so much bigger than we are."

"What don't you miss?"

"The cold, the endless wet, the hard work, putting up the sails, taking them down, fighting the wind, then praying for the slightest breeze, feeling helpless and vulnerable."

"What else do you miss? Or, should I ask, who?"

"What do you mean?" A wary note entered her voice, but Tyler paid no heed.

"Do you miss Jeremy?"

Kate reached for her water glass and took a long sip. Tyler almost regretted his abrupt change of topic. But experience had taught him to get the interviewee comfortable then strike. Whatever answer he or she came up with wasn't as important as the reaction, and judging by Kate's reaction, Jeremy was a very important subject.

"I ran into Sean earlier," Tyler continued. "That's why I was late."

"You ran into Sean? How convenient."

"Actually, I was looking for your father at the

Oyster Bar. I found Sean instead. He told me that you and his brother, Jeremy, were going to be married after you came home from the race."

Her eyes filled with shadows. "Yes, we were."

"I'm sorry."

"So am I."

"Is that why you don't want to talk about the race—because Jeremy died?"

"It's a good reason, don't you think? I won a big race, but I lost someone I loved very much. Can't you understand that I want to leave it in the past? It has been difficult to move on, but I've managed to get my life together. I don't want to go back to that place. I don't want to talk about it. I want you to drop the article idea and write about someone else. Would you do that for me?" She paused, her gaze pleading with him to let her go.

Tyler wanted to say yes. He wanted to promise her he wouldn't hurt her. He wanted to tell her there would never be a story. But she was asking him to choose between his brother and her, and he couldn't do that.

"Maybe you should go back," he said finally. "Sometimes hindsight makes things clearer. Decisions you made can be reexamined."

Each word he spoke seemed to draw the blood from her face until she was a palc version of herself. Why? What had he said? Was she thinking about a decision she'd made—maybe the decision to give up her baby? She and Jeremy had been engaged to be married. If anyone was pregnant on that boat, it was probably Kate. Then Jeremy had died, leaving her alone. Had she felt her life was over? Had she chosen to give away her baby rather than be tormented by the memory of a family that could never be?

"Is there something you wish you'd done differently?" he asked.

For a moment he actually thought she might answer him, might tell him what he really wanted to know.

Her mouth trembled slightly. Her lips parted, then closed. She got to her feet. "I don't believe in looking back. It's a waste of time. The past is the past. I'm only interested in the present."

"Maybe someone else in your family will be more accommodating."

"There's no story. Let it go."

"I can't," he said as he stood up, using his height to remind her that he was in charge of this situation.

She frowned, throwing back her shoulders and lifting up her chin, as if that could give her a few extra inches of courage. He found the gesture strangely appealing. He liked the way she didn't back down. In fact, he was liking way too much about her. He wished they had met under different circumstances. But, then again, different circumstances would not have brought them together.

"How much will this article pay you?" she asked abruptly.

"That depends on how good it is."

"What if I paid you to stop writing it? What would you say to that?"

"I'd say you don't have enough money."

"It can't be worth that much. A couple thousand dollars? Plus, you'd be done. You could leave tomorrow, earning the same amount of money for absolutely no work. It's a good offer; you should take it."

He smiled as he gazed into her blue eyes. Innocent eyes, he realized. Eyes that expressed pain and hurt and a discomfort with the whole situation. "And you should realize," he said deliberately, "that offering a bribe to a reporter raises the curiosity level. You obviously have something to hide." He reached out and let his finger drift down the side of her face. "What on earth are you trying so hard to protect? Or maybe it's not a what. Maybe it's a who. What happened during that race, Kate? What are you so afraid I'm going to find out?"

Chapter Eight

He was impossible, Kate fumed, as she strode briskly away from the restaurant. She didn't bother with her car. She needed to walk off the anger and frustration building inside her. She should have never agreed to have dinner with Tyler, never thought she could handle him by telling him just a little. A little would never be enough for a man like him. He was ambitious and ruthless, determined to get what he wanted.

Why couldn't she just accept that she had absolutely no way of making stubborn, strong-willed men in her life do what she wanted them to do? Her father had certainly never caved in to her demands. Why should Tyler be any different?

Kate stopped abruptly as three people spilled out of a local bar, stumbling across the sidewalk, obviously having tossed back a few drinks. She recognized one of them, a young man who worked in the marina office.

"Hi, Kate," he said with a cheerful slur. "Your sister is one hell of a good singer."

"What?" she asked, not sure she'd heard him right.

He tipped his head toward the bar he'd just left. "Check it out."

Kate stepped inside the doorway of Jake's. The

room was smoky, the tables packed with tourists, and the music loud enough to demand attention. Or maybe it was the singer. Kate's jaw dropped at the sight of Caroline holding a microphone in her hand. Her sister was dressed in a micro-mini denim skirt, knee-high stiletto boots, and a spaghetti-strap top that barely covered her breasts. But it wasn't her looks that took Kate by surprise, it was her voice. Her sister was belting out a pop song as if she'd been doing it all her life. And she wasn't bad. In fact, she was kind of good. Apparently the crowd thought so, too, jumping into brisk applause when the song ended.

"Thank you," Caroline said, her face aglow with excitement. "That was fun. And now more of Deke and the Devils." She waved her hand toward the band behind her, which broke into a fast beat.

Kate watched her sister step down from the stage and move slowly through the crowd, chatting with friends and strangers alike. She seemed to laugh every other minute, as if she'd never had such a good time before. It struck her then how much her sister and her father liked the spotlight. Being the center of attention was their favorite place to be.

Kate frowned as she saw a man approach Caroline. It was Mike Stanaway, and he was forty if he was a day, a rough, bearded man with dark eyes and a grim expression. She remembered Ashley mentioning something about Caroline and Mike, but she'd dismissed it as a rumor. Now she wasn't so sure.

Caroline didn't appear happy to see him. They exchanged a few words. He waved a hand toward the door, but she shook her head. After a moment, he shrugged and walked away. Caroline sat down on a bar stool, then lit up a cigarette. As she took her first puff, she saw Kate. Her smile faded, and a defensive expression swept across her face. For a moment it looked like she was going to hide the cigarette, but then she took another defiant puff, got up, and walked over to Kate.

"What are you doing here?" she asked.

"I heard you singing."

"Oh, that was just a spur of the moment thing. Deke thought it might be fun."

"You were good."

"I was?" Caroline asked, that familiar little-sister insecurity in her voice. "Did you really think so?"

"Yes. I can't remember when I last heard you sing. I think it must have been when we were on the boat."

"Probably." Caroline paused. "Are you going to hang out?"

"No," Kate said with a shake of her head. This wasn't her scene. It was too loud, too chaotic, too young. Her sister would think she was crazy if she said that. After all, she wasn't even thirty yet, but sometimes she felt a lot older. "You shouldn't be smoking."

"You're not my mother," Caroline said for probably the thousandth time. In fact, if Kate had a dollar for every time she'd heard those words from either Ashley or Caroline, she'd be a millionaire by now.

"It's bad for you."

"Maybe that's why I like it." Caroline coughed at the end of her sentence, making a mockery of her words.

"I can see how much you like it." Kate took the cigarette out of Caroline's hand and walked over to the bar, snuffing it out in a nearby ashtray.

"I'll just light another one."

"We have more important problems than your smoking." Kate pulled her sister over to a quieter corner. "I just met with Tyler Jamison. He's not going to quit. And he's talking to Sean and God knows who else. I don't know what to do."

Caroline looked at her in amazement. "You don't know what to do? You always know what to do."

"I don't this time, all right?" Kate snapped. "I need some help. I need to find a way to distract him."

"Well, that's easy. The best way to distract a man

is with sex, or the possibility of sex. In fact, anything to do with sex."

"I'm not going to have sex with him." Kate was shocked her sister would even suggest such a thing.

"He doesn't have to know that. Flirt with him, Kate. Kiss him. Get his mind off the past and on the present and the future."

"That's your advice? Why did I bother to ask?"

"I have no idea why you asked, since you never take my advice. But that doesn't mean it isn't good." Caroline laughed as a young man slipped his arms around her waist and nuzzled her neck.

"When are you going to run away with me, baby?" Curt Walker asked.

"When you let me cut your hair," Caroline said, twisting around in his arms to give him a kiss on the cheek.

"Kiss me on the lips, and I'll let you shave my head," Curt said.

Caroline looked over at Kate. "See how easy it is? You ought to try it. You might even like it."

Kate turned away as her sister gave Curt a flirtatious kiss. Everything was so simple for Caroline, so easy. She walked out of the bar, telling herself firmly there was no way she was going to kiss Tyler Jamison. It was a ridiculous idea. She didn't know why she was even thinking about it. Nor did she understand why her cheeks were suddenly warm and her heart was beating so fast. She didn't want to kiss Tyler. She couldn't want that. And even if she did, it wouldn't work.

Tyler wanted a story. He didn't want her. She'd have to find some other way to distract him. She waved a hand in front of her face, wishing for a cool breeze, but strangely enough there was not a speck of wind tonight. Another bad sign. She would have to be patient, wait Tyler out. He wasn't a man to stay in one place for long—wind or no wind.

*　　*　　*

Sunday morning had come and gone, and Tyler was getting nowhere fast. He stopped at the edge of the pier, out of breath and out of patience with himself. His run around the town had done little more than raise his pulse; it certainly hadn't brought him the peace or the answers he craved. He needed a different approach, a new plan. Kate wasn't going to tell him anything willingly. That was certainly clear. It was also clear that she was a very good candidate to be Amelia's mother. She'd been engaged to Jeremy, planning to get married, then her fiancé was killed, and she was devastated. Sounded like a good reason to give a baby away. At least the best reason he'd heard so far.

But if Kate was Amelia's mother, Mark was in trouble, because as far as he could see, Kate was a good person. She ran her own business, owned her own house, took care of her family. She didn't appear to have any overt vices. She was damn near perfect.

He scowled at the thought, knowing that he liked her much more than he should. He needed to stay objective and detached; otherwise, he would have no hope of helping his brother.

The sound of an argument brought his head around. About fifty feet away a couple appeared to be arguing heatedly about something. The man tried to pull the woman into his arms, but she pushed him away with a small cry. Tyler tensed. There was no way he would stand by and watch some jerk hurt a woman. He moved closer, assessing the situation as he did so. The woman's back was to him, but he had a clear view of the man. He was older, forties maybe, a rough beard on his face, a tattoo on his right biceps. He was strong, muscled; a man who would be formidable in a fight.

"I can't do this anymore," he heard the woman say.

"You don't have a choice," the man replied, grabbing her arm once again.

"Just let me go."

"You don't want that, Caroline. You know you don't."

Caroline? Tyler's gaze flew to the woman. Sure enough, he recognized that spiky hair. It was Kate's baby sister. He walked quickly down the path. "Everything all right here?" he called.

The couple split apart. Caroline looked upset. The man looked wary.

"Tyler," she said. "What are you doing down here?"

"Jogging. How about you?"

"Me, too," she said.

He wondered how she could have been running in a pair of flip flops and cut-off shorts, but he refrained from commenting.

"Call me later," the bearded man said. "I'll expect to hear from you."

"Sure, whatever."

"Are you all right?" Tyler asked when they were alone. He didn't like the desperate look in her eyes, and even though she shrugged off his comment, he had the feeling she was far from all right.

"You don't have a cigarette, do you? I could really use a hit right now."

"I don't smoke."

"That figures."

"Who was that guy?" he asked.

She started walking down the path the same way he had come. "A friend."

"He didn't look too friendly. What's his name?" He fell into step alongside her.

"Why do you care?"

"It's the reporter in me."

Caroline stopped and rested her elbows on the rail overlooking the boats. "Mike Stanaway," she said. "And I don't appreciate the third degree or the questioning look. I don't need a big brother. I already have two big sisters butting into my business."

"I understand." He leaned on the railing next to her. "The boats sure are pretty. Do you still sail?"

"Sometimes."

"But you don't race?"

"Not anymore."

"You don't miss it?"

"Sometimes," she said, repeating her earlier answer with a smile. "Is this the best you've got?"

"Why don't you and your sisters want to talk to me?"

"I'm talking to you right now. I had dinner with you the other night."

"And we talked about the different kinds of clam chowder. You prefer the white over the red."

"Good, you were listening," she said with a laugh, her mood obviously changing. She took in a breath and stretched her arms over her head. "It is a nice day, isn't it? Why can't I just enjoy a beautiful day without wanting more?"

"More what?"

"I don't know. More something. Do you ever feel like there's a hole in your stomach that you can't fill, no matter what you try to do?"

"Every day about four o'clock."

"I'm not talking about food. I'm talking about life."

"I'm not that philosophical. I'm usually too busy."

"Trying to get from one place to the next," she said. "You're not exactly an island-living kind of guy, are you?"

"I haven't been."

She sent him a curious look. "Does that mean this place is growing on you?"

"I make it a rule not to get too attached," he said. "It makes it easier to leave."

"What if you find somewhere you want to stay?"

"I haven't yet."

"You sound like my father."

Tyler frowned. Kate had made the same comparison the night before, and he hadn't liked it then, either. "Why do you say that?"

"He's a wanderer, a traveling man, a gypsy at heart."

"He doesn't seem to have wandered too far in recent years."

"I'm not sure that's completely by choice."

"He stays for the family?" When she didn't reply to the first question, he asked, "What's your father like?"

"Daddy is one of a kind. He's bold, brave, crazy, selfish at times, generous at others. He's complicated. He's like an upside-down cake. All the ingredients are there, but they're not in the right order. Does that make sense?"

"It's an interesting description."

"That's Duncan McKenna—interesting. Not always smart, not always right, but always interesting."

"You admire him," Tyler said, reading between the lines.

"He lives over there." She pointed to the marina. "In a small sailboat. When we first came back, he rented us all an apartment. He lasted three months there, then he bought the boat and left us on our own. He couldn't sleep on land. He still can't."

"So the three sisters stayed together?"

"For the first year or two. It wasn't easy. We'd lived together on a boat for almost three years, but we were suddenly bumping into each other and tripping over things. We argued all the time. Kate wanted a house. Ashley wanted a job. And I was trying to finish high school, but I didn't really belong there. I was a lot older than the other kids—maybe not in years, but definitely in life experience. I took an early test and got out as quickly as I could. Once I was out of school, Kate got going on her plan to buy the bookstore, and Ashley started taking classes in photography. We eventually split up and got our own places."

"What happened to the family home?"

"My dad sold the house when we went to sea. He needed the money to finance the trip." She paused. "I wish he hadn't sold it. I think we all would have liked to go back there to live, Kate especially. She loved that house."

"Who lives there now?"

"It has changed owners over the years, but the family who owns it now bought it to use only as a vacation place. It's boarded up in the winter. They usually show up sometime in July. I know Kate tried to buy it back, but they didn't want to sell. Sometimes I go out there and wander through the yard. It's on a bluff overlooking the water. We used to sit there, the three of us girls and my mom, watching for my dad's boat to sail back into the harbor." She gave a disgusted shake of her head. "That sounds pathetic, doesn't it?"

"It sounds nice."

"I'm not going to spend my life waiting for someone to come home, believe me."

Tyler smiled. "How about Kate? What can you tell me about her and Jeremy?" he asked.

"What did Kate tell you?"

"Not much. Although I did hear they were engaged to be married before he died."

"Yes." Caroline looked away. "It was very sad. He was a great guy."

"Must have been tough on Kate."

"I'm not sure she'll ever get over him."

"She loved him that much?" The idea disturbed Tyler more than it should have. It was no business of his whom Kate had loved or how deep that love had gone, unless, of course, she was Amelia's mother.

"Kate is an all-or-nothing person. She loves with her whole heart. She doesn't hold anything back, even if people don't always deserve it, like my father." Caroline paused. "And Kate doesn't tolerate anyone messing with the people she loves."

"Is that a warning?"

"I find myself liking you for some unknown reason," Caroline said frankly.

"I like you, too."

She smiled at him. "Coming from a reporter, I'll take that for what it's worth."

"One last question?"

"What?"

"Why wasn't Jeremy sailing on your boat?"

"Because my dad wanted it to be a family venture, and Jeremy wasn't family."

"So he joined the competition."

"He wanted to race; it was his best option."

"But a decision that turned out to be disastrous."

Caroline nodded, and for a moment silence fell between them. Then she said, "Can I ask you something, Tyler?"

"Sure."

"Do you think you can go back?"

"I don't think you can change the past, if that's what you mean."

"Can you change the memories? Can you ever forget things you want to forget?"

Tyler didn't have an answer to that question. He was surprised at the depth of emotion in her voice. His first impression of Caroline had been of a young, reckless woman, perhaps a little ditzy, but she was as complicated as the rest of the McKenna clan.

"Never mind," she said. "I'll have to figure it out for myself. That's the problem with life. It's not really a spectator sport."

Maybe life wasn't meant to be a spectator sport, but watching Kate had certainly become his favorite pastime, Tyler thought later that afternoon as he followed Kate's car up the hill leading away from town. He'd meant to catch her at the bookstore, but instead had found her pulling away from the curb in her Volkswagen. She hadn't seemed to notice his car behind hers. If she had, she probably would have tried to dodge him. Of course, finding her and understanding her were two different things. One was easy, the other impossible.

His eyes narrowed as she veered away from the street leading to her house. Where was she headed? Neither Ashley nor Caroline lived in this direction. A

few blocks later he had his answer when she pulled
up in front of two stone gates with a sign that read
CASTLETON CEMETERY. She drove through the gates as
if she knew exactly where she was going, and Tyler
had the terrible feeling that he also knew exactly
where she was going.

Kate's stomach began to churn as she drove up the
quiet, winding road that led through the cemetery. She
hadn't been here in a while. For years she'd come
once a week, sometimes two or three times, but lately
her visits had dwindled. Caroline would have said,
Thank heavens, you're finally getting on with your life.
Ashley would have said, *It's okay to let go. Jeremy
would want you to stop being so sad.*

Had she stopped being sad?

Had she stopped caring?

Had she finally let go?

Obviously not, since she was here. And she knew
why. Tyler.

She hadn't been able to sleep last night, thinking
about him, about Jeremy, about her father. God, all
these men. They were making her nuts.

Stopping in front of a familiar tree, she turned off
the engine and sat for a moment. Then she got out of
the car and walked onto the grass. She knelt down by the
headstone and read it for the thousandth time, tracing
the letters with her fingers. JEREMY AMBERSON, LOVING
SON AND BROTHER.

Yes, he'd been a loving son and brother, but he'd
been so much more: adventurous, carefree, bold, confident, a man who'd loved the sea, loved life, loved
her.

If only she'd done things differently.

How many times had that thought gone through
her mind?

Kate sat back on her heels. It was peaceful here,
quiet. Jeremy would not have liked it at all. He was
a man of action, a man of the water. His dreams had

always taken him to the farthest ends of the earth. She'd gone along with him in most of those dreams. He'd made the future sound wonderful. They'd travel for years, see everything they could see. They'd climb pyramids, visit holy temples, hike through the rain forest, and when they were really old—like thirty—they would have kids. She'd tried to tell him that they would need to make plans, do research, work within a budget. He'd only laughed and told her she worried too much, and she supposed she did. But, in a way, her worry and his daring had made for a nice balance.

It didn't matter that their dreams now seemed so foolish, so ridiculously young. Maybe they wouldn't have accomplished everything Jeremy wanted them to do, but Kate knew deep in her heart that they would have still loved each other. Their connection hadn't been just physical; it had also been emotional. They'd grown up together; they'd shared a deep and abiding friendship. Jeremy had held her in his arms when her mother died. He'd helped her through the worst experience of her life. And he'd been the one she turned to when she was trying to get past the grieving, trying to take care of her sisters and her father. Jeremy had listened, he'd encouraged her, and he'd promised her everything would be all right. The optimist to the very end.

Jeremy had been her everything. And she'd been his.

Upon further reflection, she realized that wasn't quite true. Jeremy had had another love—the sea. Just like her father, the ocean had called to Jeremy in a way she never could. She hadn't resented that love; she'd understood it all too well.

No, Jeremy wouldn't have liked this place. He wouldn't have wanted to be buried in the ground but rather have his ashes flung into the wind. But Jeremy's parents had wanted him here with his grandparents, with his ancestors. And Kate hadn't had the heart to argue with them. It didn't matter, anyway. Jeremy wasn't really here. Only his headstone.

Kate stiffened at the sound of footsteps. The hairs on the back of her neck stood straight up. She didn't have to look. She knew who was behind her. It seemed almost inevitable that he should be here, a sign that she couldn't continue clinging to the past, that she had to move on with her life.

Tyler wasn't Jeremy. He was a man of purpose, not a boy of dreams. She just didn't know if she was ready to let the boy go and let the man in, especially this man.

Tyler was dangerous in so many ways, on so many different levels. He was smart, he was sexy, he lit a fire in her body—a body that now seemed acutely aware of him. But he could ruin everything, destroy their carefully built house of cards.

"Kate?"

His voice was a warm, rich baritone. It ran through her like a fine wine and weakened her resolve once again.

"Are you following me now?" she asked sharply. Maybe anger could get her past this foolish attraction.

"Guilty. But I thought you were going home."

"I changed my mind," she replied, plucking at an errant weed with her fingers.

"I realized that too late." He paused. "Am I intruding?"

"Yes."

"I'm sorry."

"But you're not going to leave, are you?" Kate finally allowed herself to look at him. She immediately wished she hadn't. For most of the night she'd tried to convince herself she was not attracted to him, but dressed in blue jeans that emphasized his long, lean legs and a rugby shirt that stretched across a very broad chest, he looked as good as she remembered and so very vital, so very alive.

Jeremy's image faded from her mind. She strained to bring back the laughing, boyish smile, but she couldn't see it anymore. And she knew who had driven it away—Tyler.

"You shouldn't have come here," she said harshly, getting to her feet so fast she caught one foot on the ground and tripped.

Tyler put out a hand to steady her, and the casual gesture almost undid her.

"Don't touch me," she said.

His hand came up in defense. "I'm sorry, again."

"Why can't you just leave me alone?"

He tilted his head to one side, looking somewhat perplexed. "I've been asking myself the same question."

She saw something in his eyes, something that looked like truth, something that told her he felt this thing between them as much as she did. But he was a reporter. He wanted a story. He wanted information about her and was going to great lengths to get it. Was his supposed friendliness and attraction real or just a ploy to distract her from what he really wanted? After all, Caroline had suggested she do much the same thing.

Kate walked down the path toward her car, hoping he would just disappear, but that would be too easy. And, where Tyler was concerned, easy didn't seem to be an option.

"I have a proposition for you," Tyler said as she opened the car door.

"I'm not interested."

"Hear me out."

She shook her head.

He put a hand on her shoulder, forcing her to look at him. "I don't want to like you, either," he said, surprising her yet again. "I can't seem to help myself."

"I don't like you," she said quickly.

"Maybe *like* wasn't the right word, but there's something between us."

"Secrets and lies, that's what's between us." She took a step back. She couldn't think when he was so close. And she had to think, had to keep her wits about her.

"Whose secrets? Whose lies?" he challenged.

Kate couldn't answer that. They were both hiding something.

"I'm not sure it matters, anyway," Tyler continued. "Sometimes you find yourself attracted to the wrong person."

"I am not attracted to you." Kate was proud of the force in her voice, not so proud of how easily the lie could be told. She hadn't always been this good at deception.

"Fine, have it your way. But I am attracted to you."

She had to force back the unexpected pleasure his words sent through her. She didn't want to feel flattered. That was his goal, to get her off balance and keep her there. Too bad it was working so well.

"You'll say anything to get a story, won't you?"

"If you want to think that, I can't stop you." He paused. "Is it the fact that I'm a reporter that's holding you back? Or is it . . ." He looked back toward the grave site. "Is it Jeremy?"

"Maybe I just don't like you."

"No, I don't think that's it."

She couldn't help but smile. "You have a strong ego, I'll give you that."

"Are you still in love with Jeremy?"

Her mouth went dry. When had this suddenly become so personal? "My feelings are my own, and they will stay that way. Now I'm going home and you're going somewhere else."

"Home sounds good to me. Your home, that is."

"I won't answer any more questions."

"Any more? You haven't answered any yet. I just want to hang out with you, do whatever you're doing." He paused. "What are you going to be doing?"

"Nothing that interesting."

"Let me do it with you." He sent her a sexy, charming smile. "I think we got off on the wrong foot. Let's start over. I'm Tyler Jamison. Nice to meet you." He extended his hand.

She reluctantly took his hand, prepared to give it a brief shake, but his fingers curled around hers, and a jolt of electricity shot through her body. She looked up and saw the same awareness in his eyes. Oh, Lord. She was in trouble. The last time she'd fallen in love, she'd been a teenager filled with dreams of romance and fireworks. But this wasn't a teenage boy standing in front of her. This was a man. And she had no idea what to do with him. Actually, she did have an idea, more than one, each more unnerving than the last. She wanted to run. She wanted to stay. She wanted to let go of his hand, and yet she didn't.

"You're confusing me," she whispered.

"The feeling is mutual," he said. "Let me spend the day with you."

Kate could think of a dozen reasons why that wasn't a good idea. But the only thing she could say was yes—and hope to God that at some point she'd have the strength to say no.

Chapter Nine

Caroline walked into the Oyster Bar and paused, letting her eyes adjust to the dim light. She shouldn't have come, but her feet wouldn't go in another direction. She needed something to fill the gnawing hole in her gut. As she turned toward the bar, her attention was caught by a group of men in a far corner and a very familiar voice.

"Kate was the best at keeping us on course. She could steer by the stars," Duncan said in his big, booming voice. "And she never let herself get distracted. That girl was all purpose all the time. Ashley always had her head in a book or her eyes behind a camera. She was a watcher, she was. And Caroline, well, what can I say about my baby girl?"

Caroline wondered what he would say about her. She couldn't help but listen, hoping for something that she couldn't even put into words, but she knew it had a lot to do with approval. Duncan always raved about Kate's abilities to do just about anything, and he spoke fondly of Ashley as if she were a gentle creature that just needed to be loved. But what about her? What did he say about her when she wasn't listening? She wanted so badly to know, so she crept forward, hoping he wouldn't see her, because then he would surely shut up.

"That Caroline is a piece of work," one of the other men said. "A born hellion."

Caroline frowned. That wasn't what she wanted to hear. *Speak up, Daddy,* she silently urged. *Tell him what I'm really like. Tell him how fast I was at raising the sails. Tell him how good I was at the wheel, how important I was in winning the race.*

"Caroline was a loose cannon. I never knew what that girl was going to do. But I'll say this for her—she always kept us on our toes." Duncan laughed and took off his well-worn navy blue cap.

Caroline turned away in disgust. She'd been a fool to believe she'd hear praise from her father. He'd never been proud of her, and he never would be.

"I will say this though, she could sing like a pretty bird," Duncan added, halting Caroline in her tracks. "Some nights I'd be alone at the helm, thinking the girls were all asleep, and I'd hear this song drifting across the waves like the sea was singing to me. Caroline sounded so much like her mother then . . ." His voice broke, and he cleared his throat. "Another round for the boys," he called to the bartender.

Caroline blinked back the unexpected moisture in her eyes. She'd never heard him compare her voice to her mother's. At least he'd noticed something about her, something good instead of something bad. That was probably a first. What he never seemed to notice was how alike they were, how comfortable they both felt in dark, smoky bars, how much they'd both loved the sea. Because she had loved it.

Sailing around the world had been terrifying but thrilling, too. Maybe she needed to get back out there. What was she doing, spending all her days on this island? It was home, but it wasn't enough. She wanted more, but more what? Nothing seemed to fill the emptiness inside of her. God knows she'd tried filling it with just about everything she could find.

She cast another look at her father, wondering if she should join in their conversation.

"Did I tell you about the time Kate sewed up my hand with a needle and a thread?" Duncan asked his captivated audience. "It was incredible. I'd cut my hand, a huge gash, bloody as hell, dripping all over the deck. Caroline screamed bloody murder and Ashley looked like she was going to faint, but Kate just calmly went for the first aid kit . . ."

Caroline sighed as her father's story took off. Another tale about Kate. She was definitely not in the mood to sing praises to her sister. Not that she could blame Kate for being her father's favorite. She'd certainly tried to do that in the past, but it was impossible to hate Kate for long. She was too damn nice. And, in truth, Kate had been more of a mother than a big sister. She'd taken care of them all, even when they didn't want her to.

"Caroline, can I get you something?" Will asked as she passed by the corner of the bar.

She was about to answer when her cell phone rang. She reached into her purse and pulled out the phone. "Hello."

"It's me, Ashley. Are you busy? I'd like to talk to you."

"About what?"

"I don't want to do it over the phone. Can you meet me at the Habit? I'll buy you the greasy fries you like so much."

"This must be serious," Caroline said, not liking the nervous edge in Ashley's voice. Although she should be used to it by now. Since they'd stepped off the *Moon Dancer* eight years ago, Ashley's nerves had grown tighter and tighter until the least little thing seemed to make her anxious. She was terribly afraid that one day Ashley might just snap.

"Where are you?" Ashley asked. "How long will it take you to get here?"

"A few minutes. I'm at the Oyster Bar."

"What are you doing there? It's the middle of the day. You're not drinking, are you?"

"No, but Dad is." She cast one last look at her father who was so wrapped up in his storytelling that he still hadn't noticed her.

"Maybe you should try to get him to go home," Ashley suggested.

Caroline thought about it for a moment. Deep in her heart she knew that her dad's alcoholism was getting worse by the minute, but she also knew that drinking was the only thing that seemed to make him happy these days. In fact, he looked happier now than she'd seen him in a long time. How could she take that away from him? If she tried, he'd only get angry with her. He wouldn't leave. All she would accomplish was chalking up one more black mark by her name. And she didn't want any more black marks.

"He won't go," she said shortly. "You know he never listens to me."

"I guess not," Ashley replied.

Caroline didn't like the way Ashley agreed with her. Perversely, she'd wanted her sister to tell her that Dad would listen to her, that she was probably the only one who could get through to him. But Ashley didn't say that.

"Maybe you should call Kate and let her know," Ashley said instead.

"I'm sure she'll get called soon enough. I'll meet you at the Habit in a couple of minutes. Make sure you get a double order of fries. I'm starving."

"Leaving?" Will asked as she ended the call.

"Yes."

"Good."

"Why do you say that?" she asked curiously.

"You've been in here a lot lately, Caroline. I don't want you to end up like your dad."

"That won't happen. My dad and I are nothing alike. Just ask him—he'll tell you that."

*   *   *

Ashley tapped her fingernails against the top of the
redwood table in Caroline's favorite hamburger joint,
the Habit. As she waited for her order, she stared idly
at the Rose Harbor marina spread out before her like
a picture postcard. It was a beautiful summer day, with
plenty of boats out on the water and tourists strolling
along the pier. It was a day to be carefree and happy,
to let loose of the worries of everyday life and just
enjoy the moment. But she couldn't enjoy this moment because she was worrying about the next moment and the one after that, not to mention the
moments she'd shared with Sean the night before. She
hadn't handled that well at all. No surprise there. Han-
dling Sean well seemed to be impossible.

"Where are my fries?" Caroline demanded as she
sat down at the table.

"They should be ready in a minute."

"So, what's up with you?"

Ashley paused as the waitress set down a basket
of fries and two diet sodas. "I did something stupid
last night."

"Wow. You did something stupid, and you're telling
me about it? Oh, wait." Caroline snapped her fingers.
"You're telling me about it because you don't want
to tell Kate. Am I right? Ooh, this must be bad."

"Sean's mother asked me to talk him out of racing
in the Castleton next week."

"And did you?" Caroline asked as she squirted
ketchup into one corner of the basket. "Mmm, these
are good. Salty, just the way I like them."

"I tried to tell him that his family really didn't want
him to race, and that I thought chasing Jeremy's wake
was a bad idea. I emphasized how dangerous it could
get out there."

"But Sean doesn't care what his family thinks or
whether or not it's dangerous," Caroline said. "Did
you really think he would buy that argument, Ashley?
The last thing he wants to look like is a wimp, especially in front of you. And you made it sound like you

didn't think he was capable of doing what you did. How do you think that made him feel? Don't you know anything about men, Ash?"

Ashley stared at her younger sister in surprise. She obviously didn't know as much about men as her sister did. "I never meant to imply that I thought he was a wimp or a coward or incapable. I just want him to be safe."

"I'm beginning to think being safe is highly over-rated." Caroline leaned forward, an odd look in her eyes. "Don't you miss it, Ash? Don't you feel like the years we were racing were the most thrilling years of our life? Look at us now, traveling the same few blocks day after day, seeing the same people, doing the same things at the same time. Don't you ever get bored with this island? Don't you ever want more?"

Did she want more? Was that why there was an ache in her body that never went away, a yearning for something she couldn't have? "Sometimes," she muttered. "But that's beside the point."

"Which is what?"

"Sean and the Castleton."

"It's not your problem. So what if he races? You two aren't a couple anymore. And, look at it this way: He'll be gone. Won't that be easier for you?"

Easier in some ways, harder in others. Since he'd come back to town she'd been intensely aware of his presence on the island, and she'd realized how much energy he brought into her world. Her life was like a black-and-white photograph that burst into full color with Sean's arrival. Seeing him, talking to him, getting so close she could touch him, had aroused all the old buried feelings. It would be easier if he left, but she'd miss him again. She'd go through that whole horrible cycle that she'd gone through the last few times he'd come and gone. It was exhausting—this love she had for him, a love that could never be. Maybe that's why she had told him about Jeremy. She'd needed another barrier, another wall to throw up between them.

"I told Sean that I kissed Jeremy," Ashley said abruptly.

"You did what?"

"You heard me."

"Why would you tell him that?"

"I don't know. Maybe because I wanted to make sure it was really over. I wanted to put something between us that he couldn't forgive."

Caroline muttered something under her breath, then popped another fry in her mouth.

"He just got up and left after I said it," Ashley continued. "Not a word, not a question; he just walked away."

"That was a stupid thing to do," Caroline said flatly. "Because when Sean gets over the shock of it all, he might just come back and ask you where the hell you were when you kissed his brother. Then what are you going to say?"

"I know. I keep screwing things up." She shook her head, feeling frustrated and annoyed with herself. "I just want him gone. I want to get back to my normal little life."

"Then you shouldn't be trying to talk him out of racing."

"But I don't want him to race, Caroline. I don't want him to get hurt. Even though we're not together anymore, I still care about him. I don't want to spend the next few weeks worrying about every storm hitting the Pacific between here and—" Her words were cut off by Caroline's sudden gasp. "What's wrong now?"

"Look," Caroline said, pointing to something in the distance. "Look there, out on the water."

Ashley followed her sister's gaze and her stomach did a flip-flop. "The *Moon Dancer*," she breathed. "She's back."

"So, this is the backyard," Tyler mused as he stood in the middle of Kate's overflowing garden.

"This is it," she said with a smile and handed him a pair of garden gloves. "You'll need these."

"For what?"

"Weeding, deadheading, planting."

He looked at her as if she were speaking another language, and she couldn't help but laugh, pleased to have thrown him off balance for a change.

"Excuse me?"

"We're going to garden, Tyler. You said you wanted to do whatever I was doing. This is what I'm doing." She led him over to the rose bushes that lined the fence on one side of the property. "Let's start with these." She handed him the shears. "You can use these to cut off the dead blossoms."

"I was thinking more along the lines of having a beer and a burger together, maybe listening to some music."

"You can always leave," she said. "No one's forcing you to be here."

He frowned. "You deliberately picked this activity just to get rid of me."

"Not at all. This is what I do on Sunday afternoons. It may not be up to your usual level of excitement as a hotshot reporter, but it's just fine for me. Are you going or staying?" She was barely able to control the smile tugging at her mouth.

"You find this amusing, don't you?"

"As a matter of fact, I do. So get to work, unless you're afraid of getting your hands dirty."

"I get my hands dirty all the time," he replied as he began to snip awkwardly at a prickly stem. "Ouch." He rubbed at his forearm. "This thing has thorns."

"Haven't you ever gardened before?"

"I've mowed lawns. That's about it."

"This will be a new experience, then. You could even write about it. In fact, if you want to interview me about my adventures in gardening, I'd be happy to reply."

"Adventures in gardening," he said with a wry

smile. "That sounds like fascinating, turn-the-page stuff."

"It can be. Just last year I had to put blankets on the roses to protect them from the frost. And then there was the fungus that attacked the fruit trees, the pesticide that killed more than the pests."

"Stop, stop," he said, holding up his hand. "I will snip off the dead roses, but I will not listen to you talk about fungus. A man has his limits."

She grinned back at him. "So, tell me about one of your exciting adventures, if you find my life so boring."

"Let's see. I jumped out of a plane over Paraguay."

"Where is Paraguay? I always get it confused with Uruguay."

"Then there was the time I got thrown into a Mexican jail for interviewing the wrong person."

"That sounds like a fitting punishment. How did you get out?"

"I bribed the guard."

"A jack-of-all-trades, cunning as a fox, slippery as an eel," she said with a laugh. "You could have your own television show—the life and times of Tyler Jamison. I can see you jumping into one of those red convertible sports cars."

He waved a finger at her. "You're making fun of me."

"Not at all. I'm very impressed."

"Yeah, right."

"Did you really jump out of a plane?"

"Did you really put blankets on your roses?"

"I might have exaggerated a little bit," she admitted. "What about you?"

"I really did jump out of the plane. But, if it makes you feel any better, I sprained my ankle when I landed."

"It doesn't matter to me at all. Our lives aren't in competition. I don't really care how brave or daring you are."

"You were probably more brave and daring during your ocean-racing days than I've ever been."

She shrugged, disappointed that the conversation had returned to sailboat racing. Tyler was like a dog with a bone; he just didn't quit. It was a shame, too. Because she hadn't met a man so fun to talk to in a long time. "You should get back to work," she said, ignoring his question. "All this chatting isn't getting my roses pruned."

"You're a slave driver."

"Don't make me take out my whip." She put a hand up to ward off what was sure to be a sexy reply. "Don't even think about it."

"Yes, ma'am."

Kate knelt on the ground a few feet away from Tyler and spent the next twenty minutes clearing away the weeds that were threatening to suffocate her holly-hocks. The familiar task should have relaxed her, but she was all too aware of Tyler's very male presence. She wouldn't have been a red-blooded woman if she also hadn't noticed that he had an incredible body, including a fairly spectacular ass that was clearly evident when he bent over to toss some blossoms into a trash bag at his feet.

She blushed when he caught her staring.

"See something you like?" he drawled.

"Just making sure you were doing it right."

"I've never had any complaints."

She rolled her eyes. "You are one cocky—"

"Son of a bitch," he finished. "I know. I've been told that a few times. So, what's next? I think I got all the dead roses." He sat down on a nearby redwood bench. "You really love this, don't you? Your face is practically glowing."

"It's the sun."

"If you say so." He smiled in an odd way.

"What?" she asked. "Why are you looking at me like that?"

"I haven't met many women in my life who were

content with simple pleasures like the joy of weeding a garden."

"What kind of women do you usually meet?"

"The ones I work with are ambitious, determined, ruthless."

"The female version of you."

He tipped his head in acknowledgment. "Possibly."

"What about the women you don't work with?"

"Most of them have careers as lawyers, accountants, marketing whizzes."

"So, you like women in power suits?"

"Actually, I prefer them in a lot less clothing than that," he said with a teasing grin.

"Bathing suits, lingerie."

"Sure," he said agreeably. "You must have spent a lot of time in a bathing suit, living on a boat."

"Sometimes, but it wasn't always warm. In fact, we often had to wear heavy weather gear on deck when we were racing. It was not very attractive, as Caroline used to say, but it was necessary."

"I still wonder how three girls and a slightly crazy father could beat the best sailors in the world."

"Slightly crazy?" she asked with a rueful smile. "My father has never been slightly anything."

"How did you do it?"

"With a lot of hard work, determination, stubbornness, and luck. We had a good boat, too. The *Moon Dancer* did us right." She paused, suddenly curious about Tyler's own background. "Have you ever been sailing?"

"Never."

"Really? How is that possible?"

"I spent a lot of time in the middle of the country. Nobody I knew owned a boat."

"Everybody I know owns a boat," she said with a sigh.

"Is that so bad?"

"It's hard to get away from it when everyone is so involved."

"Then why stay? Why not live somewhere else?"

"This is where I was born. The land is in my blood, my heart. Most of my family, the people I love, are buried in that cemetery on the hill."

"You stay for the people who are gone?"

"No, I stay for myself. Everything I need, everything I want, is here. I know it's not enough for most people, but it is for me. Every time I leave, even for an afternoon or an overnight trip to Seattle, I can't wait to get back. This is home. And I guess I'm a person who needs a home, a place to plant seeds and watch them grow."

"This is an amazing garden," Tyler said, sweeping his hand toward the bounty of flowers, bushes, ferns, berries, and trees. "I've never seen anything like this outside of an arboretum or a magazine cover. You have a green thumb, that's for sure."

"Do you have a house somewhere?" she asked.

"I have a tenth-floor apartment in downtown San Antonio, but I'm rarely there. I'm usually on the road somewhere. It's the only way I know how to live," he said on a somber note.

And the only way he wants to live, Kate thought, intensely aware of how different their lives were, and how different they would always be. She got to her feet. "I'm thirsty. I think I'll make some lemonade."

He smiled. "I haven't had lemonade in years."

"I like my life, Tyler. Don't make fun of it."

"I wouldn't dare. The truth is I like it, too." He stood up, blocking her way into the house. He moved in even closer, so close her breasts were almost brushing against his chest.

"You don't like it," she said, cursing the breathless note in her voice, but she could barely speak. Her breasts were tingling. Her heart was racing. And all she could think about was lifting her face to his and pressing her lips against his mouth.

"I do," he said, his mouth covering hers. His lips

were warm, coaxing, and she could no more resist kissing him than she could resist taking her next breath. A wave of heat ran through her body, creating a deep ache within her as she pressed closer to him, running her hands up his back, feeling the taut, powerful muscles beneath her fingers. He was a solid man, a man who could sweep a woman off her feet and carry her upstairs.

"Kate, open your mouth this time," he whispered.

Her lips parted on command, and his tongue swept inside, deepening the intimacy between them. Dazed, she kissed him back with a need that grew more demanding by the minute. She wanted this man, wanted to slip her hands under his shirt, touch his bare chest, slip her legs between his, and get even closer to the hardness pressing against her belly.

"Again," he muttered as he allowed her a small breath.

She should have said no, told him to stop. This was madness. He could ruin her. He could ruin everything. But he tasted good and felt even better, reminding her that she was a woman who hadn't been kissed like this in a very long time—maybe never.

"Let's go inside," he said, lifting his head.

She wanted to say yes. But how could she? This wasn't right—it wasn't anywhere close to right. "I can't."

"Kate, this isn't—"

"It's a mistake, that's what it is." She forced herself out of his arms and put a good two feet between them. "I don't have casual affairs with men who are leaving in the morning."

"I'm not leaving in the morning."

"Close enough."

"Kate—"

"Tyler, listen to me. I'm the kind of person who gets emotional and attached. That's not the kind of woman you want to get involved with, is it? Don't you like things easy and simple and uncomplicated?"

"I used to," he muttered.

"That's not me. It never will be. I think you should just leave."

He hesitated, then said, "I probably should." He walked toward the back door of her house, then paused, casting one last longing look in her direction that almost made her run into his arms and beg him to take her into the house and make love to her. To hell with the morning or the next day or the day after. She didn't always have to do the right thing, did she? Why couldn't she be reckless and impulsive like some of the other members of her family? Why did she always have to be the good girl?

The kitchen phone began to ring, a reminder that she had responsibilities and people in her life who needed her to do the right thing. "I better get that." She moved past Tyler and into the house, reaching for the telephone on the kitchen wall. "Hello?"

"It's Caroline, Kate. You need to come down to the marina right away."

She didn't like the tense note in her sister's voice. "Why? What's wrong? Is it Dad?"

"It's the *Moon Dancer*. She's back."

Kate hung up the phone with a shaky hand. She'd known the boat was coming back, hadn't she? So why was she so shocked?

Tyler stood in the doorway, staring at her. "Does your father need another ride home?"

"What? Oh, no." She grabbed her keys off the counter. "I have to go." She urged him down the hall and onto the front porch. "Don't follow me this time," she said as she ran across the yard to her car.

"You know I will," he called back.

"It's none of your business."

"It is now."

She slammed the car door on his words and pealed out of the driveway. With any luck she could lose him on the way to town.

*   *   *

"It's none of our business," Ashley whispered as Caroline dragged her down the sidewalk leading to the marina. "We should stay out of it."

"None of our business?" Caroline asked in amazement. "K.C. Wales bought our boat and brought it back here to sail right in front of us. I think we're supposed to be involved in this. That's why he's sticking it in our faces."

"We should wait for Kate." Ashley stopped walking. It was the only way to slow Caroline down. "What exactly are we going to do? What are we going to say?"

Caroline tapped her foot impatiently. "I don't know yet."

"Let's think about it for a minute."

"I want to know why K.C. brought the boat back here. I'll just ask him."

"That's not a good plan."

"What's wrong with it?"

That was the problem with Caroline, Ashley thought. She never thought before she acted. "K.C. knows things, remember? There's a reporter in town, remember? We have to be careful. Let's wait for Kate."

"Fine. But if K.C. comes down this path before Kate gets here, I'm asking him what's up. I'm not afraid, even if you are."

It wasn't fear Ashley was feeling right now but uneasiness and maybe a hint of . . . longing? Was it possible that she wanted to see the *Moon Dancer* again? No, that was crazy. That boat had been the site of her worst nightmare. Their home at sea had turned into a living hell. She couldn't possibly want to see it again, so why was she craning her neck, hoping to catch another glimpse?

"I'm calling Dad," Caroline said, taking out her cell phone. "He needs to know. We can't let him be blindsided."

"Maybe he already knows. Kate was going to tell him."

"I don't think she did. She's been so caught up with that reporter."

"Let's wait and ask her."

"It's ringing," Caroline said. "Damn. No answer."

"Would you just take a breath, Caroline? We don't have to talk to Dad yet."

Ashley wasn't up to dealing with her father on top of everything else. Her relationship with Duncan had always been awkward. She didn't have Caroline's faith in her father or Kate's unending loyalty. In fact, sometimes she didn't care for him at all.

Ashley was relieved to see Kate's car pull up in a nearby space.

"You didn't talk to him yet, did you?" Kate asked breathlessly as she stopped in front of them.

"Not yet," Ashley replied.

"Good." Kate cast a quick look over her shoulder. "Tyler is probably on his way here right now. I tried to ditch him, but I don't think I succeeded. He drives very fast."

"Did you talk to Dad about K.C.?" Caroline asked.

"No, I meant to, but he caught me off guard when I saw him last night. He was meeting Rick Beardsley, who wants Dad to race with him. Can you believe that?"

"The way things are going these days, I can," Ashley said. "But Dad promised he wouldn't race again."

"We all know how seriously Dad takes his promises," Kate replied.

"Maybe he just wants to move on," Caroline offered. "There's nothing wrong with facing our past, saying good-bye and getting on with our lives."

Kate stiffened. "It looks like you're going to get your wish, Caroline. Here comes one person from our past right now."

Chapter Ten

K.C. Wales was a tall man, well over six feet. In younger days, his hair had been sandy brown. Now it was stark white. His dark eyes blazed against his ruddy complexion; his skin bore the weathered look of a longtime sailor. In his mid-sixties, he was still an imposing man, with a wiry strength about him and a sense of purpose. He was followed by another man, who appeared to be in his twenties and looked familiar. K.C.'s son, David? Kate hadn't seen David in years, but then David had been raised by his mother in California.

Kate felt Ashley and Caroline draw close to her, forming a united front as the men stopped before them. There was instant recognition in K.C.'s eyes, despite the lapse in time since they'd last seen one another.

"Ah, Katie," he said with a pleased nod of his head. "Ashley, Caroline. I hadn't expected that you would be part of my welcoming committee. You're all looking well."

"And we never expected you to come back here, especially in our boat," Kate said.

"The *Moon Dancer* hasn't been your boat for years."

"You know what I mean. Why did you buy it?"

"Because it was for sale," he said simply. "I'm sure your father must have seen it listed in the magazines. If he'd wanted it back, he could have bought it."

Kate wasn't about to tell him that her father didn't have the kind of money to buy back a world-class racing yacht. Instead, she said, "He's moved on in his life. I thought you had, too."

"Things change. Life changes. No day is ever the same as the last. You should know that, Katie."

"There are hundreds of better boats, especially if you're racing again."

"But the *Moon Dancer* is a winner, isn't it, girls?" He paused. "I've been remiss. You remember my son, David, don't you?"

Kate turned her head to take a better look at David. Her first impression was of a rebel in blue jeans. With a cigarette hanging out of his mouth and long brown hair, he looked like a punk. He had none of the sophistication of his father. And he was too pale to be a sailor. She wondered what he'd grown up to be. Aside from the few summer vacations he'd spent with his father when they were children, she knew little about him.

"Hello," she said.

David just shrugged.

"You look more like Nora than I remember, Katie," K.C. mused, studying her face. "Quiet strength suits you well."

Kate wasn't quite sure how to respond to his compliment, if in fact it was a compliment. Maybe it was a warning that she would need strength.

"Where is your father?" K.C. asked.

"He's around."

"It shouldn't be too difficult to find him, I'll just look in the nearest bar."

Kate wished she could tell K.C. that her father had changed, that he wasn't so easy to predict, but she doubted she would be right. Duncan probably was at the nearest bar.

"As much as I'd love to stay and catch up, David and I have a meeting to get to," K.C. said. "We'll talk again. We have things to discuss—unfinished business, you might say."

"I can't imagine what," Kate murmured.

His smile was silky smooth. "I'm sure you can imagine. As I recall, Katie, you had the best imagination of all the girls."

K.C. and his son moved away before Kate could reply.

"I don't think you had the best imagination," Caroline said after a moment. "I'm very imaginative. And Ashley has seen ghosts and all kinds of supernatural phenomena, so you might have the worst imagination."

"Caroline," Ashley said in frustration, "didn't you just hear what K.C. had to say?"

"He didn't say anything. He just implied things."

"That's what bothers me." Kate watched David and K.C. walk down the path toward the marina office. They passed by a familiar man as they did so. Tyler was leaning against a post, watching them. "Damn, he's persistent." Kate was surprised when Tyler walked away. For some strange reason she felt disappointed. Why hadn't he come over? Why hadn't he asked who the two men were? It seemed out of character for him to just leave without saying a word. What was he up to now?

"What are we going to do about K.C.?" Ashley asked. "Do you think he really knows something, or is this just about sticking the *Moon Dancer* back in our faces?"

"I don't know," Kate replied. "I guess we should speak to Dad, and he probably is down at the bar."

"I can't go," Caroline said abruptly. "I have something else to take care of. I'll catch up with you later."

"What do you have to do?" Kate asked.

"Stuff," Caroline said, refusing to give any more details before she walked away.

"I guess it's just you and me, Ash."

"I wonder if Dad knows about K.C."

"If he's thinking of racing, he probably knows who else is in the race." Kate snapped her fingers. "That's why he suddenly has to get back in the game. He wants to race K.C. That's what this is all about. Finally, a connection that makes sense."

"I need to talk to Amelia," Tyler said when Mark answered the phone.

"Why? What's wrong?" Mark asked.

Tyler sat back on the park bench, staring at the boats before him. How could he explain to Mark that he needed a shot in the arm, a kick in the butt, a reason to stay in the game? Mark wasn't here. He didn't know that Kate was a beautiful woman with a great smile and a big heart, a woman who loved and protected her family. Mark didn't know that Ashley was quiet and vulnerable and looked like she'd lost her best friend. And he didn't know that Caroline was a spunky young woman who seemed more of a confused innocent than a determined troublemaker.

Frankly, Tyler couldn't quite decide which of the girls was the most likely candidate to have given up a child. He had some ammunition to use if it was Caroline or Ashley. With a little creativity, he could probably make a case that Caroline was a reckless, irresponsible party girl with lots of vices and that Ashley was a head case, probably in need of a good psychiatrist. Kate still seemed clean as a whistle. Damn. He did not want Amelia's mother to be Kate. He did not want to have to take her down in any way. How could he? Ten minutes ago he'd wanted to make love to her, and whether or not she was Amelia's mother had been the last thing on his mind.

"Tyler, talk to me," Mark commanded.

"Sorry. I was thinking."

"Why do you want to talk to Amelia?"

"I miss her. Is she home?"

"Yeah, she's home," Mark said, a catch in his voice. "She's taking care of me, Ty. She's eight years old, and she's taking care of me. I don't know what I'd do without her."

There it was, the shot in the arm he needed. Before Tyler could tell Mark he didn't need to speak to Amelia, her sweet, girlish voice came over the phone.

"Hi, Uncle Ty. Where are you?"

"I'm looking at some boats. What are you doing?"

"I was reading Daddy a story. But now I'm making him a milk shake, because Shelly says he needs milk for his bones to get better."

"You're a good girl."

"I know," she said breezily.

Tyler's heart squeezed again at the familiar note in her voice. Did she sound like Kate—or was that just his imagination?

"I'm going swimming later," Amelia continued. "I can go all the way down and touch the bottom in the deep end now. And yesterday I got all three rings without coming up for air."

"That's terrific."

"Uncle Ty?"

"Yeah?"

"Can I ask you a question?" Amelia's voice dropped down as if she didn't want her father to hear.

"Sure, honey."

"Do you think Mommy can see us from heaven?"

"I know she can."

"Do you think she's mad because Daddy and I didn't go with her?"

"Oh, no, absolutely not. She wants you to be happy, Amelia. Then she can smile down at you from heaven."

"I'm going to take care of Daddy for her."

"I know you will. Can I talk to him again?"

"Bye, Uncle Ty."

Tyler drew in a desperately needed breath as he waited for Mark to come on the line. Amelia was strong and courageous. And he had a terrible feeling he knew whom she got it from.

In a moment Mark's voice came over the line. "Any other news?" he asked tensely.

"Not really. Every time I think I've got it figured out one way, I see another possibility. Has there been any more contact between George and the other lawyer?"

"Yes. George got a registered letter from Mr. Watson basically stating that if he didn't come up with a name and address of the baby's adoptive parents, he was going to make sure that there was a thorough investigation into George's practice."

"Damn. What did George say?"

"Nothing yet. But if this Mr. Watson found George, he might be able to find me, too. You have to figure out which one of the McKenna sisters is the mother. For God's sake, I thought you were a hotshot reporter. What's taking so long?"

"What do you want me to do—come out and ask them? Don't you think that will raise some questions? And whoever has hired Mr. Watson will then turn him loose on me. Our relationship won't be that difficult to discover. You have to be patient. You have to let me handle this my way."

"Just get her, Tyler. Dig deep. Be the ruthless son of a bitch I know you can be."

"I'll call you when I know more." Tyler closed the phone and debated his next step.

He knew there was something going on with the McKennas. The two men who had met with Kate and her sisters a few minutes ago were obviously part of whatever that something was. And there was still Caroline to follow up on. He could check out her party-girl reputation at the Oyster Bar, maybe run into Duncan and find out what was up with the infamous K.C. Wales and the *Moon Dancer*. Relieved that he had a plan that did not involve Kate, Tyler got to his feet and headed toward the bar.

Duncan felt better than he had in years, and it wasn't just because of the whiskey sliding down his throat; it was the taste of a challenge. In one week he'd be the skipper on the *Summer Seas*. He couldn't wait to feel the wind in his face, hear the roar of the ocean, smell the fish and the salt. God, he ached for those smells, those sounds, those sights. He'd paid his penance. Katie would just have to understand that a sailing man couldn't stay in port forever. Nora would have understood. She'd always known without him telling her that he needed the sea almost as much as he needed her. He could hardly believe eight years had passed since he'd sold the *Moon Dancer*.

Duncan raised his glass to his lips once again. K.C. had come just as he'd expected. It hadn't taken a rocket scientist to figure out that K.C. would buy the *Moon Dancer*. Maybe the girls would be surprised, but Duncan knew better. He'd known K.C. would come back eventually, and returning in the *Moon Dancer* would fit K.C.'s sense of drama.

It didn't matter. The boat's return added to the challenge, and Duncan felt exhilarated by the thought of it all. He was living again. He was calling the shots. He'd had plenty of time over the past few years to think. And he knew what he wanted now. A twinge of conscience stabbed him as he recalled the horror in Kate's eyes when he'd told her he was racing again, but he ignored it. He'd suffered enough.

"Mr. McKenna?"

Duncan looked up to see a young man approaching him. "Do I know you?"

"Not yet. I'm Tyler Jamison. I'm a reporter, and I'd like to do a follow-up story on your family's impressive racing victory in the Winston Challenge."

A reporter? Perfect. This day was getting better and better. "You've come to the right place."

"Can I buy you a drink?"

"Let's grab a table." As Duncan pulled out a chair, he saw Kate and Ashley walk into the bar. "Don't tell me that fool bartender called you already. I've only had two drinks."

"What are you doing here?" Kate asked Tyler.

Apparently, his daughter had already met the reporter. Probably tried to steer him away from the family. Well, not this time. A reporter suited his purposes just fine.

"You're interrupting," Duncan said, taking a seat. "Mr.— What was your name?"

"Jamison."

"Mr. Jamison and I are going to have a drink."

"Dad, he's a reporter."

"I know who he is. I just don't know what he's drinking."

"I'll have a beer," Tyler said to the nearby waiter. "What about you, Kate? Are you staying?"

Kate looked undecided, Ashley even more so.

"Sit or go," Duncan said impatiently. He would have preferred that they go, but he suspected that no matter how uncomfortable Kate felt, she would not leave him alone with the reporter.

"I'll stay," Kate said firmly. "Ashley will stay, too."

Ashley looked like she'd rather do anything else. But then that's the way Ashley looked most of the time, Duncan thought. His middle daughter had always been more of a mystery than the other two, and always so damn sensitive.

"Now, then, what can I tell you?" Duncan asked Tyler.

"I'd like to hear about your experience racing around the world."

"That could take awhile, son," he said with a laugh.

"I'll bet." Tyler leaned forward. "I've read a great deal about the race, but what I'd really like to know is how it felt to sail through one of the most terrible storms in ocean-racing history."

"Ever had someone hold your head underwater?" Duncan asked. "I thought God had his hands on our heads that night. The waves got so bad we couldn't tell if we were sailing or if the boat was just filling up with water."

"It must have been terrifying," Tyler commented.

"It was the worst we'd ever been through." Duncan knew there had to be limits to this conversation, but, dammit, some day he wanted to tell the world just how hard it had been to sail through that monster. "But we survived."

"Were you close to the boat that didn't make it?" Tyler asked.

"Who could tell?" Kate said quickly. "We couldn't see past our noses out there."

"But they kept shouting Mayday over the radio," Ashley said. "I can still hear their voices filled with panic, begging for help. I don't think I'll ever forget those voices."

Duncan shifted uncomfortably in his seat. He didn't want to talk about those voices; he wanted to talk about the roller-coaster waves and the strength it had taken to keep the boat from going under.

"When did you know that one of the boats had gone down?" Tyler asked Duncan.

"The next day, when it was over."

"I understand one man survived."

"Yes," Duncan answered. It was all a matter of public record, at least that part. He looked up as the door to the bar opened and his onetime friend and nemesis walked into the room. "Well, if that isn't right on cue. There he is now."

Duncan got to his feet, watching the man he had once loved as a brother, then hated as an enemy, walk into the room. K.C. looked good, too good. There was a glint in his eye, a spring in his step. He wanted the challenge as much as Duncan did. Two old gunfighters looking for a last shootout.

"Duncan," K.C. said.

"K.C."

The room grew quiet, as if everyone knew something was coming, but they weren't sure what.

"It's been too long," K.C. said.

"Has it? I haven't noticed."

"You haven't missed me?"

"Not at all," Duncan replied.

"I hope it's not difficult for you to see your boat being sailed by your old friend."

"I hope it won't be difficult for you to lose to your old friend yet again." Duncan felt his temper rise despite his best attempts to stay calm. God, he hated K.C.'s smug, smirking face and that slimy voice of his, pretending to be sophisticated and rich, when they both knew he'd come from nothing, same as Duncan. He didn't understand how Nora could have ever been taken in by this man.

"That's right. I just heard you were racing," K.C. continued. "I'm glad. It's only fitting. After all, the last time we raced in the Castleton, it was against each other. I remember Nora—"

"Leave her out of this." He couldn't stand the sound of Nora's name on this man's lips.

"That would be impossible. Nora was always between us. Just like the *Moon Dancer* was always between us. She feels good under my hands, Duncan, almost as good as—"

"You son of a bitch." Duncan lunged for K.C. but missed, landing on his knees. He heard K.C.'s mocking laughter and felt a terrible rage. He would make this man pay, if it was the last thing he did.

Kate ran to her father. He pushed her away, his pride stinging more than his body. "I'm fine."

"You were always so predictable," K.C. said, "so easy. I thought things might have changed, but they haven't. I'll see you on the water, old friend." And with a wave he was gone.

"Are you all right?" Kate asked as he got to his feet.

"I just tripped, that's all. What are you looking at?" he asked the other customers, who finally turned away.

"What was he talking about?" Ashley asked when he returned to the table.

"Nothing. He just likes to shoot off his mouth. Forget about it."

"That won't be easy to do," Kate said slowly. "Is there something you need to tell us about Mom and K.C.?"

"There's something I need to tell you about the boat," Duncan replied. "I'm going to win it back."

Kate looked at him in surprise. "What?"

"K.C. is going to make a bet, and he'll lose."

"What's the wager?" Tyler asked.

"If I win the Castleton, he gives me back the *Moon Dancer*."

"Oh, my God," Kate said. "You can't be serious. What if K.C. doesn't agree?"

"Are you kidding? A chance to beat me? He'll agree."

"What happens if you lose? What does he get?" she asked.

"I won't lose."

"You can't guarantee that."

"I can. Rick Beardsley gave me carte blanche to pick my own racing crew." He looked his daughter straight in the eye. "I want you, Katie girl. You and Ashley and Caroline. I want us to take back what was ours. Say yes."

Chapter Eleven

"You're out of your mind," Kate said, shocked to the core. "I'm not going to race. And neither is Ashley." She glanced at her sister, who looked sick at the thought of it.

"Not even to get back our boat?" Duncan challenged. "It's mine, Katie. I won't have K.C. living my life, sailing my boat. I'm getting it back. I want you girls to help me. We're a family. We stand together."

Kate saw Duncan turn to Ashley, whose eyes had filled with unimaginable terror. Even Duncan could see it. He opened his mouth to speak, then closed it. He put out a tentative hand to Ashley, but she pushed back her chair.

"I—I can't," Ashley stuttered. She ran out of the bar as if the fires of hell were chasing after her. Kate could understand the feeling. She wanted to flee, too, but she didn't have the luxury. She couldn't walk out on Duncan—not with Tyler so close, waiting, watching, listening.

Duncan motioned for the waitress to bring him another drink. "You think about it," he said to Kate. "You were always my best sailor. I know I could do this with you at my side. And talk to Caroline. She'll come along. She'll want to help. She always does."

"Because she wants your approval."

"She'll definitely have it, if she comes onboard."

"You knew he was coming back, didn't you?" It suddenly became clear to Kate that Duncan had not been surprised to see K.C.

"Yes." Duncan paused as the waitress set down his drink. "I knew that as soon as he saw the *Moon Dancer* was for sale, he'd find a way to buy it."

"Because?" Kate was almost afraid to ask, but she couldn't stop the question from breaking through her lips.

"He always wanted it. He couldn't stand that Nora and I built it together."

"So this does have something to do with Mom. Just like he said. Something happened between the three of you. I remember when he was your best friend. He spent all the holidays with us, then he was gone. Instead of being our favorite uncle, he was someone you didn't even speak to. What happened?" Kate couldn't bring herself to ask if there had been an affair. It sounded so disloyal. Her mother wouldn't have had an affair. She had too much character and integrity, and she had loved Duncan. Kate would have bet her life on it.

"That's between K.C. and me. What you need to be concerned about is someone else sailing our boat."

"Someone else has been sailing our boat for eight years."

"Not this someone."

"You'll have to give me a better reason." She turned to Tyler. "Would you mind giving us some privacy?"

Tyler simply smiled in return. "I don't think so."

"K.C. bought the *Moon Dancer* to show me up," Duncan said, obviously not caring that a reporter was listening in. "He wants to make me think he's the winner and I'm the loser, but he's wrong. And I'm going to prove it."

"Hasn't the time for proving things passed? Haven't you both lost enough?"

"I want my boat back. Our boat. Our home. Think about it. It's the last place we were together, and I mean your beautiful mother, too. We designed and built that boat, decorated it in our own way, spilled sweat, blood, and tears on that deck. I won't have K.C. in it. I won't have him living my life. Help me, Katie."

Kate didn't like the idea of K.C. sailing the *Moon Dancer,* either. But to race again? To compete for a boat that held so many memories, both bad and good? She couldn't do it. It would be too painful. "I can't."

"Katie, please."

"You'll have to do this one on your own. I really wish you'd forget it. Let K.C. take the *Moon Dancer* and sail to Hawaii. He'll be gone in a few days, and we can get back to normal."

"Normal? You call this normal—this life we're leading? Hell, Katie, I haven't felt normal in eight years."

Kate watched as he drained his drink. "Maybe it's all the booze. Maybe that's why you don't feel normal."

"Fine. Whatever. Go on, get out of here. You know, Katie, your mother was never so judgmental. So hard. Everything with you is black and white. People are good or they're bad; there's no in between." His eyes bored into hers with anger and frustration. "You can't stand to be wrong, and you can't stand it when people don't measure up to your lofty standards. Some of us are human. Some of us have weaknesses."

Kate felt incredibly hurt by his harsh words. She wasn't judgmental or hard. And she *was* human. She cared. She cared too much, if he only knew the truth. "This isn't about right or wrong—"

"I thought you were leaving," Duncan said, cutting her off. "I've got business to discuss with my new friend here." He tipped his head in Tyler's direction.

Kate saw concern in Tyler's eyes—or was it guilt? No, he didn't feel guilty. He'd already told her he didn't waste time on that emotion. This was the opportunity Tyler had been looking for, a chance to get the inside scoop from Duncan. And there was not a damn thing she could do about it. If she protested, it would only make Tyler more suspicious, and Duncan was hell-bent on living out his glory days one more time. Sometimes she wondered why she bothered to protect him. But it wasn't just him, she told herself firmly. That's what she had to remember.

"I'll call you later," Tyler said quietly.

She got to her feet. "Don't bother. I've said all I need to say—to both of you."

Ashley dragged an old duffel bag off the top shelf of her closet. It came down with a layer of dust and a couple shoe boxes. She coughed, sneezed, then nearly burst into tears when an old and terribly familiar smell wafted through the room. It was the smell of the sea, the smell of the boat, the smell of fear. She stared at the duffel bag in dismay. It had been eight years since she'd used it. Too long for the smells to still be there. Was it just her imagination?

Oh, what did it matter? Her life was falling apart.

She couldn't believe her father wanted them to race again. She couldn't believe that K.C. had somehow been involved with her mother. What was that all about? Was it a lie? Or something more? And did she really want to know? She had to get away. The walls were closing in. Just like before, during that terrible storm, when she'd seen the water slipping in under the door. She'd had the terrible feeling they were already underwater. She wouldn't be able to get out. She wouldn't be able to breathe. She'd die slowly, suffocating, the way she was suffocating now.

"Ashley—open up." She heard a male voice and a pounding on the door. The voice brought her back to reality, and she ran out of her bedroom before the memories could come back.

"Sean? What are you doing here?" she asked as she opened the door.

"I want to know what happened," he said, anger etched in tight lines across his face.

"I don't know." She waved her hand in the air. "K.C. showed up with the *Moon Dancer*. My father wants to race him, and he wants me onboard. It's crazy. I don't know what's happening. Everything is changing."

"What the hell are you talking about?"

Ashley stared at him. "What are *you* talking about?"

"Jeremy. I'm talking about my brother, and that little bombshell you dropped last night."

It seemed like a million years ago since she had spoken to Sean. Had it only been last night?

"You said you kissed him." Sean planted his hands on his hips. "I want to know why and when and all the rest. So start talking."

"I don't have time," she said, making a quick decision.

"Make time."

"I can't. I'm leaving." She walked into the bedroom and began emptying her drawers into the duffel bag.

"Where are you going?" Sean asked from the doorway.

"Away."

"Why?"

"You always have so many questions for me," she said, pushing her hair out of her face.

"And you never have any answers."

Sean crossed the room as she yanked open another dresser. "Stop it, would you?" He grabbed her by the arm. "Stop packing and talk to me. I want to know what happened between you and my brother. And why you decided to tell me now."

"Let go of me." She tried to free her arm, but he held on tight, so tight she felt trapped. Acute panic set in. "Let go!" she yelled. "I have to get out of here." She finally yanked her arm free.

"Ashley, wait! Where are you going?"

"I don't know." She tossed more clothes into the bag, some falling on the floor, some on the bed, but she didn't care. "I have to get out before I lose what little is left of my mind. If you care at all for me, you'll help me."

"Ash, I don't know what you want me to do."

What did she want him to do? "I know the last ferry left an hour ago. But you have a boat. You can take me to the mainland, can't you?"

"You're willing to get on my boat?"

"I just said that, didn't I?" But could she? It was dark now. The water would be black. She wouldn't be able to see the horizon or where she was going.

Sean looked as indecisive as she felt. "Maybe you should talk to someone, call Kate or Caroline. You're obviously upset about something."

"Upset? You think I'm upset?" Was that her voice screeching like a maniac? It must be, because Sean was staring at her like she'd gone over the edge. "I'm sorry. I can't do this anymore. It's too much for me." She felt overwhelmed, exhausted, terrified, and almost wished she could cry to release some of the tension, but her eyes were dry. Her tear ducts as empty as everything else.

"Look, I don't understand half of what you said before, but just take it easy, okay? Don't do anything rash. There's always tomorrow, if you still want to go."

"If I don't go now, I'm not sure I will ever go."

"Then that's a good reason to wait."

Ashley sank down on the edge of the bed, feeling defeated.

After a moment Sean sat down next to her. "Do you want to talk about any of it?"

"No." There were too many thoughts crowding her head to make sense of any of them.

"All right, then. "

Sean put his arm around her shoulders. Ashley tensed, but when he didn't make another move, she gradually began to relax, taking precious comfort in his embrace. He wasn't asking anything of her. He wasn't demanding that she do something or say something. For the first time in a long time, she felt safe. This was Sean, her first love, her only love, if the truth be told. No one else had ever come close. She'd tried to put her love away, because she didn't deserve him. But he was here, and she was weak. She needed to lean on someone.

"Don't go," she whispered, resting her head on his chest. The beat of his heart was strong and steady. "I know I shouldn't ask."

"It's about time you did," he muttered.

"You must hate me."

He let out a heavy sigh. "Sometimes I wish I did. It would make it a whole lot easier."

Kate just wanted a closer look. It wasn't a crime, she told herself, as she walked down to the docks. She was human after all, despite her father's earlier criticism, which still stung. She'd tried to work, but sorting inventory at the bookstore hadn't proved a big enough distraction, and there was no way she was going back to the Oyster Bar. She'd had enough of her father, and Tyler, too.

She just wanted a few minutes alone with something that had once been a very important part of her life, the *Moon Dancer*. They'd come together as a family when they'd first set sail, the close confines of the boat forcing them to talk to one another, to share the workload, to rely on one another for everything from food to survival. They'd learned a lot on the water with only themselves to depend on. When the racing had begun, the experience had taken on a new dimension.

The competition had created an excitement, a rush as they barreled into the wind, trying to go as fast as they could. The ports of call had been filled with parties, celebrations, and tall tales of what had happened during each leg of the race. In the beginning, she had soaked it all up as if she were a hungry sponge. She'd loved being part of it, loved seeing her father in his element, and Jeremy, too, sharing the same excitement and joy. She should have realized that two such strong men would come into conflict.

Looking back, she could see where the first thread had begun to unravel. Unfortunately, she hadn't noticed that loose thread until everything fell apart.

Shaking her head, Kate moved closer to the siren that called her name. The *Moon Dancer* sat proudly on the water, bobbing gently with the swells. Her breath caught in her throat. It was a magnificent boat, a lightweight, forty-seven-foot speedster guaranteed to give a spirited yet comfortable ride. Her parents had designed the boat and had it custom built at a yard in Seattle. Their idea was to use race technology to build a cruiser that could win races. And the *Moon Dancer* had more than lived up to the challenges they'd put it through. She'd not only won for them, she'd sheltered and protected them.

Kate drew in a breath and slowly let it out, allowing the emotions to sweep through her soul. There was no point in trying to hold them back; they were overflowing. She felt joy at seeing the boat; she also felt incredible sadness for a time in their lives that had been both the worst and the best. Maybe life would always be like that, offering something good, only to counter it with something bad.

"Boo!"

Kate jumped at the sound behind her. She whirled around in surprise to see David laughing at her. "David. You scared me."

He pulled the cigarette out of his mouth and flicked the ashes into the water. "That's what you get for trying to sneak onto my boat. Or do you still think it's yours?"

"I wasn't trying to sneak onto the boat. And I know who owns it."

"I hope so. If not, I can always show you my daddy's pink slip. That's right, my daddy. Not yours, Kate, even though you used to think of him as a second daddy, didn't you? Uncle K.C., isn't that what you called him? Didn't you give him a big fat kiss every time he brought you candy or toys or whatever else you wanted, little princess?"

There was an animosity in David's voice she hadn't expected. "You sound like . . ."

"What? What do I sound like?"

"Like you hate me." She laughed as if the thought were absurd, but he didn't laugh back, and a chill washed over her body.

"Of course I don't hate you," he said smoothly. "I don't even know you. Isn't that right? We only spoke a few times over the years when I came to visit my father. You were all too busy to hang out with me."

"I didn't think you were interested in hanging out with us."

"Oh, I don't know. I was always curious about the girls who spent more time with my father than I did."

"That wasn't our fault."

"Did I say it was?"

She didn't like the thread of their conversation. "I'm leaving now."

"Don't you want to go onboard?"

"No." Kate shook her head, even though his unexpected invitation had sent her heart racing.

"You're not interested in seeing what the inside looks like?"

"Not really."

He stepped in front of her as she turned to leave. "It's the first time in my life that I got something of yours, instead of the other way around."

Kate frowned, seeing not just anger in his dark brown eyes but also pain. "What are you talking about?"

"I'm talking about holidays and birthdays, Christmas presents that my father gave to you and your sisters instead of to me. He wanted your family, your mother. He wanted your life."

"That's not true. He was a friend, that's all."

"Really? You think that's all he was?"

"Yes." She hated the doubt that once again crossed her mind. First K.C., then her own father, now David. Did they all know something she didn't?

Uncle K.C. had always been around when she was small. So many videos showed him standing by the Christmas tree or laughing with her mother in the kitchen. Then it had changed. Something had happened. She did not want to believe it had anything to do with her mother.

"I thought you were the smart one," David said. "I must have been mistaken."

"You don't know anything. You're just trying to annoy me."

"I might be," he admitted. "Or I might not."

"Why did you and your father come back here? So you could have this little moment of triumph in front of us? So you could say you're better than us? Is that what it's all about?"

David didn't answer right away. Then he said, "I'm not sure." There was a touch of uncertainty in his voice.

"What? Now you're pretending ignorance? I thought you knew everything about the relationship between your family and mine."

"I know more than you, obviously."

"Like what? What do you think you know?"

"My father and your mother had an affair."

"That's not true." A sense of impending doom lent little strength to her words. "It can't be true."

"You look a little like him—my father."

The implication flashed through her like the sharp edge of a knife. "You are sick."

"Why don't you ask him?"

"I wouldn't believe a word your father said."

"Then ask Duncan." David's mocking comment followed her all the way back to the edge of the pier. She didn't have to ask Duncan. She knew who her father was. Didn't she?

Chapter Twelve

K.C. Wales, born Kendrick Charles Wales in San Francisco, California, was the only son of a fisherman and a high school English teacher. Tyler skimmed the data appearing on the screen of his laptop computer. He wasn't sure exactly what he was looking for, but he knew it wasn't in K.C.'s childhood. The connection with the McKenna family had come later. Sure enough, as his fingers flew across the keys, checking various search results, Tyler came up with the sailing connection. K.C. Wales and Duncan McKenna began racing each other in competitions during what had to be the early years of Duncan's marriage. Their rivalry had continued into the Winston Around-the-World Challenge, in which K.C., the skipper of the *Betsy Marie,* had been the only survivor of the ship that went down in the storm.

Tyler frowned, searching for what happened next. There didn't appear to be any further reports. The man seemed to disappear after the race. Tyler supposed that wasn't unusual for someone who had almost drowned. Then again, K.C. had looked in fine health when he'd confronted Duncan in the Oyster Bar several hours earlier.

Tyler tapped his keyboard impatiently. What he

really wanted to know was what K.C. had done between the race and now. He'd tried to get the information from Duncan, but Duncan had been strangely quiet on the subject, despite consuming enough whiskey to float a boat. While Duncan had spewed forth endless tales of racing victories, he'd refused to say anything about the girls or K.C. Every time Tyler tried to redirect the conversation, he heard yet another unrelated sea story. Finally, Duncan had run out of steam. Tyler had tried to take him home, but Duncan had insisted on staying, joining yet another group of sailors.

Giving the bartender a twenty-dollar bill and instructions to make sure Duncan got a cab ride home, Tyler had returned to his hotel, hoping that Kate wouldn't be called out yet again to rescue her father. Not that she'd thank him for getting in the middle, but he was there, no doubt about it. And he was more than a little curious about K.C.

Who was this man? Duncan's friend? His rival? His enemy? Had there been something going on between K.C. and Kate's mother, Nora, as K.C. had implied? And what was K.C.'s motive for bringing the *Moon Dancer* to Castleton?

"It doesn't matter," Tyler muttered to himself. So what if K.C. had slept with Kate's mother? They weren't the ones who'd given Amelia up for adoption. He had to get his focus back. Rubbing the tense muscles in his neck, he rolled his head back and forth on his shoulders. He closed his eyes, trying to relax and de-stress, but with his eyes closed all he could see in his mind was the hurt look in Kate's eyes when her father had criticized her.

A quiet knock at the door brought his eyes open. The clock read just past nine. He got to his feet and opened the door. Kate stood in the hallway. As always seemed to be the case when he saw her, his body tightened and his heart began to race. It was ridiculous, the way she made him feel tense and uncertain.

He knew what he had to do with her, and it wasn't at all what he wanted to do with her, which was to drag her into the room and make love to her.

Seeing her now, wearing blue jeans and a pale pink sweater, and her hair loose about her shoulders, she could have passed for younger than twenty-eight, until one looked closer and saw the tiny lines around her mouth and the shadows under her eyes. She'd lived a long life in those three years at sea. Maybe a longer life since then, as she'd tried to hold the family together.

"Hello," she said with a weary note in her voice. "I bet I'm the last person you expected to see."

"You could say that."

"Can I come in?"

"Sure." He stepped aside and motioned for her to enter.

"It's nice," Kate said, looking around the room.

He followed her gaze. It was a basic hotel room, although the Seascape Inn had provided a nautical-themed wallpaper trim as well as some interesting sea-scapes on the walls. "It's okay. You've seen one, you've seen 'em all."

Kate nodded, standing awkwardly in the center of the room. "Is the bed comfortable? Sometimes they're so hard in a hotel you can bounce coins off the mattress. Caroline used to do that . . ." Her voice drifted away. "I didn't come here to talk about hotel rooms."

"Do you want to sit down?" he asked.

She glanced over at the desk where his laptop was open. "Are you researching me?"

"Why are you here, Kate?"

"I need a favor."

Now he was surprised. "What kind of a favor?"

"Information."

"About what, or should I say whom?"

"K.C. Wales." She walked over to the computer and stared unabashedly at the screen. "I see you're ahead of me. Why are you researching K.C.?"

"Because he's tied to your family in some way. I also find it interesting that he was the sole survivor of the ship that capsized during your race."

"Why is that interesting?"

"Oh, I don't know. A sole survivor might have a different story than everyone else."

"He doesn't remember what happened. He had a severe head injury and amnesia after the tragedy. The last thing he remembered was the start of the race almost eleven months earlier. Everything else was gone."

Tyler straightened, sensing that this was the piece of information he'd been waiting for. "He had amnesia? I thought that only happened in books."

She shrugged. "I'm not a doctor. He was unconscious for several days, and when he woke up he couldn't walk or talk. The doctors said it wasn't surprising that he didn't remember a big chunk of his life, especially the recent memory. I guess the long-term memory stays longer. What else did you find out about him?"

"Probably nothing you don't already know. What are you looking for?"

She hesitated for a long moment. "I want to find out about K.C. and my mother."

"I don't think that answer will be on the Internet."

"I don't, either." She turned and walked back to him, digging her hands into her pockets. "But you could talk to him. You're a reporter. You'd know how to get that story, wouldn't you?"

"Maybe. What would I get in return?"

She sent him a pleading smile. "My deepest gratitude."

"Try again."

"Forget it. I knew you wouldn't help me. I don't know why I bothered to ask. In fact, I don't even know why I came here."

"If you want to know if K.C. and your mother had a personal relationship, you should ask your father.

There's something between those two men, something deep and very intense."

Her eyes lit up with his words. "You saw it, too. It wasn't just me?"

"It wasn't just you."

"I went down to the docks a little while ago to look at our old boat. I ran into K.C.'s son, David. He was really weird. Acted like he hated me. Like he was jealous of the time I'd spent with his father when I was a kid."

"David didn't live with his father?"

Kate shook her head and sat down on the edge of the bed. Tyler took a seat on the lone chair across the room.

"David lived with his mother in San Diego. K.C. and his wife divorced when David was just a little kid, maybe two or three. I never met his mother. But David would come and spend summers here on the island with his father."

"So K.C. used to live here?"

"Part of the year, when he wasn't sailing somewhere. He and my father ran charters for a while or worked for other people. "

"Did K.C. come back here to recuperate after the race?"

"No. He was originally airlifted to the hospital in Oahu. After that he went to San Diego to be with David, I guess. I don't know. We didn't keep in touch."

"Why not?" Tyler asked sharply. "Your families were best friends, then that's it? It's over?" There was something she wasn't telling him. Probably a big something.

"My father and K.C. had a falling out long before that race. In fact, I think one of the reasons we entered was so we could beat K.C. and his crew. I can't help wondering now if that falling out had something to do with my mother, which I never considered before. The last time K.C. was friendly to me or my sisters was just before Mom died." She paused. "I remember he spent a good hour or two with her the day before she passed away. He didn't stay for the funeral. Said he couldn't handle it or something. I don't remember exactly."

Kate got up and paced restlessly around the room. "I should be talking to Caroline or Ashley, not you."

"Why aren't you talking to them?"

"Because . . ." She waved her hand in the air as if the answer would magically appear.

"Because why?"

"David said something to me that is ridiculous. I don't believe him, and it would really upset everyone if I even mentioned it."

"Are you going to tell me? Or make me guess?"

"I shouldn't tell you."

Tyler saw the indecision in her face. "Come on, spill it. It can't have anything to do with whatever you're hiding, or else you wouldn't be here. I already know you well enough to know that. It has to be personal, because you'd protect your family no matter what the cost. But yourself? That's a different story."

"I'm that easy to read?"

"I've been studying you for a while now." If she only knew how much.

"You're right. It was about me. David said, actually he implied, that K.C. might be my real father. Isn't that just way out there? I mean, I am my father's daughter, right? I certainly don't look like K.C. And it's just ludicrous, because my father and mother were madly in love with each other, especially when they first got married. There's no way there could have been an affair so early on. But then again . . ." She paused, sending him a desperate look. "Say something, Tyler."

"I don't know what to say," he muttered, more than a little surprised by the twist in events. "I guess anything is possible."

"That's not what I wanted to hear."

"Hell, Kate, I have no idea if K.C. slept with your mother, or if he fathered you. It seems to me you have only two choices: ask your father or ask K.C."

"I doubt my father is in any condition to ask, if he continued drinking after I left him earlier."

Tyler tipped his head at her silent question.

"That's what I thought," she said grimly. "And I wouldn't give K.C. the satisfaction of the question. I know he's got something up his sleeve. I could see it in his eyes earlier, but I didn't think it was something like this."

"No, you thought it had something to do with your other secret," Tyler said, taking a wild guess.

"I don't have another secret. I wish you'd let that go. At any rate, I have enough to worry about without concerning myself with you. I'm afraid your presence here is no longer going to make the top ten on my worry list."

He smiled. "I'm hurt. I thought I was at the top of your list."

Her returning smile was weak at best. "I'll have to talk to my father. Boy, I do not want to have that conversation."

"I think it's your best option."

"To tell you the truth, I don't know how my mother got mixed up with either one of them. She was kind and honest, with tons of integrity, which is why this is so unbelievable. I always knew my father wasn't one to lean on, but my mom, she was rock solid. She always knew right from wrong, and she always did the right thing."

"And she raised you to do the same." Tyler was beginning to understand how Kate had become so conflicted. With her mother out of the picture, she'd been left to temper her father and his penchant for disregarding the rules. Duncan was a man who made exceptions for himself, a man who could talk his way in or out of any situation.

"My mom tried to raise me right. But I've let her down."

"I find that hard to believe."

"I promised I would take care of my sisters and my father, that I would make sure the family stayed together, but I didn't do that."

He heard the regret in her voice, the blame, and he was moved by the torment in her eyes. He knew what that kind of guilt felt like and how it could eat away at your soul. He didn't want to see that happen to Kate.

"She asked me that last day," Kate continued, her voice somewhat dreamy as she recalled the memory. "I didn't know she was so close to the end. I guess a part of me still thought she'd get better. But she was so thin, and her hair was gone, just little wisps of reddish blond on the top of her bald head." Kate's mouth trembled.

"You don't have to tell me," he said quietly.

She gazed into his eyes with so much pain it almost hurt to look at her. "She took hold of my hand. She could barely lift her arm, but somehow she managed. I can still feel the pressure on my fingers. It was like she was trying to hang on to life through me. And I didn't want to let her go, but I didn't know what to do. Then she asked me to promise to keep the family together, to watch out for my dad, and to protect my younger sisters. She told me that I had to be the strong one. I had to take her place. And I said yes, I'd do it. She closed her eyes then and she let go—" Kate stopped as a tight sob broke through her lips. "I'm sorry."

"It's okay." He put his arms around her and pulled her against his chest.

"It's hard to be strong all the time," she whispered. "Sometimes I get so tired."

"I know. I understand." He stroked her back, hoping she would let herself lean on him for at least a moment.

"You do understand, don't you?" she said, looking up at him. "You're the strong one, too."

"Oldest-child syndrome."

"I want to keep my promise."

"I know you do. And you will. I'm sure of it."

She shook her head. "I wish I could be sure of it. I've already made so many mistakes."

"Don't be so hard on yourself, Kate. You were a young girl when you made that promise to your mother. And maybe she shouldn't have asked you."

"It was the least I could do. She suffered so much at the end. I would have promised her anything to ease her mind." Kate took a deep breath, then stepped out of his arms. "Thanks for the shoulder to cry on."

"Anytime." He paused. "I mean that, Kate."

"Thanks. I guess I'll go home and forget about this until tomorrow."

"Things usually look different in the morning."

"I hope that's true. I suppose I should just go to my father and ask him straight out. But . . ."

"But what?"

"What if he lies? How will I know? It's so hard for me, Tyler." She looked at him with a pair of baby blues that made it difficult for him to think clearly. "I can't always tell when people are lying. I look into their eyes, and I think I see the truth, but I'm often wrong. Caroline tells me I'm the suspicious one, always looking over my shoulder, always suspecting the worst. It's because I don't trust myself to know what's the truth and what's not. And my father is very good at bending the truth. Even if he's sober, I won't know for sure if he's telling me what he wants me to know or what I should know. Will I believe his answer either way? Or will it eat away at me forever? Will I have to live with something else I can't stand to live with?"

Which was what? Her own love affair? A baby she'd given up to a stranger? Was that what haunted her? But would she protect her own secret so ferociously? She'd just told him something very personal.

If she'd given up a baby, wouldn't she tell him that, too? It had to be Ashley or Caroline. It had to be. Or maybe he just wanted it to be one of them.

"I'm done," she said, breaking into his thoughts. "You're probably relieved. I don't think you've said anything in the last five minutes."

"You needed to talk," he prevaricated.

"And you were hoping I'd drop something juicy for you to bite into."

"I thought you were starting to trust me."

"Like I said before, I can't let myself trust anyone. Now you know why."

He looked directly into her eyes. "I don't trust easily, either, Kate. My father lied endlessly to me, and I bought most of his sorry stories, I'm sad to say. But you live and you learn, and eventually you figure out who you can trust. You stop making those mistakes."

"Really? You think so? Because I just trusted you by telling you something I don't really want anyone else to know. Was that a mistake? Did I just make another one?"

He wanted to reassure her, but was she wrong? What if push came to shove? What if he needed to find a way to discredit Kate in order to help his brother? Would he take it? Of course he would. That's why he was here, wasn't it?

"I see," she said with disappointment when he didn't answer her. "Thanks for the chat. Good night." The door shut firmly behind her and Tyler punched his fist against the wall with a muttered curse.

This was not going right. He only wanted to help his brother and his niece, not hurt Kate. But she would be hurt as soon as she found out just how far his lies went. She'd never be able to trust him after that. She'd never be able to trust herself.

Yanking his wallet out of his pants, he pulled out the photograph of Amelia and stared hard at it. Her sweet, innocent face, blond curls, and blue eyes reminded him of Kate. But Amelia wasn't Kate; she was

a child who had already lost her mother and almost
her father. He had to stay strong. He had to protect
Amelia. Kate could take care of herself.

"Is there anything I can help you with?" Kate asked
a young woman browsing the bestseller rack early
Monday morning.

"I'm looking for a good mystery for my father. He
doesn't like the mystery to be too easy or the love
scenes to be too graphic or for there to be too many
female characters. He's a little on the picky side."

"At least he knows what he wants."

"Unfortunately I don't, and his birthday is today.
I'm running out of time."

Kate selected a book from the rack. "This is by
Stuart Lawson. He writes about contemporary pirates
on the high seas."

"Oh, he would love that," the young woman exclaimed. "He's an avid sailor. In fact, we're here because of the Castleton Invitational."

"I figured," Kate said with a smile. "Most everyone
is." She walked behind the counter and rang up the
sale, including a complimentary bookmark and store
flyer. "We're having a local author book signing all
day Sunday, if you're still in town. We have quite a
few excellent writers who spend their winters or summers here on the island penning their latest bestsellers.
There's a list on the flyer."

"Thanks, that sounds great. I love this store. It's so
homey; I feel like I could hang out here for a while.
Unfortunately, my mother wants someone to entertain
her while Dad is practicing his sailing."

"Good luck."

"Thanks, I think I'll need it."

Kate glanced around the store, checking to see if
any other customers needed assistance, but there were
only a few people browsing the shelves. Most people
were probably down by the water. Race week had
officially begun an hour ago. Today's races were for

twelve-foot Beetle Cats. Each day's races would feature a different class of boats. In between the races, the larger sailboats would also make practice runs before the big race around the island on Saturday. And every evening there would be parties and celebrations for the winners.

Race week brought in a tremendous number of tourists to Castleton. The hotels, inns, and private cottages were booked solid. All the local businesses, including her bookstore, benefitted from the influx of summer money, as they called it. Business would probably pick up later when the sailors returned to the marina.

Kate walked over to the door and stepped onto the sidewalk in front of the store. It was a bright, sunny day, and from her vantage point she could see dozens of colorful sails out on the water. She felt a slight pang at the sight of all those sails, and she didn't understand why. She didn't want to be out there. So why did she feel strangely wistful? Why did the light breeze brushing against her face make her yearn for something when she'd thought she was content with her life? Her father had always said it was impossible to get the sea out of your soul. Sometimes she thought he might be right.

The door to her bookstore opened behind her, and her assistant, Theresa, stepped out. "Hey, there. What are you looking at?"

"The boats," Kate said, giving her sweater a quick zip as the breeze picked up.

"Do you miss sailing?"

"I never thought I did. But I must admit I have a silly urge to wander down to the water to see who wins."

"So go. Maybe you'll run into that cute reporter again."

Lord, she hoped not. She still couldn't believe she'd confided in Tyler. She should have her head examined. Anyone else would have been a better choice. Although she didn't want either Caroline or Ashley to hear about David's theory until she had a chance to figure it out for herself.

"Kate," Theresa said. "Did you hear me?"

"Something about a cute reporter. But, cute or not, I'm not getting involved with a guy who's only in town for a few days, another week at the most."

"You could just have some fun. Not every relationship has to be serious."

"I'm not in a relationship with anyone, especially him."

"Whatever you say. Why don't you go down to the water, take a break. It's slow right now. I can handle things on my own."

Kate hesitated, wondering if it wouldn't be better to fight this urge to go down to the docks and instead bury herself in inventory in the back room. Work had always been a good distraction before. But she couldn't seem to make herself go back in to the bookstore. Something was drawing her to the sea, the call of the wind, her father would have said. Maybe it was true, because Kate found herself walking down the street, turning her back on the life she'd built. Not forever, she told herself, just for an hour or two, but it was a step, a step in the wrong direction. She took it anyway.

Ashley was probably still asleep, Sean thought when he woke up stiff and disoriented from a night spent on her hard couch. Stretching, he swung his feet to the ground and stood up. He only wanted to check on her, he told himself as he walked toward her bedroom. The door was open, and all was quiet. He paused in the doorway, catching sight of her in bed.

Lord, she was pretty. Her long blond hair spread across the covers like it had been prearranged for a photo session. She wasn't wearing anything sexy; a long-sleeve, gray knit T-shirt could be seen where the covers had slipped off. Still, she was gorgeous, her face like one of the porcelain dolls his mother collected, not a blemish or a wrinkle marring her skin. She looked like an angel.

A deep ache centered in his gut. He wanted her so much it was painful just to look at her. It had always been this way. He couldn't remember a time when he hadn't been fascinated by her, when he hadn't wanted to spend every minute of every day talking to her or looking at her. It had all started out so innocently. They'd met in kindergarten. He could still remember sitting at her table, watching her color. She'd always liked to color. And she'd been so careful to stay between the lines.

As they grew up, their friendship deepened, despite the fact that they had different personalities. He'd always been active, energized, unable to sit anywhere for very long. Ashley could sit for hours if she had a good book or something to color. The rest of the world could be spinning around her in utter chaos, but there was always a peacefulness about her. Maybe it was that peacefulness that had called to him. With Ashley he could relax, he could be himself. He lost some of the nervous energy that made it impossible for him to stay on track or on task or whatever you wanted to call it.

When she'd gone to sea with her dad and sisters, he'd felt like someone had cut off his right arm. He probably hadn't realized until that moment that he was in love with her. Oh, sure, they were only fifteen and no one thought it was anything more than a crush or an infatuation, but he'd always known it was more. He'd dated other girls while she was away, but no one had ever made him feel the way she did. And he'd thought she'd felt the same.

But she'd kissed his brother. That was something Sean hadn't known, something he wished he didn't know now. When had that happened? And why? It didn't make sense. Jeremy had loved Kate. He wouldn't have fooled around with Ashley. There must

have been something else going on. Maybe someone
had had too much to drink or something.

Oh, hell, it didn't matter now, anyway, he thought,
running a hand through his hair. It had been eight
years. And he wasn't really all that interested in the
past; he was more concerned with the present. He'd
held Ashley in his arms last night. She'd turned to
him for comfort, and even though he still didn't know
exactly what had gotten her so upset, he'd been grateful that whatever it was had driven her back into his
arms.

He'd tried to stay away. He'd tried to make a new
life for himself. He'd dated every kind of girl he could
find, redheads, brunettes, tall girls, short girls, smart
women, ditzy blondes. A few had made him laugh. A
couple had made him horny. But none had really gotten under his skin the way Ashley had.

Shaking his head, Sean moved farther into the
room, wondering if he should wake Ashley or just go.
But he didn't want to go. He wanted to talk to her.
He wanted her to trust him with whatever was bothering her. He hadn't realized how messed up she was
until last night. He'd known there was something
going on with her and the water, but there was obviously more that was wrong, and he wanted to know
what it was. She'd always been cautious but never so
afraid, so fragile. He wanted to help her. He wanted
to take care of her. He wanted her to lean on him the
way she'd once done.

He sat down on the bed beside her. Ashley moved
slightly, murmuring something in her sleep. He put a
hand on her shoulder. Her eyes flew open. Startled by
his presence, she hit her head on the headboard as
she hastened to sit up.

"Easy there," Sean said. "Everything's cool."

She tucked her hair behind her ear in a self-
conscious gesture as she came fully awake. "What
time is it?"

"Almost eleven. We both slept in."

"You stayed all night? I thought you'd left."

"I slept on the couch. I didn't want to leave you alone in case you decided to take a midnight sail to the mainland."

"I'm sorry I was such a basket case last night. You must think I'm nuts."

"I think something is bothering you. Would you tell me what it is?"

She looked at him with her heart in her eyes, and he saw the indecision there, the hesitancy. She wanted to talk but something was stopping her.

"Is it your family? One of your sisters? Your father? Is someone upsetting you?"

Ashley shook her head. "I'm all right. It's not anything like that. You should go now."

"You know the reason I came here last night was to talk to you about Jeremy," he said, changing the subject.

She pulled the sheet up over her chest, twisting the material with her fingers. "Right."

"Just tell me one thing. Did you break up with me eight years ago because of this big kiss between you and my brother?"

"Not exactly."

"So that wasn't the reason? Then, just out of curiosity, why do you think I would care about a kiss that happened eight years ago, even if it was my brother? Or was it just one more brick to throw at my head to remind me that you never wanted me as much as I wanted you?"

"No, I didn't say it to hurt you."

"Then why say it at all? What possible difference could it make now?"

"Maybe I just wanted you to see me for who I really am."

He stared at her for a long moment, absorbing the pain in her eyes. "Who are you, Ash? Do you even know?"

"I know I'm not that girl you put on a pedestal all

those years ago. I've made a lot of mistakes over the years. Kissing Jeremy was just one example. I betrayed you. I betrayed my sister. And I did it out of spite and annoyance and loneliness, and I don't know what else. I hated that race, Sean. It turned my family inside out. My father became this monster competitor, and Kate and Caroline and I got caught up in it, too. When the storms came that summer, it was only a reflection of how messed up I felt inside. I'd get this feeling in my body, like claustrophobia. The walls would close in on me. I'd feel like I couldn't focus, like the world was spinning, and the air was too thick to breathe. I'd do anything to stop the feeling."

"And Jeremy was part of that anything?" He saw the apology in her eyes even before he heard the words.

"Yes."

"Did it ever go further than a kiss?"

"No, absolutely not."

He nodded, insanely relieved. It would have been hard to accept Ashley and Jeremy together under any circumstances, even though it had happened years ago. "So, what's next, Ash? What else do you have to tell me?"

"N-nothing," she stuttered. "That's it."

He didn't believe her, but maybe there had been enough revelations for one morning. "Why don't you get dressed and come with me today?"

"With you where?"

"Wherever we want to go."

She smiled at the familiar answer, and all the years, all the anger, all the silence faded away.

"You always used to say that."

"Then we'd hop on our bikes and take off down the hill, remember?"

"Of course I remember. I beat you down the hill every single time," she boasted.

"That's because your foot never touched the brake. I can still see your hair flying out behind you."

Ashley smiled somewhat sadly. "God, Sean, where did that girl go?"

"I don't know, but maybe we can find her again. Do you want to try?"

"More than you know."

Chapter Thirteen

Kate didn't walk to the marina as she had originally intended. Instead, she pulled out the old bike she kept in the back room and pedaled to Miramar Point, a spot on a bluff overlooking the Sound that gave her an excellent view of the sailboats competing below.

There were a few other locals ahead of her with binoculars in hand. One of those locals looked distinctly familiar, wearing a bright red sweater that Kate recognized as the one Caroline had borrowed a month ago and never returned. Her sister sat cross-legged on the ground, her attention fixed on the water below. Kate flopped down next to her. "Hey," she said.

Caroline looked at her with surprise. "You're the last person I expected to see up here."

"The call of the wind."

"You, too? I thought you were immune."

"Not when the breeze picks up. I'm glad you're here. I wanted to talk to you about K.C. and Dad. You took off so fast yesterday I didn't have a chance."

"Did you find out why K.C. bought the boat?"

"No. But I did find out that Dad is going to skipper the *Summer Seas*. He wants to race against K.C. And here's the kicker—Dad wants us to be his crew. He wants to make a bet on the race with K.C., and if we win, we get back the *Moon Dancer*."

"Whoa!" Caroline put up her hand. "Did you just say Dad is racing for the *Moon Dancer,* and he wants us to help?"

"I sure did. And the worst thing is that he was actually sober when he said it." Kate gazed at the water, but she wasn't seeing the boats, she was seeing the gleam in her father's eye when he'd made his announcement. He'd looked alive, happy, energized—and terribly angry when she hadn't supported the idea. She didn't want to feel guilty at sticking a pin in his happy balloon, but, dammit, she'd changed her life once for him, and she didn't want to do it again.

"It's not completely crazy," Caroline said slowly. "I hate to see someone else sailing our boat. It doesn't feel right."

"Caroline. Snap out of it. Dad isn't fit enough to race. He's old, and he's drunk half the time."

"He still exercises—sometimes," Caroline said with a frown.

"Don't be ridiculous. Walking down to the Oyster Bar doesn't count as exercise, nor does stumbling home."

"Just because I have a different opinion than you doesn't mean I'm wrong."

"What is your opinion exactly?"

"That maybe encouraging Dad to sail again isn't such a bad idea."

"We're not talking about sailing, we're talking about racing. They're two different things, and you know it."

"I know he's not happy, Kate. He hasn't been for a long time. You know what frustrates me the most? I can ask him out to dinner or stop by for a chat, and we always start talking about you. No matter where the conversation begins, it always ends with you, the one who doesn't respect him, the one who doesn't like him, who treats him like a child."

"I don't do that. Or, if I do, it's because he acts like a child."

"The point is, Kate, you're the one whose respect and friendship he wants the most. I could tell him it's fine for him to race. I could even join him. But he wouldn't be happy if you weren't there, too. You're the one. You're it."

"Caroline, I don't think any of that is the point."

"Well, you wouldn't." Caroline took off her sweater. "It's getting warm. So much for the breeze. It seems to have died down as fast as it came up. There will be a lot of disappointed sailors down there."

Kate glanced at her sister, about to say she was more concerned about her father's disappointment, when she was struck by the sight of several dark purple bruises along Caroline's left arm. "What happened to you?" she asked with concern.

Caroline followed her gaze. "Oh, I just banged my arm on something. It's nothing."

"It doesn't look like nothing." Kate didn't like the way Caroline averted her eyes. "Did someone hurt you?"

"I'm fine."

"Was it Mike Stanaway?"

"No." Caroline slipped the sweater over her shoulders, hiding the bruises, but the damage was done.

"Then who?"

"It wasn't a who. It was a door. I just banged my arm, that's all. Leave it alone."

"I think I've been leaving you alone for too long. Caroline, you have to tell me if you're in trouble."

"Would you stop being the big sister and let me be an adult?"

"Not when I see that someone has hurt you or that you've hurt yourself. I want to help. Let me help," Kate said in frustration.

"I don't need your help. I've got it under control."

"You call dating an ex-con under control? I heard that Mike hit his wife. That's why she left him."

"That's not why she left. But, I told you before, Mike didn't hurt me, and I'm not dating him. So drop it."

Kate didn't want to drop it, but pushing Caroline wasn't getting her anywhere. Maybe she'd have a talk with Mike Stanaway instead.

"Tell me more about Dad and this race," Caroline said. "He really gets to pick his own crew? I'm surprised Rick Beardsley doesn't want more say in it."

"Who knows what Dad told him."

"Is Dad going to race to San Francisco and on to Hawaii, or just around the island on Saturday?"

"I didn't even ask him that." The thought had never occurred to her. Was her father leaving Castleton for good?

"So Dad could be gone in a week. That will be weird."

It would be strange without their dad in town. Even though he was often a nuisance, he was still their father, still their checkpoint, still the only parent they had left. "We have to stop him from doing this, Caroline. We both know what a maniac he can be. There are no rules out on the sea, no sense of what's right or wrong, especially where Dad is concerned. For his own protection, we need to take a stand, all of us together. Are you willing to say no to him? That's what I need to know."

"I'm not sure. Maybe if I race with him . . ." Her voice drifted away.

"He'll like you better? Is that what you were going to say? Dad loves you, Caroline. I don't know where you got the idea that he doesn't. You're his baby, his princess."

"I'm the one who disappoints him the most. It's okay, Kate. I get it. I've gotten it for a long time. What you don't get is that we can't outrun the past. It's catching up. Every day it's getting closer. Don't you feel it?"

Kate did feel it. Even now she had goose bumps running down her arms. "We set our course a long time ago. We have to stick with it. No uncharted waters, remember?"

"I think Dad will race no matter what we say."

"We have to try, Caroline."

"Fine. If you want me to go with you to talk to him, I will."

"Thank you."

For a moment they sat in quiet, looking out at the boats, then Kate felt Caroline stiffen next to her. "What?" she asked.

"Don't you see her? Look. She must be on a practice run." Caroline pointed to the water below.

Kate squinted against the bright sunlight. Sure enough, there was the familiar bright blue sail with a white dove soaring toward the sky. "The *Moon Dancer*," she breathed. "K.C. can't be using the same sails, the same colors. He can't be."

"They wouldn't be in good enough condition," Caroline agreed. "Unless he had them copied."

"Why would he do that? Mom designed those sails. She was so proud of them being one of a kind."

"I don't know why he's doing anything. I'm the younger one, remember? Usually the last to know."

"Did Mom ever talk to you about K.C.?"

Caroline shrugged. "I don't know. I don't think so. He was a friend. He was always around when we were little. And sometimes he brought that annoying son of his with him. That's about all I know."

"You didn't like David?"

"Hell, no. He was an annoying, irritating asshole most of the time."

"I don't remember him being around much."

"That's because you were older. I was the one who got stuck with him when he came to visit. He didn't like us. He was jealous of his dad spending time with us. I remember one time when K.C. brought you one of those snow globes. David was so pissed off he tried to break it when you weren't looking. But I stopped him. So you can thank me now."

"Why didn't you tell me then?"

"I don't remember why. Probably because I wasn't supposed to be in your room."

Kate thought about Caroline's words. They certainly painted David as a person with a grudge—a big enough grudge to make up a lie about K.C. being her real father? She so desperately wanted to believe that it was a lie.

"Don't you miss it just a little?" Caroline waved her hand toward the *Moon Dancer* streaking proudly across the water. "We should be on that boat. She's ours. She doesn't belong with K.C. and his nasty little son."

Kate had to admit it was difficult to watch their boat under someone else's hands. Especially someone who had made their life difficult during their very long race around the world.

Caroline turned to her with the same gleam in her eye that their father had had, and Kate felt every muscle in her body tighten.

"Don't say it," Kate warned. But Caroline wasn't listening.

"I think we should do it, Kate. I think we should help Dad win her back."

Tyler climbed onboard the small boat that several people had mentioned belonged to Duncan McKenna. "Hello," he called, hoping he was in the right place. The boat swayed slightly beneath him. It was an odd feeling. He couldn't remember the last time he'd been on the water. His life for the past few years had been airplanes, fast cars, and maybe a train or two in Europe. Boats were foreign to him. Especially sailboats. He couldn't imagine waiting for the wind to change before you could move. He needed control, a good solid engine that could take him where he wanted to go, wind or no wind.

"Hello, there," he called again. He jogged down the stairs and peered into the empty cabin. The interior was small, with an unmade bunk in one corner and newspapers, magazines, and clothes strewn about. The air was filled with the smell of cigarettes and booze, but there was no sign of Duncan McKenna. Damn. He'd hoped Duncan was still sleeping off what surely must have been a hangover from the night before. Walking back up the stairs to the deck, he looked around, noting the numerous empty boat slips. Apparently there was some sort of a race going on today.

He sighed, wondering what to do next. He'd already discovered several interesting facts this morning. Making a return trip to the library, he'd turned his attention to newspaper articles from the past eight years. He'd found a short article on Ashley's collapse at the Fourth of July Picnic one year after their return to Castleton. Apparently, she'd been suffering from some unnamed stress and exhaustion, possibly related to her years at sea and perhaps malnutrition. Combine that collapse with the antianxiety medication he'd seen in her purse, and he could probably make a case for some type of mental breakdown.

The other article had concerned Caroline, who'd twice been cited for underage drinking with several other teenagers and had been put on probation and ordered to perform community service. Granted, those citations had happened before she turned twenty-one, making it possible for Caroline to argue that she was no longer underage. But it might not matter in the long run. Especially if he could pull together more current evidence that she still had a drinking problem.

Then there was Duncan. He surely knew which of his daughters had had a baby, and he had no doubt been the one to contact the doctor who in turn contacted Mark's attorney. If only Mark had done things the right way, they wouldn't be in this mess now. But Mark and his wife, Susan, had been desperate for a child, having tried for several years, and they just hadn't wanted to wait a second longer. When the opportunity had presented itself, they'd put a second mortgage on their house and bought themselves a birth certificate and an instant family.

It wasn't completely legal, but, then again, they hadn't stolen the baby. She'd been given up willingly, according to everyone involved. Unfortunately, there were no letters or signed documents to support that assumption. Everything had been done as anonymously as possible. Duncan hadn't wanted anyone to know about the baby. And Mark and Susan hadn't dared to ask any questions that would prevent the child from becoming theirs. For eight years it had all gone smoothly, until three weeks ago when it became clear that one of the McKenna sisters had hired herself an attorney to find her long-lost baby.

He wondered now what had triggered that move. What had happened three weeks ago? Maybe that's where he should be looking instead of so far in the past.

Tyler turned his head as he heard a man singing about beer, broads, and a good boat. It was Duncan—Duncan and a friend. Duncan had one arm flung around the other guy's shoulders, and they staggered slightly as they came down the docks. Two old salts, Tyler thought, for surely there was no better description for the weatherbeaten, sunburned men who lived to sail and sailed to live.

"And she's all mine," Duncan wailed.

"All mine," the other man harmonized in an off-key, drunken voice.

Duncan stopped abruptly when he saw Tyler on his boat. "Well, now, who's come to visit but my favorite reporter. Pete, have you met Taylor?"

"Tyler," he corrected.

Duncan pointed to him. "That's right, Tyler. I remember. I bet you think I'm drunk, don't you? Now, Pete here, he's drunk, aren't you, Pete?"

The other man could have been forty or sixty, it was impossible to tell, but he was definitely not sober.

"Pete is my neighbor," Duncan said, dragging Pete down the dock toward the boat next to his. "Help me get him onboard, would you?"

Tyler hopped down on the dock and helped get Pete onto his boat and down the stairs to a cabin very similar to Duncan's. Tyler couldn't help wondering how many good old boys were living on sailboats in the harbor.

"You okay, Pete?" Duncan asked. Pete rolled over on his bunk with a snore. "He's okay."

"What about you?" Tyler asked as he followed Duncan back up the stairs. He was relieved to see that Duncan walked a straight line fairly easily.

"I'm just dandy," Duncan said, hopping off the boat with a spry step. "I ran into Pete on my way back from a meeting. Couldn't let him wander down here on his own. He's a sad case these days. Lost his wife a few months back and hasn't been the same since."

"I guess you know how that feels."

"That I do, son, that I do," Duncan said in a heavy voice. "When my Nora died, she about took me with her. I didn't think I could bear to see the sun come up without her by my side."

Tyler was touched by the depth of emotion in Duncan's voice. He sounded very much likc a man who had loved his wife deeply—a faithful, loving husband. But had Nora been a faithful, loving wife? "What was she like?" he asked. "Your wife, Nora."

Duncan lifted his face to the sun. "Close your eyes," he said.

"What?"

"Close your eyes," Duncan repeated.

Tyler hesitated, then closed his eyes, wondering what was supposed to happen.

"Feel the heat on your face?" Duncan asked.

Now that he mentioned it, yes. "Sure." There was

a warmth on his skin, a light behind his lids, the scent of summer in his nostrils. His senses were heightened with his eyes closed.

"That's what she did for me," Duncan murmured. "She made me feel everything more intensely than I'd ever felt it before."

Tyler opened his eyes and saw Duncan wipe a tear from his cheek, a dramatic, emotional gesture for a crusty, tough old man but a seemingly genuine one. Tyler frowned, not happy to have Duncan puncture Tyler's original opinion of him as a bad drunk and an even worse father with a sailing obsession. Apparently there was more to the man than he'd realized. Maybe that's why Kate stuck by him the way she did.

"You coming aboard?" Duncan asked as he climbed onto his boat.

"Sure."

"I don't have much time. I've got a race to plan. Things are finally turning around for me."

Tyler could see that. Duncan looked like a different man today, a light in his eyes, an energy in his step. "Have your daughters changed their minds about racing with you?"

"Not yet, but they will. Kate is the stubborn one. Where she goes, the other girls follow. But she'll change her mind. When push comes to shove, she always chooses family."

Duncan sounded confident. Based on past experience? Or just a hopeful wish?

"Why did you sell your boat in the first place?" Tyler asked.

"I needed the cash. And I wanted to make sure the girls had money to live on. Now, I really need to get to work."

"One more thing. I'd love to see what it's like to sail around the islands. I was wondering if you could take me out sometime."

"You know anything about sailing?"

"Not a damn thing."

Duncan laughed. "No bullshit, huh? I like that. But I can't let you race with me, too much at stake."

"I understand."

"I can take you out on this boat, though, if you want to check out some of the races. Maybe tomorrow. Come by the Oyster Bar later and we'll talk."

"Great. I'll look forward to it." As Tyler got off the boat, he saw Kate and Caroline making their way toward him. Kate hesitated when she saw him, then continued forward.

"Tyler," Kate said coolly, obviously not happy to see him with her father.

"Kate, Caroline."

"Hi, Ty. Is it okay if I call you Ty?" Caroline asked.

"Call him whatever you want," Kate interrupted, fixing her sister with a pointed stare. "We came here to talk to Dad."

"If you've come to sign on for the race, climb aboard and we'll talk," Duncan said. "Otherwise, I have things to do."

Duncan stood straight and tall, his position on the boat setting him above them. With his shoulders squared and his jaw firm, he appeared very much the master of his destiny and perhaps theirs as well, Tyler thought, casting a sideways glance at Kate and Caroline.

"We've come to talk you out of this crazy idea," Kate said.

Wrong choice of words, Tyler wanted to tell her, but he didn't have time.

"It's not crazy, and it's not an idea," Duncan snapped. "It's a fact. I'm sailing the *Summer Seas*. I'm going to win back our boat. I'd like you to help me. We lost her together. We should get her back together."

"We didn't lose her, we sold her," Kate replied.

"Actually, you two sold her," Caroline griped. "I don't think I had a say in the matter."

"Caroline, you're not helping."

"And you don't speak for me. Daddy, why is K.C. racing our boat?"

"To show us up, that's why. He wants revenge. And this is his way of getting it. But he won't succeed if we stick together. I need your help. We're a family."

Tyler watched Kate's reaction as Duncan played the family card. He could see the indecision in her eyes. She was as loyal as they came. Caroline also watched Kate. Despite Caroline's brashness and bravado, she seemed willing to give Kate the lead.

"We made a promise to one another to move on with our lives. This is moving back, not forward," Kate said.

"I don't see it that way."

"There is no other way to see it."

"I want the *Moon Dancer* back. And I'm going to get it, with or without you." And with those words, Duncan disappeared into his cabin.

"Great job, Kate," Caroline said as she blew out a large bubble of pink gum that snapped against her lips.

"What did you want me to do?"

"Not call him crazy for one."

"Racing is crazy."

"You used to love it. Kate was the bravest one of all," Caroline added for Tyler's benefit. "Utterly fearless. I admired her so much."

"I'm still here, Caroline."

"Not the person you were. That person left a long time ago. I kind of miss her. I'll see you around, Kate, and probably you, too, Tyler."

Kate sighed as Caroline left.

"Is she right? Were you once a fearless Kate?" Tyler asked.

"I was a stupid Kate. I believed in the wrong people and the wrong things. Then I grew up. I wish I could say the same for the rest of my family, but you might as well call my father Peter Pan, because he is never going to leave Never Never Land."

Tyler laughed, but his laughter only made her frown deepen.

"What are you doing here, anyway? Digging for more dirt?" she asked.

"That would be difficult, with all this water around."

"Ha-ha."

He smiled at her grumpy tone. "Don't worry. Your father didn't tell me the location of the family jewels."

"What did he tell you?"

"That I could sail with him tomorrow."

"What?"

"He said he'd take me out on his boat tomorrow so I could see first hand what it feels like to sail."

"I'd advise against it."

"I'm sure you would."

"You didn't say anything to my father about K.C., did you?" she asked, looking past him toward her father's boat. "About what I told you?"

"No. That's up to you."

"It would make sense—why they started to hate each other."

"So you believe it now?"

"I don't know, but I couldn't stop thinking about it last night."

"Just ask him, Kate. Go in there and ask him. What do you have to lose?"

"Everything. My whole identity, that's what. And he's already angry with me. I don't think it's a good time." She spun on her heel and started walking down the dock.

"Where are you going now?" he asked as he followed her.

"I don't know. Back to work probably."

"I have a better idea."

"I doubt that."

He put his hand on her shoulder, stopping her in her tracks. "It's a beautiful day. How about a picnic on the beach?"

"A picnic on the beach?" she echoed, as if she'd never heard the words before.

"You know, wicker basket, fried chicken, potato salad, blanket, maybe a little wine. I was reading a brochure I found in my hotel room about a beach with a waterfall. I'd like to see it."

She cleared her throat. "I don't think so. Things didn't go very well yesterday when we spent time together."

"Today is another day."

"I don't know, Tyler. There's no point."

"Does there always have to be a point?"

"For you, I would think so. You came here for a reason, to write an article. I've already told you I'm not going to help in that regard, so I'm not quite sure why you're still hanging around."

He considered her point. It was something he'd spent a lot of time thinking about, in fact. The suggestion of an article had been the easiest way to get into the McKenna family, but it hadn't played out the way he and Mark had intended. Maybe it was time to change the plan.

"I've actually decided to do as you originally suggested."

"Which is what?" she asked, surprise in her voice.

"Talk to some of the other sailors, find some interesting anecdotes. Maybe I should ask Ashley if she has any photographs that might go with a general story on sailboat racing."

There was a skeptical glint in her eyes and he was reminded of the night before when she'd told him how difficult it was for her to tell when someone was lying. At least this wasn't completely a lie. He had never actually intended to write an article, only to find out who was Amelia's mother.

"If that's true, then I still don't see what you're going to accomplish by spending the day with me."

"I could tell you that I'd like to ask you for some names and perhaps have you point me in the direction of some good people to talk to. But I really just want to spend more time with you."

She licked her lips, lips he would love to taste again, but if he told her that, she'd surely say no.

Kate didn't answer for a moment. Then she said, "You better put together the best picnic basket I've ever seen, which will definitely include potato salad, some kind of fancy Brie cheese, and chocolate. Got it?"

"I got it." Whistling, he headed down the street in search of the perfect delicatessen.

Chapter Fourteen

"Your chariot awaits," Tyler said an hour later as he pulled Kate out of her bookstore and pointed his hand toward the street where he'd rented two bicycles. The picnic basket was strapped somewhat precariously on the back of a sleek, fifteen-speed racer. Tyler supposed he could have chosen something more modest, but, hell, he was a guy, and certain macho tendencies couldn't be denied.

Kate raised an eyebrow when she saw her matching bike. "Are we riding in the Tour de France or pedaling around the island?"

"Too much?"

"You think? These have to be the most expensive rental bikes I've ever seen."

"Probably, but they were also the coolest."

She walked over to the bicycles. "I know all about boys and their toys. Bikes, boats, cars, it's all the same where men are concerned. They want the fastest, the biggest, the best."

"And what do girls want? Surely big and best is a requirement at times."

He saw the faint blush cross her cheeks and smiled. Sometimes she looked as innocent as a teenage girl.

"But not always fast," she replied. "Some things are meant to be enjoyed more slowly."

"Some things." He knew they weren't talking about bicycles anymore, and so did she.

"Well." She cleared her throat. "Let's go."

"You can lead, since I'm not sure where we're going."

"Fine. I just hope you can keep up."

"Don't worry. I have no intention of losing you." He got on his bike and followed her down the street.

Kate rode with a purpose; no meandering, no stopping and looking at the view. She zigged and zagged through the downtown village, cruised along the wharf, then led him through a residential area before turning back toward the water. It was a beautiful summer day, the kind of day Tyler hadn't stopped to enjoy in years.

How long had it been since he'd ridden a bike that wasn't stationary in some twenty-four-hour gym? He couldn't remember. How long had it been since he'd actually stopped and looked at the scenery? Years, probably.

Since that day, more than twenty years ago, when his father had picked him up from school, he'd been on the move, never calling one place home, never making more than casual friends, never letting himself get attached to any place, any person. He supposed he could have stopped sometime in the past fifteen years and made a home for himself, bought some land, put down roots, but the concept was foreign to him. It was easier to go on living the way he'd grown up, reporting on life, watching other people live instead of living himself.

Shit! Way too heavy thoughts for a simple bike ride. What the hell was the matter with him? He didn't psychoanalyze his life. He didn't have the time, the patience, or the desire. He was what he was. He didn't need to change. It was just this decadent lazy island lifestyle that made him think of change. Normal people didn't ride bikes and have picnics on Monday afternoons unless they were on vacation. He wasn't on vacation. He was on a mission, a mission he did not intend to fail. He simply had to get Kate relaxed, catch her off guard, and go in for the kill. He did not intend to end this day without a solid lead or maybe, if he was lucky, a definitive answer.

They stopped about fifteen minutes later, walking their bikes over a rough patch of grass that led down to a sandy, secluded beach.

"Hey, where's the waterfall?" he asked, looking around.

Kate pointed to a small stream of water dripping down between two rocks on the far side of the beach.

"That's it? I'm not impressed."

"It's low tide. When the larger waves hit the other side of those rocks is when you get the waterfall. Disappointed?"

Actually, he wasn't disappointed at all. He liked the intimate atmosphere. The beach was almost deserted—a mother and her toddler at the water's edge, a couple on a blanket down by the rocks, and a man throwing a stick to his dog. "Where is everybody? Isn't it summer?"

"They're watching the boats. You can't see them from here."

"Do you want to go somewhere else?"

"No, I like this beach. It's small and quiet, peaceful. We get so many tourists nowadays. I miss the years when nobody came to Castleton."

"That wouldn't be good for your business." He unstrapped the picnic basket and set it down on the ground. "Damn. I forgot a blanket. What is a picnic without a blanket?"

"We'll survive." Kate plopped down on the sand and took off her tennis shoes, running her toes in the fine sand. "This is nice."

Nice wasn't the right word. *Sexy* was. He loved the flash of hot pink polish on her toes; it seemed at odds with her very practical personality and hinted at her passionate side, a side he wanted to see more of.

"What is this love affair you have with dirt?" he asked as he knelt down on the ground next to her.

Kate laughed. "I don't know. I just like the feel of the sand. Why don't you take your shoes off?"

"I don't think so."

"Why not? Is something wrong with your feet?"

"No, there's nothing wrong with my feet."

"Then let's see 'em."

"Fine. But if I'm taking off something, so are you."

"I already took off my shoes."

He grinned at her. "I wasn't talking about your shoes."

She shook her head. "You have a one-track mind."

"Well, I am a man."

"So I noticed," she muttered.

"Good."

"Stop flirting and settle down. Get comfortable. Take off your shoes."

Shoes again. He stretched out on the ground and slipped off his tennis shoes. His white socks followed. "Are you happy now?"

"Not even an extra toe. I'm disappointed."

He flopped down on one side, letting the sand trickle through his fingers. "It's cool," he said. "Moist. Does the tide cover the sand completely when it comes in?"

"Only with a storm."

"No chance of that today. Not a cloud in sight."

"A perfect day," she agreed, and for a moment they both watched the water lap against the protected beach in small, rippling currents. "It's amazing how fast it can change, though. One minute there's nothing but blue sky and the next minute it's totally black and threatening."

"You're remembering, aren't you?" he said after a moment, watching the play of emotions across her face. "Some day in particular?"

She didn't answer for a moment. "Yes."

"It's a bad memory. It makes you sad."

"How do you know that?" she asked, turning to look at him.

"The shadows in your eyes, the way your voice drops down a notch when you talk about the sea." He reached out and stroked the side of her cheek. "Your mouth draws into a grim line as if whatever you're going to say is so distasteful you can barely spit it out."

"You're very observant."

"That's how I make my living."

She caught his wrist and pulled his hand away from her face, but she didn't let go. Instead, she interlaced her fingers with his. "You have strong, capable hands. I like that about you."

"I'm glad there's something you like about me, but I think you're changing the subject. We were talking about storms."

She looked away from him at the water, at the horizon, at the past—he wasn't quite sure what she was seeing. He just knew that her fingers had tightened around his.

"I was washed overboard during the storm," she said finally.

"You were?" He was surprised. "I don't remember reading about that."

"My father pulled me back in. There was no official rescue or anything."

"So no need for a report," he said slowly, his mind wrestling with the implications.

"I wasn't the first, the last, or the only person to go overboard. It actually happens fairly frequently."

"I thought you wore safety harnesses."

"We did, but I had taken mine off for a minute. It was stupid," she continued rapidly. "A mistake. Anyway, it took me a long time to forget the feeling of water rushing over my head."

Tyler sensed there were still pieces of the story that were missing. But at least she was talking. "That must have been terrifying."

She tilted her head as she considered his words. "I was dazed at first. I wasn't sure if I was dreaming. It was an odd feeling. Was the boat underwater, or was I? Then I saw the boat drifting away from me. That's when the fear hit. The waves were so high it would completely disappear from my view. I tried to swim, but I got disoriented." She paused, drawing in a long breath and slowly letting it out. He could see the fear in her eyes and knew that her words had taken her back to that place. He was almost sorry he'd asked. "Then my dad managed to get a line out to me, and he pulled me in. He saved my life."

"Is that why you're still saving his?"

She met his gaze, and the truth passed between them. "I guess I am trying to do that. It might be a lost cause, though. I keep throwing lines to him, but he doesn't grab on to them. He doesn't want me to pull him in."

"Maybe he needs to rescue himself."

"Maybe." She drew in a breath and slowly let it out. "Well, this conversation has gotten heavy. How about some food?"

"If you let go of my hand, I might get you some. That is, once the blood starts flowing back to my fingers," he said, flexing his hand as she let go.

"I'm sorry. I didn't realize. So, what's for lunch?"

"Everything you said. Fried chicken, potato salad, French Brie, wine, and chocolate." He sat up, opened the basket, and began pulling out containers.

"Very good, but I don't think I said wine. I'm not a drinker. My dad drove that desire right out of my head."

"Unlike your baby sister."

"What do you mean?" she asked sharply. "Caroline

likes to party, but she's not out of control or any-thing."

"Sorry, I guess I read her wrong." But he wondered if Kate wasn't protesting a little too much.

"You did read her wrong. I'd know if Caroline had a problem." She paused, worry in her eyes. "I would know, don't you think?"

"You know your sister better than I do."

"Exactly. I'll take one of those mineral waters."

He handed her a bottle of Crystal Geyser. "I'm not a drinker myself," he said. "I like to keep my wits about me. Stay in control. Part of that oldest-child syndrome, I think. Always be the responsible one."

"Is your brother irresponsible?"

How did he answer that one? And why had he even mentioned his brother? Mark was a dangerous subject. Then again, Tyler wondered if he could gain her sym-pathy by telling her about the terrible tragedy that had befallen his brother. But if he told her anything, she might one day use it as ammunition against Mark. He couldn't take that chance. "He's more impulsive than I am," he said finally. "Now, what do you want to eat?"

Kate pulled off her sweater and spread it out be-tween them. "We can put the food on this."

"Are you sure? It might get dirty."

"I like dirt, remember? And I have a washing machine."

"You're a very low-maintenance woman, aren't you?"

"I'm used to taking care of myself."

"And other people, too—your sisters, your father, your friends, your customers. Don't you ever get tired of being so independent?"

"Even if I did, I haven't seen any fairy godmothers hovering about ready to turn my pumpkin into a carriage."

He smiled, liking her wit, her sense of humor, her lack of pretension. "What about handsome princes?"

"Not a one in sight."

"Are you sure about that?"

"You're not suggesting you have one of my glass slippers?"

He picked up her abandoned tennis shoe. "Will this do?"

"I'm afraid not. There are several dozen women who could wear that shoe and do. It's not one of a kind."

"But you are," he said impulsively, leaning over and kissing her on the lips. Her mouth was cool, moist from the water she'd been sipping. He wanted to linger, wanted to warm those lips, taste her more deeply, but she was already pulling away.

"Why did you do that?" she asked.

"I wanted to," he said simply.

"You make it all seem so easy, the flirting, the kissing. It's second nature to you, isn't it?"

He saw the question in her eyes, heard the hint of insecurity in her voice. "Maybe you just make it harder than it has to be."

"That's funny."

"Why?"

"Jeremy used to say the same thing. He thought I worried too much, thought too long, planned too hard." She shrugged. "But that's just me. I can't help it."

"Why should you have to change? As long as you're happy with who you are."

"For the most part, I am. Not that I don't have my faults, and I certainly haven't lived an error-free life, but I try hard. Does that count?"

"Enough to get you a chicken leg." He handed her a drumstick.

"Hmm. This looks good. Jack's Deli?"

"I heard it was the best."

"You heard right." She took a bite and sighed as if she'd just tasted ambrosia. He was fascinated by the way she ate, so dainty and feminine, and he loved watching her lick her fingers in between bites. Made him want to lean over and take a taste himself.

"You're staring," she said. "I hate it when people watch me eat."

He smiled at that. "It doesn't seem to be stopping you."

She took another bite. "Okay, it doesn't bother me that much, but, if you don't eat, there may not be anything left. I am the fastest eater of the McKenna sisters. Although we're all pretty speedy."

"It must have been fun growing up with sisters." He'd had a good time with Mark when they were little. He'd missed that when he'd become an only child.

"It was wonderful. Even though they often drove me crazy, especially when we lived on the boat together."

"What was that like?"

"Ashley taking our pictures every other minute. Caroline sneaking into the food rations. Card games that went late into the night, flying fish that landed on our deck when we least expected it, dolphins that were so friendly we could swim right along with them." She let out a sigh. "We were a tight group. We got used to having only one another. We didn't need anyone else."

And apparently they'd kept everyone else away, Tyler thought, especially while one of them was pregnant. Otherwise, someone somewhere would have said something about it.

"Sometimes it's hard to let go—even now," Kate continued. "But I know we have our own lives to live. Caroline reminds me of it often enough. And Ashley has been pulling away lately. With my father wanting to race again, I think I'm the only one trying to keep us together."

"Everyone grows up and sometimes apart. That's the way of families."

"I know you're right. I've actually been thinking about making some changes in my own life."

"What kind of changes?" he asked with interest.

"Well, when I turned twenty-eight three weeks ago, I looked at all those candles on my cake and thought about the years that had passed. Maybe it wasn't a midlife crisis, but it was a wake-up call to break out of my little cocoon, take a look around, figure out what I want to do, where I want to be, that kind of thing."

Three weeks ago? She'd had this revelation three weeks ago? The same time that Mark had received the first contact from Steve Watson? Tyler's pulse sped up. It had to be a coincidence. It had to be.

"What kind of things, exactly?" he asked carefully, trying not to sound too eager.

She hesitated, then said lightly, "I signed up for an exercise class for one."

"That's it?"

"What did you expect?"

"How about a trip or a move, maybe looking up an old friend, someone you hadn't seen in a while?"

She looked at him through narrowed, thoughtful eyes, and he realized that he sounded much too intense for what she probably thought was a casual conversation.

"Sorry," he said quickly. "It's not for me to say how you should change your life. But I thought you meant something on a grander scale than an exercise class."

"I think I'm ready for the potato salad now."

He handed her the container and a fork.

"What about you?" she asked. "Ever had one of those life-changing moments?"

"Not while blowing out the candles on my birthday cake," he replied. "But, yes, I did have one. Fairly recently, in fact."

"What happened?"

He shouldn't tell her. He absolutely should not tell her. He tapped his fingers against his thigh. "My brother was hurt in a car accident," he said shortly. "He could have been killed. And I realized how little time we'd spent together lately. I'd spent years of my life wanting to be with him, and then wasted the opportunity when I had it. I won't let that happen again."

"Is he all right now?"

"He's getting better."

"Why are you here, Tyler? Why aren't you home with your brother?"

Damn. He'd known confiding in her was a mistake. He tried to think of a plausible excuse. "My brother is very interested in sailing and sailboat races. He's the one who first told me about you and your big victory."

"So I have your brother to thank for your intrusion into my life?" she said with a dry smile. "I hope I meet him someday."

He offered a weak smile in return. "Hey, aren't you going to share some of that potato salad with me?"

She handed him the container. "Help yourself."

He looked down at the potato salad and set it back in the basket.

"What's wrong? Why aren't you eating?" Kate asked.

He cupped her face with his hands. "I just realized it wasn't potato salad I wanted."

"What do you—"

He cut off her question with a long, deep, wet kiss that turned into another and another. He liked the way she kissed him back, the way her tongue played with his. He ran his fingers through her hair, trailed his lips across her cheek to the corner of her ear. She smelled like vanilla, and she tasted even better. He ran his hands down her back, grabbing her by the waist and pulling her up against him. He wanted to feel her soft breasts. He wanted to touch every inch of her.

"Oh, God," she murmured as his mouth moved down the side of her neck. "We have to stop."

"We're just getting started."

"I— This is crazy," she said breathlessly, pulling away from him. "We're on a public beach. Tyler, stop."

He sat back, knowing she was right. He watched her fidget with her blouse and her hair and whatever else seemed out of place. He wanted to tell her to stop. He liked her loose and messy and a little out of control. He liked her passion and her spirit and, well, pretty much everything else about her.

"You're staring again," she said. "And I'm embarrassed."

"Why? We just kissed."

"It felt like more than just a kiss." She darted a quick look at him, then glanced away.

He flopped down onto his back, closing his eyes against the bright sun. She was right. It hadn't felt like a kiss; it had felt like a promise.

"Tyler, can I ask you something?"

"Sure."

Her words didn't come right away. "Are you connected to K.C. in some way? Are you part of a plan to get back at my father? Is this about revenge?"

His eyes flew open, and he sat up. "Why would you think that?" he asked, genuinely surprised at her conclusion.

"You both show up here unexpectedly. You want information about the race. You're going to sail with my father. It all adds up."

"That adds up? How far did you go in math?"

"You didn't answer my question."

"No, I'm not connected to K.C."

"Good." She put her arms around her knees and stared out at the water. "This is getting complicated, isn't it?"

"Yeah."

"What do you want to do now?"

"Believe me, you don't want to know the answer to that question."

She turned her head to look at him, her gaze drifting down to his mouth. "I really want to kiss you again."

"Then come here," he said softly.

"I can't. I seem to go up in smoke every time you touch me."

"It's one of your most appealing qualities."

She scrambled to her feet. "I need to walk."

"Walk? You need to walk?"

"Exercise would be good right now."

"I can think of a more interesting form of exercise."

"Come with me," she said. "There's a cave on the other side of those rocks. I'll show it to you."

"Now you're talking." He held out his hand. "Help me up."

A smile curved her lips. "Do you think I'm going to fall for that?"

"Please."

"Fine."

She slipped her hand into his, and, for a moment, he was tempted to pull her back down on the sand and kiss her senseless. But two young children chose that moment to run by him, kicking up sand with their bare feet, and he knew this wasn't the time nor the place.

Once on his feet, he didn't let go of her hand, and, after a momentary resistance, she relaxed, and they walked along the water's edge together. Tyler had never been so aware of the details of his existence than he was at this moment with Kate. All of his senses were engaged. The sand was cool beneath his bare feet, the sun was warm on his head, and the woman beside him was soft, feminine, desirable—and he was as hard as a rock. He needed to relax, too, he told himself, but the tension wouldn't go away. All he could think about was how easy it would be to lean over and kiss her again. He picked up the pace.

"Hey, what's the hurry?" Kate asked as she jogged to keep up with him.

"I'll race you to the cave."

"You don't know where it is," she called after him, but he didn't care. He needed to run along the shore-line. He needed to burn off the sexual energy that was making him crazy.

He heard her footsteps behind him, then felt her draw alongside. Damn, she was fast. She flung him a smile and passed him by. He pressed on harder, but he couldn't catch her, not until she finally slowed down and waited for him.

"What the hell was that?" he asked breathlessly.

"That was a sprint. I beat you."

"I let you win."

"Liar."

He could think of only one way to shut her up. He tackled her. It wasn't pretty, it wasn't coordinated, but it was effective. Because her soft, squirming body was now under his, exactly where he wanted it.

"Tyler, I can't breathe," she gasped.

"I'll have to give you mouth-to-mouth," he said, moving his weight off of her at the same time his mouth came down on hers.

So much for burning off the tension. It was back with a vengeance, and now he was acutely aware of her legs and her thighs and her hips moving beneath his. He wanted to get closer. He wanted to touch her bare skin. He wanted—

"Oh, my God!" he yelled as a blast of cold water hit his legs. He rolled to the side abruptly, realizing his pants were now soaking wet.

Kate laughed. "That's what we call a rogue wave."

"That's what I call bad timing."

"Better than a cold shower."

"You can say that again." The water had definitely cooled off a very important part of his body.

Kate got to her feet. "We'll dry off as we walk. The cave is just up ahead."

He followed her down the beach, now very much aware of how cold and wet he was. But Kate didn't seem bothered at all—probably due to all those years of living on a boat. The cold and wet were second nature to her. A moment later they rounded a curve, and he followed her pointed finger to a cave set into the rocks.

"There it is," she said. "When the tide comes all the way in, it fills completely with water. My mother used to warn me over and over again not to get caught here."

"Did you listen to her warnings?"

"Absolutely. I'm the cautious one, remember?" She walked over to the rocks. "It's still here." She traced the carving of two names.

"Kate and Jeremy," he murmured. "Hard to compete with that."

She looked at him in surprise. "What do you mean?"

"It seems clear that Jeremy is still very much a big presence in your life. You go to his grave. You can see your names carved into rocks, probably all over this island. How can anyone compete with that?"

"Do you want to?"

He should say no. Because that was the truth. He didn't want to compete for her. In fact, he wasn't really interested in anything more than a casual fling. His life wasn't going to take place on this island, that was for sure. Once he found Amelia's mother, he'd be gone. Kate would be just a memory. He'd probably forget her in a week. And she'd forget him, too. It wouldn't be like their names would be carved into a rock anywhere.

"Never mind," she said quickly. "I don't know why I asked you that. Anyway, this is the only place that we carved our names." She walked farther down the rocks. "There are lots of other names, as you can see."

"Sean and Ashley, Mark and Connie, Paul and Rita," he murmured. "I guess this was kind of lover's lane, huh?"

"It was a good place to get a kiss. And once you'd gotten one, you carved your name into the rock." She put her hand up as he started to speak. "But we're not going to do that. That kind of permanence probably terrifies you. Let's go back to our picnic. I've worked up another appetite."

So had he, but it wasn't for food. And it wasn't even for a kiss. He cast a somewhat wistful look at the names and hearts scratched into the rocks next to him. For some damn stupid reason, he wanted to put his name there, too. His name right next to Kate's. Something that would last forever.

"That was fun," Kate said an hour later as Tyler took her bike and handed it back to the manager of Bill's Bicycles. "I can't remember when I've spent such a lazy Monday. I feel guilty."

"It's good to play hooky once in a while."

"But now it's back to reality. Unless . . ."

"Yes?" he asked with a raise of his eyebrow.

"The world's best ice cream parlor is just down the street."

"You can't possibly still be hungry."

"You've found out my biggest secret. I'm a pig."

He laughed. "I'd love some ice cream from the world's best ice cream parlor. Although I think that might be an exaggeration."

"Wait until you taste it. You'll see I'm right." She didn't resist when he took her hand. In fact, she liked it. She liked it all, the kissing, the touching, the laughing. She hadn't had such a good time in years. And, with Tyler, she felt free to be herself. It was nice to be with a man who didn't know everything about her. They didn't have a history, only a present, and the future wasn't important. Tyler would eventually leave, and she would stay. But today they were together.

Maybe that was enough. Maybe she could stop planning, stop worrying, stop analyzing for five seconds and just let it all be. It had been working pretty well so far, so well she didn't want it to end. She didn't really care if she had ice cream or not; she just wanted more time with Tyler. Now that he'd agreed to drop the article, she could relax even more. The fact that he'd made that agreement niggled a bit at her brain. It didn't seem entirely logical or probable that a man who had such determined purpose a few days earlier could so quickly change his mind, but she was reluctant to bring the subject back up.

They walked down the street, stopping at the corner as the light in front of the ferry terminal turned red.

"Doesn't it bother you that you can only get off this island at certain times of the day?" Tyler asked.

"Not at all."

"I live ten minutes from an airport that can get me to any country in the world about as fast as I can buy a ticket and board a plane."

"And you find that comforting?"

"I guess I do," he admitted. "I used to feel trapped as a kid. I couldn't get away from my father, couldn't get back to my mother. I spent a lot of time looking desperately at exit signs. Old habits die hard."

"You really had a terrible childhood, didn't you?"

"Not completely. My father didn't abuse me. He just wanted me with him in the most selfish way possible." He cleared his throat. "But we don't need to talk about him. Hey, isn't that Caroline?"

She followed his gaze to where the ferry was loading. Sure enough, there was Caroline. Her sister was with Mike Stanaway. Kate tensed, not liking the way Mike had his hand on Caroline's arm. "What is she doing with him?" Worry gripped her as she watched them board the ferry. "I don't like the look of that. We need to stop her."

"What?"

Kate began walking rapidly down the street, breaking into a run when she realized that the ferry had finished loading and would no doubt pull away any second. Sure enough, it was fifteen feet into the harbor by the time she arrived at the dock. "Damn."

Tyler caught up with her a second later. "What were you going to do?"

"I don't know, exactly."

"Aren't you being a little overprotective? Caroline is a grown woman."

Kate turned to face him. "She has dark purple bruises all over her arm. I saw them earlier today. She said she banged her arm, but I think she was lying. Rumor has it that Mike's wife left him because of abuse. I'm afraid he might have hurt Caroline."

"Did you ask her about it?"

"She said he didn't do it."

"Maybe you should believe her."

She ignored that. He didn't know Caroline as well as she did. He didn't know how many lies Caroline had told in the past. "Can I use your cell phone?"

He handed her the cell phone without comment.

Kate punched in her sister's cell phone number and silently prayed Caroline had it with her and had it on.

"Hello," Caroline said a moment later.

"It's Kate. I just saw you get on the ferry with Mike."

"Are you spying on me?"

Kate ignored the outrage in her sister's voice. "Where are you going?"

"None of your business, Kate. I'm hanging up now."

"When will you be back?"

"When I feel like it."

"But—" Kate's words were met with a click. "She hung up on me."

"I can't say I'm surprised. Are you going to call her back?"

"She'll probably just hang up again." Kate handed him back the phone. "If I tell Caroline not to jump, the first thing she wants to do is jump. I should know that by now." Kate stared after the rapidly disappearing ferry. "I just hope she'll be all right."

"I saw them together yesterday," Tyler said. "They were arguing, but he backed off when I approached them."

"Why didn't you tell me?"

"Because Caroline wasn't upset, Kate. She wasn't scared. She didn't act like she was in trouble."

"Maybe she didn't want you to know. Damn. I wish they hadn't left the island. I'd feel better if she was within shouting distance."

"She has her cell phone. She can call you if she needs help."

Kate let out a sigh. "I guess there's nothing more to do."

"Except have some ice cream."

"Except that. Then I really have to get to work. What are you going to do with the rest of the day?"

"I'll probably wander down to the marina, talk to some sailors, figure out a new angle for my story. Unless you have another idea, one that might involve your house, your bedroom, maybe some candles?"

"It's not going to happen," she said with a smile, knowing he was only teasing. And she was glad that he wasn't serious, because if he had asked her seriously . . . In fact, if he'd kissed her instead of asking, they might be on the way to her house right now. Talk about acting crazy; apparently Caroline wasn't the only one making foolish decisions right now.

"Well, tomorrow is another day." Tyler put his arm around her shoulders. "You never know what the future will bring."

Chapter Fifteen

Tuesday was far too quiet, Kate thought as she checked her watch for the sixth time in an hour. It was almost five thirty, and she hadn't heard from anyone—not Caroline, not Ashley, not Duncan, and not even Tyler, who had been her constant shadow the last few days. She wondered if he'd gone sailing with her father. He would love being on the water. She knew that, even if he didn't. The wind rushing, the waves rolling, the boat flying. He'd be hooked. He'd never again be able to say he wasn't a boat person. She almost regretted that fact. It had been nice to know someone different, someone who didn't eat, sleep, and breathe sailing.

"I'm leaving," Theresa said, stopping in front of the counter with purse in hand. "I know it's early, but everyone is down at the square for the annual clam chowder cook-off."

"I know. I was thinking we should close up early." Kate smiled at her assistant. "You must be eager to see how well you'll do against your mother-in-law's clam chowder."

"I doubt I'll beat her this year, but, one of these days I will. She still doesn't think I cook as well as she does."

"She's wrong. You're a terrific cook."

"But not good enough for her little boy. Just wait till you get married, Kate. Pray for a good mother-in-law, preferably a non-cook, non-homemaker type, who doesn't criticize or interfere. And make sure you also pick a husband who stands up for you and doesn't become Mommy's little boy as soon as she steps in the room."

"Are we talking about me or you?"

"Me. Sorry. By the way, I saw the *Moon Dancer* when I had lunch at the marina today. She's a beauty. Everyone in town is talking about your boat and your family. I heard the name McKenna everywhere I went on my errands."

Kate hated to hear that, but she'd expected as much. It was one of the reasons why she'd brought a turkey sandwich from home and had her lunch in the back room. "It will all be over on Saturday. I just keep telling myself that."

"Why don't you put the *closed* sign out and come have some clam chowder with me? We haven't had a customer in more than an hour."

"I'll be down in a bit."

The door shut behind Theresa, and the silence was suddenly deafening. Her cozy store of fantasy felt empty and lonely. Kate sat down at the desk in front of her computer. She clicked on her inventory program first, checking on upcoming releases and preorders. She supposed she could have gone through all the titles, but she just didn't feel like it at the moment. In fact, she hadn't felt like working all day. Switching from inventory to the Internet, she pulled up one of her favorite gardening sites and read through the headlines for the latest articles. Tyler would have a field day with these subjects: introducing toads into your garden, getting rid of unwanted pests, growing the best vegetables. He probably couldn't fathom how anyone could be interested in such things. She smiled to herself, thinking of his minor adventures in gardening with her. He'd been a good sport. Her smile turned into a sigh as she clicked off the gardening site and started a search engine.

Even though Tyler had told her he was dropping the article, she wasn't entirely convinced they were out of the woods. Maybe acting friendly, flirting with her, pretending he was interested in her was just another way to get her to open up. She still didn't trust him, but she had to admit she sure did like him.

The door opened, and Kate looked up in anticipation. She'd known he would come. She'd been waiting all day. And there he was. But she wouldn't tell him that. She forced herself to stand up slowly and casually, as if she had her mind on other things, as if she hadn't expected him, didn't care if he dropped by.

"Hi," Tyler said. His voice was low, intimate, as was the look he gave her, a look that said, *I missed you.* At least that's what she wanted it to say. Because she'd missed him, too. Foolishly, stupidly, recklessly missed him.

"I thought you were out on the water," she said as she got to her feet. She was grateful to have the counter between them. It provided a much needed distance.

"Your father begged off. He said we'll go out on Thursday. Apparently he's busy interviewing potential crew members."

"I wouldn't set my heart on it," she told him. "My father isn't known for keeping his promises."

"So what have you been doing all day?"

"Working. What about you? Have you found a new angle for your article?"

"Well, let's see. I spoke to, I think her name was Molly, down at the dollar store. She sold me this pen." He pulled a pen out of his pocket and held it out for Kate's inspection. "If you turn it this way, the boat has sails, and if you turn it this way, it doesn't. Pretty cool, huh?"

"At least it's not the one with the lady who loses her clothes."

"Now, that I might have found more interesting, but to answer your original question—no, I haven't come up with another article subject as fascinating as yours. Are you sure you won't reconsider? Don't you trust me enough yet to tell me your story? I'm not a bad guy. I won't crucify you."

It wouldn't be up to him, she could have answered. Telling her story would affect far too many lives, and at this point there was nothing to be gained and everything to be lost. She was moving forward with her life. She was making positive changes. Discussing the past with Tyler would not be in any way productive.

"I should introduce you to Mitchell Haley. He competed in the Whitbread ten years ago. I'm sure he has a lot of stories to tell. He actually lives in Seattle, but he usually comes to Castleton for race week. If he's here, I'm sure my father will know where to find him. They're old friends."

"I'll keep that in mind." He took a step closer, resting his arms on the counter between them. "You look good."

"I— Uh, thanks." She tucked a piece of hair behind her ear, feeling distinctly uncomfortable with his intimate perusal. She was suddenly very aware of how empty the store was, and how very much she wanted to kiss him again.

"Kate," he said in a husky voice.

"What?" She looked into his eyes and saw them darken with desire. "Tyler. We can't start that all over again."

"Why not?"

She couldn't think of an answer. And it didn't seem like she really needed one. Words were passing back and forth between them and yet not a one was spoken aloud.

"I was sent here to get you," Tyler said.

"By whom?"

"Caroline. She was setting up a clam chowder booth or something like that down by the marina."

"Oh." Her baby sister's name broke the intimate connection between them like a burst of cold water on her head. So much for fantasy. Reality was right here, right now. "I can't believe she sent you. She's been avoiding my calls all day."

"Maybe *sent* wasn't the right word."

"I didn't think so. What did she say, exactly?"

"That you should stay out of her business or she won't tell you which of the clam chowders Mrs. Rayburn made. Whatever that means."

"Mrs. Rayburn sent ten people to the clinic last year for using bad clams."

He nodded. "Your sister doesn't pull her punches."

"I just hope she's not taking any."

"She looked fine, Kate. Really."

"Some scars aren't visible."

He sent her a curious look. "What does that mean?"

She couldn't begin to tell him. "Nothing. It doesn't mean anything. I'm glad she's fine, and I'll tell her I'm sorry when I see her."

"Good, then let's go."

She wavered. She'd spent most of the night tossing and turning in her bed, reviewing all the reasons why she needed to keep her distance from Tyler. Those reasons had nothing to do with his job as a reporter and everything to do with who he was as a man and the way he made her feel like a woman who might just fall madly in love if she let herself.

He leaned across the counter and kissed her on the cheek. It was the most casual kiss he'd given her yet, but in some ways it felt even more intimate, as if they had already crossed the lines of polite acquaintance and become friends, good friends, maybe more than friends.

"You think too much, Kate," he murmured. "It's just a bowl of clam chowder I'm offering you."

"Is that all it is?"

"What are you asking me?"

She shook her head. "I don't even know. When you're around, I have trouble remembering my own name," she confessed.

"Kate McKenna," he offered, his expression a bit grim, his voice a little harsh as he said her name.

"Why did you say it like that?"

"Like what?"

"Never mind." She reached into a drawer and pulled out her purse. "Let's get some clam chowder." She turned off the lights, changed the sign to *closed*, and locked the door behind them. That's when the wind almost knocked her off her feet. "Goodness, where did that come from?" she asked with a shiver.

"The weather turned about an hour ago. You hadn't noticed?"

"I've been inside."

"I'll keep you warm," he said, putting his arm around her.

That's exactly what she was afraid of.

"Hold on tight," Sean yelled as the wind caught his words and threw them back at her. "Let's see how we do on this hill."

"It's too steep," Ashley cried, tightening her arms around Sean's waist as he stopped at the top of Sorenson's Hill. "And we're not on a bicycle. We're on a motorcycle."

Sean took his helmet off and turned his head so he could look at her. "I won't let anything happen to you, I promise."

"I'm scared," she muttered.

"You can trust me."

She wanted to believe him so badly. She wanted to let it all go, the worries, the fears. She wanted to be that girl again who could soar down a hill with her hair flying out behind her. But he was asking too much of her. Wasn't it enough that they'd spent the last two days together, that they'd explored some of their favorite haunts and gorged themselves on fish-and-chips? Wasn't it enough that she'd actually agreed to get on the motorcycle with him today? Did she really have to agree to this, too?

"Remember what you used to say to me?" he asked her, his eyes warm with understanding.

She shook her head.

" 'Just take your foot off the brake. That's all you have to do.' "

"I can't believe I ever said that. I really wish I had a brake right now. I'd stop you from doing this."

"I won't do it, if you really don't want me to. But I think there's a part of you that wants a fast ride. Come on, Ash."

"All right. Do it before I change my mind," she said, squeezing her eyes shut.

She heard him laugh, then he put on his helmet, revved up the motor, and they were off.

She hugged herself to Sean's body, tightening her legs around the bike, praying they wouldn't lose their balance or hit a big bump. Sean was nuts, and she was even nuttier for not having gotten off the motorcycle when she had the chance. But there was no more time to think. The speed, the wind, the motion of the bike were all terrifying and exhilarating. She felt like she was flying. She felt like she was sailing, racing into the wind on a glorious day.

Within a minute they were down, back on even ground, the bike slowing faster than her heart. She opened her eyes to see that the world was still upright. The sun was still shining. Life was good. Sean stopped the bike on the side of the deserted road. He got off, threw his helmet onto the ground, and said, "Wasn't that fantastic?"

She took off her helmet with shaky fingers. She wasn't sure she could actually get off the bike. Her legs were shaking. Sean must have read her mind, because he helped her off the bike, put his arms around her, and spun her around in a dizzying hug.

When he finally put her feet back down on the

ground, his grin went from ear to ear. She couldn't help but smile back. His joy was contagious.

"That was amazing," he said happily. "Tell me you loved it as much as I did. Tell me."

"I liked it."

"You loved it."

"I was scared out of my mind at first, but then it was like before, better than before. I felt like myself again," she confessed. "I didn't know it was possible to have courage again. It's been so long." Her eyes filled with tears. "You gave it back to me, Sean. I don't know how you did it, but—"

He cut off her words with a kiss, a demanding, hard kiss that was as impatient and reckless as he was—and just the way she wanted to be.

He was in the mood to do something outrageous, Tyler thought. Two hours of clam chowder tasting, chatting with Kate's friends, and listening to local bands had done nothing to quiet the reckless feeling in his gut. He wondered if Kate felt the same way. She'd glance at him, then look away without saying a word. She'd barely touched her food, which was unusual, because in his experience she was not shy about eating. And then there was the way her fingers tapped nervously, or was it impatiently, on the red-checkered tablecloth. He wanted to put his hand over those fingers and pull them to his lips in a silly, old-fashioned kiss.

Maybe it was the small-town party atmosphere that made him feel like a stranger in his own body. Or maybe it was the magic of a summer night. He wasn't a romantic, but he suddenly wanted to tell Kate how beautiful she looked in the deepening twilight, how the music made him want to take her in his arms in a long, slow dance. He drew in a deep breath and let it out, wondering how he could feel so hot when the evening air was decidedly chilly.

"You haven't said a word in a long time," Kate remarked.

"Neither have you."

"Do you want to go back to your hotel?"

"Only if you're going with me."

She quickly looked away. "That's not what I meant. I thought you might be bored. This can't be very exciting for a big-city reporter."

"It's so exciting my heart is beating double-time." He grabbed her restless hand and pressed it against his chest. "Feel that."

"You're definitely still alive," she said somewhat breathlessly as she tried to pull her hand away. "Let me go. People will look. They'll talk."

"And what will they see? What will they say?"

She thought about his questions for a moment, and when she gazed back at him, her expression was somber. "They'll see the local bookstore owner losing her head over a sexy stranger. They'll shake their heads and whisper, 'Poor, Kate. Doesn't she realize it's just a summer fling? He's not going to stay here. He's not going to fall in love with her. Why can't she see that? Why can't she just tell him no right now and go find herself a local man who'll treat her right and not break her heart?'"

Tyler heard everything she was saying and more, all the fears, the worries. This wasn't any more casual for him than it was for her. Nor did it make any more sense. Even less, because he knew all the things he wasn't telling her.

"I won't let you break my heart," Kate continued. She took a deep breath, and he sensed she'd made some sort of decision. "But I won't send you away, either. I can't. I should, but I can't. I want to spend time with you, however long that time may be."

It was a gift he shouldn't accept, but how could he turn it away? He wanted this time with her, too. They couldn't have a future, not with the way their families were fated to clash, but they had right now. Maybe she'd hate him later. Hell, she'd probably hate him either way for all the lies he'd told, even if they were mostly lies of omission.

"I want to spend time with you, too," he said simply. That at least was the truth, the only truth he could speak.

She hesitated, then got to her feet. "Do you want to see one of my favorite places on the island?"

"Absolutely. It's not your bedroom, is it?"

She smiled as he'd meant her to. Things had gotten far too serious in the past few minutes. "No, it's not my bedroom, but nice try."

They walked back to Kate's store and picked up her car. Ten minutes later they pulled onto an uneven dirt road on the other side of the island. There were no streetlights out here, no houses, just tall, thick trees that didn't allow him to see the water until they finally reached an open bluff. That's when he saw the strange-looking building. Only it wasn't a building; it was a castle with a drawbridge, towers, and turrets.

"What the hell is that?" he asked.

"The Castleton Castle, also known as Frank's Folly. Frank Castleton was one of the original settlers on the island. He built the castle on a whim. At one time he envisioned an entire island filled with castles. Fortunately no one else shared his vision. It's not just a castle; it's a lighthouse. Do you want to go inside?"

"Sure."

"No one lives here anymore," she said as they got out of the car. "Frank was the only one who actually spent time in the castle. Apparently he'd hoped for a Cinderella to share it with, but as the legend goes he was more of a toad than a prince."

Tyler followed her across the drawbridge that lay over a dry gully, which he surmised was supposed to be a moat. The huge wooden door opened to Kate's gentle push. It was dark and dusty inside.

"There's a kitchen down here, a small dining area,

and a bedroom. But the best room is upstairs." Kate took his hand and led him up a staircase that opened onto one very large, round room. The walls were glass, and the only furniture was a wooden bench window seat that encircled the room. The rising moon sent shafts of light through the windows, creating an atmosphere of dark, romantic intimacy. So much for changing the mood. Tyler's heart sped up at the thought of what they could do in this quiet, secluded room.

"What do you think? Doesn't it feel magical?" Kate asked, doing an impulsive little twirl that reminded him of Amelia.

He chased that thought right out of his mind. The last person he wanted to think about right now was Amelia. At least he was doing one thing Mark had asked him to do; he was sticking close to Kate.

"It does," he agreed, but he had a feeling the magic had more to do with Kate than with the room.

She walked over to the windows. "The Sound is there. You'll be able to see the water when the light goes on."

"There's a light?"

"It's automatic. It comes on around nine o'clock in the summer. But I prefer it like this, the moon dancing around the room, lighting up the shadows."

Suddenly Tyler understood. "The *Moon Dancer*. This is where the name came from."

"Yes. This was my mom's favorite place. We always came at twilight, just as the moon was coming up. She'd tell us stories about the island. She was born here and knew all the history. Sometimes we'd bring a picnic. Sometimes we'd bring music and laugh ourselves silly trying to figure out how to dance. I always wanted to lead instead of follow."

"Why am I not surprised?"

"There are a lot of memories here," she said with a wistful sigh. "My dad never came here with us. For him, the magic was always out on the water."

"Am I trespassing on sacred female ground, then?"

"I think it will be all right. I sense that despite your outwardly cynical appearance, there is a bit of the dreamer in you."

"I will never admit to that. It's very unmanly."

"Why do you say that? Do you think dreams are only confined to females?"

"We men believe in practical goals." He knew she wasn't buying his macho act for a second. "Will it help if I pound on my chest now?"

"I still won't believe you. My father is a dreamer. Anyone who sails across the world is a dreamer at heart. And any man who roams the world in search of news stories has to be a dreamer, too." She paused. "You like a big canvas to paint on, and so does my dad. Nothing unmanly about that."

"You liked it, too, didn't you, Kate? Wasn't there a part of you that enjoyed that trip around the world?"

"Oh, yes, there definitely was," she said, surprising him with her answer. "But it wasn't so much about battling the water that thrilled me, it was that first glimpse of land off in the distance. Was it a mirage, born of boredom and loneliness? Was it a deserted island? Would there be people living on that island, lost to the world? Would we be their rescuers?" She smiled at him. "We never did find anyone on a deserted island, but every time we saw land, I thought it could happen. And when we'd sail into some foreign port, I'd stand on the deck of the *Moon Dancer* and soak it all in. I loved hearing the different languages, seeing faces of people I'd never seen before and never would again. I remember this little girl on the docks in South Africa. She was begging. I'd never seen such poverty in my life. I gave her my sunglasses, and her face lit up like a miracle had just occurred. That's what I miss, Tyler. Those little miracles that you don't expect."

"And yet you're happy to stay here on this island, reading about other people's adventures?"

"Yes, I am. I'm not saying that someday I won't

travel again. But for now what means the most to me is predictability, security. Maybe it's just part of getting older. I don't want to be a gypsy. I want to be a part of something that takes root and grows. What I did on the *Moon Dancer* was enough for me. But I bet you can't say the same. You're still a wanderer. You're still in search of something."

He considered her words thoughtfully, sensing a very definite feminine undercurrent. "What are you asking me, Kate?" He thought he knew what she was asking, but who could be sure when dealing with a woman? He'd mistaken female intentions before. And no doubt he would again.

"I'm not asking you anything," she said quickly. "We're just talking, aren't we?"

"If you say so."

"Do you want to go?"

What he wanted was for them to get back to the easy conversation they'd had a few minutes earlier. "I have another idea." He extended his hand to her. "Would you dance with me?"

"There's no music," she said practically, but he saw the desire in her eyes.

"Do we need any?"

Kate hesitated, then put her hand into his. "I told you before I have a problem with slow dancing. I usually like to lead."

"That's not a problem." He pulled her up against his chest and gazed into her eyes. "Just take me wherever you want to go."

She cleared her throat, a slight blush washing across her cheeks. "Uh, well, I guess we can just move around in a circle."

Tyler allowed her to set the pace, which was awkward and not at all graceful. In fact, Kate stepped down hard on his foot, and he had to bite back a wince. "I'm sorry," she said immediately, dropping her hands from his shoulders. "I think I need a beat."

"How about if I sing?"

"You can sing?"

"Don't sound so surprised. I'm a man of many talents."

"What do you sing?"

"Frank Sinatra mostly. My dad was a huge fan. Played Frank's songs over and over again." He began to hum a tune, because he couldn't remember the words. But, then again, it was difficult to remember anything with Kate in his arms. Picking up the pace, he moved her rapidly around the room until they were both laughing.

"Oh, my God!" she said breathlessly. "I feel like I should be wearing a chiffon dress with a big skirt that swings around my legs when I spin."

"You should," he said, twirling her again.

"This reminds me of one of my favorite movies. There's a scene in *The King and I* where Anna teaches the king how to do a polka. And they go flying around the room, spinning and spinning and spinning."

"Like this?" Tyler asked. He spun her around until they were both too dizzy to do anything but collapse on the window seat.

Kate held up her hands. "Time out. I need a breather."

"Hey, I'm just getting started."

"You're not a bad dancer," she admitted.

"I still have a few moves I haven't shown you yet." He gave her an exaggerated wink, and she laughed.

"You are terrible. A natural-born flirt." She paused, her expression turning serious. "I can't remember when I've had so much fun."

"Neither can I. It's been awhile, that's for sure."

A charged silence fell between them, the coziness of the room and the darkness of the night drawing a blanket of intimacy around them.

"If we wait a few minutes, we'll have a spotlight to dance under," Kate said somewhat nervously. "When the light comes on, this room will be as bright as day."

"I kind of like the moon shadows." The moonlight

had turned her from pretty into beautiful, from an ordinary woman into an angel. He wanted to take her in his arms and make love to her. "Kate," he murmured.

"We shouldn't," she said quickly, obviously reading his intentions. "We have nothing in common. You're a wanderer. I'm a homebody. This has disaster written all over it."

Her gaze left his eyes and moved toward his mouth. His pulse jumped. She was looking at him like she wanted him. "Kate," he said again.

"I know. I can't seem to stop wanting . . ." She touched his face with her fingers, and his breath caught at the tender, womanly caress. "You must have to shave every day," she murmured as her fingers brushed against his jaw.

He didn't know what she was saying. All he could think about was how good it felt to have her touching him and how very much he wanted to touch her. But he was afraid to move, terrified she'd stop.

"I want to kiss you again." She surprised him with her boldness.

"What's stopping you?" he asked, but in her eyes he saw the conflict of duty versus desire.

"Who you are. What you want with me and my family."

"I thought we'd moved past that." He turned his face into her hand and kissed her palm. He looked up and saw the spark of desire in her eyes. It was all the encouragement he needed. Leaning forward, he kissed her on the mouth, slowly, deeply. He didn't want to rush, wanted to take the time to savor the taste of her mouth, the scent of her hair, the wonderfully feminine curves of her body.

But Kate seemed impatient with the slower approach. She slipped her hands under his shirt, her fingers glancing off his abdomen, running through the hair on his chest. His muscles tightened at every touch.

"Yes," he muttered with encouragement.

"You feel so good, Tyler."

"Say my name again," he ordered.

"Tyler, Tyler, Tyler," she said against his mouth, punctuating each word with a kiss. "Maddening, annoying, frustrating Tyler."

"Don't get carried away, now."

"I want to get carried away," she said with a longing that removed the last of his doubts.

He moved his hands under her sweater. Her skin grew warmer the higher he traveled, until he met up with a lacy bra that thankfully had a clasp in the front. He didn't realize how much he wanted that bra undone until his fingers fumbled with the clasp, once, twice, before opening. He cupped her breast with his hand, the softness of her skin sending him over the edge.

He caressed her fullness, brushing his thumb over the taut peak. She was as excited as he was. It wasn't enough to touch her like this. He wanted more, much more. While his hands explored her breasts, his mouth moved from her lips across her cheek and down the side of her neck. God, she was sweet. Sweet and sexy and willing.

Kate tugged at his shirt. "We need to get rid of this."

"My pleasure." He pulled the shirt over his head and tossed it on the floor. He liked the way she looked at him, wanting him with her eyes, but she hadn't touched him again, and he wanted that more than anything. "Kate," he said, willing her to come the rest of the way.

She didn't move for probably the longest minute of his life. Then she slowly lifted the sweater over her head and slipped off her bra. Her hands came up to cover herself, a shyness that he liked but didn't want now.

"Don't." He put his hand on hers. "Let me look at you."

Her hands slowly moved back to her side. "You are one beautiful woman," he murmured.

She stared back at him without moving. "Touch me, Tyler. Put your hands on my breasts, the way you did before. I want to make love to you."

Now he was scared, his feelings of incredible lust getting mixed up with a little bit of guilt. There was trust in her sweet blue eyes. And he didn't deserve that trust.

"Tyler, what are you waiting for?"

"I—" Before he could answer, a shockingly bright light hit the room like a spotlight on center stage. Kate gasped and covered her breasts.

"Oh, my God. I forgot about the light," she said. "It's so bright!"

Shockingly illuminating, Tyler realized, and it had probably just stopped them from making a huge mistake. Tyler handed her the bra and sweater from the bench. "Do you want to put these on?"

"I don't look so good in the light, do I?"

He hated the sudden doubt in her voice. "It's not that. I just think this light is showing us a reality that we were trying to deny." He paused, his mind finally getting back into gear. "I don't even have anything with me, Kate. Believe it or not, I wasn't exactly counting on this happening."

"What do you mean?" Realization came slowly into her eyes. "Oh, right. We should have thought of that."

"It's hard to think of anything when we're together."

She put on her bra and pulled her sweater over her head with swift, jerky movements. "I don't know what came over me. I don't usually do stuff like this."

"I'm glad you don't. I'm glad it was just for me."

She stared at him. "Maybe you should put your shirt on, because this light isn't working on me quite as well as it worked on you."

"Trust me, it didn't do anything to diminish what I feel." He took her hand and guided her toward his rock-hard erection. "Whatever you're thinking in that head of yours, don't think I don't want you. But not tonight. Not like this."

Not until he knew the truth. Not until he didn't have to lie to her anymore.

Kate pulled her hand away and got to her feet. She looked out at the water that was now lit up by the light. "When you're on the ocean, a light like this can be a savior, the promise of a safe harbor. I never thought I wouldn't be happy to see the light." She turned to him. "I know it was smart to stop. I just kind of wish we hadn't. Because it felt good, and it's been a long time since I felt that good. I wanted to be selfish. It's a family trait, you know." She headed toward the stairway. "Let's go home."

Home? Where was that? he wondered. Logically, he knew his address in San Antonio. That's where his things were, where his friends lived, where his brother and niece made a life. So why was he starting to feel as if this island was home, as if wherever Kate was going was where he wanted to be?

Chapter Sixteen

Kate dropped Tyler off at his hotel without even turning off the engine. She muttered a good-bye and took off as soon as he'd shut the door. It was just as well. He regretted tonight almost as much as she did, not for what they'd done, but for what they hadn't done. He'd never been caught so off guard before. Dating had always been fairly traditional—dinner, drinks, maybe some dancing, then he'd take the woman back to her house or whatever hotel room he was in, and they'd make love or have sex or whatever you wanted to call it. He was always prepared for that eventuality, and, like any man, always hoping for that end result.

But not this trip. He didn't even know if he had a condom in his shaving kit, much less his wallet, pocket, or anywhere else that might have been handy. This trip wasn't supposed to be about anything but finding Amelia's biological mother.

Maybe sleeping with Kate would have helped discredit her as a candidate for overturning the adoption. No, he thought with a frown, it probably would have done more to discredit him. He was here under false pretenses. And while he'd done some things he wasn't particularly proud of in the name of reporting, he'd never taken advantage of a woman in that way. It was good that they'd stopped. At least he could still live with himself. Sleep was a different matter altogether.

He felt wired, jazzed, and too unsettled to even think about returning to his quiet hotel room. Most people in Castleton apparently felt the same way, Tyler realized, as he walked back through the town square. The food booths were being dismantled, but there were still crowds of people gathered around small tables, talking and laughing. A few people called out hello, people he'd met through Kate or on his own. He'd only been in town a few days, but they were making him feel like part of the community, part of their lives, and it was a nice feeling, almost too nice.

The thought worried him. A small island in the Pacific Northwest was not the place to get attached to. There were no earth-shattering news stories here, no need for tough investigative reporting. It was a tourist destination, a place for fishermen and sailors, bikers and hikers, honeymooners and retirees, a place for people to relax, smell the flowers, enjoy life—not a place for him. He liked to be on the go, flying in fast jets over countries whose names he could barely spell. He liked the nonroutine, the unpredictable, the never-ending adventure.

Didn't he?

Then why was this scene so appealing? Why did Kate's small house charm him so? Why did he feel so attracted to a woman who had made it clear she was never going to move? Why did he suddenly wonder what it would feel like to have a house of his own and friends who would welcome him home, who would butt into his business and protect him from strangers' questions, who didn't expect anything from him? Why did the idea of one woman, one long-term relationship, one marriage suddenly sound so attractive?

Hell, he was out of his mind. He didn't want any of those things. What he wanted was a drink. Thankfully, the Oyster Bar was just around the corner.

It was fairly crowded for a Tuesday night. Tyler

stood for a moment, checking out the room for familiar faces. Sure enough, there were two: Caroline and Duncan sitting at a table in the corner. His eyes narrowed at the sight. He wondered what they were cooking up. There was an intensity to their conversation that was apparent in their body posture, the way they leaned in toward each other, the sharp look on Duncan's face as he said something to Caroline.

Tyler moved closer so he could hear what they were saying.

"I want to help you, Daddy," Caroline said. "You know I do. But Kate won't race again, and Ashley can't even get herself on a boat these days."

"You have to convince them, Caroline. I'm counting on you," he said loudly, firmly.

"I'll come with you. I'll race. I'll be your partner. Maybe that will be enough. We can get a good crew. There are plenty of strong, willing sailors around. We don't need Kate or Ashley."

"Of course we need Kate. She's—" He waved his hand in the air as if searching for the right word. "She's the one who makes it all work."

"I can make it all work."

Duncan called to the waiter to bring them two beers.

"I don't want a beer," Caroline said. "Look, why don't you take me out on the practice run tomorrow? You'll see how good I am."

"You haven't sailed in years."

"Neither have you," she argued. "But I've kept in shape. I'm still really strong."

The waiter set down two beers in front of them. Duncan picked his up and drank like a man who hadn't tasted water in a week, but, judging by the empty glass on the table, this was not his first beer. Nor would it probably be his last. As he set down his glass, he saw Tyler and motioned him over.

"There you are, my favorite reporter. What are you drinking?"

"Beer, I guess."

"Will, bring me another for my friend," Duncan called out. "And put it on my tab."

"How's it going, Caroline?" Tyler pulled out an empty chair at their table and sat down.

"Fine," she said with an expression that was not particularly welcoming. "You sure do get around."

"She's upset," Duncan told Tyler. "She wants to race with me, but I need Kate, too."

"I still don't get why," Caroline retorted.

"Well now, honey, I don't want you to get your feelings hurt, but you're kind of a jinx."

Caroline sat upright in her chair. "I am not a jinx. How can you say that?"

"Trouble follows you around like a tail follows a dog." Duncan smiled over at Tyler. "If there was a bucket nearby, Caroline would no doubt step in it. If there was a drink by her elbow, she'd knock it over, accidentally of course." He glanced back at his youngest daughter. "It's okay. You can't help it, and you always try hard."

"I am not that clumsy. And that only happened a couple times," she protested.

"Oh, look, there's Rudy." Duncan waved his hand toward his friend. "Hey, Rudy, come over here and sit your sorry ass down."

A big, burly man in his late fifties ambled over to the table. "Who's your friend?" Rudy asked.

"Tyler something," Duncan replied. "He's a reporter looking for some good sailing stories."

"Don't believe a word this bastard has to say," Rudy said, giving Tyler a hearty pat on the back. "He lies so much he's forgotten what the truth looks like."

"That's for sure," Caroline said harshly as she got up. "I'm out of here."

"Hey, you haven't touched your drink," Duncan said. "Push it on over here, would you? I don't want good beer going to waste."

Caroline looked as if she was going to do what he suggested, but when her hand touched the glass she hesitated. She lifted it to her mouth and took a sip. She gave her father a hard, unforgiving look, then tilted her head back and drank the beer down to the last drop. She set the glass down on the table. "See, there are some things I'm good at," she said and turned toward the door.

Tyler wanted to go after her, but Duncan was saying something to him and Rudy put a hand on his arm, and by the time he excused himself and got to the door Caroline had disappeared. He thought about calling Kate, but, hell, Caroline was a grown woman, and it was none of his business. Still, Caroline had a dangerous, reckless look in her eye. He had a feeling she was looking for trouble. He just hoped she didn't find it.

Kate jogged down the sidewalk that ran along the marina early Wednesday morning. She'd almost made a huge mistake the night before, and she was doing penance this morning by putting her body through a punishing workout. Maybe if she got tired enough, she'd stop thinking about Tyler, stop wanting to make love to him, stop acting like a fool.

He'd been the one to call a halt to things, to remember basics like birth control and safe sex. She was the one who'd been caught up in the moment, and it still irked, even after a long, sleepless night. She liked to be in control at all times, especially of herself and her emotions, but there had been a few minutes last night when she had been completely out of control.

What had she been thinking? She barely knew him. And she wasn't sure she could trust him. Tyler seemed like a good guy, but she still suspected he was hiding something. Then again, so was she. It was difficult to call him a liar when he could throw the word right back at her. And he'd been so charming, so much fun.

He'd made her laugh; he'd made her feel emotions she hadn't felt in a long time—if ever. That traitorous thought brought her jog down to a walk.

Had it ever been that good with Jeremy? Had her senses been so completely involved? Or was it even fair to compare? Time had dimmed so many memories. And she had changed as well. She was a grown woman now. Her needs, her wants, her wishes were different.

Kate paused along the rail, looking out at the water and the boats. She'd been content before Tyler came to town. She'd told herself work and family were enough. She didn't need a man in her life, didn't want all the messy, emotional complications of love, didn't want to have her heart broken again. And she'd almost bought into all of that until Tyler had arrived.

Now she'd had a taste of what she was missing, and that taste had made her want more.

It could hurt, a voice inside her head reminded her. And could she survive another loss? Wouldn't it be better to play it safe?

While she was thinking, she caught a glimpse of a man coming out of the coffee shop down the street. It was Mike Stanaway, the man her sister had been with at the ferry landing on Monday. She'd tried to talk to Caroline about him at the clam chowder cook-off, but her sister had claimed she was too busy to chat and then disappeared.

Maybe this was her opportunity to talk to Mike. While Kate weighed her options, Mike took off at a brisk pace. She broke into a jog to follow him and came down the dock just as he disappeared onto his boat.

Climbing aboard without waiting for an invitation, she called out his name as she went down the stairs into the cabin. She stopped abruptly as she saw Mike offering her sister Caroline a cup of coffee. Caroline was sitting up in bed, wearing a black spaghetti-strap undershirt. A tangled sheet covered her bottom half.

Her hair was a mess, her makeup smeared as if she'd been crying.

"What are you doing here?" Caroline demanded.

Kate was so stunned by her sister's appearance she could barely speak. "I—I wanted to talk to Mike. I didn't know you were here."

"About me? You wanted to talk to him about me?"

"Get dressed. I'm taking you home." Kate glared at Mike, daring him to try and stop her, but he didn't say a word.

"I'm not twelve, Kate. I'll go home when I want to," Caroline snapped. "And I'd like you to leave."

"What?" Kate asked in shock.

"You heard me. I want you to leave."

"Not without you. I'm not leaving you here with him."

"I'm fine."

"You don't look fine. You look like someone who knocked back a liquor store last night."

Caroline uttered a bitter laugh. "You don't know anything."

"I know this is not a good place for you to be."

"Mike is my friend."

"She's too young for you. What are you doing with her?" Kate demanded of Mike.

"That's her business and mine," he said quietly but firmly.

"I know what I'm doing, Kate. You have to trust me."

"It's him I don't trust," Kate said, tipping her head in Mike's direction.

"He won't hurt me."

"He already has. Look at your arms."

"I told you I banged my arm. For God's sake, Kate, would you just leave? I'll call you later, or I'll come by the bookstore, just go now. Go," Caroline added, with a pleading smile. "Trust me to take care of myself."

Kate did not want to leave without her sister, but what could she do? "You better not hurt her," Kate said fiercely. "Because if you do, I will come after you."

Mike didn't reply, just tipped his head in acknowledgment. Kate hesitated, then turned and ran up the stairs. Once on the dock, she stopped, debating her options. If she stayed nearby, she could hear Caroline if she called for help. Would she even call for help? Caroline certainly didn't want her interference. But, if she left, she'd be worrying the rest of the day.

As she paced back and forth on the narrow dock, she saw a man approaching her—K.C. Just when she thought her day couldn't get any worse.

"If you wanted to take a closer look, why didn't you just ask?" K.C. said as he stopped in front of her.

"What are you talking about?"

"I'd be happy to give you a tour, Katie. I'm sure you're curious."

It was then that Kate realized the *Moon Dancer* was just a few slips down. She'd been so preoccupied with following Mike that she hadn't noticed until now. "I didn't come here to see you or the *Moon Dancer*." Although, now that she was here, maybe she should find out what K.C. was up to.

"Have it your way," he said, walking past her.

"Wait. I did want to ask you something."

K.C. smiled as he turned back to face her. "I thought as much."

"Why are you really here? Why did you buy our boat and have the sails remade in exactly the same design? I'm sure that wasn't a coincidence."

"I bought the *Moon Dancer* because I wanted it, because your mother and I designed that boat in our heads long before she and Duncan decided to have it built. It was always meant to be mine—like so many other things that Duncan stole from me."

"I assume you mean my mother."

"Nora belonged to me. He knew that."

"She went where she wanted to go. And the three of you were friends. I remember you at every important occasion in our family until my mother died."

K.C. sent her a steady, assessing look. "That was because of you, Katie."

Her heart stopped. He couldn't mean what he was implying.

"I thought you were my daughter," he said, confirming her worst fear.

"But it wasn't true." She made sure the words were a statement and not a question, but she was still holding her breath as she waited for his answer.

"No, it wasn't true," he said finally and seemingly with regret. "Nora had told me that all along. But I had reasonable doubt. We'd both slept with her within the same critical period of time."

"I find that hard to believe." She hated the thought of her mother with K.C., with anyone besides her father.

"Nora and I had been dating, but we'd had an argument, a misunderstanding. A few days later Duncan returned from one of his trips. My good friend was back," K.C. said with bitterness. "I was happy to see him. So was Nora. She'd met him a few months earlier. I didn't realize what an impression he'd made on her until he came back. They started seeing each other. The next thing I knew, they were married. I didn't know she was pregnant at the time, but then you were born six weeks too early." He paused for a long moment. "When she told me I wasn't your father, I didn't believe her. I thought she was protecting her marriage, protecting Duncan. I couldn't fight her on it, not without hurting her. So I stayed close, figuring if I couldn't have you, I'd at least see you, spend time with you."

"Give me presents that made your own son jealous," Kate added.

K.C. looked at her in surprise. "Excuse me?"

"Something you didn't realize? David still believes that you're my father, and that I'm your favorite."

"That's not true. I love him very much."

"Maybe you should tell him that. Maybe you should let go of this old hatred of yours. What's it going to accomplish to beat my father? Will you be happy then?"

"I think I might be. Duncan didn't just cheat me out of the woman I loved. He cheated me in many other ways, including our race around the world."

Kate stiffened and silently begged, *Please don't remember. Please don't remember.*

K.C. watched her closely. "Can you deny that he didn't?"

It was a risky question, one she didn't quite know how to answer, especially since she didn't know what he knew. "That race was over a long time ago."

"I was leading, going into that storm."

"How do you know that?"

"It's a matter of record. I should have won that race."

"It's not our fault your boat went down."

He didn't look like he believed her.

"We all need to move on with our lives," she added quickly. "Don't you think it's time to put this thing with my father behind you? How long will you try to make him pay for winning my mother's love?"

"As long as it takes," K.C. said coldly. "You've heard about our bet, Katie?"

"Yes. My father is racing you for the *Moon Dancer*. And he'll probably win."

"I guess that would depend on his crew. You were always a better sailor than your father. Another reason why I thought you were mine. But, no matter. When your father loses, I'll get something else I want."

Kate knew she would regret asking, but she couldn't

stop the words from coming to her lips. "What's that?"

"The portrait of your mother with you and your sisters."

"That's mine," she said tightly.

"I believe technically it belongs to your father."

Kate couldn't believe Duncan would have bet the portrait. Or maybe she could. His ego knew no bounds. He probably didn't consider it a risky bet.

Kate turned her head, hearing a commotion behind her. Caroline jumped onto the dock. She scowled when she saw them. "Waiting for me, Kate?"

"K.C. stopped to talk to me," she said, taking advantage of his presence. He might as well be good for something.

"I'm going home," Caroline muttered. "Don't follow me. I'm not in the mood for you or one of your lectures."

Kate let Caroline go, because it was obvious this wasn't the time or the place. At least Caroline was going alone. That was worth something. She turned back to K.C. "You will never get my portrait."

"Who's going to stop me?"

Kate wanted to slap the sneering smile off his face and say *she* would stop him. But she couldn't quite get the words out of her mouth. That would mean agreeing to join forces with her father and racing again. How could she do that?

"No one will stop me, Katie. You've left your father on his own this time. And we both know he can't do it without you. He never could."

Tyler flipped off the television set in his hotel room and realized he couldn't put off calling his brother for another minute. He should have called yesterday, but he'd felt so conflicted after spending the evening with Kate that he just hadn't had the heart to call Mark. He felt like a wishbone, being pulled in two directions, and it seemed like he was betraying both of them. There was no way they could all win. In the end, someone would be terribly hurt.

Picking up his cell phone, he punched in Mark's number and waited.

"Hello?" A childish voice greeted him.

"Hi, honey. It's Uncle Ty."

"Hi, Uncle Ty."

"How are you, sweetie?"

"I'm fine. Daddy just needed some water, so I got it for him. I even put ice in it."

"You're a good helper. But I thought that was Shelly's job."

"She had to go out for a little while. She's not back yet."

"Not back yet?" Tyler wondered where Shelly had gone. Mark was supposed to have twenty-four hour care at all times, especially with Amelia in the house.

"Do you want to talk to Daddy? I think he might be asleep, but I can check."

Tyler felt even more uneasy at the idea of Amelia being in the house with Mark asleep and no Shelly nearby. Amelia was only eight years old, although at the moment she sounded closer to twenty. For the first time, Tyler wondered if he was doing the right thing. Mark would have a long road back to recovery, a road that would require care, money, and time. Would Amelia be shortchanged growing up in such a way?

"Are you okay there by yourself?" he asked her.

"I'm not by myself. Daddy's here. He'll wake up if I need him."

"What if you fall or something?"

"Then I'll get up," she told him with simple childish logic.

"I guess you will."

"Daddy and I wrote Mommy a letter, and we put it on the dining room table so she could see it when she's looking down on us. I printed in really big letters, too, so she could read it from heaven."

Tyler's stomach clenched at her words. "That sounds nice."

"Do you want to hear what I wrote?"

Did he want to have his heart ripped out of his chest? "Sure," he said, knowing that was the answer Amelia wanted.

"I'll get it."

Tyler heard her set down the phone and wished he could call her back. He was torturing himself—punishing himself for getting carried away with Kate yesterday, for letting Mark down, even if only in thought not in action.

"Are you there?" Amelia asked when she returned to the phone.

"I'm here."

"Dear Mommy, we miss you a lot," she read. "We hope you're happy in heaven, but we wish you were here. I sang your song last night to Daddy, and he said I must take after you, because he sings really bad. I'm going to try to be just like you when I grow up."

Tyler's heart twisted with emotion at her simple statement, and he couldn't help wondering for the thousandth time why Mark and Susan hadn't told Amelia she was adopted, maybe not the who, why, where, or whatever, but enough so that Amelia wouldn't be shocked to find out one day that she was not who she thought she was.

"I'm talking to Uncle Ty," Amelia yelled, probably to her father. "Daddy wants to talk to you," she said. "Bye."

"Bye, honey."

"Ty? What's up?" his brother said a moment later. "Why didn't you call me back yesterday? I left you three messages."

"I didn't have anything new to report."

"Well, maybe I had news," Mark snapped. "George got another letter from Mr. Watson. He found the doctor in Hawaii who delivered Amelia. He has a signed letter stating that the doctor turned the baby over to George on the exact same date of our adoption. George sent me a copy of the doctor's letter. It's all there, Tyler. The doctor even has my name listed as the adoptive parent. But there's no signed release by the birth mother or father. George assured me he had one, but he can't seem to find it."

"He never had it, Mark, you know that," Tyler said forcefully. "That's why he charged you so much money for the adoption. That's why he told you to leave Hawaii immediately. And you did it, because you didn't want to ask any more questions."

"Yes, I did it. For Susan," Mark replied. "I loved her so much. I don't know if you can understand that. She was everything to me, and after all those miscarriages, I couldn't stand to see her in any more pain. I'd do it again, if I had to make the choice. I don't care if the birth mother signed the paper or not, she still gave her baby away."

"Or her father did," Tyler said.

But did that make sense? Wouldn't one of the girls hate Duncan if he'd stolen her baby and given it away? No one reacted that way to him, not even Ashley, who seemed to be the most distant from her father.

"I'm thinking about leaving town," Mark said, ignoring his comment. "Taking Amelia and disappearing forever."

"You can't do that, Mark. You need medical care. You're rehabilitating. How can you go into hiding? You need a full-time nurse."

"You could help. You're not getting anywhere in Castleton. Why don't you come back here and help me and Amelia disappear?"

Like he and his father had disappeared? thought Tyler. Always on the run. No chance to make friends, to feel a part of something, with uncertainty everywhere. Did he want that for his niece?

"It's my best chance," Mark added. "It's a big world. We couldn't find you for six years. I don't think it will take that long for Amelia's biological mother to give up."

"It's a terrible life. I don't want it for you, and I sure as hell don't want it for Amelia."

"It's better than giving her up. She's my life. She's all I have left."

"But you don't want to ruin her life."

"I'm not doing that. I'm trying to save us."

"You sound just like Dad." Weren't those his father's words? *I'm trying to save you, Tyler. Save you from a life of pain, living in a home where no one wants you.* But his father had been trying to save himself, not his child. Just as Mark was doing now.

"Don't ever compare me to him," Mark said coldly. "And I'll do this with or without your help. I thought you could find something out, but obviously you can't. I'll make other arrangements."

"Don't do anything yet," Tyler said, knowing he was well and truly caught. He couldn't let Mark go off half-cocked. He didn't want to lose contact with his brother again. "Give me more time. I'll find out who it is before Saturday. And we'll make a decision then."

There was a long silence on the other end of the phone.

"I'll think about it, Tyler. But make no mistake— I'll do what I have to do. If they get too close, I'll be gone."

Chapter Seventeen

Kate debated what to do next. Torn between anger at her father for betting their portrait and concern for Caroline, Kate wasn't sure which way to go. In the end, she decided to go after her father. Since her sister was no longer with Mike, she wasn't in any immediate danger. It would be smarter to track down Duncan before he went out on the practice run or drank too much to make any sense. She could not allow him to bet their portrait. It was the only picture she had of her mother and her sisters all together. And she wasn't about to let K.C. win it and hang it on his wall, as if they were his family. It was sick.

When Kate arrived at her father's slip on the other side of the marina, she found him on deck talking to Rick Beardsley, the man who had hired him to skipper the *Summer Seas* in Saturday's race. She'd met Rick a few times over the years. In his early fifties, he was younger than Duncan but close enough in age to remember Duncan at his best. Which must be why Rick had decided to give Duncan another shot at racing glory.

She paused for a moment, watching the two men talk. Her father had on his usual sailing cap, but what really disturbed her was the bright orange-red T-shirt he had on. He'd always claimed it was his lucky shirt, that it reminded him of the color of her mother's hair. She also didn't care for the way he was waving his hands, punctuating each word with obvious vigor. She hadn't seen him look so energized, vital, and completely in charge in years.

Was she wrong? Was this what he needed? Was this what they all needed?

"Katie," Duncan called out with a cheerful wave when he spotted her. "Come on up. Say hello to Rick."

She climbed aboard. "Good morning."

"Nice to see you again, Kate. I can't wait to show you my boat this afternoon," Rick said.

"The practice run, you remember," Duncan said quickly, a plea in his eye.

Kate was torn once again between family loyalty and honesty. As usual, the two didn't seem to go together.

"Right," she said, hoping it was a neutral enough word to satisfy both of them.

"I'll see you then," Rick said. "Remember what we discussed," he added to Duncan. "I'd like to see Caroline and Ashley onboard as well."

Duncan nodded. Kate stood motionless and silent until Rick stepped off the boat and was halfway down the dock.

"He thinks I'm racing with you. He thinks we're all racing with you," Kate said slowly, realizing that her father had misled Rick.

"It's a possibility."

"It is not a possibility."

"Katie, I want you with me. You're my daughter. This is a family matter. We're not just racing to race, but to take back what's ours. You must help me."

Her stomach knotted with guilt. He always did know how to push her buttons. "What did you tell Rick?" she asked, trying not to weaken. Someone had to make the tough decisions. Someone had to be logical, practical, and unemotional. And that someone had always been her. She was tired of trying to keep things from sinking or drifting away, but, if she didn't do it, who would?

"I told him I'm building a solid crew, one that will win, and that my daughters always support me."

"You don't always deserve that support."

"We all make mistakes. But we don't turn our backs on one another. And there's a lot at stake."

"I know exactly what's at stake. I ran into K.C. a few minutes ago. He told me you bet our portrait on the race. I said that couldn't possibly be true. You know how much that portrait means to us."

Duncan shrugged. "Don't get all bent out of shape. I'm not going to lose."

"You always say that."

"And I haven't lost yet, not to K.C."

That was true. But they both knew there were things they weren't saying. "What if this is the first time? How could you live with the idea of K.C. putting that portrait up as if we were his family?"

"It's what he wanted to wager against the *Moon Dancer*. I had no other choice."

"You had a lot of choices, all of them starting with the word *no*."

"He won't beat me."

"I won't give up that portrait. It's mine." The portrait had hung on her wall for the last eight years, and before that it had hung in the main cabin of the *Moon Dancer*. It had gone around the world with them, and it was one of the few things they'd taken off the boat before they'd sold it.

"Then sail with me, Katie. You were always the best of the girls. If you sail with me, I know we won't lose." His voice grew more energized with each word, the passion of his quest clearly visible in his eyes. "Don't you want to feel the wind in your hair, at your back, driving you toward the finish line? Don't you want to hear your heart pounding? Don't you want to feel alive again?"

It was the talk of an addict, an adrenaline junkie. Hearing the need in his voice awakened memories from long ago. Kate could almost hear the wind, feel the spray in her face, see the other competitors in front of her, behind her, and beside her as they raced for the finish line, willing to win, no matter the cost. She was shocked at how easily it came back to her, that thirst for victory, as if it had been biding its time, hiding beneath the surface, until she couldn't hold it back anymore.

"I can see it in your eyes, Katie. You want it as much as I do."

"I don't."

"Say yes," Duncan urged. "Help me right this wrong. K.C. shouldn't have our boat. Your mother would hate knowing he was sailing it."

"Would she?" Kate knew she had to ask. There had been too many secrets between them for too long. Perhaps if she understood this one piece, the others would make more sense.

"Of course she would hate it," Duncan said fiercely. "She was a McKenna. She was proud of that boat, proud of us."

There were so few things about her father that Kate was certain of, but his love for her mother had never been in question. Would she hurt him if she spoke the words running through her brain? He'd hurt her many times, her conscience argued. But this could go deep. Would her mother want her to speak?

"K.C. told me that Mom loved him first," Kate said, taking a deep breath. "He claims that she was with him in an intimate way, that he actually thought I was his child for most of my childhood. Did you know about that?"

Duncan's eyes turned cold and hard. "Nora never loved K.C. He lived in a fool's paradise, and he's still there, thinking he can take over my life, my boat, my family."

"That's what this is all about," she said, finally understanding the elusive missing piece of Duncan's ambitious drive and his intense, fierce rivalry with K.C. It had never been about the sailing, not really. It wasn't who was the better sailor; it was who was the better man. "K.C. couldn't accept that Mom loved you," she continued. "For a long time he convinced himself that they had a special secret: me, the daughter no one but the two of them knew about. When he realized that it wasn't true, the pretense at friendship was over."

"I won't let him take over my life, Katie. Your mother chose me." Duncan brought his hand to his chest. "Me. I was the one for her. But, even after we married, K.C. was always around. Nora said, 'Let him be, Duncan. He's lonely. He needs friends.'" Duncan's voice took on a bitter edge. "She had no idea he was trying to destroy me every chance he got."

"How did he do that?"

"He'd sabotage my boat before races or he'd bribe someone to race for him instead of for me. He'd drop hints that I was with some broad when I said I was working, just to make your mother doubt me. I didn't see it at first. I thought they were innocent remarks, but he was playing a game all along. He brought you and the other girls presents when I couldn't afford to give you what you wanted so he could be the big man." Duncan looked her straight in the eye. "He bought that damn portrait, Katie."

"But Mom got it for you, for your birthday."

"He paid for it. Said he wanted to share in the birthday present. He knew I couldn't afford it. So he arranged for you all to have it done while I was away on a fishing charter."

Her heart sank. The portrait was paid for by K.C.? Kate would never be able to look at it in the same way. And her mother had let K.C. do it. Why? Hadn't she realized that the man was still in love with her?

"Why didn't Mom tell him to go?" Kate asked. "Did she know he thought he was my father?"

"She was too softhearted. That's why she let him stay."

"I don't believe it was just that." Perhaps her mother had still felt some love for K.C., some unwillingness to completely break the tie.

"She told him a bunch of times that you weren't his kid, but it wasn't until she was on her deathbed that he finally believed her."

It made sense. Because he'd never been on their side after that.

"That was it for him," Duncan added. "He'd thought he'd have something of Nora after she died, but he wouldn't. You weren't his. You were mine. It broke him. That's why he went after us during the race. He was always in our faces, always trying to bend the rules."

K.C. or her father? Kate asked herself. Sometimes she didn't know who had bent the rules more. It was hard to remember.

"I'm not lying about this, Katie."

She wanted to believe him. But, as she'd told Tyler earlier, Duncan had a way of making everyone believe his lies, including himself, until the event became in his head whatever he'd pretended it to be.

"We can't let him win, Katie." Duncan's voice once again held desperation. "This is probably our last chance. If he even lets us have this chance."

"What does that mean?" She stared at her father in dismay. "What else aren't you telling me?"

"There's a slim chance K.C. knows something."

"About the storm?"

"I don't know if he's fishing, or if he remembers. I want to race him, Katie. I want you and your sisters to help me. Our family will take back what's ours,

making damn sure that K.C. doesn't end up with anything McKenna. Your mother would have wanted it
this way. She wanted you to help me keep the family
together. Didn't you promise her just that?"

Kate wanted to tell him to go to hell. That it wasn't
fair to put this on her. But, on the other hand, she
really hated the idea of K.C. sailing their boat. And
she hated the idea of him winning their portrait
even more.

Now that she realized there had been something
between K.C. and her mother, it made all of his other
actions—the presents, the friendly pretense—that
much more sickening. He'd had a hidden agenda the
whole time he was acting like a family friend. He'd
waited for Duncan to screw up, maybe even tried to
help that along, so he could steal Nora back.

Still, race again? It was an impossible thought. She
couldn't go back out on the water. She couldn't face
the other sailors, the boats, the crowds, the wind. She
couldn't put herself out like that, couldn't expose herself to that world again. She knew what men could do
in the heat of a race. She knew what she could do.

"I can't," she told him. "I want to move forward,
not backward."

"It won't ever be over, not until we take back the
Moon Dancer."

"We made a promise."

Duncan looked her straight in the eye. "I can't
keep it."

"Well, I can."

"Racing is who I am. I'm starving, thirsting, dying
for it. Please, I'm begging you. Talk to your sisters,
Katie. Together, we can take back what we lost. We
won't be free of the past until we do."

She should have stayed at Mike's, Caroline thought,
as she faced herself in the bathroom mirror. She didn't
want to be alone in her apartment. She didn't want
quiet or time to think. Nor did she want to have to

look at herself. But she was drawn to the mirror as if it were a car wreck, one she couldn't pass by without turning her head to see the damage. And there was considerable damage.

Her mascara was no longer on her lashes but under her eyes, giving her the appearance of a prizefighter. Her lipstick was long gone. Her hair lay in sweaty strands on her head. She looked as if she'd spent the night having sex and taking drugs, which was no doubt the conclusion Kate had drawn when she'd found her in Mike's bed.

It hurt to know that Kate's opinion of her had only gotten lower. But it was going to get worse, much worse.

Closing her eyes, Caroline took a deep breath. Her head was pounding so hard it was making her sick to her stomach. She'd made a big mistake last night, and it had begun with that one stupid, reckless drink when her father had told her she was a jinx and a klutz and basically not good for much of anything. Damn him. He'd pushed just the right buttons. He'd made her feel bad about herself, insecure, unworthy, the way he'd done so many times before.

She opened her eyes and stared defiantly at the mirror. She was just as good as him, just as good as Kate, just as good as anyone—well, maybe not this morning. Maybe this morning she was only as good as her father, who probably felt as bad as she did.

Bending over, she splashed cold water on her face. Rubbing her cheeks ruthlessly on a terry cloth towel got rid of the rest of her makeup, and the stinging sensation made her feel better. She walked out of the bathroom and stood in the middle of her bedroom, still wearing her low-rise blue jeans and black tank top. She needed to change, to go to work. She didn't feel like doing either.

How was she going to get through the next five minutes, much less the next few hours? There was so much going on in her head. So many things she wanted . . . no, *needed*. The craving started deep in her soul, an itch that couldn't be scratched. She had to do something to stop it. Before she could move, the doorbell rang, followed by a pounding knock and a loud voice that belonged to her oldest sister.

"Would you shut up already?" Caroline snapped as she opened the door. "I'm here. What do you want?"

"I want to come in." Kate walked into the apartment, shutting the door behind her. "I want you to tell me what's going on with you and Mike."

"It's none of your business."

"I'm making it my business."

Caroline flopped down on her secondhand couch. "I'm not in the mood for a lecture."

"I don't care if you're in the mood. I want to know what's going on."

"Nothing."

"Caroline Marie McKenna, you are going to talk to me. I'm not leaving until you do." Kate sat down on the other end of the couch, folding her arms in front of her chest. Caroline knew that stubborn look well. But she preferred this look to one of disappointment, disgust, and embarrassment, which were exactly the expressions she'd see as soon as she told Kate what was really going on.

"I'm an adult, Kate. I can see who I want."

"I don't care how old you are. I'm your sister, and I won't stand by and let you make a huge mistake."

"The mistake was made a long time ago."

"Talk to me, Caroline." Kate sighed. "I'm not mad. I'm worried and scared. I love you. I know this guy is up to no good, even if you can't see it."

"Because he has a snake tattoo and wears an earring?"

"No, because he has a criminal record and a history of drunken brawls. I want more for you. I won't apologize for interfering. You need someone to give you a good kick in the butt. And if I have to be the one, I will do it."

"You're so strong," Caroline said wearily. "Where do you get that from? Dad or Mom? Or maybe both of them? Maybe you got everything, and there just wasn't enough to go around for Ashley and me."

"What are you talking about?"

"I'm talking about why I never measure up. Why I can't seem to do the right thing. Why I need someone to swoop in and rescue me."

"We all need that at times."

"You never do."

Kate's face was unblemished, giving no sign that she'd been through any private battles, fought any internal demons, even though Caroline knew that Kate had done both. How had her sister managed to come out so unscathed, so unmarked by life?

"I've had my share of weak moments, Caroline. You know that better than anyone. You were there for most of them." Kate paused. "Now I want to be there for you. I know something's wrong. I won't leave here until I find out what it is."

"I don't know where to start."

"Start with Mike."

Caroline smiled at the irony. Kate was so wrong, so terribly wrong, it wasn't even funny. "I've told you a dozen times that Mike is just a friend, and that's what he is—a friend." As she finished speaking, her stomach rebelled once again, the nausea overwhelming this time. She ran into the bathroom and threw up until she was shaking. Dimly, she was aware of Kate handing her a towel and helping her into the bedroom and into bed.

"Do you want anything? Do you want me to call Dr. Becker?"

"I don't need a pediatrician. I'm grown up," Caroline grumbled.

"He's a family doctor. Maybe you have the flu."

"I don't have the flu, Kate."

"You can't be sure."

"I'm sure."

"Caroline, I don't want to argue, but—"

"Then don't." Caroline put up her hand. "I'm not sick, at least not in the way you think. Don't you get it? Isn't it clear?"

"Oh, my God! You're not pregnant, are you?"

"No, I'm not pregnant," Caroline said in exasperation.

"Then what?"

"I'm an alcoholic, Kate. Your baby sister is a drunk."

Chapter Eighteen

Your baby sister is a drunk.

Kate couldn't believe the words ringing through her head. Yet the evidence was right in front of her. In fact, faced with the actual words, she wondered why she hadn't seen it earlier. Or had she?

"I think I've left you speechless for the first time in your life," Caroline said.

"I knew you drank, but I didn't think . . . I mean, you're not like—"

"Like Dad? He's an alcoholic, too, you know."

Kate sat down on the end of the bed, feeling very tired. Of course she knew their father was an alcoholic. She'd known that for years. But Caroline? She was so young. So full of life. Had all that life and energy come from an endless supply of liquor?

"I'm trying to stop drinking," Caroline continued. "Mike is helping me. He's not my boyfriend. He's my sponsor, the person I can call when I'm feeling desperate. Most people don't realize he's been sober for more than a year because of Alcoholics Anonymous. He took me to my first meeting a few weeks ago. I was doing really good . . . until last night." She punched the pillow up under her head.

"What happened last night?"

"I went to see Dad at the Oyster Bar. I thought I could handle being in there for a few minutes, but he put a drink down in front of me. I wasn't even going to taste it until . . ."

"Until what?" Kate prodded. "What did Dad say to you?'

There was a bitter pain in Caroline's eyes when she looked back at her. "He told me he didn't want me to sail with him unless you came along to watch out for me. Apparently I'm a huge jinx."

"That's ridiculous. You're not a jinx. And he'd be lucky to have you."

"He doesn't think so. I don't know why I keep trying. I'm never going to be good enough. I'm never going to be you."

Kate frowned as Caroline slid down in the bed, pulling the covers up over her head the way she used to do when she was a little girl, when the world got too scary. The memories suddenly swamped Kate—Caroline curled up just like this in her bedroom in the middle of the day, the day their mom had died. Kate had come into the room to tell her, because her father couldn't do it, and Ashley was already crying.

Then there were all those times on the boat when it got too much for Caroline, when slipping under the covers and escaping seemed to be the only way out. Sometimes Kate had wanted to do the very same thing. But someone had to be there to pull the covers back, and that someone was her.

She did it now, pulling the blanket off Caroline's head and smoothing down her sister's hair with a loving gesture. "It's going to be all right, Caroline. We'll get through this. I'm going to take care of you."

"You can't make this better," Caroline said dully. "I can't even seem to make it better."

"You should have told me about the drinking."

Caroline turned and looked at her with a truth in her eyes. "You knew, Kate."

Kate began shaking her head. "I didn't think . . ."

Hadn't she sometimes worried about Caroline's drinking, her smoking, her need to let loose? Hadn't those worries started years ago? It all seemed so clear now.

"Last night was the first time I drank in almost a month. I know it's not much, but Mike says I just have to try again, start over from today."

Kate suddenly realized how wrong she had been about Mike. "That's where you were going on the ferry the other day."

"To an AA meeting." Caroline nodded.

"I still don't understand how you came to tell Mike."

"Remember when I told you I ran my car into a ditch on Hawkins Road because a dog ran out in front of me? There was no dog. I was drunk. Mike found me. He told me if I didn't get my act together, I was going to kill myself. But he didn't have to tell me that, Kate, because I already knew. That accident scared the hell out of me. I didn't realize how out of control everything had gotten. I could have hurt someone else, too."

"The bruises on your arm, were they from the accident?"

Caroline smiled at that. "No, that was just me tripping down the stairs and banging my arm into the door, just like I told you." Her smile faded. "Maybe Dad is right. Maybe I am a klutz."

Kate barely registered the explanation. She was still reeling with the reality of Caroline's drinking. Caroline had almost killed herself driving drunk into a tree. It was awful, beyond awful. She should have realized. She was the big sister. Shc was supposed to take care of things.

"Don't blame yourself," Caroline said. "I can see it in your eyes. You're feeling guilty."

"How can I not?"

"Because it's not your fault. It's mine. I'm the one who started drinking. I'm the one who has to stop. I let Dad get to me last night. He insisted on putting a beer in front of me, and, once I drank that, it was easy to keep going. I went over to Jake's later and downed a few cosmopolitans. Mike found me there and took me back to his boat; I was in no condition to go any farther. He didn't take advantage of me. He really has been a friend. But I feel like shit today with a god-awful hangover—it must be the result of a few weeks of clean living, because I haven't felt this bad in years."

"I'm glad you had someone to take care of you. I just wish you would have confided in me." Kate stood up and paced restlessly around the room. "I thought we were moving on, getting by, forgetting," she muttered, a thousand thoughts running through her mind so quickly they collided with one another. "But you were drinking, Dad was drinking, and Ashley was taking anxiety medication for panic attacks. I did this to us."

"No, you didn't."

"It was me. It was all me. Every last bit of it. I'm not keeping us together the way I promised Mom. I'm killing us off slowly but surely."

"Why is my drinking your fault?"

"Because it is."

"Doesn't that sound a little egotistical?"

Kate heard the words, but she ignored them. It didn't matter what Caroline said, whether or not she tried to take the blame. Maybe Kate hadn't forced Caroline to take a drink, but she'd given Caroline, Ashley, and even her father the need to find a way to escape.

And hadn't she done the same in her own way, turning a simple bookstore into fantasyland? Turning her back on the water, and all that had happened out there? Forcing everyone to keep the promise they'd made no matter what the personal cost?

"Stop it, Kate. Stop making this about you," Caroline said with irritation as she sat up on the bed. "It's about me. It's my problem. And I'll have to solve it myself."

"When is your next AA meeting? I'll go with you."

"Oh, sure, that's just what I want, strong, invincible Kate by my side, making me feel even more inadequate."

"I wouldn't do that," Kate said, feeling hurt.

Caroline made a face. "Dammit, Kate, there you go again, making me feel guilty. I know it's not you. You can't help it that you're so good, so perfect. You can't help it that you're Daddy's favorite. Or even that you were Mom's favorite. After all, you're the one she asked to make a promise. Not me. Not Ashley."

"You were too young. So was Ashley," Kate said in astonishment, then she started to get mad, too. "Don't you realize how much responsibility comes with all this favoritism that you see? Don't you think I ever get tired of worrying about all of you? Because I do, Caroline. I'm only four years older than you, but sometimes I feel like I'm a hundred years older."

"I'm sorry," Caroline said.

"You should be."

"I am. I just need to find a way to stop looking back all the time and keep looking forward. If I'm not happy, then I should make changes, not get drunk. See, I'm starting to get it. I'm going to be like you. I'm going to erase everything but today and tomorrow from my mind."

Kate didn't think she'd been all that successful in erasing the past. In fact, Caroline had no idea how much looking back she'd been doing, especially recently. "I think we should call Ashley," she said, focusing her attention on Caroline. "She'll want to help."

Caroline rolled her eyes.

"What does that mean?" Kate asked.

"I think Ashley has her hands full at the moment. I saw her last night on the back of Sean's motorcycle."

Kate sank back down on the bed and met her sister's knowing eyes. "Oh, dear."

"I'm sure she won't say anything after all this time," Caroline offered halfheartedly.

Kate hoped Caroline was right, because she wasn't sure of anything anymore.

"Hello, Ashley. Can I come in?" Tyler asked as Ashley opened her apartment door. Dressed in slim-fitting denim shorts and a sleeveless top, her long hair pulled back in a ponytail, Ashley looked young and pretty, full of life. In fact, there was a light in her eyes that Tyler didn't remember seeing before.

"Mr. . . ."

"Jamison. But you can call me Tyler."

"Right. What do you want?"

"A few minutes of your time."

She hesitated, then stepped aside. "Sure, come on in."

He was surprised at the chaos in her small apartment. She had obviously not gotten the same neat and tidy gene that Kate had. There were magazines, photos, and books spread out in the living room as well as a few items of clothing.

"I wasn't expecting anyone," Ashley said apologetically, moving some clutter from the couch. "Do you want to sit down?"

He paused by the coffee table and picked up some photos. They were pictures of boats and racing crews. "For the Castleton?" he asked.

"Yes, I photographed each and every entry."

"They're good. Nice light, excellent color, good angle."

"You sound like you know something about photographs."

"I've worked with a few photographers in my time."

"Photos to go with your articles?"

"Exactly," he said. "That's why I'm here. I was

wondering if you might have any photos I can choose
for this article."

She looked taken aback by the idea. "I— Uh, I
don't know what you mean."

He wondered if Kate had told Ashley he was dropping the article on them. It didn't appear that way,
because Ashley suddenly seemed very nervous. She
was fidgeting with a chain around her neck and looked
like she wished him anywhere but here. "Do you have
any photos of your race, shots you took on the *Moon
Dancer* of you, your sisters, and your father?" he
asked, figuring her answer would tell him just how
much she knew.

"I had some, but I don't know where they are."

"It seems funny, you being a photographer and all,
that you wouldn't have them up all over your walls."
He looked around her apartment. There were lots of
photographs but none of the family. He couldn't quite
believe that Ashley had spent nine months on a boat
with a pregnant sister and hadn't taken one photo
revealing that fact, unless she'd been the one who
was pregnant.

"I change my pictures frequently. That race was a
long time ago. And I put a lot of stuff in storage when
we got back."

Tyler sat down on the couch, deciding to switch
tactics. "I met your friend, Sean, the other day. He
told me you two were high school sweethearts."

"That's true." She perched on the edge of an
armchair.

"It must have been difficult for you to go to sea
and leave him behind."

"It was, but I didn't have a choice."

"Of course." He smiled to ease the tension he could
see tightening the muscles in her face. He sensed he
would have to go easy with her or he'd get nowhere.
"I bet the boys were all over you and your sisters at
the various ports of call. Three good-looking, adven-

turous blondes. It doesn't get much better than that. You must have been beating them off with a stick."

"Sometimes. But racing men are different. They're so focused on their boats, the other competitors, the weather, the course—everything else is unimportant. Besides, we were pretty young."

"Jailbait," he agreed. "Everyone but Kate." He paused. "What happened with you and Sean when you got back?"

"Nothing. I mean, we broke up."

"Why?"

"Because," she said with a helpless shrug. "It just wasn't going to work anymore. It's hard to come back and start over with someone you haven't seen in a few years."

"True. He still seems very fond of you, though."

She flushed. "I care about him, too."

More than a little, he suspected. "Maybe you'll get back together someday."

"I don't know." She paused, looking decidedly uncomfortable. "Is there something else you wanted? I have some things I need to take care of."

"Well, I know you said you don't have photographs of your race, but I wondered if you have anything of some local sailors or past Castleton races that might be a good accompaniment to my article. I would be happy to pay you for their use, of course."

"I have lots of photos from last year's race week. Let me get my file."

"Sure, take your time," Tyler said as she walked into her bedroom. He didn't really want any photos, but he needed a moment to think about how he could win her trust, and maybe look around a little bit. Surely this lawyer who was communicating so avidly with Mark's attorney would be copying one of the McKenna sisters on what was happening.

The coffee table didn't boast anything personal, so Tyler got up and walked over to the desk where Ashley's computer was located. His gaze caught on an envelope on top of a stack of bills with the return address CASTLETON FAMILY HEALTH. The envelope was open, so he pulled out the bill. It was dated a month ago, an office visit, patient Ashley McKenna, physician Dr. Myra Hanover. That didn't tell him much. He turned to the accompanying letter, which was much more interesting. In the letter, Dr. Hanover referred Ashley to two different psychiatrists specializing in anxiety and depression, both located in Seattle. That confirmed his earlier suspicion that she had mental health problems. He slipped the bill into his pocket, doubting she'd miss it, since she'd obviously already paid it, and he might just need it.

Hearing Ashley, he turned away from the desk and returned to the middle of the room.

She handed him a thick manilla envelope. "You can have these from last year. I have to warn you, though, that they're not action shots. There's another guy in town, Nate Raffin, who takes shots out on the water. He might have better photographs. In fact, he's doing this year's races, so you might want to talk to him."

"Thanks, I will." He took the envelope out of her hand. "How come you don't take the action shots? An experienced sailor like yourself, I can't imagine that anyone else could do a better job."

She paled at his question. "I just don't."

"Oh, that's right. You don't like to go out on the water anymore, do you?"

He could see that she remembered their first meeting at Kate's house when she'd confided her inability to get on the boat and take a picture.

"What happened to make you feel that way?" he asked, pressing deeper. He was running out of time, with Mark's threat to take Amelia and run hanging over his head.

"I . . . It's a long story."

"Was it the storm? Were you traumatized? Or was it something else? Someone you left behind, perhaps?"

Her face now turned completely white. "What do you know?" she whispered.

His heart sped up. Maybe it was Ashley. Maybe she was Amelia's mother. Maybe she was traumatized because she'd left her baby behind.

He started as the phone rang. Ashley hesitated.

"Aren't you going to get that?" he asked.

"I'm sure the machine . . ." Her voice trailed away as they listened to the message: *Ashley, it's Kate. I'm at Caroline's. You need to call me or come here as soon as possible.*

Tyler frowned at the concern in Kate's voice.

Ashley grabbed the phone. "Kate, are you there? What's wrong? Is Caroline okay?" She paused then said, "Why can't you just tell me now? Fine. I'll be there in a few minutes."

She hung up the phone and turned to Tyler. "I have to go."

"Is everything all right?"

"I doubt it. Things haven't been all right in a long time."

She picked up her purse and keys and headed toward the door. Tyler had no choice but to follow.

"I'll bring these back later," he said. "Maybe we can finish our conversation then."

"I won't be here later. Just leave them by the door. No one will take them." She hurried down the hall before he could say anything more. Short of running after her, there was nothing more he could do. Damn. He'd been so close to getting somewhere. Now he would have to wait.

Unless he went over to Caroline's apartment. All three girls would be there. But they would undoubtedly form a united front, he realized. He would have more success when they were apart. He would simply have to divide and conquer, one sister at a time.

Kate had tidied up Caroline's apartment, put on some hot water for tea, and checked on her sister for

the third time in a half hour when there was a knock
on the door. Ashley, she thought with relief. Maybe
it wasn't right to burden Ashley with this problem;
she had enough to worry about. But Kate needed to
share it with someone who would understand. Maybe
someone who could tell her that it wasn't that obvious,
that she had also been fooled by Caroline's behavior.

Kate opened the door and let Ashley in. "Thanks
for coming so fast."

"What is it? What's wrong now?"

"Caroline is . . ." How could she say it?

"She's what? Is she sick?"

"Not exactly." Kate closed the door behind Ashley.

"Why are you being so mysterious?"

"Because she's trying to find a nice way to say it,
but there isn't any," Caroline said from the doorway
of the bedroom.

Caroline looked like she was feeling better. She'd
changed into a pair of leggings and a T-shirt, and there
was color in her cheeks now. But as she sat down on
the sofa, Kate could see how thin her baby sister had
gotten. Too much booze, not enough food—another
sign she'd missed.

"Does someone want to tell me what's going on?"
Ashley asked.

"I'll say it. I think I can do it." Caroline took a
deep breath. "I'm an alcoholic, Ashley. There I did it
again. It's getting easier."

"You—you're what?" Ashley stumbled over her
words.

"An alcoholic. A drunk. A boozer. Whatever you
want to call it."

Ashley stared at Caroline for a long moment. "I
don't understand."

"Do you want me to spell it for you?"

"I understand what you're saying; I just don't understand how it happened." Ashley looked at Kate.
"Did you know?"

"Not until an hour ago. Although . . ." Hadn't there

been signs? Hadn't she worried that Caroline was partying too hard, hanging out with a wild crowd? "Maybe I did notice," she continued, "but I guess I didn't want to see it."

"Well." Ashley sat down in the chair across from Caroline. "What do you want me to do?"

"Nothing. Kate was the one to call you, not me."

"We need to support one another," Kate said, sitting down on the couch. "We're still a family." A family that had given Caroline that first drink, Kate realized. How old had her sister been then? Fourteen, fifteen? "It was that champagne we opened the first day we set sail," she murmured. "Dad wanted to toast our trip. That was the first time you ever drank, wasn't it?"

"Probably."

"You liked it a lot," Ashley commented. "I remember you sneaked back into the galley and finished it off later that night."

"Busted," Caroline said. "I guess you two are to blame for my bad habit."

"Yes," Kate agreed.

"I'm just kidding," Caroline said. "No one held my head and forced me to taste that champagne, and it's not like either of you turned into drunks because of it."

No, but that had opened a door they'd never closed. It had been easy to get alcohol on their trip. When they'd hung out with their father, there had always been glasses left unattended and sailors eager to give you a taste of this or that. Caroline had loved to sit by their father's side and listen to him tell stories. She'd always been the closest to the booze, and to the boozers, for that matter.

"You can't blame yourselves. This is my problem, and I'll fix it." Caroline stood up. "First I'm going to take a shower, then I'm going to work for a few hours and hope they won't kill me for blowing off this morning's appointments."

"You're going in to work?" Kate asked in confusion. "I thought we could spend time together."

"I need to work. So do you. Don't you have a bookstore to run?"

"Theresa is there," Kate replied, but in truth she did need to get to work.

"Look, I'll be okay. Maybe not today, maybe not tomorrow, but eventually. Mike said it will take awhile. In the meantime, I have to live as normally as I can. If you want to have dinner or something tonight, I guess we could do that, but— Oh, damn, I almost forgot, the charity picnic auction is tonight. I promised I'd put in a basket this year, and I don't have a thing in the refrigerator."

"I promised as well." Kate added that to the rapidly growing list of things she had to do. The annual picnic auction was a big fund-raiser for the local library. All of the eligible women on the island made up big baskets of food that were auctioned off to participating bachelors. The couples would then share a picnic supper together. Kate had always enjoyed the event, although some of her bachelors had been better than others. A shiver ran down her spine as she thought about Tyler. Would he come? Would he bid? Would their self-control be tested once again?

"Kate?" Ashley asked.

"What?" She suddenly realized she'd been daydreaming.

"I said that I made extra chocolate cookies if you and Caroline want to put them in your baskets."

"That sounds great." Kate looked at Caroline. "Do you think it's a good idea for you to go? It's usually traditional to include a bottle of wine in the basket."

"I can't avoid every situation where there's alcohol, or I'll never go anywhere. I'll just clue Mike in and ask him to bid on my basket. That way I won't have to pretend with anyone else."

Kate frowned, still not comfortable with the idea of

her baby sister and this much older man. "Are you sure—"

"He's really nice," Caroline said, cutting her off. "He has changed since he stopped drinking. He told me so. And he's been nothing but a gentleman. Really. I know how a guy acts when he wants sex from you. I'm not naive."

Kate realized Caroline was probably less naive than she was where men were concerned, so she supposed she'd have to let her do what she wanted. She probably couldn't stop her, anyway.

"Speaking of men who want things . . ." Caroline cast Ashley a curious look. "I saw you and Sean last night riding down the street on his motorcycle. I couldn't believe it. When did you decide to take a walk on the wild side?"

"It was just a ride."

"And?"

"It was nice," Ashley admitted with a guilty smile. "We went down Sorenson's Hill at about a hundred miles an hour. Okay, maybe not that fast, but it felt like we were flying. I can't remember the last time I did anything that thrilling or risky. I felt so alive."

Now Kate had something else to worry about. "Are you sure it's wise to get involved with Sean again?"

"I didn't tell him anything," Ashley said. "But—"

"No buts," Kate replied sharply. "Not now, not ever. If you think you can be with him and keep the past locked away, then fine, but if you can't, you shouldn't start something you can't finish."

"I really like him," Ashley said quietly. "And I've missed him. I've missed who I am when I'm with him. I'm not sure I can say good-bye to him again." She sighed. "But it may not be my choice. I think he's still planning to race not just in the Castleton but on to Hawaii."

"That might be the best thing," Caroline chimed in. "It will be easier for you if he's not here."

"That's what I thought when he left eight years ago.

But I was wrong. I think this might be my last chance with him, and I'm really tempted to take it." Ashley turned to Kate. "By the way, Tyler stopped by my apartment. In fact, he was there when you called."

Kate tensed. "What did he want?"

"Some photos of us from the race. I told him they were all in storage."

"But he told me that he dropped the article idea about us. He's working on a new angle for a story."

"Are you sure? He asked me some rather probing questions about my fear of the water and what might have happened to cause it. I didn't get the feeling he'd given up on the story at all."

Kate's heart sank. Tyler had lied to her. Why? Why was it so important for him to do a story on them?

"I gave him some photos from last year's Castleton Invitational," Ashley continued. "Maybe he'll find something interesting in there to build a story around. In fact, maybe we should think of a new angle for him, since he seems to be having trouble coming up with one of his own."

"That's a good idea," Caroline said. "Why don't you introduce Tyler to Ronnie Burns? He can tell Tyler about that shipwreck he discovered off the coast of Oregon last year."

Kate nodded, knowing it was a good idea, but her mind was still wrestling with the fact that Tyler had gone to Ashley behind her back.

"Maybe I misunderstood Tyler," Ashley said. "Maybe he was just making conversation. You should ask him about it."

"Believe me, I intend to." And this time she would force herself to listen with her head instead of her heart.

Chapter Nineteen

Hokey, silly, stupid, corny, old-fashioned. Tyler could think of a hundred adjectives to describe the auction taking place in Castleton's town square. But none of those adjectives would adequately describe the excitement of crowd. There were more than thirty picnic baskets up for bidding and at least a hundred people milling about, preparing to make their bids.

"Mr. Jamison, are you bidding on a basket tonight?" a woman named Margaret asked him. Margaret was in her mid-fifties and worked the front desk of the hotel where he was staying.

"I'm not sure yet. They look good, though. I'm starting to get hungry."

"Mine has a big pink bow," she said with a wink. "If you like crab sandwiches, check it out."

Tyler smiled as she disappeared into the crowd. Crab sandwiches didn't sound bad, but he was more interested in finding a McKenna sister, one in particular, to share a picnic supper with. He hadn't seen Kate all day, and he very much wanted to.

His cell phone rang, and he dug it out of his pocket with irritation. Mark was probably calling him for another update, another reminder that time was running out, that if he didn't get an answer soon, he would disappear with Amelia. That thought had been on Tyler's mind all day, and he knew that he did not want Amelia to live the life he had led. There had to be another solution. He would simply have to find it.

He was relieved to see a different number on his screen, that of one of the editors he frequently worked for, Kenny Weinman.

"Hi, Kenny," he said. "What's up?"

"Where the hell are you, Ty?" Kenny asked. "I've been calling your apartment for days and get nothing but your damn machine. Finally dug up your cell phone number from that cute blonde in the lifestyle section that you dated last year."

"Jenny?"

"Julie," Kenny said with a laugh. "Jesus, you haven't changed. Love 'em and leave 'em Jamison."

"Why are you calling me, exactly?" Tyler asked, somewhat annoyed with the analysis. Maybe he had been that way in the past, but things had changed.

What? What was he thinking? Things hadn't changed. He was still that same guy, wasn't he?

"I've got an article that only you can write," Kenny said. "But you have to get to Paris by Friday."

"I can't do it," Tyler said automatically.

"I haven't even told you what it is yet."

"I'm taking some time off. Family business."

"You have a family?" Kenny asked in surprise. "I didn't know that."

"Yes, I have a family," Tyler snapped. "And I'm taking care of them at the moment. I'll be in touch when I'm free."

"I'll pay you triple your usual fee. This is Paris, Ty. You'll love it."

"Send someone else."

"I can't believe I'm hearing this. You never turn down jobs."

"I'm turning this one down," Tyler said and hung up the phone. He could hardly believe he'd actually done it. Maybe Kenny was right. Maybe he had changed. When had that happened? When Mark had gotten hurt? That was definitely a turning point. But was it meeting a woman who made him want to stick around that was changing him? That was a scary thought.

The microphone on the stage in front of him crackled as the auctioneer made the last call for baskets. Tyler looked around, hoping to see Kate. Sure enough, there she was, setting a dark brown basket on the table. He noted the silver ribbon hanging from the handle. Reaching into his pocket for his wallet this time, he checked his cash. He might have to hit an ATM machine before the auction started. There was no way anyone would outbid him for Kate's basket.

"Tyler is over there," Caroline said to Kate as they put their baskets on the long tables in the front.

"Where?" Kate couldn't help asking as she took a quick look around.

"At the back of the crowd. Oh, he's gone now."

"He'll be back," Kate said. "He's like a bad penny; he keeps showing up."

"And you like him."

"It's not like that . . ."

"It's exactly like that. And it's not a crime, you know. He's a hot guy. And you're a normal red-blooded female with—"

"Please, don't say urges."

"Feelings and desires. It's been a long time since you've looked at a man the way you look at Tyler. I think it's nice."

"I think it's crazy. And I'm going to ignore those feelings and especially those desires from here on out."

"Good luck," Caroline said with a laugh.

"I can do it. I'm very strong."

"You'll have to be, because I think Tyler is one man who knows what to do with a woman."

He certainly had so far, Kate thought grimly, but

she had her guard up now, and she intended to keep it up.

"I wonder if Dad is coming," Caroline murmured as she looked around the crowd.

"Oh, I forgot to tell you, I had a chat with both Dad and K.C. earlier. Dad bet our portrait against the *Moon Dancer*."

"No way. He wouldn't do that. He knows you love it."

"He would, and he did. So much for me being the favorite child. Although, I have to admit, it made me think twice about racing with him. Not to help him, but to protect that portrait from K.C."

Caroline stared at her. "Would you do it, Kate? Could you race again?"

Kate understood what Caroline was asking; the truth was she didn't know the answer. "I'm not sure. But I realize now that there was more between Dad and K.C. than we ever knew."

"Like what?"

"It's a long story, and I think the auction is starting. I'll tell you later."

"Okay, I guess it can wait." Caroline paused. "I hope Mike gets here in time to buy my basket."

"I'm sure he will."

The auction began and grew more lively with each competitive bid as friends and strangers alike got into the mood of the event.

"Look, there's Ashley's basket," Caroline said a few minutes later. They watched in amazement as the bidding flew around the crowd fast and furiously, until only one bidder was left.

"Sean," Kate murmured, not really surprised. "I think I liked it better when Ashley was afraid of her own shadow."

"I didn't. I missed the old Ashley," Caroline said. "The one who would jump into the water with fearless abandon."

Kate nodded, remembering all the times they'd sunbathed on the boat then jumped into the water to cool off. Ashley had always loved to swim and snorkel. She'd even taken a deep-sea diving class the year before they'd started racing. "You're right," she said slowly. "I've missed her, too. And I think she might be back." For there was Ashley, greeting Sean with an exuberant hug and an ear-to-ear grin. They walked off, arms linked, as if they were daring anyone to part them ever again. "I hope she doesn't tell him anything she shouldn't."

"If she doesn't, I don't think it will be to protect our secret, but to protect her heart," Caroline said wisely. "Ashley knows deep down that telling Sean will be the end of it all. I don't think she'll risk it. I think she loves him too much."

"Love makes you do crazy things."

"That's true," Caroline said with a laugh. "Look, your basket is next, Kate."

Kate couldn't help stiffening as her basket was handed to the auctioneer. She hadn't seen Tyler all day, nor had she even hinted to him the night before that she'd be participating in the auction. There was no way in this crowd, even if he was here, that he would know which basket to bid on. She should be happy about that. No long evening of avoiding tense questions. No heart-stopping, spine-tingling moments that would make her consider acting in a reckless manner. Thank heavens.

The bidding began slowly, gathering steam as new parties entered into the auction. She had almost relaxed when she heard Tyler's voice. She couldn't see him, but she knew it was him. Her heart stopped and her spine tingled, just as she'd anticipated. How had he known? Did he know? Maybe it was a coincidence.

But when the bidding stopped and she walked forward to meet her date, she knew without a doubt that, like everything else in their relationship, this was no coincidence.

*   *   *

"I think we were supposed to have a picnic on the beach or something," Kate said as she led Tyler into her house.

"We already did that. And, since I paid for this date, I get to choose the location."

"You could have picked something more picturesque." She turned on the hall light and set her purse down on the table. She felt tense and nervous and couldn't quite believe she'd agreed to bring him home. It would have been much safer to picnic in the park or on the beach, someplace where the crowds would have prevented them from talking seriously or acting foolish.

"I like this picture," he said, looking at her face and not at their surroundings. Oh, Lord, she was in big trouble. She knew what he wanted. More important, she knew what she wanted. But they couldn't have it. Couldn't do it.

"We should leave," she said. "This isn't going to work."

"Give it a chance, Kate."

"You lied to me. You told me you were dropping the story, but then you went to Ashley and asked her for pictures."

His grin faded and his expression turned somber. "Yes, I did do that."

"Why?" She silently pleaded with him to tell her the truth. And she prayed that she'd recognize it when she heard it.

"I went to Ashley to get some photos of the Castleton from last year, but, when I got there, I started thinking about your family again, and Ashley didn't seem to realize that I'd dropped the story, so I—"

"Decided to see what Ashley would tell you," Kate finished.

"I know something happened to you during that race, Kate. Something that you and your sisters can't tell anyone. I have an instinct for a story, and I know there's one you could tell me if only you would. I can see in your eyes that I'm right."

"What you see is anger that you're invading my privacy."

"That's not what I see at all." He took a step closer, and she took a step back.

"Don't," she said, putting up a hand. "I thought I was strong, but I'm not."

He didn't say anything for a moment. "Why don't we just have our picnic and save this discussion until later?"

"I won't change my mind."

"Then you won't," he said simply.

She hesitated. "All right, fine. We'll eat. Then you'll go." She started to head toward the kitchen, but he caught her by the arm.

"Let's eat in the living room."

"There's only a coffee table in there."

"We'll eat on the floor. You'll spread out a blanket, and we'll pretend this is a grassy park."

She rolled her eyes. "Is this part of your seduction strategy? I just told you—"

"I heard you, believe me. But I paid for a picnic supper, and you owe me one."

"You're a very annoying man."

"So I've been told."

She led him into the living room and he set the basket down on the coffee table. "I'll get the blanket," she said, but he followed her down the hall. "This isn't exactly a two-person job, you know."

"I want to check out your house."

She opened the linen closet and waved her hand toward the neatly stacked piles of towels and bedding. "This is where I keep the sheets. Excited?"

"Actually, sometimes sheets do get me excited."

She couldn't help laughing at the wicked glint in his eyes. "That's a very bad line. And you, a writer, should be ashamed." She tossed him a blanket. "I think everything else we need is in the basket."

"Are you sure there isn't anything in your bedroom that we need?" he asked, stopping to peer through a half open door.

Kate grabbed his arm and pulled him along. "Bedroom tours are not part of the picnic auction."

"They should be, for the price I paid."

She ignored that, returning to the living room where Tyler spread the blanket out on the floor.

"How about a fire?" he asked.

"It's not that cold."

"I heard there might be a storm coming in this weekend. The racers will not be happy."

"Actually, most sailors love a good storm. It's the calm that makes them crazy."

"So they'll race even if it's storming?"

"Not if it's really bad. But if there's a good brisk wind, you bet. The boats will run even faster." She paused. "Are you still going out with my father tomorrow?"

"That's what he said."

"I hope it's before he gets drunk."

"So do I."

"Tell me again why you're sailing with him?"

"To get some firsthand experience on a boat. It will make my story more realistic."

"Yeah, whatever story that is—if there even is a story." She paused. Had Tyler just flinched? Maybe there wasn't a story. But he was a reporter. She'd already checked that out.

"Of course there's a story," he said. "There's always a story."

"You can probably find one anywhere, can't you?"

"Pretty much. It's just a matter of simple curiosity and a sharp eye."

"What about your story, Tyler? What if I said I was going to write an article and tell the world about your father stealing you away from your mother? Would you want that revealed to the world? Or would you be protective of your family, maybe even of your father, who you probably have a lot of mixed feelings about?"

Tyler met her questioning gaze with a small smile. "You're very good, Kate. Very perceptive. Smart. Beautiful. Sexy. A deadly combination."

Beautiful? Sexy? Smart? Did he really think she was all those things? Kate shook her head and cleared her throat, realizing he'd successfully sidetracked her once again with his unending charm. She sat down on the blanket. "Let's eat. You can serve me. I did all the cooking."

"Is that part of the date? I thought you would serve me. In fact, I thought you would feed me."

"Not likely." She slid across the blanket, resting her back against the coffee table. Tyler made the same move a second later, his shoulder touching hers, their legs stretched out in front of them.

"I'm not that hungry yet, are you?" he asked.

"Not really," she admitted. Although, if they didn't eat, they'd probably have to talk or, worse yet, they'd find something even better to do.

For a moment they just sat. Then Tyler said, "Is everything okay, Kate? With your sisters?"

"Why would you ask that?" She turned her head so she could look at him.

"You seem preoccupied. A little down, not your normally cheery self."

"Is that the way you see me? An overly perky woman?"

"I think you try to be cheerful, even when you don't feel like it. You're big on putting up a front. A don't-let-anyone-see-you-sweat kind of girl."

"You're the same. You hide what you're thinking behind those unreadable eyes."

"You mean you can't read my mind right now?"

His eyes had darkened, and his gaze focused on her

mouth. Her lips tingled. She felt as if he was kissing her, yet he hadn't even touched her.

Tyler put his arm around her shoulders and pulled her close until her head was resting against his chest. She should have pulled away, but it felt too good.

"This is better," he said

"I can hear your heart beating."

"Thank God for that."

Kate slipped her hand inside the neck of his polo shirt. "It's beating faster now."

"Want to see how fast it can go?"

"Tyler—"

"Shh." He pressed her head back against his chest. "Did I tell you what I did today?"

She relaxed a bit at the casual question. Maybe they could just sit and talk. "Besides grill my sister? No."

"I stopped at the drug store."

Her body tensed again. So much for just talking. She knew what was coming. What she didn't know was what she would do about it.

"Like a good boy scout, I'm prepared," he added lightly.

"That will be nice for whatever girl scout you run into."

"I don't want a girl scout, I want you."

"I thought we just agreed . . ."

"I think the only thing we agree on is that we both want each other."

She lifted her head and gazed into his eyes. "That's true, but—"

"No buts." He paused, his eyes very serious. "I know there are a hundred reasons why we shouldn't do this, but I can't stop thinking about you. This kind of feeling doesn't happen every day of the week, you know. I can't make any promises. I can't offer you my heart and my soul, because, in truth, I don't know what's left of my heart. It took a big hit a long time ago when my father ripped my family apart. I don't really know how to love."

"You knew how to love once," she reminded him.

"It almost killed me."

"I understand."

"I know you do. That's why we keep coming back to this place."

Their eyes met in a moment of deep connection.

"I can't stop thinking about you, either, Tyler, but I've never been one to leap without looking. And I'm afraid to look where you're concerned."

"I think there was a time when you could leap. Then you got hurt, and you grew wary, and safe seemed better than sorry."

"It still does," she admitted.

"We're a lot alike."

"In some ways."

"Whatever happens between us tonight is separate from everything else," he said. "There's no past, no future, just tonight. I want to make love to you, Kate. You and me, nothing between us, no clothes, no secrets, no questions, no lies, no memories, no ghosts. Just the two of us."

She drew in a breath and slowly let it out. She was tempted, but it was madness. They couldn't escape the reality of the morning, could they? And how would she feel then?

His hand stroked the side of her face, a gentle, tender caress that made her heart skip a beat. What was coming was inevitable; she'd known that when she'd brought him home.

She leaned forward and touched her mouth to his with a deep sense of relief. Closing her eyes, she let him take over and allowed him to deepen the kiss, sweeping her away from all conscious thought. Her brain shut down and her senses took over as she tasted his mouth, ran her hands through his hair, around his neck, down his shoulders.

No matter what happened, she wouldn't regret this night. There were plenty of things in her life she could feel sorry about, but this wouldn't be one of them.

She broke the kiss and put her finger against his lips when he started to protest. "Is that boy scout kit of yours handy?"

"As close as my pocket."

"Good, because I'm going to show you how a girl scout makes a fire without any matches." She ran her tongue along the edge of his ear and heard his swift intake of breath. "I think I just got a spark."

"I'll show you a spark," he growled, tumbling her over so she was flat on her back.

She waited for his kiss, but he didn't move for a long second; he just stared at her, stripping her bare with his eyes, looking right into her soul. Could he see everything that she was hiding? It was both terrifying and thrilling.

"Touch me," she said softly, putting her hand on the back of his neck and pulling him down to her. She closed her eyes as his mouth trailed along the side of her face, her neck, down to her collarbone. "Don't stop."

"I won't," he promised and then kissed her on the mouth.

She ran her hands up under his shirt, loving the play of the taut muscles in his back. He was a strong man, a solid man, but he was complicated; he had hidden motives and secret agendas. In some ways he reminded her of the ocean—deep, mysterious, dangerous. It was part of his appeal, and she couldn't resist. She wanted him, wanted to see his control snap, wanted to feel the power in his body, wanted to get closer to him than anyone ever had, wanted to fill that emptiness in his heart.

She helped him off with his shirt, then slipped her sweater over her head as he removed his pants and helped her slide out of her jeans. It was a blessed relief when his naked body covered hers. There was nothing left between them. They were breast to breast, hip to hip, toe to toe, mouth to mouth.

Tyler shifted slightly, taking his weight to one side

as his hand cupped one full breast, his fingers caressing, pulling, tugging. His mouth followed suit in the most delicious, wicked manner until her nerves were screaming and her breath was coming in rapid gasps of pleasure. His hands and his mouth were relentless, marking every inch of her body with passion and purpose until she was begging him to finish it.

He was in her head, in her heart, under her skin, but it wasn't enough. She pulled him on top of her body and welcomed him inside. She was finally home. And, Tyler might not know it yet, but so was he.

Chapter Twenty

She'd told him she wouldn't ask him for anything, wouldn't beg him to stay the night or make promises he couldn't keep. But Kate was still disappointed to find Tyler gone when she woke up Thursday morning. A quick glance at the pillow next to her showed nothing but a single strand of dark hair, no note, no rose, no silly sentimental anything. She smiled at her own foolishness. It was just sex, not love, not romance. But she picked up the pillow, took a deep breath, and sighed. She could still smell the musky scent of his body. And, if she closed her eyes, she could see him in her mind, could feel his hands on her body, those wonderful, magic hands.

A wave of heat ran through her. She had been a fool to think one night would be enough. At least not for her. Tyler, on the other hand, had taken off at first light. Maybe it had been enough for him. With that disturbing thought, she stretched her arms over her head and forced herself to get out of bed. Her body felt deliciously sore. Muscles she'd forgotten she had were aching, but it was a good ache, a satisfied ache. It was pointless to look for a note from Tyler, but, after putting on her bathrobe and slippers, she managed to check every table between her bedroom and the kitchen. There was nothing.

Coffee, she decided, maybe some breakfast, then off to work like it was any other day, like all the days that would come next. She didn't miss him. And she wouldn't miss him. Not today, not tomorrow . . . Well, maybe for just a few days. Then she'd move on.

They had no future together. Tyler didn't belong here. And she couldn't be anywhere else.

Kate shivered. The house seemed colder this morning. Was this the way it would feel from now on, as if someone or something was missing, some heat, some magic? She should never have brought Tyler home. It wasn't smart to have a casual affair at home. She should have kept it separate, gone to a neutral location, a place she wouldn't have to visit every day. She was sure those rules were in a book somewhere, a book on how to have a love affair without breaking your heart.

Like Tyler, she'd thought she didn't have a heart left to break, but there was a distinct ache in her chest. Had her heart somehow reawakened when she wasn't looking? Maybe when Tyler had arrived in town? Tyler, who had all the things she wanted in a man: strength, humor, compassion, and a body to die for. She smiled at that thought—a silly little smile that she would make sure never crossed her face when anyone was looking. She'd keep her feelings for Tyler a secret, just like she kept all the other secrets.

That thought immediately sent her smile packing. No matter what she felt for Tyler, there were still secrets between them. They'd both acknowledged that fact, made no pretense of believing that they were being totally honest with each other, but it had felt honest last night. It had felt like love. But how could there be love without trust?

She was doing exactly what she'd promised herself she wouldn't do: rethinking and regretting. It had to stop right now. Whatever happened from here on out,

she'd have last night. She'd know that somewhere out
in the world was a man who could touch her heart
even if she couldn't touch his.

The phone rang and Kate reached for it, feeling a
surge of ridiculous hope.

"Katie?"

The line crackled with static, but she could still
make out her father's voice. "Where are you?" she
asked. "I can barely hear you."

"I'm at the pay phone on the dock. I'm about to
take that reporter friend of yours out for a sail. I need
to know if you've changed your mind about racing on
Saturday. Rick is pressuring me. If you don't race,
then I can't race."

"I already told you—"

"K.C. is spreading rumors, talking trash about us,
smearing our name."

Rumors or memories? Kate hoped it was the
former.

"Your mother is probably turning over in her
grave," Duncan continued. "You have to change your
mind. We need to pull together as a family. I need
you, Katie. Don't let me down. Say yes."

Kate closed her eyes as her hand gripped the phone.
How many times had he said those words to her? How
many times had she gone along with him? She'd always supported him, always run interference if she
could, always been his backup—but he was asking for
too much.

"I can't," she said finally. "I can't race with you."

There was nothing but static now, his silence as po-
tent as any argument.

"Good-bye, Katie," he said with a finality that
alarmed her.

"Wait, Dad." Her only answer was a dial tone. She
stared at the phone for a moment, then dialed the
number of the hotel where Tyler was staying. Maybe
he'd stopped there to change before going down to
the docks. She wanted to tell him . . .

What did she want to tell him? *Don't go. Don't talk to my father.* Or, *Take care of my dad. He's depressed. He's not getting what he wants, and he's dangerous when that happens.*

There was no answer in Tyler's room. He must already be with Duncan. Damn. He'd probably been standing right next to her father. Kate hung up the phone feeling angry and worried. Even if she threw on her clothes and raced down to the docks, her dad would probably be gone by the time she got there. At least he'd sounded sober. Mad, but sober. Hopefully that would last.

They would probably be fine. Her father would just have to deal with her decision, live with the disappointment. It wasn't as if she hadn't had to do the same.

Kate turned on the coffeemaker. She definitely needed some caffeine to deal with this day. While she waited for the coffee to perk, she checked her answering machine for messages. There was nothing important.

She looked through the bills piling up on the counter, realizing at some point she'd actually have to pay some of them. Maybe later, when she was really depressed.

"Kate," Ashley called out, slamming the front door. "Are you here?"

Kate met Ashley in the hall. "Is something wrong?"

"Something is right, actually," Ashley said with a smile. "Sean bought my basket last night."

"I saw."

"We had a great time."

"Why don't you come in the kitchen and have some coffee with me? This sounds like a long story."

Ashley followed her into the kitchen, taking a seat at the table while Kate poured her a cup.

"So, speak," Kate said, sitting down across from her.

"We ate in the park and talked until almost midnight. Neither one of us wanted to end the evening."

"What did you talk about?"

"Mostly what Sean has been doing for the past few years. He really wants to work for his father, Kate. He loves designing and building boats; that's where his heart is. It's not in racing. And that's the really good news. He decided not to race in the Castleton. He's going to stay here on the island and build boats. I think it's what he was always meant to do."

"So do I," Kate said with a sigh. She was happy for Sean, but she knew this only meant more trouble ahead for Ashley.

"You think it's going to be a problem, don't you?" Ashley asked.

"Don't you?"

"Well, it doesn't matter. Sean shouldn't have to stay away from his family. If anyone should leave, it should be me."

"But you won't, will you?"

Ashley thought about that. "I love this island, Kate, probably as much as you do. But I want Sean to be happy. And I want him to be safe. If that means he stays here, then I want that, too. If it gets too hard, I'll figure out what to do then."

"You seem so strong all of a sudden."

"He gave it back to me, Kate. I don't know how he did it, but I feel so much better since Sean came back. I'm starting to believe my old self might still be in there somewhere."

"I hope so. I like that girl."

"Me, too." Ashley got up. "I've got work to do."

"I'll walk you out."

Kate followed her sister down the hall, realizing a second too late that she should have steered her past the living room.

"Oh, my!" Ashley exclaimed. "You had quite the picnic last night, didn't you?"

Kate was almost afraid to look into the room. She wasn't sure what state it was in, but it had to be bad. She forced herself to peek around the corner. The sofa pillows were on the floor, along with the blanket, which was completely twisted and tangled among containers of food, some still half full.

"Is that whipped cream?" Ashley asked in amazement. "Just what did you put in your basket?"

"It was for ice cream sundaes. They weren't part of the original basket."

"I bet they weren't." Ashley turned to her with amusement edged with concern. "Are you sure that was smart?"

"I am nowhere near sure. But it happened. And, before you ask, there was no pillow talk, no spilling of secrets. Just a lot of really great . . ." Kate couldn't quite find the right word.

"Conversation?"

"That's not what I was going to say."

"I'll bet. Tell me, big sister, did the whipped cream actually go on the ice cream?"

"Ashley!"

"Hey, you're supposed to be my mentor. If there's something more interesting to be done with whipped cream, I think it's your sisterly duty to tell me about it."

"I think it's time you went to work."

Ashley paused at the front door. "I'm glad you had a good time. You deserve it." She paused. "I kind of wish you would have had this emotional breakthrough with someone else, though."

"That would have been easier," Kate agreed.

"Well, easy has never been the McKenna way."

"I was selfish, though. I could have put us all in a bad position."

"It's not selfish to fall in love."

"I'm not in love."

"Oh, Kate, come on."

"It's true. I just had a fling. He's leaving in a few days. It's nothing."

"It may be nothing to him, but it's something to you. You don't give your body or your heart lightly. I don't care what you told Tyler Jamison. I know that for a fact. And if you slept with him, then you're falling for him."

"He's all wrong for me, Ash. I don't want to care for him."

"And I don't want to care for Sean. But we don't choose love. It chooses us. Once it grabs hold, it doesn't let go." She paused, bending over to pick up a piece of paper. "What's this?"

Kate's heart skipped a beat. Had Tyler left her a note after all?

"Kate?" Ashley looked at her with a question in her eyes. "Where did you get this?"

"What is it?"

"It's one of my medical bills."

A flash of disappointment swept through her, followed by confusion. "How did that get there?"

"I have no idea. I didn't even bring my purse in."

They stared at each other for a moment, both coming to the same conclusion at the same time.

"Tyler," Ashley muttered. "He was in my apartment yesterday."

"And in my house last night," Kate added. But it didn't make any sense.

"Why would Tyler swipe a copy of my medical bill? What on earth could he hope to find there?" Ashley asked, echoing her thoughts.

"He must be on the wrong track."

Ashley looked at her through troubled eyes. "Or maybe we are."

Tyler sat back in the small boat as Duncan steered them out of the marina and past the buoys that marked the beginning of the day's races. There were lots of boats sailing in the area of the start, which would take place in approximately thirty minutes, but Duncan apparently had a different course in mind. He headed them away from the racing area toward the north end of the island.

"Are you eager to be out there yourself?" Tyler asked.

Duncan stood at the rear of his boat, his hand on the tiller, his eyes on the horizon. "Nothing like a fast start to get your blood pumping."

"It must be different when the race is longer. You have to stay ahead for weeks, months at a time. Must require a great deal of endurance, not just a fast start."

"Long-distance ocean sailing is like running a marathon. You have to pace yourself and take into account changes in weather, temperature, sails, every little detail that could alter the outcome of the race."

"And you don't stop for anything, do you?" Tyler asked. "Not even if someone is sick or injured. You just keep going."

Duncan shot him a thoughtful look. "We didn't have to worry about that."

"The girls were healthy the whole time?"

"They were as fit as any of the crews out there."

Except one of them had been pregnant. Why hadn't anyone realized that fact? Tyler frowned, knowing that this tack was no better than the last. Duncan was too smart to give him an easy answer.

Looking out at the water, Tyler tried to drum up some enthusiasm for his job. But he had to admit that, after spending an incredible night with Kate, he felt even less inclined to hunt down the truth. She was an amazing woman, everything he'd ever wanted—not just beautiful but sexy, warm, funny, smart—the kind of woman a man could be friends with, not just have sex with. Although the sex had been good, very good.

Kate had made love with a sweet shyness, then with a deepening passion as she let herself go, as she gave up that tight hold she had on control. He knew she hadn't let go of that control lightly. He'd had to fight for her trust. And he'd won.

But he hadn't deserved to win. He was lying to her.

The fact that she also was probably lying to him didn't make it better. He didn't want walls between them. Then again, maybe he should be happy the walls were there. It would make it easier to do what he had to do and walk away.

And he would walk away. There was no question about that. His life and his job were miles away from this island in the Pacific Northwest. And why would Kate be willing to give her heart to a man who had come to town to destroy her or one of her sisters? She wouldn't be able to forgive someone who hurt her family. Her loyalty ran deep. It was one of the things he loved about her. Not love, he told himself fiercely. Just like. He just really liked her.

"Look, there," Duncan said, pointing to the right.

Tyler got to his feet, stunned to see two incredibly large gray whales just a few feet away. They sliced through the water with power and grace. "Amazing," he murmured. "I didn't realize we could get that close."

"They're used to the boats. They don't pay us much attention."

"You love this world, don't you?"

"Every last bit of it. But I won't be back this way for a while. It's time to move on."

"You're going to race down to San Francisco next week?"

"And then on to Hawaii. Maybe," he added, surprising Tyler.

"Maybe? I thought it was a done deal."

"Rick wants the girls onboard. I thought Kate would change her mind. She always came through before." Duncan's voice grew weary. "I guess she's finally given up on me. Hold the tiller, would you?"

"What?"

"Just steer toward those trees. I want to adjust the sails."

Tyler felt awkward with the tiller in his hands. Unlike Duncan, he did not feel comfortable on the water, especially when their progress seemed to be contingent on a couple of pieces of canvas and the stick in his hands. Not exactly high technology. But then this boat had obviously seen better days, much like its owner. They were relics from a past era. They'd never be what they'd once been, but they both had stories to tell. He'd bet his life on that.

"I'll be right back. You're doing fine," Duncan said as he disappeared into the cabin.

Doing fine? What the hell was he doing? He was just holding on to the tiller and hoping he didn't run into anything, but they were away from most of the other boats now, and the islands were getting smaller, too. He'd never realized the Sound was so large, so empty.

A shiver ran down his arms as the wind picked up and the boat suddenly seemed to take off. But the wind disappeared as quickly as it had come. Tyler relaxed as the boat's speed decreased. He liked adrenaline as much as the next guy, but he would have liked it more if he knew what he was doing.

Tyler wondered what the old man was up to. He hoped Duncan didn't have a stash of vodka in a cabinet somewhere. He suspected that was a foolish hope. Duncan didn't seem to keep much distance between himself and a bottle of booze.

Tyler reached into the jacket of his windbreaker for his cell phone. He had Kate's numbers, both the bookstore and house, programmed into the phone. He'd try the bookstore first.

"Fantasia. Can I help you?"

The sound of her voice stirred him in a way he'd never imagined. Instantly he was taken back to the night before, to the soft, breathless words she'd spoken in passion. His body hardened; his muscles tightened. He didn't want to be out on this damn boat. He wanted to be with Kate, making love to her.

"Is anyone there?"

"It's me, Tyler," he said quickly, realizing she was about to hang up.

"What? Tyler? I can't hear you."

"I wanted to make sure you were all right," he said loudly. "I wanted to say good-bye to you this morning, but I didn't want to wake you."

"I can't hear you, Tyler. Is everything okay?"

"It's fine."

"Tyler? Are you there?"

He sighed, knowing she couldn't hear him. They were too far out, and getting farther away by the minute. He'd thought this would just be a nice little sail around the island, but Duncan seemed to have other plans. "I'll call you later. I miss you, Kate. I wish you could hear that." Maybe it was better that she couldn't.

Tyler closed the phone and slipped it back into his pocket. That's when he realized that Duncan was standing at the top of the stairs, watching him.

"Was that Kate?" Duncan asked.

"Yes. She couldn't hear me, though. Bad connection."

Duncan lifted the silver flask in his hand to his lips and took a long drink. "Katie won't leave Castleton. She's dug her heels in. And you're not a man to stay in one place." He paused. "So why are you messing with my daughter?"

"I'm not messing with her. I like her."

"And she likes you?"

"I think she does."

"I thought she had more sense than that. But then, she is her mother's daughter. Nora was a sucker for a smooth line and a charming smile."

"K.C.," Tyler guessed.

"It took her awhile to realize he wasn't who he said he was. Even then she was too softhearted to push him away. Just like Katie should be pushing you away."

"She's been trying."

"Not hard enough. You're still in town." Duncan walked forward. "Move aside."

"Gladly," Tyler said, giving the tiller back to Duncan. "Are we turning back?"

"We're just getting started."

"Where are we going?"

"Wherever the wind takes us."

"That's it? We're at the mercy of the wind?"

"You like to be in charge, don't you?"

"Yes, I do," Tyler admitted.

"Then why are you working for K.C.?"

Tyler was once again surprised by the question. "Why would you ask me that?"

"It's just a coincidence that you two turn up in town the same week? I don't think so. I think you're part of K.C.'s plan to destroy me. He remembers, doesn't he?"

"Remembers what?" Tyler asked, sensing that Duncan was taking off on a tangent that might finally lead to the truth.

"What happened that night," Duncan said impatiently. "Don't play the fool with me. You can romance Katie, intimidate Ashley, or sucker Caroline into talking, but none of them knows what I know."

"What do you know, Duncan?"

"What's it worth to you?"

"I don't understand."

"We can make a deal. Something I want for something you want."

"You don't have anything I want," Tyler said.

"I have Katie." Duncan looked him straight in the eye. "You want her, don't you?"

Chapter Twenty-one

Kate was still waiting for Tyler to call back several hours later, but the phone remained silent. His voice had cut in and out, making his words incomprehensible. Had he said he missed her? Or had she just imagined that part?

And why did she care? The man she'd made love to the night before had some explaining to do, like why on earth he would have taken a medical bill from Ashley's apartment. Her mind was still wrestling with that question. Unless the bill had been in Ashley's pocket and fallen out and she'd just forgotten it was in there . . . No, come to think of it, Ashley had been wearing short shorts and a tank top, no big pockets. Maybe the bill had been there for a while—but, no, she would have seen it lying in the middle of the floor. It had to have been Tyler who'd dropped it there. Why would he care about Ashley's health? Or was it something else? Was there some type of number on the bill? A social security number? Kate didn't think so, but she supposed it was possible. Maybe that number would lead Tyler to something else, or maybe he thought it would.

Kate sighed as one of her favorite customers approached the counter with a couple books.

"Tough day?" Wanda Harper asked as she reached into her purse for her wallet. "Or do you have race fever like everyone else in this town? All those boats out there make it hard to concentrate on work and chores and all that."

"I know what you mean. I've been restless all day." Kate cast a glance toward the window and was surprised to see some clouds blowing in.

Wanda followed her gaze. "The weather is changing. They're predicting rain for tonight."

"I thought that was tomorrow."

Wanda shrugged. "You know what summer storms are like—they pop up when you least expect them. Thanks," she added, taking her books and walking out of the store.

Yes, Kate knew what summer storms could be like. Intense and powerful. She walked around the counter and stood by the window. In a way, Tyler was like a summer storm, blowing into her life without any notice and drowning her in it, completely overwhelming emotions. And just like a summer storm—gone by the morning.

The door to the bookstore opened, and Caroline walked in. Dressed in low-rise jeans and a hot pink sweater, she had a smile on her face and energy in her step. Her baby sister was back, navel ring and all.

"Hi, Kate."

"You look good."

"I feel good. I'm working, so I only have a second. I wanted to give you this." She handed Kate a white paper bag.

"What is it?" She laughed when she pulled out the carton of chocolate-chip cookie-dough ice cream. "You used to give me this when you were in trouble or when you wanted something. Which is it this time?"

"It's a thank you for not criticizing, not judging, just being my sister."

"I'll always be your sister, and I'll always love you, no matter what you do."

"Don't say that, because the down side of being sober is that I feel like crying every other second." Caroline took a deep breath. "Anyway, I stopped by the docks to see Dad, but his boat was gone."

"He took Tyler out sailing."

"Why?"

Kate shrugged. "Tyler said he wanted a sailing experience so he could write more intelligently on the subject."

"And he picked Dad to give him that experience?"

"I'm sure he had another reason."

Caroline's eyes narrowed. "You look worried, but you shouldn't be. Dad won't say anything. Sometimes I don't think Dad even remembers what happened, or maybe he's just rewritten the race in his mind so that it actually happened the way we told people it happened."

"You could be right about that. I'll feel better when they get back, though." She checked her watch, startled to see it was almost four o'clock. "They should have been back by now. They left at nine o'clock this morning."

"It's not that late."

Kate walked Caroline to the door. She was surprised at the blast of cold air that greeted them. "The wind is really picking up."

"The racers should be having a hell of a ride about now."

"Hopefully they'll have the sense to come in if it gets worse."

"Since when did sailboat racers have any sense?"

Kate smiled somewhat weakly as Caroline took off down the block. She pulled the door shut behind her and walked across the street. She could see a few boats heading for the marina. She hoped her father was on one of them.

There was no reason to worry. Her father was a good sailor. As long as he wasn't drinking. As long as he had the good sense to check the weather reports.

As long as he didn't try to do something stupid and daring. As long as he didn't let the memory of another storm creep back into his head.

Okay, so she would worry. She couldn't help it, especially since he had Tyler with him. Tyler wouldn't be much assistance to her father.

The wind lifted her hair off the back of her neck, sending chills through her. This day reminded her so much of that other day, the one that had started out so bright and full of promise.

She'd been standing on the deck when the clouds began to gather. The afternoon sun had vanished. The moon had not yet risen. It was dark. Then it got darker. The swells grew into full-sized waves that rose like dragons from the deep. The wind whipped those waves into white-capped frenzies.

But today wasn't yesterday, she told herself firmly. This storm wasn't as bad or as dangerous. Everyone would be all right. No one was going to die.

Tyler hung on to the rail of the boat, feeling his stomach take another nauseating roll. His first experience at sailing had gone on far too long. The beautiful scenery had long since faded away as thick mists descended upon them, socking them into what felt like their own personal cloud. The colors had faded to grays, blues, and blacks. It was hard to tell where the water ended and the sky began. He had no idea if they were a mile from shore or ten miles.

"We've got to get back," he said,

"We will," Duncan shouted. "Don't worry. I've got everything under control. I love it when it gets like this."

Tyler believed that. Duncan was the happiest he'd ever seen him, also the most dangerous. Gone was the weak, tired, old drunk. In his place was a man on fire, obsessed, determined to beat back Mother Nature. Determined to win at all costs. For a split second, Duncan McKenna reminded Tyler of his own father,

the man who had stolen him from his mother, taken
him away from everyone he loved, because it was what
he wanted, what he needed.

Selfish obsession—some thought it led to greatness.
It took that drive, that impossible ambition, that foolish courage to tackle insurmountable odds. But, ulti-
mately, Tyler thought it led to defeat. His father had
died a broken man. Duncan was battling to continue
a career that in reality had ended eight years earlier.

"Give it up," he said out loud.

Duncan shook his head. "Never. Never give up. Go
into the wind. It's the only way to win."

"Or go back, reevaluate, live to fight another day."

"That's the safe way."

"That's the smart way."

"I've been sailing longer than you've been alive. I
know what I'm doing."

"How far are we from shore?"

"Not far. I thought you had more guts than this—
a hotshot reporter like yourself."

Tyler was knocked sideways as the boat surfed up
one side of a big swell and down the other. He had a
life jacket on, but no safety harness, and he didn't
think it would take much to go overboard. Still, he
felt better on the deck than in the cabin below.
"Shouldn't you put on a life jacket?" he asked
Duncan.

"Only got the one."

"What? You mean you don't have a vest?"

"I won't need it. You worry too much," Duncan
added. "Just like Katie. She was always looking over
my shoulder, second-guessing my decisions, wanting
to take charge." Duncan pulled out his flask and took
another swig.

"Are you sure you should be drinking right now?"

"Just a little something to warm my bones."

"It could slow your reaction time."

"I'm fine, Jeremy, just fine."

Tyler stared at Duncan, wondering if the old man

realized he'd just called him Jeremy. But Duncan was fiddling with the sails again and not looking at him at all. Why would he call him Jeremy?

Because he was getting drunk and confused. And Tyler had been an idiot to get himself into this mess. He wondered if Kate had ever felt this helpless with Duncan, this vulnerable. But her situation had been different. She'd known how to sail the boat. She could have taken over if she had to. Tyler had no idea what to do. He had seen a radio down below. Maybe he should call for help. Duncan would probably kill him for casting aspersions on his ability to make it back to shore. Then again, at this rate, Duncan might just kill him anyway.

"Whoo-hoo!" Duncan screamed with delight as the boat went straight up a wave and down the other side.

"Holy shit!" Tyler swore, managing to hang on as water crashed over them. "What the hell are you doing?"

"Living," Duncan yelled. "Isn't it grand? I'd forgotten what it's like. I'm never going back to that life."

"But we are going back to shore, right? You can race again on Saturday. You can sail all the way to Hawaii and wherever else you want to go, but right now we're going home."

"It hasn't been home since Nora died."

"Your daughters are there."

"They hate me."

"That's not true. I know Kate loves you."

Duncan shook his head. "She blames me. They all do."

"For what?"

"I didn't mean to hurt him."

"Hurt who?"

Duncan took another drink. "Jeremy."

Tyler saw a flash of pain in Duncan's eyes. "How did you hurt Jeremy?"

"He pissed me off, telling me I was cheating, threatening to turn me in. He didn't know what was at stake."

Tyler was having a hard time following the conversation. "Cheating at what?"

"The race. K.C. had sent him to spy on me. That's why Jeremy was looking through my things. I didn't want to hurt him," he repeated. "I just shoved him. I didn't even know he went off the damn boat until I heard Kate scream. Then she was gone. I had to save her." Duncan's eyes turned wild as he grabbed Tyler's shoulders and shook him. "You understand, don't you? I had to save my daughter."

"I understand," Tyler said. Which was only partially true. What he really understood was that Duncan was getting more drunk and more agitated by the minute, his mood turning as dark as the storm surrounding them. "We've got to get back to shore. We can talk about this later." He stepped out from under Duncan's grip and grabbed the tiller as the boat began to spin. "Help me here. I don't know what I'm doing."

"K.C. knows," Duncan said, ignoring Tyler's panic. "Somewhere in his brain, he knows. And someday he'll tell. I hate the waiting. But it's part of the plan. I still think you're a part of it, too. Admit it."

"I don't have anything to do with K.C."

"You're a liar. I can see it in your eyes."

He was lying, but not about that. Before he could say so, it suddenly occurred to him that his feet were wet. He looked down and realized he was standing in three inches of water.

"Duncan. What's happening?"

"I don't know anymore. I don't know which way to turn. I'm tired, Tyler, tired of living with this awful guilt."

"I'm talking about all this water," Tyler said sharply.

Duncan's gaze finally focused long enough to understand what Tyler was saying. "Sweet Jesus," he said. "The pump must be broken."

"What does that mean?"

"It means if we don't get this water out of here fast, we're going to sink to the bottom of the Sound."

Caroline stared down at the dark water where her father's boat should have been. Why wasn't he back? Most of the racers had returned an hour ago. It was almost six o'clock, and the wind was growing wilder. The distant thunder and lightning over the water was getting closer by the minute. Something bad was coming; something bad was already out on the water—the water where her father was. The storm had come in much more quickly than anyone had anticipated.

Just like the last time—eight years ago.

The weather reports coming in over the radio that awful day had gotten worse as the morning turned into afternoon. There had been some concern from race officials and the other boats that perhaps they should turn back or change course. Her father had refused to listen. It was a beautiful day for racing, and he wanted to race. They were on a roll. He didn't want to lose their momentum. Kate had voiced some concern, but that was typical. Kate was always more conservative than Duncan. Caroline had taken pleasure in siding with their father and gained approval from him at the same time. Ashley had gone back and forth as she always did. In the end they'd continued on with the race.

The other boats had also agreed to continue. If the McKenna "girls," as they were called, were willing to stay the course, so were they.

Five men had lost their lives that night. Five men.

Caroline shuddered at the memory. She still held herself somewhat responsible for those five men, especially for one man. If she hadn't supported her father, if she'd sided with Kate, maybe together they could have convinced him to wait or at least postpone the start. But aside from wanting to see approval in her father's eyes, she had also wanted to get it all done and over with. It had gone on far too long, and she was yearning for home, desperate to get there, in fact.

"Caroline?" She turned to see Kate approaching, a worried look on her face. "Dad's not back yet?"

Caroline shook her head. It should have been obvious that his boat was not in the slip, but something prevented her from making her usual sarcastic remark. "I'm sure he's fine. It's not even raining yet."

"It is out on the Sound. And, even if it weren't, where the hell are they? This was supposed to be a little cruise around the island, not an all-day trip."

Caroline heard panic in Kate's voice, and her own tension increased. Kate was always the calm one. She was reasonable, rational, and in control. But not this time. "We can try him on his radio."

"I just did that. I stopped by the harbormaster's office on the way over here. There's no answer. And I don't even know if his radio works. He rarely takes his boat out past the first buoy. I don't know why he did today."

"Probably trying to act macho in front of Tyler."

"Tyler has never been on a sailboat before. He doesn't know a thing about them. If Dad got into trouble, he wouldn't be able to help. He wouldn't be able to make his way back here."

Caroline didn't like the chill creeping up her spine. Her father was a seasoned sailor, a veteran of bluewater sailing. He could handle a storm like this. Couldn't he? Or was she still thinking of him as a hero instead of just a man, an older man, a man who was no longer fit and drank far too much. "What should we do?" she asked.

"I don't know. I talked to the coast guard. They've had two distress calls, but neither boat fit the description I gave them of Dad's boat. They said it was getting bad out there and some of the training runs had gone farther out to stay away from the racing and hadn't come back in yet."

"That's probably why Dad went farther out," Caroline said.

Kate put a hand to her stomach. "I feel sick inside. I know something is wrong. I just know it. The last time I felt like this was eight years ago."

Their eyes met, and Caroline knew that Kate had no more forgotten that night than she had. "We can pretend all we want that it's long behind us, but it isn't really," Caroline murmured. "It's always there, waiting, ready to burst out as soon as we open the door."

"I don't want to open that door."

"I think you already have."

Kate shook her head, but they both knew it was true.

"I was just standing here, thinking about the morning of the storm," Caroline continued. "We were all so confident in our racing ability, our weather forecasting, and our gut instincts. We thought we were invincible, every single one of us. Even Ashley. She wasn't afraid at the beginning. It wasn't until later, until we realized that it wasn't going to be just a storm. It was going to be a monster, and we would have to fight it to survive."

Kate looked out at the dark water. "At least we knew how to fight. Tyler doesn't have a clue. I don't want to lose him, Caroline. I'd rather have him walk away from me than have something terrible happen to him. I don't think I could stand it."

Caroline put her arm around Kate. "You won't lose him. Tyler may not know how to fight, but Dad does."

"I wish I could have as much confidence in Dad as you do."

"McKennas don't quit," Caroline said, repeating Duncan's favorite refrain. "Dad may be a lot of things, but he isn't a quitter."

"And neither am I," Kate said. "I'm going back to the harbormaster's office. If they haven't heard anything more, I'll find someone with a boat to take me out there."

"What?" Caroline asked in amazement. Was Kate really considering going out on the water?

"You heard me. I can't sit here and do nothing. And I can't just hope that the coast guard will find them. We both know there isn't always time to rescue everyone."

"You'll be hard-pressed to find anyone to take you out in this weather."

"Then I'll go myself."

Kate turned away and started down the dock.

"Wait," Caroline called after her, making a quick decision. "I'll come with you."

Kate hesitated. "Maybe you should stay here, find Ashley. If anything should happen, she'll need you."

"Nothing will happen," Caroline said forcefully. "This is not going to be like the last time."

Ashley walked down the street, telling herself not to get worked up over the fact that the weather was changing again, the wind getting stronger with every breath she took, the thunder and lightning moving closer. She would not let the fear take her. Hadn't she flown down a hill on the back of a motorcycle just two days ago? Hadn't she kissed Sean in a way that she'd never kissed any other man? She wouldn't go back to being the scared, neurotic woman of the last eight years. She couldn't. She didn't want to live like that anymore.

But the storm was making her stomach churn, making the memories swirl. It was going to be a battle. The demons of the past were determined to get to her again and again, the way they always did. She stopped and took a deep breath, looking at the building in front of her. The Amberson and Sons Boat Works was housed in a large, barnlike building at the far end of the marina, the back door of the building leading to a boat ramp where they could launch their boats directly onto the water.

Ashley couldn't remember the last time she'd come here. It had to be years. But Sean was here. He was going to tell his father that he wouldn't be sailing away on Saturday or any other day. He would finally be taking on the role of son in Amberson and Sons. It was a role that had been empty for too long. She knew the Ambersons would be happy to have Sean at home. He was the only son they had left, and he belonged here. She'd known that all along.

In some ways, Sean's absence had only added to her guilt. He shouldn't have had to leave home. Their breakup had never been about him or even their love; it had been about all the things she couldn't tell him, things that involved Jeremy and Kate, Caroline and her father, things they had promised to take to their own graves. The only way she had been able to keep the promise was to distance herself from Sean. In doing so, she'd hurt him and herself. Hurting herself had been a just punishment. Sean, however, had never deserved that pain.

She wanted to tell him that. She wanted to say she was sorry. She wanted to let him know that if it became too difficult again, she would be the one to leave, she would be the one to sacrifice. And she was prepared to do it. It wouldn't be an empty promise. If one of them had to leave, it would be her. She still didn't know if it would be possible to be with him, to see him day in and day out, without ever talking about the past.

Squaring her shoulders, she opened the door and walked inside. The building was quiet. Maybe the employees were down at the marina or on one of the bluffs overlooking the races. Race week always made it difficult to concentrate on work.

She walked down the hallway past the business offices and into the main building. There were two boats under construction, one barely begun and one almost finished, a sleek twenty-five-foot sailboat. It was beautiful. The wood was smooth, rich, expensive. She couldn't help running her hand along the side.

The touch brought back feelings of another lifetime— the rail on the *Moon Dancer* warmed by the noonday sun, hot beneath her fingers. To cool her hand, she'd put it over the side, trailing her fingers in the chilly water of the deep blue sea. So many days of the sun, the wind, the moon, the stars. Endless hours of watching the different shades of water play out in front of their eyes. The sudden squawk of a seabird sometimes the only thing to break the endless quiet.

But it wasn't always peaceful out there. Sometimes the wind sounded like a freight train roaring down the tracks. Sometimes the night was so dark, the mist so thick, that she'd felt like she was sitting in a cloud, suffocating.

Just the thought shook her up. She turned her head, instinctively seeking air, escape. Sean was standing there, watching her.

"Hi," she said somewhat nervously.

"Hi, yourself."

He looked at her as if he wanted to kiss her again, and she couldn't help licking her lips, bringing his gaze to her mouth. Maybe this was a bad idea.

"Did you talk to your dad?" she asked, breaking into speech, anything to cut the tension between them.

"This morning. He was thrilled. I finally did something to make the old man happy."

"I bet your mom is happy, too."

"Over the moon. She's making my favorite dinner, fried chicken, mashed potatoes, and pecan pie. You're invited, by the way. She's sure you had something to do with my change of mind."

"It wasn't me," she said with a self-deprecating shrug.

"Of course it was you. It's always been you."

She swallowed hard. "I wanted to tell you something." She hesitated, not sure how to say it.

Sean held up a hand. "I don't like the expression on your face. Things are good between us right now. Let's just leave it that way, at least for today. What do you say?"

"I just wanted to tell you that I don't want you to ever go away again because of me. If anyone needs to leave, I'll be the one."

"No one needs to leave. We're grown up now, Ash. Can't we just put the past behind us?"

She wanted to do exactly that. "Do you think that's possible?"

"I know it is." He paused. "I realize that when you first came back from the race, I badgered you constantly about Jeremy and the storm and what had happened out there. It wasn't fair. You were traumatized, and I didn't see that I was making it worse. I just wanted answers. I wanted something to ease the pain, you know?"

"I know," she whispered.

"But I drove you away, and I regret that."

"You don't have anything to apologize for, believe me."

"Well, it won't happen again. A few days ago I told you I wanted to race, to follow in Jeremy's wake, to experience what he did, but the truth is I don't want any of that. I never did. I never wanted to be him. I just wanted him to be here."

"Then why did you say you were going to race?"

"Maybe I was looking for another way to get to you. It kind of worked," he said and gave her a crooked grin. "It got you talking to me again."

"Your mother did that," Ashley said with a small smile.

"I'll have to give her a big present on Mother's Day. So, do you want to go for a sail?"

She stiffened. "Uh, no, not in this weather."

"Relax. I was talking about this boat." He tipped his head toward the boat next to her. "It's as ready as you are for a dry-dock test run." He pushed the box steps over to the boat. "Want a closer look?"

"All right."

Sean climbed into the boat and held out his hand to her. After a moment's hesitation, she climbed aboard.

Sean sat down on the bench seat and patted the spot next to him. "Sit here with me."

She did as he asked, feeling an odd sense of comfort as she sat down, as if she'd come home.

"Remember when we had a picnic in Mr. Garcia's motorboat?" he asked her.

She smiled at the memory. "Your father was furious at us for getting jam on the seats. I don't think we were more than twelve."

"The good old days."

"The good old days," she echoed.

"What do you think of the boat?" Sean asked.

"It's beautiful."

"It's my design. I sent it to my father a couple years ago. He finally found a customer who wanted it."

She looked at him in surprise. "You did this? That's incredible."

"A little better than all those bad drawings I used to show you, huh?"

Ashley nodded, remembering how Sean had always been busy scribbling on pieces of paper. "As I recall, most of those boats looked like supersonic jets. You had a fascination with speed."

"I'm learning to slow down," he said, putting an arm around her shoulders.

"I don't think that's slowing down," she replied, not quite sure she was ready for what was coming. He'd taken her by surprise with his kiss during their motorcycle ride. She hadn't had time to think, to worry, to make a decision. Even when he'd kissed her good night last night after their picnic, it had been quick, forceful. But today was different.

"I'm going to kiss you now," he murmured, lowering his head.

"I know you—" she started to say, but his mouth cut off the rest of her sentence. The kiss started out slow but took off fast as Sean groaned and swept the inside of her mouth with his tongue, demanding that she give everything to him.

A door slammed shut, breaking them apart. "What was that?" she asked breathlessly.

"Just the wind," Sean said. "No one else is here. They've gone home for the night."

"I hate the wind. It makes me crazy. I feel so out of control."

"I like you out of control." He swooped down and stole another kiss.

She put a hand against his chest. "Maybe we should stop."

"Is that what you really want?"

She stared into his beautiful gold-flecked brown eyes and knew it was the last thing she wanted. But was she ready for Sean? She could feel the energy, the tension he barely had under control. This wouldn't be a gentle love affair; it would be wild and turbulent and unpredictable, exactly the way she didn't like things.

"I can't," she said slowly. "It's too much, too soon."

"Then I'll wait. I'm used to it," he said, an annoyed edge to his voice. He pushed her away and stood up. "Let's get out of here."

"And go where?"

"Someplace where there are people, crowds, noise, action. Someplace where I won't be thinking every second about making love to you."

She followed him off the boat, not particularly liking his mood or trusting it. "Maybe we should just take a break from each other," she said as they reached the hallway.

"No. No more breaks. We've had too many already. Let's go to my house. We'll be fine with my parents as chaperones."

Ashley liked that idea even less. "I'm not sure I'm ready for a family dinner."

He put his hands on his hips. "What the hell are you ready for, then?"

She glared at him. "Sean, you are being a jerk. You've been back in town less than a week. Don't rush me."

"Maybe I'm afraid you'll change your mind, that this is some bout of temporary insanity, and you'll suddenly wake up and shut me out the way you have the last eight years. Maybe that's why I'm rushing you a little."

She saw the insecurity in his eyes and could understand where it came from. "You have a right to feel that way, but we can't go from nothing to everything in five minutes. That won't work, either. We need to get to know each other again. Why don't we go down to the marina and get a soda? Then you can meet your parents for dinner, and we'll set up something for tomorrow."

He seemed to relax at the promise of tomorrow. "Okay, I guess I can do that." He grabbed his jacket off a hook and opened the front door. A blast of wind hit them right in the face.

"Oh, my God," Ashley murmured, her already tense body stiffening. "The sky is black." Her heart sped up. A shiver ran down her spine, and her breath came faster as thunder rocked the night, taking her right back to the very place she didn't want to go. She shook her head, trying to get the memories out of her head, but all she could see were the clouds, swirling, swooping, then the waves doing the same, all mixing together, bearing down on her. "I can't do this," she murmured. "Close the door."

Sean shut the door. "It's just a storm, Ashley. It won't hurt you. We'll be fine."

His voice sounded just like Jeremy's voice. She closed her eyes and saw Jeremy in her mind, his brave face lined with worry, but his eyes alight with the magnificence of it all. He hadn't been scared.

He'd been positive they would come out of the storm all right.

She opened her eyes, seeing Sean, seeing Jeremy, their similar features blurring in her mind, just as the past was blurring with the present.

"That's what Jeremy said, but he was wrong," she murmured.

"What? What are you talking about? When did you speak to Jeremy?" Sean grabbed her by the shoulders. "Did you talk to Jeremy the night of the storm? Did you hear his voice on the radio?"

"Not on the radio," she whispered, the truth pressing against her lips. She couldn't let it come out. She couldn't.

Chapter Twenty-two

"Answer me," Sean said. "If you heard Jeremy's voice on the radio, those might have been the last words he ever spoke. I can't believe you never told me this before."

Ashley winced as his grip tightened on her arms, but she deserved the pain. A flash of light illuminated the room, spotlighting the torment in Sean's eyes. The loud clap of thunder that followed seemed like a sign from the heavens that it was time to come clean, time to tell the truth.

"Ashley, I'm waiting, and, in case you hadn't noticed, I'm not very good at waiting."

Before she could speak, the door to the building burst open, and Caroline and Kate almost ran them down in their hurry.

"Thank God, you're both here," Kate said, her eyes lit up with worry and fear.

"What's wrong?" Ashley asked, her uneasiness turning to full panic. Something was wrong. She'd felt it before, but she knew it now. Even Caroline looked concerned.

"It's Dad," Kate said. "He took Tyler out on his boat today. They haven't come back yet, and the radio is dead."

"What are you saying?" Ashley asked.

"He's missing, Ashley. He's caught in the storm, and we need to find him." Kate looked at Sean. "I need a boat. I've asked everyone else, Sean, but there are three other boats missing and everyone willing to search is already out on the water. Do you think you could take me out on your dad's boat? If you don't want to do it, will you let me take the boat myself?"

Ashley couldn't believe what her sister was asking of Sean. Nor could she believe what Kate was contemplating. "Kate, you can't be serious."

"I am serious," Kate said, determination in her eyes. "It's not just Dad. Tyler is with him. They're in trouble. I know it. I'm desperate, Sean. I know I shouldn't ask, but—"

"I'll take you out," Sean said abruptly. He looked over at Ashley. "But when I get back, you and I are going to have a long talk."

"Meet us at Kate's house," Caroline told her as the three of them walked toward the door. "Bring some of your cookies. Make some tea. We'll probably need it when we get back."

That's what she had been reduced to—tea and cookies. She'd once been as good a sailor as both of them. But they didn't trust her now. She'd lost their respect along with everything else. Wasn't it about time she tried to get it back?

The three people she loved most in the world were on their way out the door when she finally found the courage to speak. "Wait, I'm coming with you."

Kate couldn't believe Ashley would actually get on Sean's boat, but she didn't want to waste time arguing. When Ashley balked, they'd simply leave her behind and deal with that problem when they came back. Right now she had to concentrate on finding her father and Tyler as quickly as possible.

"We won't be able to stop and bring you back,"

Kate told Ashley as they neared the boat. "Maybe you should just wait here."

"She's right, Ash. You don't have anything to prove," Caroline said.

"I'm part of the family. I have to go. One for all, all for one, remember?"

Ashley's words of bravado were accented by sheer terror as she grabbed Kate's arm to steady herself on the dock, which was moving up and down with the water. "Just help me get on the boat. I'll be fine from there."

"It's okay, Ashley," Kate replied. "You don't have to do this. We love you. Dad loves you. He'll understand why you didn't come."

"He won't understand. He never understood. It was my fear that caused our problems before. Dad told me to grow up, to stop crying, or someone would get hurt." Ashley looked at Kate with anguish in her eyes. "I just didn't know it would be Jeremy."

Kate caught her breath at the sharp blast from the past. "Stop it. That was a long time ago and a completely different situation." Besides that, Ashley was wrong, completely wrong. If anyone was to blame, it was herself.

"Let's go," Caroline said impatiently from aboard the boat.

"It's now or never," Kate said, glancing at Ashley's white face.

"Now." Ashley reached out her hand to Caroline, who helped her onboard. Kate untied the rope and jumped onto the boat behind her sisters. They huddled on deck as Sean started the engine of his father's thirty-two-foot cabin cruiser and steered them out of the harbor, right into the heart of the storm.

The rain was coming down steadily. Tyler wiped his eyes, wishing he could see better, but the clouds had obliterated all light. "We should try the radio again,"

Tyler said to Duncan, who continued to bail water out of the boat, which was looking to be a hopeless task.

"It's dead," Duncan said, stopping his efforts. He straightened and pulled out his flask once again. "Maybe it was meant to be."

"What was meant to be?"

"That it would end like this."

"Hey, nothing is going to end tonight. That's for damn sure."

Duncan smiled with defeat. "You and Jeremy, so much alike—strong, energetic, determined, convinced you can overcome. I used to be like that."

"You still are like that, Duncan. You're going to race on Saturday, remember? You're winning back the *Moon Dancer*. Come on, man, don't give up on me."

"I won't be able to race. Rick won't let me race without the girls. And they won't come with me."

"I'll help you change their minds." Tyler knew that he had to get Duncan out of this depression so they could fight the storm.

"It's over. I have to accept it. The girls have finally given up on me. It was only a matter of time. And this is the time."

"It's not the time. It's not the time at all. Kate will never give up on you. And Caroline is crazy about you. I don't know as much about Ashley, but I do know this: you're their father. You mean something to them."

"Ashley is a sweet girl, so quiet, so sensitive. I never know what is going on in her head. She's a mystery— has been from the day she was born." Duncan took another drink. "The only thing I do know for sure is that she doesn't like me much. Sometimes I think she hates me."

Tyler stared at Duncan, realizing the old man had just given him a big clue. "Why would Ashley hate you?" He wondered if he'd finally hear the words *Because I gave up her baby.*

"They all hate me for taking them to sea, making them race, not letting them go home when they wanted to go," Duncan said instead. "They didn't know how much was at stake. I couldn't just quit. I'd bet everything—the life insurance money, the mutual funds set up for the girls, Nora's jewelry, her wedding ring. It would all be gone if we didn't win that race. I'd made side bets they didn't know about, and I'd used some of the money to help ensure our victory. It wasn't really cheating, even though Jeremy wanted to blow the whistle on me. He just didn't understand how things were done."

"Jeremy wanted to turn you in?" Tyler asked, trying to make sense of what he was hearing.

Duncan didn't answer him. His eyes were glazed, his face and clothes soaked through with the steady rain pouring down on them. Tyler wondered if he even realized where they were.

"I thought he loved Kate," Duncan said. "But he loved the truth even more. Or maybe he just wanted to prove that he was better than me. I should have kicked him off the *Moon Dancer* when I had the chance."

"How did Jeremy get on the boat?" Tyler asked, still not sure he was following what Duncan was saying. The old man was rambling in a dozen directions at the same time, and it was hard to keep up.

"Kate snuck him aboard," Duncan said, "at the last minute, as we were leaving for Hawaii. She was clever about it. No one knew. We were underway before I realized he was there. I would have lost time kicking him off."

"So you let him stay. And then there was an argument. You fought with him about something to do with cheating."

"I just shoved him away. He was in my face. I didn't mean for him to fall. I didn't know he hit his head. I never saw that." Duncan's voice filled with anguish. "It was an accident, I swear it. I heard Kate scream, and when I turned around she was in the water. My daughter had jumped into that angry sea. My precious girl. I had to save her." His eyes begged Tyler to understand. "You understand, don't you? A man has to save his child."

"What about Jeremy?"

"He disappeared. He was there, and then he was gone. The storm was huge, far worse than this. No one could survive more than a minute or two. I didn't let him die."

"But they thought you did." Suddenly it was all so clear. "That's it, isn't it? The girls think you killed Jeremy. That's the big secret." Tyler suddenly realized why Kate had been stonewalling him all this time. It had nothing to do with a baby and everything to do with Jeremy's death. Or maybe Jeremy had had something to do with the baby? Had he come on board to help take care of Kate because she was nearing the end of her pregnancy? Hadn't Duncan said that Kate wanted Jeremy with her? What other reason could there have been? They were in the middle of a race. And they would have been together forever only a few weeks later when it was all over. Why jeopardize everything by taking Jeremy onboard on the second-to-last leg? "Wasn't that against the rules?" he asked. "Jeremy coming onboard? Wouldn't you have been disqualified as soon as you got to the next port?"

Duncan shook his head. "You could have a crew of up to six. It didn't matter who they were." Duncan paused, looking at Tyler. "I didn't kill Jeremy. I just couldn't save him."

"But he was going to blow the whistle on you. That's a good motive for letting him drown." Tyler knew it was stupid to speak so frankly at this moment. Lord knew he wasn't in a position to piss Duncan off, but he couldn't stop the words from coming.

"I couldn't find him. I tried. He must have been unconscious. Otherwise he would have been swimming."

"Why was his name listed on the other boat's manifest?" Tyler asked. "Why didn't anyone know he was with you?"

"The only people that knew were on the *Betsy Marie*. And I'm not even sure they knew Jeremy was with us. They might have thought he'd just disappeared or missed the start. When the *Betsy Marie* went down, everyone but K.C. went down with it."

"And K.C. didn't remember." It all made sense now in a terrible way. Kate's boyfriend had died off their boat, and no one had said a word. The girls had circled the wagons around their father. Loyal to the end, they'd protected him.

"I'm sorry," Duncan said, the alcohol slurring his words. "If we don't make it, I'm sorry. Tell the girls I loved them."

"No good-bye speeches. We're both going to make it. Tell me what to do, Duncan."

Duncan's eyes began to drift shut. His hand let go of the tiller, and the boat went into a spin. The boom came flying across. Tyler tried to get out of the way, but it caught him on his back and sent him sprawling onto the floor of the boat. Dazed, his only real thought was that he was going to drown, and he didn't even like to sail.

Kate and her sisters stood in the weather-protected cockpit next to Sean, watching as he steered the motorboat through the rough swells. They could see a search plane off to the right, its lights blazing across the water. There were Mayday calls on the radio, but none from her father's boat. She told herself it would be all right. Just because his radio was out didn't mean they were in severe trouble. She had to keep the faith. She couldn't let the fear overtake her, but it was there in every breath she took. This was too much like the last time. Maybe not the size of the storm, but certainly the stakes.

"Where to?" Sean asked briskly.

"Captain's Cove. He loved that spot. He might have tried to get a break from the wind over there."

"No, I think he'd sail straight into the wind," Caroline said. "The way he did before. Remember? He wouldn't listen to us. He was convinced that the only way out was straight ahead."

Sean looked from one to the other, then over at Ashley, who was huddled in the small space with them, her face white, her eyes huge, her grip on a nearby rail as tight as she could get it. "You okay, Ash?" he asked her.

"No." She shook her head.

"It's going to be fine. I won't let anything happen to you."

Kate felt her breath catch in her throat. Sean looked so much like Jeremy right now, confident, strong, sure of himself. He had no idea . . .

"Captain's Cove or straight ahead?" Jeremy asked Kate.

"Straight ahead. Caroline always understood the way Dad thought better than I did."

"Jeremy didn't want Dad to sail into the wind," Ashley murmured. "He thought we should go east, don't you remember? But Dad said we'd lose even more time, and it was just a summer storm. It wouldn't get that bad."

Kate stiffened. If she was closer, she would have given Ashley a good swift kick, but she couldn't reach her. Already Sean was turning toward her with a question in his eyes.

"What are you talking about, Ash?" Sean asked.

"She's confused," Caroline said quickly. "Look at her, she's terrified."

"They were arguing so loudly," Ashley continued as if neither Sean or Caroline had spoken. She looked at Kate. "I'm sorry."

"Was Jeremy talking to your dad over the radio? I thought there wasn't any contact during the storm."

Kate met Ashley's anguished glance. She sensed her

sister was at the breaking point. The current storm
was bringing it all back into her head.

"He was on our boat," Ashley burst out. "I'm sorry,
Kate. I can't keep it in anymore. I'm so tired of lying."

"What did you just say?" Sean demanded, looking
from Ashley to Kate. "Jeremy was on the *Betsy Marie*.
He went down with that boat. That's the truth."

Kate took in a deep breath, knowing it was over. If
she didn't tell him, Ashley would. "I brought Jeremy
on board the *Moon Dancer* just before that leg of the
race. I wanted him to sail with us, Sean." Her stomach
twisted into a knot as she thought back to those awful
days. "I needed him with me. No one knew, not even
my father, until it was too late to turn back."

The boat bounced and Sean stiffened, his hands
jerking the wheel. "I don't understand. If Jeremy was
on your boat, then what happened to him? You all
survived. Why didn't he make it, too?"

"So many things happened all at once," Kate murmured. "I'm not even sure I know the sequence of
events."

"It started with me," Ashley said. "I was down in
the main cabin, and I was crying. I wasn't—I wasn't
feeling well, and I was scared. The storm was just
starting then. It wasn't that bad yet. Jeremy told me
it would be all right. Just like you did a minute ago,
Sean." She paused. "That's when he put his arm
around me, and I kissed him. I wanted to distract myself from the storm. I wanted to forget where I was.
Then Kate walked in." Ashley looked at her sister.
"You had the most awful look in your eyes when you
saw us, like I'd just stabbed you in the heart."

"I couldn't believe it," Kate said painfully. "I misunderstood the situation. I went a little berserk, and
I said things I shouldn't have." Her eyes watered as
guilt swamped her. She'd never had a chance to tell
Jeremy she was sorry.

"But he knew you didn't mean it," Caroline interrupted. "Because I talked to Jeremy right after that.

He understood that tensions were running high. We were all on edge. We had been for months, but when Jeremy came onboard, it tipped the scales. Dad was furious. I think that's why he started drinking. He'd been so good the rest of the time. But, that night, it all came to a head."

"Yes, it did." Kate wished the memories weren't flooding back, but they were, and she couldn't stop them. "Dad and Jeremy were fighting about something. I don't even know what really. I was too mad at Jeremy to talk to him about it, and then I was too busy trying to keep the boat afloat to worry about it."

"Jeremy accused Dad of cheating," Caroline said. "I was down in our cabin, and I heard them talking about it. Jeremy said Dad had been cheating all along, bribing some of the crew members of the *Betsy Marie* to slow K.C. down, stuff like that. Then Dad accused Jeremy of coming on board for K.C. and not for Kate." Caroline looked taken aback by her own words. "I just remembered that. He thought Jeremy was K.C.'s spy."

"You never said that before," Kate said.

"I guess I forgot."

"Get back to how my brother ended up in the ocean," Sean said harshly, drawing all three womens' eyes back to him.

"It was later that day," Ashley said. "Kate was at the wheel. Caroline and I were down in the cabin. I don't know which one of us was crying more." She exchanged a poignant look with Caroline. "Jeremy came down to check on us. I guess that's when he took off his safety harness."

"And when he came back up, Dad started shouting at him," Kate continued. "I told them to stop fighting and come help me with the sails. They started toward me, and then they collided." Kate saw the scene unfolding in front of her eyes. Jeremy rushing toward her, then Duncan getting in his way, the shove, hands, fists, arms, legs flying, Jeremy landing on his back with a crack. She had turned in horror, and as she'd done so, the boat was hit by a huge wave, and suddenly Jeremy was sliding away, right over the side of the boat and into that awful, monstrous sea. "Jeremy fell. And then he was gone, over the side," she muttered.

"Oh, my God!" Sean said, horror in his eyes.

"I remember unhooking my safety harness. I ran to the side, and I saw him in the water," Kate continued.

"And then you jumped in after him," Ashley said. "I couldn't believe it. Dad and I went running for the lines so we could rescue you both."

"I had Jeremy's hand in mine." Kate looked at the brother of the man she had loved so fiercely. "I jumped in after him. I tried to save him, Sean. I swear I did." Her voice broke. "But I couldn't hold on. It was too wet. His hand was too slippery, and he wasn't conscious. His eyes were closed. I screamed at him to look at me, to talk to me, but he wouldn't. And then he was gone." Kate saw the awful pain in Sean's eyes, but it was nothing to the pain she'd felt when Jeremy had disappeared. A tear ran down her face as she took in a breath and let it out. "The next time I came up, I saw the *Moon Dancer* in front of me, and I managed to get to the life preserver Dad had thrown out to me. He and Ashley pulled me onboard."

"We looked for Jeremy, but we couldn't find him," Ashley said. She put a tentative hand on Sean's arm, but he threw it off in anger.

"How hard did you look?"

Kate flinched. "We looked, Sean. Don't you think I would have saved Jeremy if I could have? I loved him. He was everything to me."

"But not to your father. Your father hated him. Maybe he made a choice that night. Maybe it was easier to let Jeremy's accusations drown."

"That's not true," Caroline said. "Dad wouldn't have done that. He might be a drunk, but he's not cruel."

"Why didn't you say something?" Sean cried. "All

these years, you let me and my parents believe that
Jeremy went down with the *Betsy Marie*. How could
you do that?" Sean stared at them as if he'd never
seen them before. And he hadn't—he was seeing them
for the first time the way they really were. Kate felt
naked and ugly and totally ashamed.

"We didn't set out to lie," she said. "But when we
got back to shore, everyone was talking about the guys
who went down on the *Betsy Marie*. They were comforting me, knowing that I was involved with Jeremy.
Dad asked us not to correct them. When it became
clear that no one knew Jeremy had been with us, it
was too late to come clean."

"Because you were afraid that your father might
have been held accountable," Sean said roughly. "He
killed my brother. He shoved him, knocked him out,
and then didn't try to rescue him."

"That's not what we just said," Kate said.

"Isn't it? That's what I heard. And then the three
of you covered it up."

"Because Jeremy was dead, and nothing we said
would change that," Caroline explained.

But her explanation didn't satisfy Sean. Kate could
see it in his eyes, eyes that were so much like Jeremy's. Only Jeremy's eyes had never condemned her,
never wished her to hell as Sean's eyes were doing
now. She couldn't blame him for the hate. It was the
same hate she'd felt for herself every day for the last
eight years.

"I loved Jeremy," she said. "If I could have died in
his place, I would have."

"But your father saved you, so you saved him in
return." Sean shook his head. "What the hell am I
doing out here with the three of you? How could you
even ask me to do this?"

"I asked you because I was desperate," Kate said.
"That's why. Because it's not just my father who is
missing. Tyler is with him, a man I care very much
about. A man I don't want to lose the same way I

lost Jeremy. You can hate me, Sean. You can hate all of us. We probably deserve it. But there's an innocent man out on the water who has no idea about any of this. And he doesn't deserve to die because of something that happened eight years ago, something we can't take back no matter how much we want to."

Sean stared at her for a long moment, then turned his attention to the water in front of him. "We probably won't be able to find them, anyway. They could be anywhere."

"But you won't turn back, will you?" Kate asked, holding her breath for his answer.

"Not yet," he said finally.

For a few moments no one spoke. The only sounds were those of the increasingly furious storm. Kate, Ashley, and Caroline huddled together, arms linked, drawing strength from one another as they stood behind Sean, their father's fate resting in his angry hands.

They peered through the darkness. The spotlight running from the top of the boat illuminated patches of water, but it was difficult to see much of anything. The radio continued to relay distress and rescue calls, but none that fit the description of their dad's boat.

It couldn't end like this. *Not like this,* Kate prayed. There were too many things she wanted to tell Tyler. And even her father. Too many questions left unanswered. Too many feelings left unspoken.

"There they are!" Ashley shouted, drawing her attention back to the water. "Look, there's Dad's boat."

Sean seemed to hesitate. For a split second Kate wondered if he would turn back, leave her father to save himself.

"Sean?" Kate questioned.

"I don't leave anyone in the water," he said abruptly, turning in the direction of Duncan's boat.

When they drew closer, Kate could see Tyler, waving and shouting something, but the wind took away his words. Not that it mattered. Kate could see they were in trouble. The boat was sitting precariously low in the water and going lower by the second. Each swell seemed to push it even farther down.

Sean steered them as close as he could, but the waves pushed them apart.

"I need someone to take the wheel," Sean said urgently.

"I'll do it," Caroline offered.

Sean hurried out onto the deck, and Kate followed quickly behind him.

"We'll throw them a line and try to tow them closer to us," Sean yelled to her.

The rain seemed to pick up as their efforts intensified, creating a thick curtain between the two boats. Kate barely felt the water or the wind. She was too focused on Tyler and her father, who just seemed to be sitting there. Why wasn't he helping? Why wasn't he trying to grab the line?

The first few attempts fell short. Finally the line made it into Tyler's hands. Kate let out a gasp of relief as Tyler tried to tie the line to the boat. But he couldn't do it. The boat was sinking, she realized in horror. Her father and Tyler were going underwater. And her father didn't have on a life jacket. Why not? Had her father gone completely crazy? Unless he only had the one, and he'd given it to Tyler.

As she watched, Tyler began to shrug out of his life jacket, clearly intending to put it on her father. She clapped a hand to her mouth, realizing that he would be completely vulnerable if the boat went down. "The life preserver," Kate shouted to Sean.

Sean was already tossing a life preserver to Tyler. Tyler caught it and tried to get it over Duncan's head.

What was wrong with her father? He seemed completely out of it. Was he drunk? The horrifying thought made her sick to her stomach. Was that why they hadn't come back? Had her father taken Tyler along on some drunken joyride? Damn him!

"Dad must be hurt," Ashley said as she came on deck. "Or sick."

"Or drunk," Kate said bitterly.

"What are we going to do?" Ashley asked as they watched Tyler try to wrestle their father into the life preserver.

"I'm going in," Kate said decisively. "I'll swim over there and help Tyler."

"You can't," Ashley said. "Not again."

The last thing Kate wanted to do was jump into that black, swirling water, but she couldn't stand by and do nothing, not when another man she loved was in danger of drowning.

"I have to," she said.

"I'll go." Sean put his hand on Kate's shoulder. "You went after my brother. I'll go after your father."

"No, Sean!" Ashley screamed, rushing to the side as Sean went into the water. "No, don't go," she cried, sobbing as they waited for Sean to come up.

"He'll be okay," Kate said, putting her arm around her sister and holding her close. She was relieved to see Sean's head pop out of the water and the beginning of a strong freestyle. But it seemed to take forever for Sean to reach the boat. He was swimming in a life jacket, his movements hampered by the bulky vest, and he had his arm hooked around another life preserver. Despite the fact that he was a good swimmer, the waves kept pushing him back toward their boat.

"This is just like before," Ashley said. "I was watching you struggle in the water. Dad was trying to save you, and I didn't think I was ever going to see you again."

Kate pulled Ashley into a tight hug as they both started crying. "You can't get rid of me that easily," she said. "And Sean is just as stubborn as I am, probably more so. He'll make it, and he'll save Dad and Tyler."

Kate looked toward the other boat. Sean was almost

there. So close. And then Tyler was leaning over. He grabbed Sean's hand and pulled him onboard. Together, they put the preserver around Duncan's body. But he seemed to be wrestling with them, arguing, shouting something.

Please, Dad, Kate prayed. *Please, just let them save you.*

A huge swell came up, crashing over all three of them. One minute they were on the boat, the next they were in the water, and the boat was gone.

Kate heard screams. She didn't know if they were hers or her sisters', but they echoed the screams of the past. The storm had returned. The day of reckoning had come.

"I don't see them," Ashley cried. "Oh, my God, Kate! I don't see any of them."

Chapter Twenty-three

It was just like before. One minute he was there, the next he was gone, Kate thought. She shook her head, wiping the rain and tears from her eyes so she could see better.

"They can't be gone," Ashley sobbed. "I love Sean. I never told him."

She'd never told Tyler she loved him, either, Kate realized. She'd let the opportunity pass by, afraid to put her heart on the line, afraid to even admit to herself that she'd fallen for him. Now it might be too late. And what of her father? Had she protected him all these years, only to lose him now?

Then the clouds suddenly parted. The moon peeked through, lighting up the water next to them like a spotlight on center stage.

"There they are!" Kate shouted. The bodies drew closer, but she couldn't tell how many. Were there two or were there three?

Finally they reached the boat, and she could see Tyler and Sean, each with a hand on the life preserver holding her father afloat. She threw the rope ladder over the side and Tyler pulled himself halfway out of the water. Then, with what looked like a superhuman effort on his part, he managed to get Duncan to the ladder.

Kate and Ashley both reached out for their father. Duncan's movements were awkward and slow. His eyes were open, but he seemed barely conscious or aware of his surroundings, and his body was like a deadweight. With Sean and Tyler pushing him up, they managed to pull Duncan over the side and onto the deck of the boat. Caroline ran up the stairs from the cabin below, her arms full of blankets. While she wrapped a blanket around her father's shaking shoulders, Kate reached out to Tyler.

He grabbed her hand and she held on tight. She would not let this man go. He would not slip from her fingers. As he climbed up the ladder, their eyes met, and she almost burst into tears, knowing that she could have easily lost him forever. Then he was over the side of the boat and holding her in his arms, his cold lips touching hers in a passionate kiss that warmed them both from the inside out.

"Are you okay? Are you hurt anywhere?" she asked, pulling away from him long enough to take a good look.

"I'm fine." He turned toward Sean, who was wrapped up in Ashley's arms. "Thanks to your friend here."

Sean drew back from Ashley and stared at all of them, his gaze finally settling on Duncan, who was half lying, half sitting on the deck, his breath still coming in ragged gasps.

"You should have let me drown," Duncan said, looking at Sean. "It's what I deserved."

"Probably," Sean agreed. "But, unlike you, I don't let people die." He stomped into the cockpit, ignoring the blanket in Caroline's hand, and a moment later the engines roared to life.

Kate squatted down next to her father. "He knows everything. We told him on the way out here."

"And he still jumped into the water?"

"He's a good man."

"Just like his brother," Duncan muttered. "I never wanted Jeremy to die, Katie. It was an accident. I didn't like him, but I didn't mean to hurt him."

She'd heard it all before. But the words of forgiveness wouldn't come. "What about Tyler? Did you mean to hurt him when you brought him all the way out here? What the hell were you thinking? Why didn't you turn back when the weather changed?"

"Katie, I—"

"You were drinking, too. Drinking and sailing without a working radio, without two life jackets! It's madness, and you know it. You taught us the rules years ago, but you keep breaking them. Over and over and over again. How many times do you think I can rescue you? How many times can I keep doing this, Dad?"

He looked at her with intense pain in his eyes. "I'm sorry. I'm sorry for everything, for Jeremy, for the cheating, and for the lies I asked you and your sisters to tell." He looked over at Ashley and Caroline. "You girls were the best thing that ever happened to me after marrying your mother. I know I didn't raise you right, taking you out of school and sailing around the world. I made a lot of mistakes. I'm still making them. But I love you, girls. If you don't believe anything else, I hope you'll believe that. And I hope you'll forgive me." His sentence ended with a fit of coughing that turned his face red.

Caroline came over with a bottle of water. Kneeling down beside him, she took off the cap and lifted it to his lips. "Here you go, Daddy," she said. "Don't talk anymore. You need to rest."

More tears came to Kate's eyes at the emotional scene. Caroline loved Duncan so much, in spite of everything.

"I don't know if I can ever forgive him," Ashley said quietly to Kate. "Apologies are fine and good, but what happens tomorrow when he picks up another drink?"

Kate couldn't give her an answer, because she didn't know. But she did know one thing: Life wouldn't be the same after this night. Sean knew the truth, and, turning her head, she could see that Tyler knew it, too.

Two hours later, Kate and her sisters tucked their father into Kate's bed, then returned to the living room where they collapsed on the nearest available sofa or chair. No one said anything for a long time. There had been too many words spoken already.

Sean had taken off as soon as they docked. Tyler had headed to the hotel in search of dry clothes. And the McKenna sisters had come home. As Ashley and Caroline looked at Kate, she knew it was her job now to say something wise and reassuring, but for the life of her she couldn't come up with a single thing. Who knew what would happen now that the awful truth was out in the open, and in front of a reporter no less? The story could be all over the newspapers, sailing magazines, and online sailing chat rooms in twenty-four hours. Everyone would know that the McKennas had covered up the death of Jeremy Amberson. And if someone probed further, they might find other discrepancies, incidents of cheating that her father had tried to cover up. She hadn't been aware of that part of it until Jeremy had come onboard and mentioned to her that he thought Duncan was paying off crew members on the *Besty Marie* to slow things down. She still didn't know if that was the truth or not; her father had been unwilling to ever admit to that, and no one had ever come forward. Perhaps K.C. still had something up his sleeve, something else they would have to face before this week was over.

Kate sighed wearily at the thought of more drama. She looked at the portrait hanging over the fireplace and saw her mother's smiling face. Nora McKenna looked beautiful, innocent, happy. What would she have thought of all this?

Maybe her mother wouldn't have been surprised. She'd lived with Duncan for almost seventeen years; she'd known her husband wasn't all good or all bad. But he'd been different with her, Kate thought. He'd changed after her mother's death; he'd crossed lines that before he'd never crossed. Without Nora, without his anchor, he'd gone adrift, and Kate hadn't been able to pull him back—until tonight.

But what had she pulled him back to? That was the question. Would he change? Would this brush with death finally make him realize that it was time to stop drinking? Would he see that it was time to stop racing, that he had to give up the glory days of the past, that he couldn't recapture them? He had to find some other way to be happy, but how? And would he even have the opportunity if the consequences of this night resulted in criminal or civil charges?

"What do you think will happen now?" Caroline asked, obviously reading Kate's mind.

"I don't know. We'll have to talk to the race officials and whoever else needs to know. We won't have a choice."

"I didn't mean to blurt it all out," Ashley said, a guilty expression on her face. "It just came out. I couldn't stop it."

"You wanted to tell Sean. You've wanted to tell him for a long time," Caroline said with her usual bluntness. "I knew you couldn't keep it in forever."

"I tried. I tried for eight years. But tonight with the wind and the rain—all the memories—it just came out."

"I'm not blaming you," Caroline said. "I'm kind of glad, in a way. It's almost a relief. And hopefully the consequences won't be too horrible."

"I suppose the race victory could be overturned, although it wasn't illegal for Jeremy to be onboard, but we did cover up his death," Kate said. "And I guess his death might be investigated as something other than an accident. If the other allegations of cheating and bribery come to light, then maybe that will make what happened look more sinister."

"You don't think Dad could go to jail?" Caroline asked in alarm. "It was an accident. We know it was."

"Sean's family may not be so certain," Kate replied. She offered Ashley a sympathetic glance. "It won't be easy for him, Ash. Jeremy and Sean were very close. The whole family was. They're going to be furious with us, and rightly so."

Ashley nodded, her face tight, her mouth set in a grim line. "I know. We need to talk to Mr. and Mrs. Amberson as well as to Sean."

"Tomorrow," Kate said. "We'll do it tomorrow. We'll do it together, the way we should have done before."

"I don't want Dad to go to jail," Caroline said. "The rest of it I can handle. If we have to give back the trophy, who the hell cares? If we have to find a way to repay the money we won, we'll find a way to do it. But I don't want Daddy to go to jail."

"We'll do everything we can to make sure that doesn't happen." Kate pressed her fingers together, hoping it wouldn't go that far. Her father would never be able to survive such an experience. And, in truth, he didn't deserve a jail sentence. He was a lot of things, but he wasn't a killer. Jeremy's death had been an accident. If she had ever believed anything else, she would have made sure her father had paid for it a long time ago. "One thing that surprised me tonight," she said, "was that the two of you blamed yourselves for what happened to Jeremy. Why didn't you ever tell me that before?"

"You never wanted to talk about any of it," Ashley said quietly. "And who could blame you? You were going to marry him. You had so many plans. Remember all those bridal magazines we bought at every port? Every time you took a break, you were poring over wedding dresses, flowers, and cakes."

Kate remembered. After two years at sea, she and Jeremy had found each other again, just before the start of the Winston. For three weeks they'd been in the same port, and they'd discovered that the love they'd kept alive by phone calls during the past two years was just as strong as ever. Those three glorious weeks had been spent in love and laughter, and, just before the start of the Winston, Jeremy had asked her to marry him. They'd set the date for a month after the race. Their families and friends had been thrilled.

Actually, that wasn't true. Her father had not been happy at all. He liked Jeremy, but he had visions of the McKenna family racing into the history books. Kate had thrown him a bone by telling him that Jeremy would race with them after they were married; he would be a useful addition to the family and to the crew.

"You're thinking about Jeremy, aren't you?" Ashley asked quietly.

"Yes, I guess I am."

"I'm sorry I hurt you by kissing Jeremy that night."

Kate waved her hand dismissively. "I knew it was nothing, even then. Maybe momentarily I saw red, but I knew you and I knew him. The stress of the situation was getting to all of us." Kate turned to Caroline. "And just because Jeremy took off his safety harness to check on you, Caroline, doesn't mean you were responsible for him not putting it back on when he came on deck. Besides that, neither of you had anything to do with the argument between Jeremy and Dad. I'm the one who created the situation. If I hadn't asked Jeremy to come onboard, none of it would have happened."

"But he might have died that night, anyway, on the *Betsy Marie*," Caroline said. "Who knows what would have happened? If he would have survived along with K.C., or if he would have drowned with the others."

"I know what you're saying. I've thought of that a thousand times, but—"

"But it always has to be about you." Caroline gave Kate a smile that took the edge off her words. "Some things are just fate, accidents, circumstance. Some things you can't control, no matter how hard you try."

Kate let out a sigh. "Lord, what a long day it's been." She checked her watch and realized it was almost eleven o'clock. It was quieter now, too. Glancing out the window, she could see moonlight. The storm had passed as quickly as it had come.

"I could really use a drink right now," Caroline said. Then she added quickly, "Relax, Kate, I was thinking along the lines of some tea or hot chocolate with marshmallows."

"I agree." Ashley stood up. "I'll make the hot chocolate."

"I think there are marshmallows in the cabinet," Kate said as her sisters headed toward the kitchen. "And cookies, too, if you're hungry."

Kate sat back in the chair as her sisters left the room. She appreciated the momentary peace and quiet. She needed to think about all that had happened. And she probably needed to start thinking about what to do next, how to deal with the consequences of their confession. But not now. Maybe tomorrow.

The doorbell rang, putting an end to her ruminations. She got to her feet, knowing it was Tyler even before she opened the door. She just didn't know what on earth they would say to each other now.

Tyler had changed into dry blue jeans and a gray sweater. His hair was still damp, his face red from a long day in the wind.

"Hi," she said softly, not sure how to greet him this time. "I didn't think you'd be back this soon."

"But you knew I'd be back," he said without smiling.

"I figured. Do you want to come in?"

"Where's your dad? Your sisters?" he asked as he stepped inside.

"My dad is asleep in my bed, and my sisters are foraging for food and drinks in the kitchen." She led him into the living room and took a seat on the sofa. She could hardly believe she'd made love to this man in this very room only twenty-four hours earlier. She'd lain naked in his arms, been as intimate with him as anyone in her life, but now he seemed almost a stranger. The day's events had put a distance between them that she wasn't sure how to cross. "I guess you finally got your story."

"I guess I did." He sat down on the chair by the coffee table and stared at her for a long moment. "Duncan told me about Jeremy. He even called me Jeremy at one point. He said we were a lot alike." He offered her a grim smile. "Of course, that didn't make me feel any better when I realized he'd shoved Jeremy overboard in the middle of a storm."

"It wasn't like that. It was an argument that got out of control."

Tyler leaned forward, resting his elbows on his knees. "Okay, let's say I buy that. Duncan gave Jeremy a shove, and he ended up in the water. In the confusion, Duncan was only able to save you, his daughter, and not Jeremy. A terrible choice for any father."

"Don't you think I've kicked myself a hundred times for jumping in that water? If I hadn't, if I'd kept my cool, maybe I could have gotten the line to Jeremy, or my Dad and I together could have found a way to save him."

"Not if he was unconscious, which he apparently was. He wouldn't have been able to grab a line. Your only hope was to jump in after him. You didn't have time to think about all that, but instinctively you knew it was the right thing to do. And very brave, too," he added quietly. "I can't even imagine having a woman love me enough to jump into a raging sea to save me. Jeremy must have been a hell of a guy."

"He was, but I would have gone in after *you* tonight, Tyler, if Sean hadn't done it. I let him because I thought he was stronger, and I didn't want to make the same mistake as last time. I didn't want to cause a bigger problem, with Sean having to rescue me instead of you and Dad."

"I know you would have jumped in, Kate. Your bravery has never been in question." He paused. "Only your judgment. Why did you cover it up? Because your father cheated during the race? Because Jeremy had something on him? What? What was the reason?"

She could have told him that it hadn't started out as a cover-up, that they'd just let people believe what they already believed, that Jeremy had died going down on the *Betsy Marie,* but was that really the truth? Or just the truth she'd told to herself? Hadn't a part of her always known that things hadn't been done quite right, that if there was an investigation, her father might be in serious trouble?

"It was family loyalty," she replied finally. "I was afraid my father might go to jail."

"Because Jeremy didn't just fall overboard. He was pushed. And if the cheating came out, what was an accident could have looked like murder. So you chose to protect him."

"Yes, I did," she said fiercely. "Ashley and Caroline, too. I was the oldest. I had to watch out for all of us. And he was our father, the only parent we had left."

"How could you look Jeremy's parents in the eye? How could you look Sean in the eye, knowing what you knew?"

"Weeks passed before that happened. His parents were notified by the race officials long before we ever got home. In fact, they held Jeremy's funeral and placed his headstone before we sailed back into the harbor. They had come to terms with what happened, believing that he'd gone down with the ship, that he'd died heroically trying to save others on the boat. The

Mayday calls painted those sailors as heroes. It was easier to let it be, to leave it alone. It was too late to tell the truth. Jeremy was dead, whether he'd died off of our boat or not."

Tyler frowned. "Do you really believe that, Kate? Do you really believe you were right?"

She met his gaze and saw the sharp, ruthless pursuit of the truth in his eyes. "Not completely," she admitted. "But I wasn't thinking clearly at the time. I did love Jeremy. I was emotionally distraught when he drowned. I couldn't believe it at first. I thought it was a horrible nightmare. But I couldn't wake up, and every time I closed my eyes I saw Jeremy's head going under the water. I felt his hand slipping out of mine." She took a breath, emotion threatening to overwhelm her. "I've seen two people die, two people that I loved very much. I guess I didn't want to lose anyone else."

"Like your father?"

"Like my father," she agreed. "I can say I'm sorry, but it won't change the facts. I lied, whether it was by omission or not. I am sorry, though. I didn't realize how one lie could spiral so far out of control, how our lives would be forever influenced by that one hasty decision."

"You must have been worried that K.C. would recover his memory. He knew Jeremy hadn't been onboard his boat. That must have given you some sleepless nights. He could have recovered his memory at any time and blown the whistle on you all. In fact, your father thinks he does remember, that's why he's come back now."

"Then why hasn't he said anything?"

"I have no idea. Maybe he's waiting for the right moment." Tyler paused. "Your father wanted to die out there tonight. He gave up. He knew you weren't going to race with him on Saturday. He knew he wouldn't ever get the *Moon Dancer* back. He was going to let us drown."

His words horrified her. "Oh, my God, Tyler! I had

no idea. I just thought the storm came up too fast or he drank too much and couldn't get the sails going right. I didn't know he quit on you. That's a first. McKennas don't quit," she said with a bitter sadness. "You don't know how many times I've heard those words spoken."

"But you don't quit, do you?" Tyler sent her a hard look that she didn't understand.

"What do you mean?" she asked hesitantly, sensing his anger had just gone up a notch and not sure what had triggered it.

"I just want to know one thing, Kate. Why, after screwing up your own family, did you go looking to screw up someone else's family?"

"Who are you talking about? Jeremy's family, the Ambersons?"

"No."

"You mean, you?" Kate asked in confusion. "You mean, why—why did I sleep with you?"

"I mean, why did you go looking for the child you gave up eight years ago?"

Kate's breath fled from her chest as the last secret came to the surface. "You know about the baby? My father told you that, too?"

"He didn't have to. That baby is my niece. Her name is Amelia. She was adopted by my brother, Mark, in Hawaii eight years ago. She has a locket with Nora McKenna's name on it."

Kate put a hand to her heart. She'd never expected this. "Amelia? Her name is Amelia?"

"That's right. And she's happy, healthy, and she loves her father."

"What about her . . . her adoptive mother?"

"You mean her *real* mother—the one who took care of her, stayed up with her at night, that woman?" His voice was unforgiving. "What does it matter, Kate? You gave your baby up. You can't have her back." He shook his head. "I still can't believe you did it. But Jeremy was dead, so it all makes sense now. He came onboard to be with you when you had the baby. After he died, you couldn't bear the thought of keeping his child. So you gave it away. You pretended it had never happened, just like everything else you denied."

"You must think I'm a terrible person," Kate murmured, seeing the hardness in his eyes.

"I think you've had second thoughts and decided to hire a shark attorney to get your daughter back, but you can't have her. I have enough on all of you to thwart any efforts to take back Amelia. So don't even try."

"You have enough . . ." Her voice trailed away as her brain finally caught up. "You came here to find your niece's mother, not to do a story about us winning the Winston, didn't you?"

"That's right, Kate. I couldn't care less about the damn race. I only care about what happens to Amelia. I won't let you take her away without a fight."

Kate snapped her fingers. "That's why you took that medical bill from Ashley's apartment. And you mentioned that you thought Caroline had a drinking problem. You were collecting evidence. What about me? What did you find out about me when you made love to me last night?" A terrible pain stabbed at her heart as she realized the truth depth of his deceit.

For the first time, Tyler looked guilty. "Last night wasn't about Amelia. It was about us, but we both knew there were secrets between us."

"Yes, we both knew," she said wearily. Her heart was as heavy as a stone.

His eyes softened just for a minute. "Why couldn't you tell me, Kate?"

"I didn't even know that was your question. I thought you were probing into what happened during the race. I had to protect my family."

"And I have to protect mine. I'm sorry if it hurts, but you made the decision to give your baby up. Now let her be."

"It wasn't Kate's decision, it was mine."

Tyler turned to the woman standing in the doorway. "What did you say?"

"She isn't the mother. I am."

Chapter Twenty-four

Tyler was stunned to see Caroline standing in the doorway. Caroline? No. That wasn't right. Kate was the mother. It had to be Kate. Kate and Jeremy. Was this just another ploy to confuse him? The McKenna sisters sticking together, no matter what?

"That's right, Tyler," Caroline repeated with a forcefulness he couldn't ignore. "I'm the one who got pregnant and gave up a child." Caroline walked into the room, her head up, her step purposeful.

"You? But I don't understand," Tyler said. "You were only—"

"Sixteen years old." Caroline held up a hand as Kate started to interrupt. "It's okay, Kate. I want to tell him. I want to be done with the secrets. It's true. I had a baby, and I gave her away."

"Willingly?" Tyler asked. "Or did your father make the decision for you?"

"It was a combination of both," Caroline said tightly.

Not exactly what he wanted to hear, but close enough. "Then you had no business hiring an attorney to go after my brother. Do you know what kind of pain and turmoil you've caused by threatening to take away his child? Do you have any idea what it's like to spend eight years loving and raising a daughter only to find out that the birth mother suddenly wants a second chance?"

Caroline appeared shocked by his comments. Her eyes had grown wider with each word. Was it all an act? Or had she just not considered the consequences of her actions?

"I didn't," she said finally. "I didn't threaten to take her away."

"Your hotshot attorney did."

"Steve? He must have done that on his own."

"You hired an attorney?" Kate asked. "When did you decide to do that? Why didn't you tell me?"

So Kate didn't know about the attorney. For some reason, that made Tyler feel better. Maybe if Kate had known, she would have advised Caroline not to do it. Maybe there was still some hope that he and Kate might wind up on the same side.

"What's going on?" Ashley asked, returning to the room with a tray of hot drinks. "Don't tell me something else is wrong."

"Tyler came here to find out which one of us gave up a baby," Kate answered her sister. "I can't believe that possibility never even crossed my mind."

"You were too busy covering up the Jeremy story," Tyler said. "Ironic, isn't it?"

"Sorry, I'm a little too tired to appreciate the irony." Kate paused. "His brother adopted the baby," she added for Ashley's benefit.

"I think I'd better sit down." Ashley put the tray down on the coffee table and took a seat on the couch next to Kate. Caroline sat down on the other side of her big sister. They were a united front, but Tyler wasn't intimidated.

"I'd really like to know how you became pregnant with Amelia," he said.

"Amelia? Is that her name?" An eager light blossomed in Caroline's eyes.

"Answer the question."

"Don't interrogate her," Kate said sharply. "She's not on trial here."

"It's okay," Caroline said. "I want to tell. In fact, I've been dying to talk about the baby, but I knew I couldn't talk about it with Kate or Ashley."

"Why not?" Kate and Ashley asked at the same time.

Caroline looked at both of them and shook her head. "Because we never talk about the past, especially that night."

"We didn't want to cause you more pain," Kate said. "We figured if you wanted to talk about it, you would."

"To answer your question," Caroline said, turning her attention back to Tyler, "I was a little wild back then. I started drinking on the boat, swiping some of my dad's stuff, and it was easy enough to drink on-shore, too. I just sat by my dad at the bar, and people were always willing to give me sips of this and that. Kate and Ashley tried to keep the reins on me, but I was a rebellious teenager, and we were living like gypsies. One night I got into trouble. I wound up going further than I wanted to. It wasn't like rape or anything," she added quickly. "I let things get out of control. I didn't try to stop until it was too late. The worst thing is that I didn't even know his name or who he was."

"I'm sorry," Tyler said sincerely. Despite Caroline's brave words, he had a feeling the night had been more traumatic than she was saying. "That must have been a terrible night for you."

"Thanks for saying that. It was."

"How could you keep it a secret? That's what I don't understand. Didn't anyone see you?"

"We wore heavy weather gear a lot of the time," Caroline explained. "And once I was showing, I didn't really go off the boat much. Besides that, I was a teenager in great shape. I wasn't eating that much. We were racing. We were working hard. I didn't even know I was pregnant until I was five months along."

"That doesn't seem possible," he said.

"It was, believe me. My periods weren't that regular. I never threw up. And if I felt queasy, I just chalked it up to being on a bouncing boat. But my growing stomach finally got my attention, and I had to tell Kate and Ashley that I thought I might be pregnant."

"It must have been some conversation," Tyler commented, looking over at Kate.

"It was pretty scary," she replied. "Caroline was so young, and I wasn't that much older. I had no idea what we were going to do."

"Kate bought me a pregnancy test at the next stop, and we found out for sure," Caroline continued. "Kate thought we should drop out of the race."

"Of course you should have dropped out of the race," Tyler said sharply. "What did your father say when you told him?"

"He said no," Kate replied, answering for Caroline. "Caroline wasn't due to deliver until after we got back, and at the moment we were in second place. We were very close to everything he'd dreamed about. Later, I discovered that there was some money involved in the race, some creative financing that my father had done."

"With your mutual funds and your mother's jewelry," Tyler said with a nod. "He told me about that."

"You had quite a chat out there, didn't you?"

"It's amazing what a man will say when he thinks he won't see tomorrow. But, let's get back to a pregnant teenage girl on a world-class racing boat with only her father and sisters to take care of her. You were miles from land at times, days from help. What if something had gone wrong? What would you have done?"

"I don't know," Kate answered. "It's easy to look back now and say we were crazy, but you don't realize how powerless we all felt. My father was in charge. Caroline was underage. I couldn't take her and run away, even if I wanted to. I didn't have any money. We'd been living on a boat for more than two and a half years. I had to listen to Dad. I didn't have another choice. None of us did."

"Why keep it a secret? Would it have disqualified you?"

"No, but Dad didn't want Caroline to be the focus of a lot of unwanted attention. He was protecting her."

"Bullshit!" Tyler leaned forward. "He didn't tell anyone because he didn't want to lose the spotlight. He didn't want the press to be sidetracked by a pregnant teenage girl hard-luck story. Isn't that the truth?"

"Yes, that's the truth," Ashley said, speaking for the first time. "Dad was obsessed with that race. He was a different person during those eleven months. He wouldn't let anything get in the way of winning. I don't remember having one conversation with him that didn't include some worry about the course, the sails, the boat speed, or the weather. He was on one track and one track only. When we told him about Caroline, he barely blinked. His response was 'All right, we'll deal with that later, when we get home. Right now we have a race to win.' "

"Dad didn't want to deal with the fact that Caroline was pregnant," Kate added. "He knew he was responsible for what happened, for not keeping a better eye on her, and I think he felt guilty about that, even though he didn't say so. I believe that deep in his heart he felt he'd let Caroline down."

"Really? Do you think so?" Caroline asked. "Do you think he felt bad? Because he always seemed angry. Then he got distant and pulled away from me until we barely spoke. I figured he was just so disappointed he could barely stand to look at me."

Tyler couldn't believe what he was hearing. Actually, he could believe it. Having spent the day with

Duncan, he now had a better understanding of just how difficult and complicated a man he could be. He was extremely likable at times, and a real bastard at others. "So, your father wouldn't let you tell anyone. He made Caroline hide away on the boat and swore you all to secrecy."

"He did buy me a stack of baby magazines and baby books," Caroline said.

"Bully for him." Tyler shook his head in disgust. "He didn't treat you right, Caroline. He should have made sure you had proper medical care. He should have tracked down the boy who got you pregnant. There were a hundred things he should have done that he didn't do, and you all know it. But you're still protecting him, even now."

"You don't know him as well as we do," Caroline said with a soft plea in her eyes. "He could be a great dad at times. He could be the best time you ever had."

"But mostly he was a terrible dad and the worst time we ever had," Ashley said. "Don't you agree, Kate?"

Tyler waited for Kate to speak. He had a feeling her viewpoint fell somewhere in the middle of theirs.

"He's our father, Tyler. And you're judging our actions eight years after the fact. In retrospect, things always look a lot more clear than they did at the time," Kate said.

"I'll give you that," he conceded. "Tell me about the birth. It must have happened right after the storm. Was it after you got to port?" The three sisters exchanged looks that made him even more curious. "Well?" he prodded.

"I went into labor during the storm," Caroline said. "I don't know if it was the stress or the fear or whatever, but there it was. I started having contractions about ten minutes into the storm. That's why I stayed down in the cabin. I was in a lot of pain. Jeremy kept coming back and forth to check on me."

"Jeremy," Tyler echoed, realizing this was another

piece of the puzzle. He turned to Kate. "You wanted him on board to help you with Caroline and the baby in case it came earlier."

"That was part of it," Kate admitted. "I was scared. Caroline had been having some smaller contractions, and while it didn't seem possible she would deliver that early, I was worried something might happen. My father wasn't seeing very clearly back then. I couldn't even talk to him about it."

"When did the baby come and who delivered her?"

"She was born at dawn, and it was a group effort," Kate replied. "Ashley did the most. She'd read all the books. Frankly, I was still in shock from losing Jeremy to be much of a help. Dad was around, too. Jeremy's death had sobered him up quickly. But it was mostly Ashley who talked Caroline through it."

"I can't even imagine that night. First you're fighting for your life, then you lose your fiancé, then your sister goes into labor." He looked at Kate and shook his head in amazement.

Kate gave him a grim smile. "It all happened so fast. In twenty-four hours we saw someone go out of the world and someone come in. It was almost surreal. That morning was eerily quiet. The sun seemed to mock everything we'd gone through, as if we'd imagined that awful storm, as if it had all been a bad dream. But Jeremy's things were on his bunk, and he wasn't coming back to get them. And Caroline was holding her baby in her arms as we limped into port, ravaged, exhausted, overwhelmed." Kate's voice petered out, and Tyler saw Ashley put a hand on her sister's knee. Then she looked at Tyler and continued the story.

"When we got to Hawaii the next day, there were lots of reporters waiting," Ashley said. "We were one of the first boats to arrive. But already news had spread like wildfire that the *Betsy Marie* had gone down. That's all anyone was talking about. Dad went out first and gave interviews. Then he sent Kate and me out to run interference. As long as the news people could talk to the 'girls,' as they liked to call us, they were satisfied. I kept waiting for someone to ask us about the storm, about Jeremy, but no one did. In fact, people came up to Kate, trying to comfort her. A lot of the other crews knew that they had gotten engaged just before the start of the race. It quickly became clear that no one knew Jeremy had switched boats at the last minute."

"And you didn't tell them?"

"No, we didn't."

"Dad took me to the hospital to get me checked out," Caroline said. "Actually, it wasn't a hospital. It was a clinic, I think. I don't remember, exactly. I do remember the doctor telling Dad that he knew someone who would love to take the baby." She drew in a deep, emotional breath at the memory. "I gave her one last hug and said good-bye, and I put the locket around her neck. I wanted her to have something of mine, and that locket was given to me by my mother." Caroline paused. "I cried for three days straight."

"We all did," Kate added. "I wanted to help Caroline raise the baby. I didn't want to let her go, but my father convinced Caroline that it wouldn't work. Maybe if Jeremy hadn't just died, maybe if the race had been over and we'd been home, I would have been able to make him see that we couldn't give Caroline's baby away. She was part of our family. But that wasn't how it was, and when Caroline came back to the hotel room alone, we didn't know where the baby had gone or who had adopted her. The decision had been made, and we would have to live with it."

"Exactly. So what happened three weeks ago, Caroline?" Tyler demanded. "What made you decide to try and take your baby back now?"

"I didn't decide to take her back. I just wanted to know if she was all right. That's all. I swear."

"Your attorney—"

"My attorney is a friend of a friend. I don't know

what he told you or what he did, but all I asked him to do was to see if he could find out if my baby was okay. You see, a few weeks ago, I came to terms with the fact that I have a drinking problem. I went to AA and listened to all the talk about taking responsibility for your actions and saying you're sorry and all that. That's when I decided that I needed to know that the baby was all right." Caroline looked at Tyler with her heart in her eyes. "Is she all right, Tyler?"

Tyler hesitated, knowing he was about to take a step his brother probably would not want him to take, but he was leaning toward believing Caroline's story. She had no reason to lie to him now. She could just have easily told him that she thought her baby had been taken illegally, and she wanted to get her back. But Caroline seemed genuine in her concern and remorse. "Yes," he said finally. "Amelia is fine. She's a happy and healthy little girl. But she did suffer a huge tragedy a month ago when her mother was killed in a car accident."

Caroline put a hand to her mouth in horror. "Oh, no."

"My brother, Mark, was badly injured, but Amelia was fine. A few scratches, that's it. I'm only telling you this because I believe you when you say you don't want to hurt Amelia. She doesn't know she's adopted. She doesn't know anything about you. She loves her father, and she misses her mother, and the last thing she needs is to find out she's adopted. Not right now, anyway. Not while her world is so shaky."

"I understand," Caroline said. "What is she like? Is she pretty?"

Tyler smiled. "Yeah, she's pretty." He reached into his pocket and pulled out his wallet. "Would you like to see a picture?"

"Would I ever."

Tyler took a photograph from the wallet and handed it to Caroline. "That's last year's school picture."

"Oh, my God!" Caroline whispered. "Is that really her?"

"She's you, Caroline," Kate murmured.

"Only the best parts of me, I hope." Caroline traced Amelia's sweet face with her finger. "She's real, isn't she? Sometimes I lie in bed at night and think I imagined the whole thing. But then I remember how it used to feel when she'd kick me, first a little flutter, then I could actually feel her toes or her fist. I'd never experienced anything like that, never done anything so incredible as I did the day I gave birth to her. She was my greatest achievement and yet my worst failure."

"No," Tyler said. "You didn't fail. She already means so much to a lot of people. She's bright, loving, kind, smart. You would be very proud of her."

"Because of your brother," Caroline said. "I wish I could thank him."

"Why didn't your brother come himself?" Kate asked.

"He's still rehabilitating from the accident," Tyler answered. "And he didn't want to leave Amelia at home or bring her here."

Kate nodded, a gleam of understanding in her eyes. "In case one of us recognized her. Just out of curiosity, why was your brother so worried? I mean, he adopted her legally and all."

Damn Kate for being so smart, so perceptive.

"It was legal, wasn't it?" she continued.

"Close enough."

"I don't think so, or you wouldn't have come here. I'm not surprised things were done in an underhanded way. After all, my father was involved."

"Look, Mark might have played loose with the rules, but, like you said, so did your father. You can be assured that Mark and his wife, Susan, desperately wanted a baby. And they loved Amelia from the first second they saw her. They devoted themselves to her.

She has had a very good life. Mark only became worried because of his wife's death and his injuries. He didn't think any of that would help if your sister came calling. He was afraid that whoever was looking for the child would use the accident to her advantage in trying to overturn the adoption. I didn't think that could happen, but I wasn't sure, and Mark wasn't willing to take the chance."

"So your whole reason for being here was to find out which one of us was Amelia's mother. There was never any story, was there?" Ashley asked.

"No, that was just my way of getting to meet you. All we knew was that one of the McKenna sisters was the mother. We didn't know which one. And frankly, Caroline, this jerk of an attorney that you hired made it absolutely clear that you wanted your baby back. I couldn't just come out and ask which one of you had a baby. I was afraid it would lead you straight to Mark, and I needed to find out who you were and what you wanted before that happened."

"I understand," Caroline said. "I didn't mean to cause such turmoil. I know it's too late for me to be Amelia's mother. I won't try to take her away. I won't even try to see her. I just want to know about her, if that's okay."

Before he could reply, he was interrupted by Kate, who now had a very purposeful look in her eyes. "You lied," Kate said. "Or omitted the truth. Amazing how easy that can be, isn't it, when you're trying to protect someone you love."

"It's not the same. We're not the same." He got to his feet, feeling suddenly restless and edgy. He'd known it would come back to him and Kate. The race, the baby, all of that had been explained, but not what had happened between them.

"Aren't we?" Kate asked as she stood up to face him. "Wouldn't we both do just about anything for our families?"

"I didn't cover up a murder."

"It wasn't a murder. It was an accident. And you were willing to cover up an illegal adoption."

"It wasn't illegal. It was just not done quite as properly as it should have been done."

"You're making excuses."

"So are you."

"Why did you sleep with me?" she demanded.

"Why did you sleep with me?" he returned.

Their heated exchange sent sparks flying between them. Kate couldn't look away. Tyler couldn't, either.

"I don't think you need us anymore," Caroline said.

Tyler was dimly aware of Ashley and Caroline leaving the room. His entire focus was on Kate.

"Answer the question," he said.

"I asked you first."

He saw a flicker of uncertainty in her eyes then and knew that the time for half-truths and evasions had long passed. "I made love to you for one reason, Kate, and one reason only. I wanted you more than I've ever wanted a woman in my life. You got under my skin, into my head. I couldn't stop thinking about you. I told myself not to get distracted, but every time I saw you that thought flew right out the window."

"That can't be true," she said.

He saw the indecision, the reluctance to believe him. She'd told him once before that she couldn't distinguish a lie from a truth, and he could see it was happening now. But he had to make her believe him. One thing he'd learned out there on the water was that he didn't want to die without telling her how he felt about her.

"It is true," he said again. "I love you, Kate. I fell in love with you probably the first time I saw you. I didn't know it then. I didn't know it last night, if you want to know the truth. But I knew it today, when I thought the world might end. I finally saw what meant the most to me, and it was you." She blinked rapidly, moisture pooling in her beautiful blue eyes. "Believe me, Kate. Please."

"I want to," she whispered. "But how can I believe anything you say when you've lied to me the whole time you've been here?"

"Not the whole time. Not the times I kissed you, not last night when we made love. That was the real me, Kate."

"But you came here to discredit me. Maybe this is still part of the plan, to make the oldest sister believe you love her so she won't put up a fight."

He shook his head. "No, Kate. The desire to do you wrong left a long time ago. You have to understand that when I came here, you were just a name in a news article, a picture on a magazine cover. I didn't know you. But I did know my brother and Amelia. I knew how much they had suffered. I knew how much they loved each other. I couldn't let anyone hurt them. Especially Mark. He had just lost his wife, the woman he loved more than anyone in the world. You know how that feels, don't you? You, more than anyone, know how that feels."

"Yes, I know," she admitted.

"Mark threatened to leave. He said he'd take Amelia and disappear before he'd give her up. I didn't want that life for her, the kind of life I had led, always on the run, always hiding from someone."

"So you set out to ruin each one of us. And we made it so easy."

"You didn't. I had nothing on you. You were smart and caring, kind and compassionate, beautiful, nurturing, loyal to a fault." He reached out, unable to hold himself back from touching her. Her soft hair drifted through his fingers, and he rested his hands on her shoulders. "I couldn't think of one reason why you wouldn't be a terrific mother. You're an incredible woman. Don't you know that?"

"Keep talking."

He smiled, sensing the battle was half won. "All I could think about on the water today was getting back to you, asking you to forgive me."

"I don't think I've actually heard the words."

"Will you forgive me, Kate?"

She made him wait a long, tense moment, then her lips, her beautiful, generous lips curved into a tender smile. "Yes, I'll forgive you. I love you, too, Tyler. That's why I made love to you last night, even though there was more to be discovered between us. Deep down inside, I knew you were a good man. Maybe you weren't being completely honest, but then I hardly hold the title for honesty myself."

"What else did you know?" he asked, teasing her cheek with a soft kiss. He liked the way she caught her breath, and he did it again, just to hear that small sound.

"I knew— You're distracting me, Tyler."

His tongue swept the curve of her ear. "I'm listening, Kate."

"I knew you could make me feel like this, crazy, reckless—not that those are necessarily good things, but they sure feel good," she said with a sigh. "You make me laugh, and you make me think about the future, and I've never let myself think about the future. Not in a long time. I'm not proposing or anything," she added with a nervous laugh. "It's too soon for that."

She kissed him again, and he wrapped his arms around her, pulling her up against him until he could feel every inch of her. Only it wasn't enough. It would never be enough. "Did you say your father was in your bed?" he grumbled.

She grinned. "Yes, and my sisters are in the kitchen."

"This house is way too crowded, but I know where there's a hotel room with lots of privacy."

"Will you show me?"

"Oh, I'll show you lots of things." He grabbed her by the hand and pulled her toward the door.

"Tyler, wait, I need my purse, my coat, my—" He cut her off with a deep, passionate kiss.

"Hey, where are you two going?" Ashley asked as she and Caroline came out of the kitchen.

Tyler swept Kate up into his arms. "She'll see you tomorrow," he told them. "We have a few things to discuss in private."

"You're leaving us with Dad?" Caroline asked in shock. "You can't leave us with Dad."

Kate laughed. "As a matter of fact, I can. Good night."

Tyler kicked the door shut behind them and looked down into Kate's smiling face. "You're okay with this, right?"

"I'm more than okay. I'm madly in love, and tonight is ours. Tomorrow I'll worry about tomorrow."

"Well, what do you think of that?" Caroline asked in dismay. "Kate just runs off with the sexy reporter when we've got a huge mess on our hands."

"Sounds like something you would do," Ashley replied.

Caroline didn't appreciate the smug look in Ashley's eyes. "Very funny. Do you think it's serious between them?"

"I hope so. I haven't seen Kate look so happy in a long time."

"It would be great if they got together, because then I'd have a chance to know Amelia, not as her mother but as her aunt. Wouldn't that be cool? Not that I don't want Kate just to be happy, but this could work out well for everyone."

"Certainly for you," Ashley said, but she smiled to take the sting out of her words. "I hope you do get to know Amelia. That would be very cool."

"Amelia is beautiful, didn't you think? Like Mom."

"Like you."

"Thanks. That's nice to hear." Caroline's eyes narrowed when she saw Ashley glance at her watch, then

the door, then her watch again. "Where are you thinking of going?"

"I want to talk to Sean."

"Maybe you should let him cool off."

"That would probably be smart, but I feel like time
has never been on our side, and maybe waiting would
be more of a mistake." Ashley opened the hall closet
and took out one of Kate's coats. "I'm going to bor-
row this. I'll see you tomorrow."

"Tomorrow?" Caroline echoed in alarm. "Hey, you
can't leave me here with Dad."

"You always wanted to be his favorite," Ashley told
her. "Now is your chance."

Before Caroline could reply that both of her sisters
were being totally unfair, Ashley was gone. The house
was suddenly quiet, too quiet. Caroline was alone.
Well, not exactly alone. Her gaze turned down the
hall toward Kate's bedroom. Maybe she should check
on her dad, make sure he was all right.

She walked down the hall and pushed open the door
to see her father asleep in Kate's bed. His face was
red, his hair still damp, but he appeared to be sleeping,
breathing normally. It suddenly occurred to her that
everything her father owned was gone. Even his favorite cap had sunk into the Sound. All he had were the
few items of clothing he'd left at Kate's house over
the years. The rest of it had disappeared into the sea.

She walked farther into the room and sat down on
the rocking chair next to the bed. She wondered if he
was dreaming or reliving the experiences of the day.
His breathing seemed to have quickened, and his chest
was moving up and down more rapidly. Whatever he
was thinking about was disturbing him in some way.
She was tempted to put her hand on his shoulder and
tell him to relax, that everything would be all right.

Weren't those the very same words he'd told her
when the pain of labor had grown too much to bear?
When she hadn't thought she could go on? He'd held
her hand the morning Amelia had been born. He'd

cut the umbilical cord and held his grandchild in his arms. There had been something in his eyes that morning, something that looked like love, but still he'd taken them both to the hospital and given away her child. She'd hated him for it. But she'd loved him, too, because he'd taken care of her after that, and he'd told her how proud he was of her, how strong she had been. For the first time in a long time, she'd felt worthy of his love.

She'd jumped right back into the race, helping them finish in first place. She didn't really know how they had sailed that last leg. She had been weak and hurting. Kate had been grieving. Ashley had been traumatized by seeing Jeremy die. But somehow they had pulled through for this man—this man who wouldn't let them quit, who aroused so many mixed emotions in their hearts.

Her father's breathing caught, changed, and then he turned over on his back. His eyes opened as he awoke. "Where? Where am I?" he asked in a thick, slow voice.

"You're at Kate's house." Caroline pulled her chair closer to the bed. "I'm here if you need anything."

"Where's Kate?"

Caroline should have figured that would be his first question. "Kate is sleeping with Tyler at his hotel, I imagine. Any other questions?" She supposed she could have sugarcoated it, but why bother? They'd told too many lies already.

Duncan sighed wearily. "She's angry with me, isn't she?"

"For almost killing her second love? Yeah, I'd say she's angry. By the way, Ashley and I aren't too happy about what happened, either. Not that you care."

He turned his head to look at her, and for a long moment he didn't say anything. The silence almost undid her. It made her want to jump into speech, offer an apology for whatever needed to be apologized for so he wouldn't be angry. But she forced herself not to speak, not to give in. She wasn't in the wrong. He was.

"I didn't set out to hurt anyone," he said.

"You never do, but somehow people always seem to get hurt."

"You most of all."

"Yes," she agreed. "The worst time was when you took my baby out of my arms and gave her away to that doctor. You ripped my heart in two that day. I wasn't sure I'd ever feel whole again."

"Hardest thing I ever did. I knew I should have let you keep her. Nora must have turned over in her grave when she saw me give our grandchild away." He shook his head. "But I was barely keeping us afloat. I didn't think we could manage a baby, too. And you were just a kid yourself."

"It wasn't about that. It was about the race. You didn't want to stop, and if I'd kept the baby, we would have had to stop. It took me a long time to realize that was the real reason I had to give her up." She paused. "It's over, you know. Tyler knows everything, and Sean, too. By morning the rest of the world will be talking."

"You all should have let me drown out there tonight."

"That would have been too easy," she said sharply.

His gaze flew to hers. "Now, you listen, young lady—"

"No, you're going to listen to me for a change. You made some huge mistakes in your life, and it looks like you'll have to pay for some of them, just like I've had to pay for giving up my child, and Kate for losing Jeremy, and Ashley for having to lie to Sean. You don't get to drink yourself into oblivion anymore. You have to face the consequences of what happened. Maybe that means we give back the trophy and pay back the money. Hopefully, that's all it means. But we need to move on, and we can't be worrying about you every second, especially Kate. She's in love with

Tyler, and she deserves a chance to start over. So you're going to have to pull yourself together and fast." She looked him straight in the eye. "We need a father, and you're it. Starting tomorrow, you're going to start acting like a father. But tonight you get to sleep."

Caroline smiled as her father's eyes drifted shut. He probably wouldn't remember their conversation, but she would. She'd meant every word—words she should have said a long time ago. Now the dam had burst. Little did her sisters and father know that from here on out, she probably wouldn't shut up.

No more going along with the family. She was standing up for herself. She would stop drinking, keep working, and find a way to be proud of herself—and hope that someday her daughter, Amelia, might be proud of her, too.

Ashley walked down the damp, dark streets of Castleton wondering if this would be the last time she spoke to Sean, or if she would even have the chance to speak to him. Would he send her away without a word? Would there be only anger and hatred in his eyes? She deserved nothing more than that. She just wanted a chance to say she was sorry.

Doubting that he would have gone home to his parents' house just yet, she went back to the marina, hoping he'd be on the boat. She suspected he would need time to think about how to tell his parents what had really happened to Jeremy. Besides that, it was past midnight; his mom and dad were probably asleep.

As she walked down the dock, she thought how odd it was that everything was quiet now. No more wind, no more rain. The storm had passed. Just like that.

Ashley climbed onto the Ambersons' motorboat without a second thought for the water below. That fear had been well and truly vanquished. She realized now that it was never really the water she'd been afraid of, but all the things buried beneath it, like

Jeremy's death and Caroline's baby, her father's lies, their cover-up. She'd been terrified all the secrets would come up and hurt them all, so she'd stayed away from the water. Now the secrets were out, and the water was just water.

She walked down the stairs to the cabin and found Sean sitting on the couch, a bottle of beer in one hand. He'd changed into an old sweatshirt and a pair of jeans. But it was his face that had changed the most. There were new lines in his forehead, new shadows under his eyes, and a new hardness in his gaze.

"Can I come in?" she asked.

"Looks like you're already in." He took a swig of his beer.

She sat down on the edge of the couch, careful to keep some space between them. "I wanted to tell you I was sorry."

"Yeah, well, it's a little late, isn't it?"

"Yes. But I still mean it." She paused, not sure what to say now that she had a chance to say it. "Jeremy—"

"I don't want to hear any more lies about Jeremy," he said sharply.

"What about some truths?" she challenged. When he didn't reply, she continued, "Jeremy spent the last day of his life doing what he'd always done, taking care of Kate and her family."

"He shouldn't have been with you."

"I know, but he was. He was with the woman he loved, Sean. Those days before the storm hit were good ones for both of them. They were finally together. They'd wanted to be together for so long. I'm glad they had that time. And I think Jeremy was, too."

"He shouldn't have died."

"You're right. He shouldn't have died. He didn't deserve to die that night. But it was an accident."

"Your father pushed him."

"Not overboard. They were arguing, yes. And my father shoved Jeremy, but Jeremy hit his head, and the storm did the rest. The water crashing over the boat is what swept Jeremy over the side." She paused, taking a breath as she forced herself to relive that night. "I saw Kate jump into the water after your brother. And I helped my father try to rescue them both. I wish I could have done more. You don't know how much I wish that. I've blamed myself for not trying to get Jeremy while Dad was getting Kate, or not being able to spot Jeremy in the water. If only I'd done something differently, maybe the result wouldn't have been the same. I know Kate feels the same way, and I suspect my father does, too."

"Your father hated Jeremy."

"My father and Jeremy were a lot alike. They lived for the sea. They butted heads because they both cared deeply about what they were doing. Sailing and racing was as much a part of Jeremy as it was a part of my father."

"He still shouldn't have died," Sean repeated with a hitch in his voice. He rubbed a hand across his eyes. "He was so young. He had his whole life ahead of him. And he lost it for what? A stupid sailboat race."

"He didn't think it was stupid. He thought it was the most exciting thing he'd ever done in his life and the most exciting thing he might ever do. We spent a lot of time together at the various ports along the way. Jeremy loved what he was doing. If you don't believe anything else, I hope you'll believe that. He also loved you very much. He talked about you all the time to me. He knew I was missing you." She stumbled over the words as emotions swamped her. "I loved you so much, Sean. The only reason I broke up with you was because I couldn't stand to lie to you. I knew eventually we would come to this point, when you would look at me and know the truth, and you would hate me. It was inevitable."

She paused, wishing he'd say something, but he was staring at his bottle of beer. "Anyway, I just wanted to say I was sorry. I still love you, Sean, but I'm going to leave the island. I'm going away, so you don't have to look at me every day or, worse yet, try to avoid me. I want you to be happy. I really want that." She got to her feet, but he reached out and caught her hand in his. She looked into his eyes and saw what looked like forgiveness and so much more.

"Don't go," he said, pulling her back down on the couch. "Don't ever go." And his mouth covered hers before she could tell him that the last thing she wanted to do was leave.

Kate rolled onto her side and ran her hand down the center of Tyler's chest. His eyes were closed, but she knew he wasn't sleeping. He'd already tensed with the slightest brush of her fingers against his skin. They'd made love twice already, but it wasn't enough. She wanted to feel him inside her again, filling all the empty spaces in her heart and her soul.

"You're living dangerously, Kate," he murmured.

"You may not know this about me, but there was a time when I liked to live dangerously, and I'm beginning to want to do it again." She lifted her head and smiled as he opened first one eye then the other.

"How dangerous are we talking?"

"Really dangerous." She hesitated, not sure he was as ready as she was to talk about the future. "But we can discuss that later."

"Why wait?" he asked. "I'm right here. I'm not going anywhere."

"Maybe not today," she said slowly, "but I suspect soon." She put her head on his chest and closed her eyes, listening to his heart beat steadily beneath her ear. She wished she hadn't said anything. She could feel the tension in his body now, tension she'd created by wanting to talk about the future.

He gently stroked her hair. "Kate?"

"What?"

"I don't know the best way to work things out between us. But I do know that I want to make it work, more than anything."

She lifted her head and turned over on her stomach so she could look him straight in the eye. "I want that, too. I love you."

"I love you back," he said with a gaze so tender, so full of promise, she felt tears in her eyes.

"Wherever you want to live," she said, "I'll go with you. I want you to know that."

"You'd give up this island, your garden, your little house in the hills? You'd give that up for me?"

She didn't answer right away, because she wanted him to know that she was taking this question seriously, that her answer mattered and meant something. She saw his eyes darken with uncertainty. "Yes, I would," she said finally. "I'd give up everything for you. I would have jumped in the water for you tonight, if I'd needed to. I don't want to lose you. If my grip gets too tight, you'll have to let me know."

"I'll be holding on to you just as tightly, Kate." He put his hand behind her head and pulled her close for a kiss. "You're the best thing that ever happened to me. I'm not going to ask you to give up anything for me. We'll find a way to work it out." He kissed her again, then set her aside.

"Hey, that wasn't enough," she complained.

He smiled as he reached for his cell phone on the bedside table. "There's one call I need to make."

"To your brother?"

"Yes, I need to let him know that Caroline is no threat to Amelia. He'll be very relieved."

Kate frowned. "How do you think he'll feel about you being involved with the sister of Amelia's birth mother? That could be complicated."

"He'll deal with it, just as Caroline will. I think Amelia is a lucky little girl to have so many people love her. And hopefully one day she can know the true circumstances of her birth. I think it's important, and I hope Mark will realize it, too. Amelia should know her biological family."

"Even my father?"

Tyler groaned. "Well . . . all right. But, I warn you, I will never sail with that man again. In fact, I may never sail again."

"Fine by me." Kate sat up in bed, wrapping the sheet around her bare body. "Before you make that call, there's something else I wanted to talk to you about."

"What's that?"

"I've been thinking, and this will sound crazy, but I want to race in the Castleton on Saturday and try to win back the *Moon Dancer*." Her words came out in a rush, and she waited for him to say she was a fool, it was a ridiculous idea. But he didn't say anything, he just smiled at her.

"I think that sounds like a terrific idea."

"Really?"

"It's the last bit of unfinished business, isn't it?"

"As long as K.C. has our boat, he'll always be in our lives. I want him out. I want all of the past to be over with." She sighed. "Now I just have to convince Caroline and Ashley to sail with me."

Chapter Twenty-five

"All for one, one for all," Caroline held out her hands to Kate and Ashley as they stood on the dock in front of the *Summer Seas,* the boat they would race against the *Moon Dancer* in just a few minutes. Rick Beardsley had agreed to let them participate in the race around the island with a few of his crew, who would then take the boat on to San Francisco and eventually to Hawaii.

Kate had persuaded her father to sit the race out. Yesterday she'd notified the race officials from the Winston Around-the-World Challenge of the true events of eight years ago. There would be an investigation and probably some type of recompense to be made in terms of the prize money they'd already spent. Kate had no idea where they'd get the money to pay it back or whether her father would suffer any further penalties, but it didn't matter. It was a relief to have it all out in the open.

They'd also faced the Amberson family and had come clean on every detail of the last few days of Jeremy's life. The Ambersons had been understandably furious and hurt, the pain once again as fresh as it had been eight years ago. But hopefully in time they would understand that Jeremy had still died a hero.

He'd come aboard the *Moon Dancer* to help and support the McKenna girls, and he'd done exactly that right up until the last minute.

It didn't take long for the news to race around the island, and gossip and speculation were running rampant. The McKennas had been the talk at every bar and on every boat on the island. But today was a new day. A new race. And, like all good sailors, they weren't looking behind them. Their eyes were fixed on the horizon.

"I can't believe I'm doing this again," Ashley murmured.

"Me, either," Caroline said with a dimpled smile. "But it feels good. I feel good."

"So do I," Kate said.

"That's because you're in love," Caroline teased.

Kate was in love—lust, infatuation, she had it all. She still didn't know what the future would hold. Loving a man like Tyler would no doubt offer its own set of challenges. He was a roamer at heart, and, even though he claimed he wanted roots, she wasn't sure how the reality of island living would fit him. Something else she'd deal with as she went along. She could live anywhere. She knew that now. She no longer needed a place to hide, but a place to live.

"Hello, girls," a familiar voice said.

They turned to see K.C. and David bearing down on them.

"Hello," they said in unison.

"It's been quite a week, hasn't it?" K.C. said, looking at Kate.

"Yes, it has."

"I didn't remember, you know. I almost wish I had. I almost wish my plan had been as devious as you no doubt thought it was," K.C. said. "I realize now that Duncan thought I came back here to torture him with the possibility of revealing the truth. But I just came back to rub his face in the sight of me sailing his boat."

"Not for long," Kate said. "We're going to win it back. The bet still stands, right? Whether my father races or not?"

"Why would you want the *Moon Dancer*? You girls don't want to race or even sail."

"Because it's ours. It's our home, our legacy. My mother would want us to have it."

K.C. met her gaze with a long, serious look of his own. "I wish you luck, then," he said, tipping his head.

"We won't need luck. We're McKennas," Kate called after him, repeating her father's favorite phrase.

"I'm not so sure we don't need luck," Ashley said somewhat darkly. "We haven't raced in eight years. We're a little out of practice."

"That's true, but we're still strong and fit, and, frankly, I think it's ingrained in us, don't you? There was a time when we could do this in our sleep. I'm hoping it comes back. But, if it doesn't, at least we will have tried our best." Kate paused, giving her sister a curious look. "How is Sean?" Ashley blushed and Kate had her answer. "That good, huh?"

"We're working things out."

"I'm so glad."

"I left him a message that we were racing today, but I'm not sure he wants to be a part of it." Ashley looked around. "I thought Dad might come down to see us off. Although he's probably angry with us for finally speaking the truth."

"He is, but he brought a lot of it on himself. He told Tyler quite a bit of it when they were on the boat together. I think in a way he was almost as relieved as we were to speak the truth. At any rate, I told him I didn't want him here today unless he was sober. We have to make some changes in our lives, starting now," Kate added, but since her father was nowhere in sight, she had a feeling he hadn't been able to do as she requested.

"That's a lot to ask."

"It's past time to be asking," Kate said. "It's bad

enough, all the risks he took with us by his side, but I can't forgive him for endangering Tyler's life the way he did. We're not going to lie to one another anymore. We're not going to pretend things are right when they're wrong."

"He may not be capable of changing," Ashley said.

"I know. But I am capable of changing how I deal with him."

"Let's go, girls," Caroline said, waiting for them on deck with two other crew members whom Kate had met the day before. "It's time to get this show on the road."

Kate and Ashley climbed onto the boat, and within minutes they were in the familiar groove of race day preparations.

The starting line was crowded with boats. Kate felt a rush of excitement as the boats jockeyed for position. Then they were off. It was a tight race to the first buoy marker. The boats were neck and neck. There were barely inches between them at times.

The next two hours were exhilarating, exhausting, and renewing. Turn after turn, tack after tack, into the wind with speed and grace. Their lives had come full circle. As they turned and headed for home, the *Moon Dancer* by their side, Kate knew that the victory was theirs.

"Look, Ashley," she said with a wave of her hand. Standing on the bluff were the two most important men in their lives, Tyler and Sean. "They're waiting for us."

"I can't believe it," Ashley said, tears coming to her eyes.

"Me, either." Kate wished there was someone waiting for Caroline, too. But her sister wasn't looking at the bluff; she was concentrating on the finish line. For Caroline, it wasn't about love—it was about the future. She also felt a bittersweet sadness that Duncan wasn't there, but perhaps he couldn't bear to see them race without him. Maybe it was better this way.

They'd finally cut the ties between father and daughters. They were on their own, for better or for worse.

"Stay focused," Caroline said. "We haven't crossed the finish line yet," she added as the *Summer Seas* and the *Moon Dancer* battled back and forth for position.

Kate adjusted the sails and ran the boat boldly and bravely into the wind, remembering who they'd once been and who they would be again.

Epilogue

Ship's log, *Moon Dancer*, July 14
Wind: 8–10 knots
Sea Conditions: calm, peaceful
Weather Forecast: clear skies

Kate McKenna picked up her pen with a smile. It had been eight years since she'd written in this log—this weather-beaten, storm-battered log that had been stored in her attic until today. She was supposed to write down only the facts, but she couldn't help herself, not this time. She turned to the last empty page in the book.

I never thought I would write in this book again, but today the Moon Dancer *will sail around Castleton Island, a proud victory sail for my sisters, my father, and myself. We have taken back our boat. We have taken back our lives. That terrible storm of eight years ago destroyed much, but it did not destroy us. We are stronger now. We have learned to let go, to forget and to forgive, but, most important, we have learned how to love again.*

Kate set down the pen and closed the book. She took it up on the deck where her sisters were waiting, along with her father, Tyler, and Sean.

"What do you have there?" Tyler asked, a curious glint in his eyes.

"The ship's log. The history of our trip around the world. And the forecast for today's sail."

"Did you embellish?" her father asked with a slightly grumpy smile. He'd been sober for almost twenty-four hours, so he was bound to be a bit out of sorts. Kate didn't know how long it would last, but they would take it one day at a time.

"Just a bit." She handed him the book. "I think this belongs to you, Dad. So does the *Moon Dancer*. Caroline, Ashley, and I agree that you should live on it here in the harbor. But we'd prefer that you don't take it out unless you invite one of us along for the ride."

"Would you go?" he asked, sounding slightly astonished by the idea.

"I would," Caroline said quickly.

"I would, too," Ashley replied a bit more slowly.

Kate simply nodded.

"Well, then . . ." Duncan shook his head in bemusement. "You girls always come through for me, don't you? I'm not sure I deserve it. Actually, I'm sure I don't deserve it. But I'm going to try harder." Duncan looked over at Sean and Tyler. "I guess you two will be hanging around, huh?"

"I certainly will," Sean said firmly, putting his arm around Ashley.

"What about you, Mr. Hotshot Reporter? What's your story?"

"I think my story is just beginning," Tyler replied, sending Kate a tender smile. "Or should I say *our* story?"

"Our story," Kate agreed. "So, are we ready to set sail?"

Duncan held up a hand. "First," he said, walking

over to the side of the boat, "we need to get rid of this."

Kate gasped as Duncan tossed the ship's log into the harbor. She rushed to the side in time to see it sink beneath the surface of the water.

"What did you do that for?" Caroline asked.

"It's over," Duncan said simply, directing his words to Kate. "Isn't that what you've been trying to tell me?"

Kate blinked back a happy tear. "Yes, Dad. It's finally over. Today, we begin again."